BLUE SKIES OF EL DORADO

Carl J. Barger

Strategic Book Publishing and Rights Co.

Strategic Book Publishing and Rights Co., LLC
USA I Singapore

For information about special discounts for bulk purchases, please contact Strategic Book Publishing and Rights Co. Special Sales, at bookorder@sbpra.net.

ISBN:978-1-68181-587-9

Book Design: Suzanne Kelly

CHAPTER 1

Early winter hit Autauga County, Alabama, in the worst way—or at least, the worst I'd seen during my lifetime! On December 1, 1862, we have already experienced two snows. I can still remember what my deceased father, James Bradford, said about snows before Christmas: "We're going to have a bumper cotton crop this coming year." He was normally right in his predictions.

I've struggled with my sleeping lately. I'm assuming it's because I have too many things bearing on my mind. I fall asleep thinking of the upcoming move to El Dorado, Arkansas, and wake up thinking about it.

This morning, I awoke unusually early and couldn't go back to sleep. I said to myself, *enough of this nonsense. I'm getting up! I've got too much to do to lie here in bed and toss and turn.* I rolled out of my warm bed, dressed, and went directly to the kitchen to get coffee.

On this brisk, cold morning, I decided to carry my coffee to the front porch. I knew it was going to be cold, but every now and then I like to bundle up with a heavy coat, a cup of hot coffee, and a warm blanket and sit in my rocking chair on the front porch.

As I entered the kitchen, Mattie, Betsy, and Big Jim were preparing the family breakfast.

I said, "Good morning, everyone!"

"Good morning to you, Obadiah," Mattie and the others said.

"Mattie, I'm going to get me a cup of your fresh-brewed coffee and take it to the front porch. Do you think you could bring me some more in a few minutes?"

"I'll have you some right out, Obadiah," Mattie responded.

As I sat down in my rocking chair, I glanced out over this beautiful plantation. We moved to Twin Oaks when I was a young boy. It has been my home for many years. I have many fond memories of my life here.

In two weeks, the move to El Dorado will happen.

Mattie's coffee was extra good that morning. Maybe it's because I was sitting there freezing. As I sipped my coffee, my thoughts went back to my boyhood and young adulthood at Twin Oaks.

It was at Twin Oaks that our devoted slave George taught me how to ride my horse General. It was at Twin Oaks that George and my father taught me how to fish. It was when I turned twenty-one that my father took me to Selma to buy a replacement for our dear household maid Mamie, who died of natural causes.

It was at the slave sale in Selma, Alabama, that I purchased Mamie's replacement. I picked Mattie and her beautiful daughter, Penelope. On the way home to Twin Oaks, I realized I had strong feelings for Penelope. I believe I loved her from the first time I laid eyes on her. She was so beautiful. She looked white, standing by her mother of light-brown skin. Her blue eyes were captivating. I don't know how to explain it, but it's like she had some kind of spell over me.

It was at Twin Oaks that the Bradford family came together to celebrate Christmas. The entire James Bradford family was present when my father read the Christmas Story. My father was big on establishing traditions. He always made his annual speech to the grandchildren before Christmas dinner. His speeches were always inspirational and encouraging. He put his heart and soul into making it enjoyable and entertaining. Father's Christmas Story was definitely the highlight of Christmas Day!

"Obadiah, I bet you're ready for some hot coffee," Mattie said as she poured steaming hot coffee into my empty cup. I took my coffee black, so she didn't have to worry about bringing cream or sugar.

"Thank you, Mattie!"

"You are more than welcome, Obadiah."

"Mattie, are you looking forward to our trip?"

"To be truthful, Obadiah, I love Twin Oaks. I know the real reason you're leaving Twin Oaks, and that's okay with me. I'll be happy wherever my family lives. You do know that, don't you?"

"Yes, Mattie, I do know how much you love your family. I will miss Twin Oaks as well. I'm optimistic that when we get to El Dorado, we will be happy there as well."

"I hope so, Obadiah! Can I pour you more coffee?"

"No, thank you! I'm getting ready to go inside."

"Breakfast will be ready in about fifteen minutes. Mrs. Catherine and Penelope are up and around, getting Charles and Belle ready for breakfast."

"I'll be in shortly!"

My thoughts returned to Twin Oaks and the move to El Dorado. There are several people I will miss dearly. Among them are my brothers, John and Dent, and my sisters, Tanyua Ballard and Sarah Crawford. I will especially miss my good friend, Dr. John David Banister.

Dr. Banister had let me shadow him at the age of eighteen and had made me his assistant. It was because of him that I became a doctor. How would I ever be able to repay this man? I thought.

As I sipped coffee from my cup, I began to reflect on other blessings that have led up to this move to El Dorado. The bullet injury to my shoulder in the battle of Corinth, Mississippi, was now healed. I have no pain, and I'm getting stronger daily.

In my short time back from the war, I have managed to achieve several things in getting ready to depart for El Dorado.

I sold Twin Oaks to my brothers, John and Dent Bradford. This gave me a sense of peace, knowing that Twin Oaks would stay in the Bradford family.

I also made a quick trip to El Dorado to visit my sister, Mary Shadrack, and her husband, Virgil. Virgil and Mary own a general merchandise store on the town square, and Virgil runs Daniel Pratt's cotton gin.

While in El Dorado, I was able to close a deal on a planta-tion located between Norphlet and El Dorado. The plantation came with a beautiful antebellum home, which is located right in the middle of six hundred acres.

With some work, four hundred acres could be used for cultivation. The other two hundred acres are covered with tall virgin pine, and in a few years, the pine can be harvested. There is a sawmill near Camden, Arkansas, not far from my new plantation.

The principle crops for the area are cotton, corn, and beans.

I view the plantation as a prime piece of property and was able to purchase it at a bargain price.

The house is not as nice as Twin Oaks, but with a little repair work, it will look good. I'm sure Penelope and Mother will find it quite charming and will soon make it one of the better homes in Union County.

I left instructions with Virgil what I wanted repaired. Some of the slave quarters needed repairing as well. I'm hoping Virgil will be able to have the repairs completed by the time we arrive in El Dorado.

I don't know how I could have made this happen without Virgil and Mary's help. They have been wonderful, and their willingness to help is truly appreciated.

After I returned home from Tupelo, Mississippi, I promised my beautiful bride-to-be, Penelope, that our day will soon come. In two weeks from now, we will be exchanging vows in holy matrimony. They will bind us together for the rest of our lives!

I made God a promise that I wouldn't compromise my faith and convictions by taking privileges with Penelope before marriage. I stuck to my convictions. I've always believed every good thing is worth waiting for, and every good thing comes from the Lord for those who love, trust, and obey Him. It has been hard on both of us not to stray and give over to our profound love and passion for each other. But with God's help, we were able to keep his commandments and will soon be rewarded with a life of happiness and joy as husband and wife.

We had planned to be married on a train, leaving Selma, Alabama, for Monroe, Louisiana. From Monroe, we will board a steamboat on the Ouachita River and travel to our new home in El Dorado.

Those plans got changed when I asked my mother to handle our wedding arrangements. My mother, Catherine Bradford, who would be moving to El Dorado with us, has always been dedicated to any assignment she accepts. She loves arranging family get-togethers, weddings, and parties.

When I asked her if she would help with our wedding arrangements, her reply was, "I thought you would never ask."

I had previously told my mother I had planned to marry Penelope on the train to El Dorado. I knew from the frown on her face that she didn't like that idea. She didn't say anything right then, but later she asked me if she could discuss the subject with me. Naturally, I didn't dare say no to my mother.

"Obadiah, you and Penelope have been waiting for this special day for several years. There are so many family members who would be sadly disappointed should you get married on a train and they missed a wedding celebration."

"Okay, Mother. What have you done?"

"I've spoken with the director of the Selma Community Building, and I have arranged for the wedding to take place there on the day we leave for El Dorado. I've checked with all the family members, and they think it's a great idea. What do you think?"

How could I possibly object? My mother had gone to a lot of trouble, and I certainly wasn't going to disappoint her. My mother is seldom wrong. I knew she loved Penelope, and I knew she was thinking of Penelope as well.

"Have you talked to Penelope about your plans?"

"Yes, I have, and she thinks it's a wonderful idea."

"In that case, I agree also. You do remember we are only two weeks away from our departure date?"

"You don't worry, Obadiah. Everything is going to work out just fine."

CHAPTER 2

In the deed agreement on the sale of Twin Oaks, I agreed to sell John and Dent one-half of the slaves I own at Twin Oaks. All of the details were noted in the agreement, along with a clause that Mother would continue to get her 10 percent of the gross proceeds of Twin Oaks as long as she lives.

My father, James Bradford, had included that clause in his will. Dent and John had no problem honoring father's will.

It took a little negotiating with Dent to work out the details on which slaves I'd be taking to El Dorado. I've always been a firm believer that slave families shouldn't be split up.

My father once told me that he had been present for slave sales where black family members were sold separately. He said it was heart breaking. How could people do that to other human beings? I thought. This same thing happened to Mattie. Because she was light skinned, intelligent, and attractive, she was bought by a plantation owner who had other plans for her, other than working in the fields. Her mother and brothers were purchased by other plantation owners, and she has not seen them since.

I will always admire and respect Mrs. Charlotte Thompson of Dallas County, who was the previous owner of Mattie and Penelope. She made it clear to the auctioneer that Mattie and Penelope had to be sold together at her estate sale.

I was twenty-one years old the day I went with my father to the slave auction in Selma. He approved of my decision to bid on Mattie and her daughter, Penelope, to replace our beloved Mamie, who had died a few weeks earlier.

I had been in a bidding war with a Mr. Samuel Bishop for Mattie and Penelope, but he had finally dropped out, and my father had purchased them along with four black males ranging in age from nineteen to twenty-three.

One of the males, Hank, and I became good friends over the years. Hank later married a slave girl named Nanny and moved to Dent's plantation.

Dent and I traded Hank for Big Jim, who fell in love with Mattie and married her.

After much discussion with Dent and John, it was decided that I would take Hank and Nanny, Big Jim and Mattie, and all their children, along with Bill, our carriage driver, Betsy, and enough of the field hands to care for the plantation in El Dorado.

The El Dorado plantation doesn't have a name right now, but with the help of Penelope and my mother, I'm sure we will be coming up with a charming name.

I spent at least an hour on the front porch, sipping coffee and reflecting on the past and planning for the next two weeks. I was just getting ready to get out of my rocking chair and go inside when the front screen door flew open and out came Charles and Belle. They both jumped on my lap and said, "Good morning, Father!"

"Good morning, angels," I said as we exchanged hugs and kisses.

"Granny said to tell you that breakfast is being served," Charles said.

"I'm ready. Are you guys hungry?"

"I am," said Charles.

Belle just nodded her head in the affirmative.

I picked Belle up and carried her into the dining room and put her in her high chair next to me. Charles took his seat on the other side of me. He sat in a big chair all by himself.

In a few minutes, Penelope entered the room. She came immediately and stood behind me, bent over, and gave me a kiss on the cheek.

"Good morning, Obadiah," she said softly.

"Good morning to you." I reached up and took her hand in mine. She then took her seat by Belle, where she would assist in feeding her breakfast.

Penelope's responsibility each morning was to get the kids dressed and ready for breakfast. She had been doing this since the death of my first wife, Audrey Denton, the mother of Charles and Belle. Because they were both babies, Penelope is the only mother they have known.

Big Jim came through the door and handed me a copy of the Selma newspaper. Like my father, I had become accustomed to reading the paper every morning. Every day the paper carries stories of the Civil War, with most battles still being fought in Mississippi and Virginia.

The last person to enter the room was my dear mother. Although her age is showing a little, she still carries her good looks and a pleasant charm.

"Good morning, everyone," she vibrantly said as she went from one side of the table to the other, giving the kids a hug and kiss. She always sits next to Charles so she can assist him if he needs help.

In a few minutes, Big Jim, Mattie, and Betsy came in carrying our breakfast.

CHAPTER 3

Our wedding day finally arrived. In the community room at Selma, Alabama, I will be exchanging vows with the most beautiful woman I have ever known. Penelope and I have waited seven years for this day to come. I am the luckiest man in the world, I thought as I slipped out of bed and got dressed.

As I shaved, I felt comfort knowing that a lot of our household goods and farm equipment was previously shipped to the city of Champagnolle, Union County, Arkansas.

I made arrangements for Virgil to pick the items up at the river port in Champagnolle and transport them to my plantation near El Dorado, Arkansas.

In my previous trip to Champagnolle, I was impressed with the beauty of the town. It was once the county seat for Union County, until the county seat was moved to El Dorado because of El Dorado's central location. Champagnolle was a thriving shipping center located on the bluffs of the Ouachita River. At its peak in the 1850s, thousands of bales of cotton were shipped yearly by steamboat as far away as New Orleans, Louisiana.

Champagnolle was home to several prominent settlers during the 1850s. Since there was no railroad to El Dorado, the steamboat up the Ouachita River from Monroe, Louisiana, was the chief form of transportation.

We were leaving behind some household items for John and Elizabeth. After John and Dent jointly bought Twin Oaks, John decided it was best for him and his family to move from Prattville to Twin Oaks so he could better manage the affairs of the plantation.

As I finished dressing, I was reminded we needed to leave Twin Oaks in time to get to Selma's community center by two o'clock p.m. I certainly didn't want to miss my own wedding.

I felt confident that John would be on time. I've never known him to be late for anything. He and his moving crew should be here any time to load our personal belongings. There will be several wagons and carriages arriving in Selma at the same time. I'm sure people in Selma will wonder what is going on.

I had previously obtained Penelope's and my marriage license from Dallas County. Dent's pastor from First Baptist Church of Selma agreed to perform the wedding ceremony. Dent accepted my invitation to be my best man, and Sarah, my sister, will be Penelope's maid of honor. As soon as the preacher signs the marriage license, our marriage will be official. Penelope will become Mrs. Obadiah Bradford.

The two years Penelope spent at Mrs. Adams' Boarding School in Boston, Massachusetts, was one of the best things that could have happened to her. She was trained well for this new adventure in her life. She now possesses all the characteristics of a Southern lady. In my opinion, she is perhaps the most educated slave in Alabama. My father and mother were financially responsible for her schooling. I know if my father was here today, he would be quite proud of Penelope. Not only is Penelope beautiful and intelligent, she is a gifted pianist.

In Boston, her performances at social gatherings earned her the title of one of the best piano players in Boston. Penelope has worked hard and has achieved much during the ten years she has been with the Bradford family. I know, beyond doubt, she will be able to hold her own with anyone in El Dorado, Arkansas.

I previously made arrangements for boarding passes on the Alabama-Tennessee Railroad for my family and my slaves. I also made arrangements for a private car for Penelope and me. I know a railroad car is not the best of honeymoon suites, but I'm counting on any inconveniences being minor.

I can remember clearly the first time Penelope and I rode on a train together. It was when I accompanied her to Boston to enroll her in Mrs. Adams' Boarding School for Young Ladies. It was an overnight trip, and I had rented two berths, one for Penelope and one for myself. Oh, how I longed to share Penelope's berth during the long night of traveling, but because of my religious convictions, that didn't happen.

Tonight will be completely different. Tonight we will be husband and wife, and what happens tonight will be blessed by God. Penelope and I have waited a long time for this day to come. God has put us together, and when we stand before Him today to exchange our vows, we will carry no guilt.

As John and his men showed up to load our personal goods for the trip to Selma, Mother entered the parlor. "Obadiah, I need a minute with you," she said.

"What is it, Mother?"

"There will be two carriages going to Selma today. I want Penelope to ride with me. I want you to ride in the other carriage with Sarah and Tanyua."

"What's going on here, Mother?"

"I just don't want you to see Penelope before the wedding ceremony. We will get her dressed, and she will be ready for the wedding ceremony at two o'clock sharp."

"I guess this is one of those traditional things?"

"Yes, it is! It is something I feel strongly about. I don't think the groom should see his bride on the day they marry until she walks down the aisle."

"Whatever you wish, Mother, is perfectly all right with me. Does Penelope know we will be riding in separate carriages?"

"Yes, we've discussed that already."

"So I don't even get a peek at her until two o'clock?"

"That's right!"

"All I ask is, take care of my beautiful lady and have her there on time," I said, smiling.

"What you see at two o'clock will make you the happiest man on earth," she said as she turned and left the parlor.

As she left the room, I thought, My mother is having the time of her life getting Penelope and me married. I feel certain she has done everything humanly possible to make our wedding ceremony the very best. The caravan reached Selma at 1:15 p.m. Mother and Penelope's carriage had arrived around 1:05. Penelope had been rushed into the community room by my mother.

My sisters were there to help Mother get Penelope ready. All was working as Mother had planned.

Dent and I arrived about the same time, and in a short few minutes we had our suits on and were ready for the big event.

Mother had arranged a section of the community building for the wedding reception. She invited all our slaves and all family members to the wedding. The reception would last about two hours before we had to board the train for Monroe, Louisiana.

We had decided not to invite anyone outside our family to the wedding. We didn't want to take a chance that word would get back to Autauga County or El Dorado, Arkansas, that I had married a slave girl. I was not ashamed of my love for Penelope, nor was that she a slave. I felt it is best for her peace of mind that our future years in El Dorado are free of ridicule and embarrassment, should anyone find out about her background.

What the residents of El Dorado didn't know certainly wouldn't hurt them. I want Penelope to become an active part of El Dorado's social life and enjoy the finer things of life. I want her to be addressed as Mrs. Penelope Bradford, the wife of Dr. Obadiah Bradford. It is my sincere belief that she will be able to hold her own under any circumstance that might arise.

At two o'clock, I heard the big bell at First Baptist Church strike two times. Dent and I took our places by Dent's pastor, Mark Daniels. As the piano player began to play, Sarah was the first to walk down the aisle. She took her place opposite Dent and me.

The next person to walk down the aisle was my handsome son, Charles, as the ring bearer. Charles took his place by me. In a few minutes, Tanyua walked down the aisle leading my beautiful, little girl, Belle, who was the flower girl. She got tired walking about halfway down the aisle, and Tanyua picked her up and carried her. Belle continued to drop flowers on the floor as Tanyua approached the front. Tanyua ended up standing with Belle in her arms.

As the music changed to the traditional "Wedding March," everyone in the room stood. Looking down the aisle, I saw Penelope. She was wearing the most gorgeous white dress that my Mother had spent hours making. I then knew what my mother meant when she said, "You will certainly like what you see!"

Penelope's wedding veil covered most of her beautiful, black hair. The smile on her face brought out the beauty in her blue eyes. My heart was pounding faster and faster as she came closer and closer to me. As she approached, I stepped forward and took her hand. She handed the flowers to Sarah, who was standing near Tanyua and little Belle.

She then turned to me and looked directly into my eyes and whispered, "I love you, Obadiah Bradford!"

I smiled back and whispered to her, "I love you too!"

Penelope and I had written our own wedding vows.

She looked straight at me with those beautiful, blue eyes and said, "Obadiah Bradford, I've waited ten years for this day. I love you with all my heart. When I'm near you, I feel safe; I feel loved. I will dedicate my life to making you happy. I promise you, I will always be true to you, until death do us part. Where you go, I will go. I will be your wife until the day I die, my love."

I looked into her blue eyes and said, "Penelope, I've loved you from the day I first laid eyes on you. You are my joy in the morning, my rest in the evening, my dream come true. God has surely been good to me by sending you to me. I promise you, as well, that I will dedicate my life to making you happy. I will take care of you in sickness and health. I will be faithful to you, protect you, and live with you until death do us part."

We then turned to Pastor Daniels for the ring exchanges. That went very well, after I bent down to pick up Penelope's ring that Charles had accidentally dropped when he unpinned it from the pillow. Everyone in the building laughed, except for Charles.

Pastor Daniels said, "You may now kiss your bride." This, too, was something both of us had been waiting for. Then Pastor Daniels said, "Now, I introduce to you, Mr. and Mrs. Obadiah Bradford."

CHAPTER 4

At the reception, which Mother had so beautifully planned, I had the pleasure of the first dance with my beautiful bride.

It wasn't long before my brother Dent touched me on the shoulder and said, "Would you mind if I dance with your lovely bride?"

I hesitantly stepped aside as he started swirling Penelope around the dance floor. Soon my brother John broke in on Dent, and then Marion, Dent's older son, broke in on John. I was beginning to wonder if I would ever get my bride back.

Penelope was having the time of her life. She was certainly a hit with all my family. It didn't matter that she had gone from being a slave to a plantation owner's wife. The family wanted me to be happy, and they had always known I loved Penelope and desired to marry her.

While Penelope was being swirled around the dance floor by my brothers and nephews, I found Mother, and we danced. Although Mother is getting up in age, she still dances eloquently. Her Southern upbringing had taught her well.

I spotted my sister Sarah dancing with her husband, Jim Crawford. I went over and asked if I might cut in. Jim, being the nice guy he is, was polite enough to let me dance with my little sister.

Sarah and I have a strong relationship, one of trust and admiration for each other. We have shared our innermost feelings in days past. She, above all the rest, knows me better and gives me lots of good advice. She was the one who suggested I send Penelope to Mrs. Adams' Boarding School in Boston. She knew that if anything ever happened to Audrey, I would want to marry Penelope. She knew also, as long as Penelope was present on the plantation, there would be a constant temptation tearing away at my heart. She knew it would be the same for Penelope.

Before Sarah and I finished the dance, I made her promise me that she and her family would come and visit us in El Dorado. She promised, even though she was aware of the vast traveling distance between Prattville and El Dorado. She knew that, because of our mother's age, she'd be the one who needed to do the traveling.

"Obadiah, I look forward to traveling to El Dorado. From what you've told me, the town and plantation sound exciting. When I come, I'll get to visit with your family, our mother, and Mary's family, as well."

"We will treat you like royalty every time you come."

"Obadiah, I've always looked up to you. I spent lots of sleepless nights at the plantation thinking about you and Penelope. I was afraid that Audrey would discover your love for Penelope. If that had happened, it would have broken her heart."

"Sarah, I loved Audrey deeply, and I could never take privileges with Penelope as long as Audrey was my wife."

"Obadiah, I know that now, but at the time, I wasn't sure you'd have the faith and strength to deny your love and passion for Penelope.

"But I was wrong; God has blessed you in so many ways. You denied yourself, and God has surely saved this day for both of you. I'm so very proud of you, Obadiah!

"You've fought a good fight, and you won the battle, and now God has given you an opportunity to love and cherish the girl you've always loved. I wish you and Penelope all of God's grace and blessings. I know, beyond any doubt, Penelope will make you a wonderful wife. I can't wait for you to start your family with Penelope."

The time to say goodbye came too quickly. The wedding reception was a success, just like Mother planned it. She was right, once again. It would have been wrong to have gotten married on the train and denied my family this wonderful occasion.

As I was leaving the community center with Penelope, Dent came to me again and asked Penelope if he could steal me away for a minute. He said, "I'll bring him right back to you."

We stepped aside and he handed me our father's gold watch.

"Dent, what is this?"

"Father gave this watch to me before he died. Being his oldest, he wanted me to have it to remember him by. I don't ever carry it or use it. It just sits in the drawer at home. I've noticed that you don't have a watch. A doctor has to have a watch, doesn't he?"

"You're right about that. I do need a watch, but I can't take Father's gift to you."

"Obadiah, I want to give it to you. It is my gift from my heart. Someone needs to use it, and that someone is you. You have made me very proud, little brother. The times I tried to persuade you to take privilege with Penelope, you were strong enough to stand up and say, 'It's not right, big brother; it's just not right in God's eyes.' I shall always remember those words."

"Dent, I'll take Father's watch and accept it with honor, coming from you. You need to know that my love and respect for you have grown so much over the years. I've always known you wanted the best for me. You and John were so gracious and understanding when Father left me Twin Oaks in his will. Both of you could have rebelled and turned on me, but you didn't. I knew then that the Bradford blood ran strong within our veins. Family is very important, and I'm going to insist that you and Sara come see us in El Dorado, Arkansas."

"All I ask of you, little brother, is that you take good care of our mother and your beautiful bride, Penelope. I swear, Obadiah, Penelope is the most beautiful woman I've ever seen. Now, don't you ever tell Sara I said that!"

"Your secret will be between you and me as long as I live."

"Well, I guess we'd better get you on the train. This is your and Penelope's night, the one you've been waiting for. Enjoy it to the fullest!"

My slaves had never ridden on a train before. I had rented two boxcars so that everyone could have a seat. It didn't take long for them to settle down. It was so quiet! I felt sorry for them. They just sat staring out the window, fear written all over them. I finally decided I would ask Hank if he could do something to entertain them or get them involved some way.

It didn't take Hank long before he had them singing and full of laughter. I knew right then it was a wise decision to take Hank and his family to El Dorado.

Charles, Belle, Little Jim, and Hank's little boy were up and down the aisle, enjoying every minute of their ride.

Including several stops along the way, the trip by train would take two days to get to Monroe, Louisiana. At Monroe, we would board a steamboat that would carry us to Champagnolle, Arkansas.

After sharing a light supper with the family, Penelope and I excused ourselves and went straight to our boxcar. The train car was small, and our bed couldn't come close to being as comfortable as the beds at Twin Oaks. I had already resolved in my mind that neither of these inconveniences was going to matter.

I know now that God wanted my mind to be absent of any guilt I may have had, should I have made love to Penelope out of wedlock. God knew this night was going to be something special for both of us. It was His gift and His blessings that we now reaped in pleasure.

Sometime during the night, I can't say when, Penelope fell asleep in my arms with her head on my chest. I don't know how long she had been lying there, but both my arms had gone to sleep. The first thing I thought about doing was to gently wiggle out from under her, so I could free myself from my aching, lifeless arms. As I lay there looking at her, I just couldn't do it. What if I awakened her? She might think I was already tired of her. I enjoyed her body being next to mine and decided to abandon any movement that might awaken my lovely bride.

I must confess, I did pray to God that I needed a little help from Him regarding this situation. My arms were killing me.

Again, God responded to my prayer. It wasn't long after that Penelope roll off my chest, and I was able to free both of my arms.

I had just fallen asleep again when I heard the train steward saying, "Breakfast will be served in fifteen minutes."

For some unknown reason, I was very hungry! I didn't know about Penelope, but I was ready for some breakfast. I reached over and touched her soft face with my hand. She opened her beautiful, blue eyes and smiled. I looked at her and smiled back.

"Are you hungry, my love?"

"I'm really hungry," she said as she moved close to me and gave me a kiss.

"Don't get up. I'm going to have the steward bring our breakfast to our car. We are going to have room service, my love!"

"I've never had room service before, Obadiah."

"I wanted you to know what it's like. I believe you will love it."

"I need to get up and wash my face. I don't do very well with sleep in my eyes."

"You go ahead and wash the sleep from your eyes and come back to bed. We are just going to lounge around!"

While Penelope was freshening up, I caught the steward in the hall and ordered room service for Penelope and me. I also handed him a note to be delivered to my mother. I wanted her to know all was well and told her to contact me if she needed help with Charles and Belle. Mother has been so helpful with the kids. She had previously told me she wanted to take care of Charles and Belle while Penelope and I enjoyed the first hours of our honeymoon together. My mother knew both Mattie and Betsy would be available to help her with the kids as well.

CHAPTER 5

The transfer from train to steamboat in Monroe, Louisiana, was completed without a hitch. We were soon headed up the Ouachita River to Champagnolle, Arkansas.

A big part of our traveling success was due to Hank, my loyal and faithful servant-friend. I had assigned Hank, George, and Bill the responsibilities of looking after the slaves during our trip from Selma to Champagnolle. They had done an excellent job.

Standing on the deck of the steamboat, in the quietness of the morning, I found a real sense of solitude as I breathed in the fresh air coming off the Ouachita River. The beautiful bluffs that lined the banks of the river were a beauty I hadn't seen in Autauga County.

As I stood there, I began to reflect upon some of the last few weeks' events. Before leaving for El Dorado, I announced to Hank that I was making him my overseer on my new plantation in El Dorado. I don't think I had ever seen anyone more excited.

The first question he asked me was, "Why me, Master Obadiah?"

I gladly responded, "Because, I trust you. I trust you with my life. We've been fishing buddies. We've studied God's Holy Bible together. We've ridden horses together. You're a preacher of God's word. What else can I say? You are my man!"

"That's very kind of you, Master Obadiah. I can promise you one thing, I will do my very best, and I'll make you proud of me."

"There's no doubt in my mind that you will do an excellent job."

"Can I ask you one more question?" Hank asked.

"What is it, Hank?"

"Well, I was just wondering. All the overseers I've seen have been white folks. They spend lots of their time dealing with white folks. Do you think I will be able to represent you with white folks?"

"Hank, for some reason, I knew you were going to ask me that question, and I'm prepared to answer it.

"First of all, I will be letting business people whom I deal with know you are my trusted overseer. They will know you represent me. That will make things easier for you. You will soon establish yourself in the community, and people will know who you are and what role you play on the plantation. Now, does that answer your question?"

"Yes, Master Obadiah, that helps a lot!"

There were several reasons I wanted Hank as my overseer.

He is admired and respected by the slaves, and they look up to him. He is intelligent and a hard worker. These qualities come natural to Hank. He is also their preacher. He can raise a roof with his preaching. They love him!

I had seen some terribly mean overseers who were hated by slaves on some of the plantations in Autauga County. Leadership and respect have everything to do with gaining the confidence of those who work under authority. Hank possesses those qualities and more.

I remember the first time I met Hank. It was the day we purchased Mattie and Penelope in Selma, Alabama. Hank was sold by himself, and my father was the successful bidder. He was a stout-built man, one who was not scarred from being flogged. He didn't flinch when plantation owners pulled open his mouth to look at his teeth. He just stood there like a brave soldier, with ankle braces and chains, and didn't say a word.

I gained a lot of respect for him that day and was glad my father was the successful bidder. After returning to Twin Oaks, Hank and I became best of friends. He was a deep thinker, one who reached out for knowledge and soaked it in. We spent a lot of time lying on the river bank fishing and discussing the Bible. Sarah and I took Hank under our wings, so to speak, and taught him how to read. He was smart and caught on quickly. He read everything he could get his hands on.

I remember when Hank came down with malaria. He was so sick. I thought we might lose him. I prayed for God to heal my friend, and by His grace He did. I thought then, God has a purpose for my friend. He will be a man of importance someday.

I was in deep thought when I felt a gentle hand touch me on my shoulder. I turned to see my lovely bride looking at me with those piercing, blue eyes and a smile that made my legs weak.

"Good morning, Obadiah!"

"Good morning to you, my love," I said as my lips met hers. I wondered how long it would be before my heart wouldn't skip a beat when I kissed her. Maybe never, I hoped!

"Obadiah, I came out here at your mother's request. She wanted you and me to join her for some breakfast. Are you hungry?"

"Yes, I am. Let's go inside and join Mother, Charles, and Belle," I said.

Penelope took my arm, and we went inside, where we found our family. Mother had already arranged for seating for the five of us. She had ordered our breakfast, and as we sat down, the servants came through a French door, carrying our plates. I would miss my tall glass of milk, but that didn't matter. I can have my cold milk after we settle in at our new home.

"What time will we be arriving at Champagnolle?" Mother asked.

"The captain says we should arrive around three o'clock."

"I can't wait to see Mary and her family."

"They will be there waiting for us. Virgil will have our wagons and carriage there. I told him not to bother getting drivers. We will let Hank, George, and Bill handle the driving."

"I would like to go out on the deck and sit when we get closer to Champagnolle," Penelope said.

"We can do that!"

"I want to see the little town on top of the big bluff that you described," Penelope said.

"Champagnolle is certainly a nice little town. You will be seeing some of the beautiful homes on the bluff as we approach the port area. There are some rich people living there," I said.

"Daddy, after we eat, can we play on the deck?" Charles asked.

"Yes, but you can't be running all over the place. You will have to stay close to us."

"Can little Jim and Obi play with us?" Charles asked.

"I'm sure Mattie and Nanny won't mind them playing."

Charles was so excited that he ate everything on his plate. He wanted to get out on the deck as fast as possible. He was so energetic. I don't know where a four-year-old gets that much energy. Charles's best friend is Little Jim. They played together before they started walking. Their friendship is free of prejudice. They have not yet reached the time in their lives when they would notice that slaves are treated differently from whites.

We were sitting on the deck when the captain of the big steamboat pulled the rope that unleashed the loud whistle, which indicated we were approaching Champagnolle. The whistle reminded me of when I was a kid living at our plantation, Black Oaks, in Cahaba, a little town near Selma.

My father let me go to Selma with him to watch the steamboats come in and go out of Selma. Selma was one of the state's leading and busiest river ports for shipping cotton and other farm products. I always wanted to ride on one of those big steamboats but never had the opportunity, until now.

When we arrived in Champagnolle, we were tired and ready to get off the steamboat and head to our new home. It will take about two hours by wagon to get to the plantation. We should arrive there before dark, giving us plenty of time to get settled.

As we stepped off the steamboat and onto the wooden dock, we heard kids running up the boardwalk yelling, "Grandma Bradford."

I looked at Mother and said, "Mary's kids want to see their grandma."

Mother said, "If I could run, I'd meet them halfway!"

"Don't try that. Let them do the running."

Matthew, Mary's oldest, was the first to get to Mother. He wrapped his arms around her as she bent down and gave him a hug and a kiss on the forehead.

"Matthew, you are growing up too fast, big boy," Mother said.

"I'm seven years old now, Grandma," Matthew replied.

By this time, Mary, Virgil, Annie, and Susie had made it to Mother. Annie, Mary's second child, was five, and Susie was three. They were very well behaved.

After we greeted each other and everything was loaded into the wagons, we drove through the little town of Champagnolle so everyone could see it. We traveled along the Champagnolle road until we came to a junction that was about two miles from El Dorado. At the junction, Penelope and I joined Bill on the driver's seat of our family carriage. I wanted Penelope to get a good view of her new home as we approached.

At the junction, we traveled a different road for about four miles, and then we turned onto a smaller, narrow road.

When we turned onto the narrow road, we could see our plantation house about a quarter of a mile away. It was a beautiful antebellum home, with a big porch with columns running up to a second balcony level.

The carriage seat was crowded, with three of us sitting in a driver's seat meant for one person. Realizing that Bill was having problems navigating the reins of the horses, Penelope slowly positioned herself in my lap. She wrapped her arms around my neck and gave me a quick kiss. She looked straight ahead and said, "Oh, Obadiah, I'm so excited!"

The expression on her face was like watching someone opening a Christmas present on Christmas Eve. It was a time Penelope and I would never forget.

As I looked at the plantation house from a distance, a thought came into my mind. I suddenly realized this was Penelope's first real home. She had always been in someone else's house, someone who was in authority over her. Now she would be in her own house, under her own authority, and loving every minute of it.

This is what I wanted for her. This is what we both had wanted for several years, and now our day had come. Today would be another day in history for me and Penelope. A day that we will always remember and cherish. A day that our God had made special for us. It felt so good!

As Bill pulled up in front of the house, I got down and helped Penelope from the carriage. In the meanwhile, Bill was helping Mother and the children down from the carriage.

I looked at Penelope and said, "Penelope, in the South, when a newly wedded couple enters their home for the first time, the groom carries his bride through the front door, puts her down on the inside, and gives her a lingering kiss. This custom brings good luck to the couple."

I picked Penelope up and carried her through the front door, put her down, took her in my arms, and gave her that promised kiss. We stood there and just held each other for the longest time, gazing into each other's eyes and smiling. She finally said, "Obadiah, you've made me the happiest lady in the world. Thank you, my love!"

"In this house, Penelope, we will raise our children, and I'm hoping there will be several. Our love will grow daily for each other. We will take care of each other in sickness and health, and be there for each other until God takes one of us home to Heaven. You are my precious angel and partner in life. You are truly my soul mate!"

CHAPTER 6

After touring the entire house from bottom to top, every inch of it, I was exhausted. Penelope had dragged me all over the house, asking questions and telling me what needed to be done here and there. I didn't realize that it was going to be like this. She had energy that I've never seen in a lady. I have to admit, it was all worth it. I was so happy she liked the house. I couldn't wait until she and Mother got their heads together and gave our plantation a name.

There are eight bedrooms, three toilets, one bathroom, a parlor, a large living area that look like a ballroom, a formal dining room, a kitchen, a screened-in back porch, and a large stairway leading up to the second floor.

The five downstairs bedrooms will be used by Penelope and me, our kids, my mother, and Big Jim, Mattie, and their kids. There is a small room, off from the kitchen, for Betsy.

The plantation grounds are well landscaped. There is a flower garden that I am sure will be pleasing to Mother. She can have her rose garden, just like the one she had at Twin Oaks.

The plantation has several slave houses and one large bunkhouse for the single slaves. Those slaves who have families will get the family units, while the single slaves will be placed in the bunkhouse, just as we did at Twin Oaks. The bunkhouse has a bedroom and a bathroom for the cooks, John and his wife, Lolo.

The slave houses are not bad, but need some repair work. The bunkhouse and the family units are located within one hundred yards of the main plantation house. This gives us a closer accessibility to Hank, George, and Bill when we need one of them.

Virgil and Mary had been a tremendous help to us. Prior to our arrival, they filled our pantry and the bunkhouse supply room with several food items, which will be utilized as we figure out what our future needs are.

It will take a few days to settle in. During that time, Penelope, Mother, Old John, and I can do an inventory to determine what we have and what we need for the winter months.

This will certainly be a big change for me. I've always had my mother and father to do all of those things. Now it will be different. I am now the bread winner, so to speak, for everyone.

My first concern, of course, is for my immediate family. Secondly, I now am responsible to feed and clothe fifty slaves. In my mind, I was convinced I could do it but smart enough to know I couldn't do it without help. I have my mother to fall back on should I fall flat on my face. She has done this kind of planning before, and she is experienced at it. If I run into a problem, I will consult with Mother.

It was the middle of December, and the nights were already cold. With all the timber on our land, we had no problem finding wood for the stoves and fireplaces. The first thing I wanted to do was make the repairs to the slave quarters. I didn't want my slaves to have to go through a winter like some of the slaves did in Autauga County. Every winter, there would be a number of slaves die because of not having proper clothing and heat. I don't think I could live with myself if I was guilty of not providing warm clothing, ample food, and a warm habitat for my slaves.

After a few days, we'd settled into our new home. Mattie, Betsy, and Big Jim had become well acquainted with the kitchen. The meals were as good as, or better than, what we had been accustomed to at Twin Oaks.

Penelope and I continued to enjoy our honeymoon together. We couldn't seem to get enough of each other. When our lips touched, everything seemed to explode. If two people were ever in love and meant to be together, it was Penelope and me. We were sure our love would bring the pitter-patter of little feet into our home in the near future. I am so blessed to have Penelope as my wife. My feelings for her are indescribable. God, with all

His wisdom, surely knew what He was doing in preparing us for these wonderful days and nights that we've been experiencing.

Today we will be going to El Dorado to visit Mary and her family. I asked Bill to have our carriage ready at ten o'clock. After breakfast, we dressed in our winter clothing and met Bill on the porch to make the trip into El Dorado. This would be the first time for Bill, Mother, Penelope, and the kids to see El Dorado.

On the way, I reminded Mother and Penelope that we needed a name for the new plantation.

"We've been discussing that, Obadiah," Mother said.

"So, have y'all decided on a name yet?"

"We have narrowed it down to four choices but have not yet decided on a name to present to you."

"Oh, no; you two are to pick out the name. I've already told you, this job is yours."

"We want your input in the decision as well," Mother said.

"What are your four choices?"

"Our four choices are Pine Grove Plantation, Tall Timbers Plantation, Bradford Plantation, and Three Oaks Plantation."

"What do you think?" Mother asked.

"I like all four!"

"Obadiah, you're not getting off that easy. Let's analyze the possibilities. We thought that, since there are four hundred acres of tall virgin pine trees, Pine Grove Plantation or Tall Timbers Plantation might be appropriate. We also like the Bradford Plantation, because it's our name. Once we're settled in, people will hear of the Bradford Plantation and will know who we are. The last possibility is Three Oaks Plantation, because of the three big oak trees in our front yard," Mother said.

"I can see your dilemma. This is harder than I thought. I was thinking about the Tall Timbers and Pine Grove names. If you want my opinion, I would eliminate those two. Let me explain why. If you look around Union County, you will see thousands of acres of pine trees. Our plantation looks like most of the other plantations in this county."

"See, I told you; we needed your help. I hadn't given that any thought, but you're right. What do you think, Penelope?" Mother asked.

"I agree. I vote not to consider those two names," Penelope said.

"I agree as well. Now we're getting somewhere. We are down to two. What is your feeling about the other two?" Mother asked.

"I like both of them!" I said.

"Come on, Obadiah! You're not putting this back on us!" Mother said.

"If you can't agree, let's just flip a coin. If heads come up, we will call the new plantation Bradford Plantation. If it's tails, we will call the plantation Three Oaks."

Mother and Penelope nodded their heads in the affirmative. We were now getting somewhere.

I suggested we let Charles flip the coin; when it falls on the carriage floor, we can clearly see whether it's heads or tails.

"How does that sound to y'all?" I asked.

"That all right with me," Penelope responded.

"Me, too," Mother said.

I showed Charles how to flip the coin. He was so excited to be able to participate in this big decision-making process. He took the coin and put it on top of his finger and flipped it neatly into the air. When it hit the floor of the carriage, it rolled a short distance and landed on tails. As agreed, tails meant we would call the new plantation Three Oaks. I liked the sound of that. It was almost like saying Twin Oaks, our old plantation in Autauga County, Alabama.

We arrived in El Dorado, where Bill hitched the horses to the hitching post in front of Mary and Virgil's store. Mary and Virgil were glad to see us. After a short greeting, Mary said, "Who wants a tour of the store?"

"I do," Mother said.

"Me, too. Me, too," Charles said excitedly.

Mary walked us through their well-stocked store. It was a big store with lots of nice merchandise. They had about anything a customer might want to purchase. Virgil is a good business man, and the store is doing quite well financially.

Virgil also manages the big cotton gin for Daniel Pratt of Autauga County, Alabama. The cotton gin was the main reason that Virgil and Mary moved to El Dorado. Daniel Pratt had heard that Union County was the leading cotton-growing county in Arkansas. He, being a good businessman, asked Virgil to move to El Dorado and run the gin for him. It was a good opportunity for Virgil and Mary. During the cotton season, Virgil divides his time between the cotton gin and the store.

Charles wondered where Mary's kids were.

"Where are Matthew, Annie, and Susie?" he asked.

Mary explained that Matthew was in school and Annie and Susie were at home with their baby-sitter.

"Can we go to your house to play with Annie and Susie?" Charles asked.

I explained to him that we would have to wait until a later time to visit with his cousins. He wasn't too happy with my answer, but when Mary distracted him and Belle with candy, the problem was resolved.

El Dorado is the county seat of Union County. The founding fathers built a courthouse right in the middle of town. Mary and Virgil's store is located on the street to the south of the courthouse. Since most of the businesses are located around the courthouse, Mary offered to escort us on a tour around town.

"I need a break, so let me give you a walking tour of our lovely, little town," she said.

We were more than glad to accompany Mary on the tour. She introduced us to several people as we went up and down the streets of El Dorado. Mary and Virgil's family attend the First Baptist Church in El Dorado. A lot of the business owners are members of their church.

I could tell Mary was having the time of her life introducing us to her friends. She was so happy that we had moved to El Dorado.

On the north side of the courthouse, Mary stopped and pointed to an empty building. "This building is for sale, Obadiah. I believe it would be an ideal building for your doctor's office. Take a good look at it. Jake Jones, next door, owns the building, and I'm sure he wouldn't mind giving us a quick tour if you have time," she said.

"We will take time, won't we?" I asked, as Mother and Penelope answered in the affirmative.

Mr. Jones showed us throughout the building. The building had the necessary qualities needed to be converted into a doctor's clinic. I thought that Mr. Jones's asking price was reasonable, but I planned to offer him a little less than his asking price. I figured he'd either accept my offer, or counteroffer. If he counteroffered, I would try to get him to split the difference. One way or another, I wanted this building.

Mary was right. It is an ideal location, one that will get a lot of street traffic. There is only one other doctor in town, and his office is located on the west side of the courthouse. His name is Doctor Samuel Weaver. He and his family live in the Mahoney District, which is known as the area where the wealthiest residents lived.

I thanked Mr. Jones for his time, told him I was impressed with the building, and that I would get back with him in a few days. I didn't want to take the time to discuss business with him as Mary continued her tour of El Dorado.

We passed Jake's Restaurant, which reminded me of the restaurant where Audrey and I used to meet for lunch in Prattville, Alabama. I asked Mary if she had eaten there.

She said, "Yes, Virgil and I eat there quite often, and their pies are just out of this world!"

Mary insisted that we go home with her and Virgil for lunch. She explained that today was the day she and Virgil went home to eat. She said, "I left instructions with Maggie to cook extra food today. There will be plenty food for everyone. I want to show y'all our home here in El Dorado. Although it's not located in the Mahoney District, it's nice enough for us. We like it, and it's in a good neighborhood, close to our church, First Baptist."

Mother was excited because she wanted to see Mary's house and see her grandchildren as well. This would certainly please

Charles and Belle. They would get to play with Susie and Annie, after all.

After visiting with Mary and her family over lunch, we returned to their store and placed an order for lumber, as well as some household items for our new home. The lumber order would be delivered to Three Oaks by Virgil, upon its arrival to his store. While I was there, I ordered our sign for the Bradford plantation, which will be placed at the entrance of our property and will read 'Three Oaks Plantation'.

While in El Dorado, I subscribed to the local newspaper, *El Dorado News-Times,* which is a daily paper. Like my father, I have grown accustomed to reading my newspaper. A newspaper is a good way of keeping up with the outside world. I want to keep up with what is happening in the Civil War.

There isn't a day goes by that I don't think about my good friend, Dr. Henry Dotson. Henry was my best friend at the Old Military Academy in Augusta, Georgia, where we both got our doctor's degree. I later served with him in Corinth, Mississippi, during the battles of Shiloh and Corinth. Henry commanded the Confederate Army Medical Corp while I was in Corinth, Mississippi.

Henry signed my honorable discharge in Tupelo, Mississippi, after I was wounded in the battle of Corinth. He is the one responsible for me being here today. I had died on the operating table, and he brought me back to life. I shall always be indebted to him. Not only did he save my life, but he gave me my release from service so I could come home and marry Penelope, the love of my life.

God has been so good to me. I hope my faith and trust in Him will be enough for His continued blessings as I start my doctor's office in El Dorado. I have dedicated my life to helping the sick and to serving my Lord. He has blessed me with knowledge and understanding of medicine and the skills I possess. I want very much to please Him.

As Bill guided our horses and carriage down the road to our new plantation, I felt honored to be sitting arm in arm with Penelope.

CHAPTER 7

For a few weeks, we were extremely busy at Three Oaks, and in El Dorado renovating my new doctor's clinic. Mr. Jake Jones accepted my offer to purchase the building without a counteroffer. If the business does well, I might add another doctor. There is certainly more than enough room for other doctors.

Virgil delivered the lumber for repairing the slave quarters, and those repairs have been finished. The slaves are happy with the much-needed repairs. They can now rest assured that the roofs don't leak, and the windows now operate correctly.

Mary has introduced Mother and Penelope to the women's social clubs in El Dorado, and from all conversations, I believe they are adjusting rather well.

We joined First Baptist Church in El Dorado and love the pastor and the church. We have been members now for two weeks.

Pastor Darrell Johnson is truly a man called by God. He is well prepared each Sunday and always preaches a thought-provoking sermon, one that focuses on the scripture. One can easily see he relates his scripture passages to our everyday circumstances. I like that! I get more out of a message when it relates to something I can identify with.

Every morning, Bill goes down to the end of our road and picks up my daily newspaper. Every morning when I go to breakfast, my paper is lying on the breakfast table, just as it was for my father, in Twin Oaks.

Almost every morning as I unfold the paper, there is an article related to the Civil War. Right now the Civil War is a hot topic for everyone. The headline this morning read, "The Confederacy, Victorious at Fredericksburg."

I had just begun to read the story when Charles and Belle came running into the dining room, shouting, "Good morning, Father!"

"Good morning to you, my angels," I said as we hugged and kissed.

By then, Penelope and Mother entered the dining room. Mother helped Belle into her high chair as Charles took his seat at his usual place, by Penelope. We were seated as a family, and how proud I felt. I decided to lay my newspaper aside, to be enjoyed later in the parlor. I wanted breakfast to be special, just like it was at Twin Oaks.

As usual, Mattie, Betsy, and Big Jim had cooked a nice breakfast. I am always hungry when I get up in the morning. Maybe a little more so, since I married my beautiful Penelope!

After breakfast, I retired to the parlor to read my paper. Penelope told me she would keep the kids out of the parlor so I could concentrate on my reading. She knew the kids were very lively during this time of the day.

I carried my coffee cup with me, knowing that Mattie would be around with fresh coffee in a few minutes. She knew my routine and had her timing down just right in refilling my cup with hot coffee.

Mattie is a beautiful woman. Her mother had fallen victim to the selective breeding practice, which was practiced on some Deep South plantations. Mattie herself was impregnated by a white man, and that was the reason Penelope is so light. Looking at Penelope, one would never guess she is a Negro.

Another article in today's paper was titled, "General Lee Teaches Burnside Lesson." The article consisted of a summary of the battle:

General Ambrose Burnside, commander of the Union Army of the Potomac, invaded the city of Fredericksburg, Virginia, on December 11, 1862. General Burnside built five pontoon bridges across the Rappahannock River in order to get to the city.

On December 12, the Federal army crossed over the river, and on the 13, General Burnside mounted a series of futile frontal assaults on Prospect Hill and Marye's Heights, which resulted in several casualties for both the Union and Confederate armies. For a time, General Meade's division on the left flank briefly penetrated Stonewall Jackson's line but was driven back by a counterattack.

It was Burnside's plan to use General William B. Franklin's 60,000 men to defeat General Robert E. Lee's position behind Prospect Hill, but that too failed."

The Army of the Potomac suffered nearly 13,300 casualties; nearly two-thirds of them were killed at Marye's Heights.

In comparison, General Robert E. Lee's army had suffered 4,500 losses. The engagement in the Battle of Fredericksburg's involved some 200,000 combatants. No Civil War battle had drawn such a large number of soldiers in one location.

At the end of the battle, the Union army had lost two key generals: General C. Feger Jackson and General George Bayard. Generals from the Confederacy who lost their lives were General Thomas R. R. Cobb and General Maxey Gregg.

This quote, coming from General Robert E. Lee said, "It is well that war is so terrible, or we should grow too fond of it."

On the morning of December 15, 1862, General Burnside called off the offensive, crossed back over the Rappahannock River, and ended his campaign at Fredericksburg.

After reading the article on the Battle at Fredericksburg, I laid my paper down and started praying. "Lord, help us! How many more lives will be sacrificed before this terrible war comes to an end? Lord, what can be done, or what needs to be done to stop this brutal killing? Please Lord, intervene and do something to stop this killing. If we, your people, have done something to be punished for, please forgive us, and revive us so we can again start new and bring our country back together. Oh, Lord, please hear my plea!"

While praying, the thought of losing over eighteen thousand men in this battle made me cry. Although, those eighteen thousand could be the lucky ones! How many more were wounded and lying in some unsanitary house, hospital, or makeshift building or tent, being treated by a small number of doctors? *There are never enough doctors. It makes me sick to think about it. What's going to happen to them?* My thoughts returned to the Battles of Shiloh and Corinth. I thought these battles were bad, but according to this account, they wouldn't measure up to Fredericksburg.

Just as I finished my prayer, Penelope entered the room. She knew I had been crying.

"Obadiah, what's wrong?"

"It's all right. I'll be okay!"

"Obadiah, please tell me why you've been crying. I want to be a part of this, whatever it is. I know something has hurt you."

"There is an article in today's paper about the Battle of Fredericksburg, Virginia. It's quite disturbing!"

"May I read it?"

"Surely you may, but the content of the article reminds me of the battles of Shiloh and Corinth. It makes me wonder whether I should be there, helping attend to the many wounded."

"Oh, Obadiah, please don't think about reenlisting in this terrible war!"

"Penelope, don't you worry, I won't do that. My place is here in Union County, with my family and doing God's work through healing the sick. I can promise you, I won't be reenlisting in a war that no one really wins."

"Oh, my love," Penelope said, as she sat down on my lap and gave me a kiss. That was the type of medicine I needed.

"Penelope, I have to go into town today and check on my office building. Would you like to go with me? We could have lunch with Mary and Virgil, and do Christmas shopping afterwards."

"I would love to," she said.

"Why don't you change clothes while I have Bill bring around the carriage?"

We said goodbye to Mother and the kids, and headed out to El Dorado.

The office building would soon be ready to move into. The painting had been completed, and all that was left was polishing the floors. We should be able to move in right after Christmas.

After having lunch with Virgil and Mary at Jake's Restaurant, we went Christmas shopping. We had been so busy with other things that Christmas shopping had been put on the back burner.

As we went from store to store, I realized this was Penelope's first Christmas to shop. She would look at a price tag and shake her head. I finally walked up close to her and whispered, "Penelope, I've got money to buy whatever you want to buy, within reason." I laughed.

She looked at me and smiled. "I've never done this before. To tell you the truth, Obadiah, I think some of these prices are unreasonable. I see several things I'd like to have for the kids and family members, but they're really costly."

"Let's don't worry about the price until you find an item you like. We will look at the tag together, and then decide if we want to pay that price. How does that sound?"

"That's good for me, boss!" she said with a smile that melted my heart. She is such a joy!

The shopping took longer than I thought. Bill kept carrying things to the carriage. I finally asked him, "Are we going to have any space to sit, going home?"

"Yes, Master Obadiah! I've kept your and Miss Penelope's seat clear of all them packages."

I smiled and said, "Good for you, Bill!"

Mother and Penelope, with the help of Mattie, Betsy, and Big Jim, had put up a beautiful Christmas tree in our parlor. Our Christmas presents would certainly take up a lot of space under the beautiful tree.

As Bill and I carried in the Christmas presents, Charles, Belle, Jim, and Mattie's kids were right under our feet. Charles wanted to help carry the presents in. Belle wanted to tear one open. Mother was excited and asked, "Why wasn't I invited?"

I quickly replied, "Because we didn't want you to see what we were buying you for Christmas! But, tomorrow is your day, and I'll go to El Dorado with you. You can have Bill accompany you around in the stores so none of us will know what you are buying."

"Obadiah, how will I get my grandchildren's Christmas presents back to Prattville? I'm afraid they won't get there until after Christmas!"

Mother was right. With all the things that occupied our time lately, we had completely neglected Christmas shopping.

"You may be right, but I think they will realize the distance and the shipping problems. I expect they won't mind getting their presents a little late. Come next year, we're going to start shopping earlier."

"I certainly hope so! We always had our Christmas presents ready on Christmas Day when we were at Twin Oaks."

"I can promise you that next year it will be different."

"I'm going to hold you to that promise, Obadiah," she said with a big smile and a hug.

CHAPTER 8

I awakened to a frosty Christmas morning. At least it wasn't snowing, although it was plenty cold. The fire in our fireplace had died down, so there was little heat. I could hear chatter in the hallway. The chatter was coming from Charles, Belle, and Mother. I heard Mother say, "Let's give your parents a little more time before we wake them up."

As soon as I heard those words, I knew it was time to get up. I didn't want my kids to have to wait any longer than necessary to tear into their presents. I remembered how much Christmas morning meant to me when I was a kid. I was very excited, and I know they must be as well.

I turned over and looked at my beautiful Penelope. She was sleeping so soundly, I dreaded waking her up, but I didn't want the kids to worry Mother any longer than necessary. I knew Penelope wanted to be a part of this special family day as well. She had invited Mattie and her family to celebrate Christmas with us. Why shouldn't they? We were now one family, under one roof. Mattie is Penelope's mother, and there are no real connotations of slavery in my household, other than the papers I hold in my safe on Mattie.

The talk around El Dorado is that President Abe Lincoln will be utilizing his executive powers in issuing a document entitled the "Emancipation Proclamation" in January, 1863. This document will set in play freedom for all slaves in the Confederate states.

An article in the *El Dorado News-Times* says that President Abe Lincoln can enforce the proclamation, which falls under his power as commander in chief, and that the freedom of the slaves would be maintained by the Executive Government of the United States. Right now, it's the feeling of slave owners in

38

Union County that, as long as the Civil War is going on between the states, slavery will still exist in the Confederate states.

I had previously promised Penelope that someday I would free her and Mattie from being slaves. In one way, I've carried through on my promise to Penelope, when she became my wife.

On the day we married in Selma, Alabama, and boarded the train headed to Vicksburg, Mississippi, I reached in my duffel bag, pulled out the slave document, lit a match, and burned the slave document that my father had given me on the day we purchased Penelope and Mattie in Selma, Alabama.

On that glorious night, I held Penelope in my arms as we both watched the slave papers burn. I shall never forget that moment in time. Penelope gently wiped away the joyful tears from her eyes and looked at me with a smile that melted my heart. The burning of the papers meant that there was no written legal proof that she had ever been a slave. She is now, and shall always be, my beautiful and charming wife.

I've searched my heart many times trying to decide what to do about Mattie's freedom. Right now, Mattie has it good. She's married to a nice man, and they have two children, Little Jim and Benjamin. She lives under my roof and is considered family. There are no threats to her and her family. She and Penelope are together, and that's very important. Someday, when the right opportunity arises, I'll free Mattie and her entire family.

As I lay there watching Penelope breathe in and out, I took my hand and begin to gently brush Penelope's soft cheek. I wanted to awake her gently. She soon opened her eyes and smiled.

"Merry Christmas, Penelope, my love."

"Merry Christmas to you, my handsome husband!"

"I think it's time we got up and got ready for the big day. I've been hearing chattering in the hall. Mother is trying to encourage Charles and Belle to wait until we wake up to open their presents. I'm afraid she's going to need some help real soon!"

"Give me a few minutes, and I'll be ready."

"Do you want me to check on Mattie and Big Jim?"

"Would you, please? Mama knows they're to share Christmas activities with us, but she may need to be reminded."

39

"I'll take care of it," I said.

As soon as I walked into the hallway, I smelled the aroma of bacon cooking in the kitchen, so I made my way down the hall and entered the kitchen. I found Betsy, Mattie, and Big Jim cooking.

"Merry Christmas! What's cooking in here?" I asked.

"Breakfast will be ready in just a few minutes," Mattie answered.

"I came to remind you that we're having Christmas together today."

"I do remember that, Master Bradford, but we thought everyone would want breakfast before opening presents."

"That may be a problem! Mother and the kids have been up for some time and are excited about tearing into those presents."

"We can leave everything in the warmer if you want us to, but it's not going to be fresh."

"Let me go talk to Mother and the kids. I'll be right back."

Charles and Belle were disappointed, but Mother made them understand that having breakfast first would allow them the opportunity to play with their toys all day long, should they choose to do so. Her explanation worked, and we had a nice breakfast together.

Big Jim and Mattie's family, Betsy, Mother, and my family took our seats at the dining table for the first time ever as a family in our new home at Three Oaks. Oh, what would the neighbors back at Twin Oaks think about this? I thought!

Before passing out the presents, I read the Christmas Story, just like my father, James Bradford, had done on Christmas morning for many years. I don't think anyone in my family could ever top my father's performance in reading the Christmas Story. All of us Bradford children, as well as the older grandchildren, loved the Christmas Story and looked forward to Father reading it each year.

How I miss hearing his voice! I decided after his death I would continue this Christmas Story tradition with my family, as long as God allows me to live.

As I watched the kids tear open their presents and heard the joy and excitement in their voices, I couldn't pass up the opportunity to bow my head and softly whisper, "Thank you, Lord, thank you!" I couldn't remember a time in my life that I have been any happier.

God has blessed me with the love of my life, a new home to share with Penelope and my mother, who chose to leave Twin Oaks to come live with us. What else could He bless me with? I wondered!

CHAPTER 9

On January 5, 1863, we had the grand opening for my new doctor's clinic in El Dorado. People came from all over Union County and as far away as Columbia and Ouachita Counties.

Without the help of Penelope, Mary, and my mother, the open house wouldn't have been the success it turned out to be. They spent countless hours sending out invitations and running ads and articles in the *El Dorado News-Times*.

The event was a come-and-go event, with refreshments served in the large waiting room. I had never seen so many people. There was standing room only. The big turn-out was a good indication that they were checking me out. I was in hopes that the open house would boost my chances of getting a good clientele of patients.

It was during the open house that I first met Dr. Samuel Weaver, the only other doctor in El Dorado. When I shook his hand, I felt a sense of acceptance, both in his voice and facial expression, as we engaged in conversation. He welcomed me and said, "Dr. Bradford, I believe God has sent you here to help me."

"How's that, Dr. Weaver?"

"My workload is making me old before my time," he said.

"I understand you have a big following of patients."

"Yes, I do! Too many, I'm afraid."

"Well, if you have too many just send them over here," I said jokingly.

"Dr. Bradford, you shouldn't have any problems getting your practice started here in El Dorado. Since I don't do house calls, and since you've advertised you do, I expect you will get more business than you can handle."

"Why don't you do house calls?"

"I used to when I was younger, but as I've grown older, I had to drop that part."

"I do enjoy house calls. To me, there is something special and exciting about reaching out to folks from both the city and county," I said.

"Dr. Bradford, I've got to get back to my office, but if I can be of help to you, just let me know."

"There is something you can do for me!"

"How can I help?"

"I'll be interviewing for a receptionist and a head nurse position in the next few days. Do you know of anyone who might be interested in applying for those positions?"

"I believe I can help you with that," he said, as he jotted down some names on a piece of paper and handed it to me.

"After you get settled in, I'll buy your lunch," he said as he set his glass down and proceeded to leave to go back to his office.

I felt the day had gone well. Now all I needed to do was employ a receptionist and a head nurse.

With the help of Dr. Weaver, I was able to find two ladies who had excellent credentials for the two positions. For the receptionist position, I chose Elizabeth Parker, who had recently moved to El Dorado from Memphis, Tennessee. She had previous experience as a receptionist in a doctor's clinic in Memphis. Her people skills appeared to be excellent, and she was certified as an LPN, which made her even more valuable.

For my head nurse, I employed Beth Ann Johnson, who was a dedicated Christian who attended the First Baptist Church. Beth Ann once worked for Dr. Weaver but had taken a leave of absence to stay home with her twin boys for a few years. She is ready to return to work. She brought with her a wide range of medical experiences, such as birthing babies and working as an assistant in the operating room. Dr. Weaver said Beth Ann could do about anything, and does it well.

I missed my practice, and getting back to work was going to be exciting and good for me.

Dr. Weaver was right. After three weeks on the job, I was booked up every working day. I couldn't take on any additional patients, except for emergencies.

I had certainly done well in selecting good office personnel. Elizabeth and Beth Ann were working themselves to death. If I want to keep them, I have to do something and do it fast.

Elizabeth's nursing skills were so good that I trusted her to do things I would normally do. Therefore, she became my go-to nurse when Beth Ann and I were tied up with patients. This was good in one way, but bad in another, because the front reception-ist desk duties were being neglected.

Every day as I returned home to Three Oaks, I found myself worn out from a taxing day at the office. Something had to be done. I was neglecting the plantation as well as my family. I also had to consider doing something for Elizabeth. If I was going to continue to use her as a nurse, I needed to find someone to help with the receptionist job.

After sharing my office dilemma with my two most trusted companions, Mother and Penelope, Penelope came up with an intelligent solution.

"Obadiah, I have an idea. Do you want to hear it?" Penelope asked.

"By all means, speak up!"

"Catherine and I have noticed the stress you've been under. We didn't know all the circumstances until tonight, but I think we have a solution."

"All right; let me hear what's on your mind."

"Let me come and be your receptionist. I can do that job. When I was in Boston, we had training in this type of work. I know I can do it!" Penelope said with persuasion.

"Penelope, I really appreciate your offer, but I need you here with the kids."

"Obadiah, I think Penelope's offer is worth consideration. She's very smart, you know. Besides Betsy, Mattie, and I can handle the kids. You don't have to worry about the kids," Mother said.

"Penelope, you really want to do this?"

"Obadiah, I would love to try. At least give me a chance. I want to help. In one way, I'm being selfish; I want to be with you more. I only see you late at night. This way, we can at least have lunch together. Come on, let me try it!"

"I want to sleep on this overnight before I give you an answer."

"Maybe I could do it for a while until you can locate someone else to take my place. Please consider it!"

In my heart and mind, I knew Penelope could do the job. In fact, with her personality, writing, and math skills, she probably would be as efficient as Elizabeth.

I honestly didn't know if I wanted my wife to do this type of work. Although, if I agreed to let her try, she would finally have the opportunity to utilize and practice the skills she learned at Mrs. Adams' Boarding School in Boston, Massachusetts.

In knowing she was contributing to the family's livelihood, this job could be good for Penelope in regard to her self-esteem and personal pride.

Dr. Obadiah Bradford, what are you going to do? I thought!

After retiring to our bedroom, Penelope, sensing I was still under lots of stress, proceeded to do what she did best. We had a very interesting night.

Before giving Penelope and Mother my answer to Penelope's proposal, I wanted to sit down with Elizabeth and see if she objected to taking on a nursing position full time. If she had no problems with that, I would give Penelope the job.

Everything went well with Elizabeth. She was excited that she would be doing full-time nursing, a job she'd always wanted to do. She was pleased to know that Penelope would be coming aboard, and that she would have an opportunity to train and get to know her. *Things are looking up,* I thought!

After Penelope became my receptionist, I felt free enough to start scheduling trips to the different plantations in Union, Columbia, and Ouachita Counties. I had been approached by several big plantation owners to look after their families and slaves. I was able to negotiate a retainer's fee with those who had contacted me.

The first plantation on my weekly schedule was the Silas Arlington plantation, which was located just over the Union County line, in Ouachita County. As I slowly traveled down the Champagnolle road that led from El Dorado to the little town of Champagnolle, my mind began to reflect upon my days in Autauga County. I was in hopes of having pleasant experiences in Union, Ouachita, and Columbia Counties, not like the ones I experienced back in Autauga County.

What would I say, or do, if I found slave abuse going on? My mind was filled with questions. Would I be able to speak my mind to Mr. Arlington? Would I encourage him to treat his slaves better? Would I be able to warn him of the consequences of abusing his slaves, or would I treat it as none of my business?

As I pulled up at the plantation house, I could sense that Mr. Arlington took pride in keeping his place looking good. The grounds surrounding his plantation home reminded me of Twin Oaks. The lawn was well groomed and the garden on the east side of the house was well kept, free of grass and weeds. Someday Three Oaks would look just as good, I thought.

As I was stepping down from my carriage, a nice Negro man dressed in black pants and a white shirt greeted me. I started up the stairs leading to the front porch.

"How may I help you?" he asked.

"I'm Dr. Obadiah Bradford. I'm here to see Mr. Arlington."

"You come on in, Dr. Bradford, and I'll let Master Arlington knows you are here. You have a seat in the parlor," he said as he pointed toward the parlor.

"Thank you!"

The parlor had several beautiful pictures hanging on the wall. One of the pictures was a beautiful portrait of Mr. and Mrs. Arlington. The picture appeared to be new. I had never met Mr. Arlington. His overseer was the one who came by my office and worked out a retainer's fee.

I heard steps coming down the hall. I thought I heard a cane hitting the floor as well. I had no sooner gotten out of my chair when Mr. Arlington came through the door, leaning on his walking cane.

"You must be Dr. Bradford?" he said.

"Yes, sir, I'm Obadiah Bradford."

"I'm please to make your acquaintance," he said as he reached out his hand to greet me.

"I'm please to meet you as well, Mr. Arlington."

"Just call me Silas. Everyone around here calls me Silas."

"Silas it will be," I said.

"Dr. Bradford, I'm happy you accepted my offer to look after my family and my slaves. As you can see, I'm not getting around very well.

"One year ago, I was thrown from my horse and, as a result of that fall, I've suffered a lot of damage to my back, hip, and left leg. The pain and agony I've gone through has been a big challenge for me."

"First, let me say, I'm sorry about your accident. I hope I can be of some help to you."

"I'm hoping the same," he said as he sat down in a nearby parlor chair.

"Dr. Bradford, I have three grown sons and one daughter. Two of the sons have gone away to college. My oldest son is handicapped. He lives here with Melody and me. He was born mentally deficient and performs somewhere around a second-grade level of education.

"My daughter, Susan, is a beauty. She's eighteen and she's the apple of my eye. She, too, lives here with Melody and me. You will surely meet her before you leave today. I warn you, she pretty much rules the household!

"My wife, Melody, is in the garden. She loves the outdoors. She's the healthy one. Don't think she will need any medical attention any time soon."

"What about your slaves?"

"I've had pretty good luck with my slaves, but some of them are getting up in age and need some attention. I have forty-one slaves altogether. I would like for you to do a quick assessment of them when you can schedule it in your work day."

"If you can arrange it, I could see some of them during this trip and schedule the others at a later date."

47

"I'll call Joe, and he can get started on seeing how many are not tied up in the fields."

Mr. Arlington called Joe, who came quickly into the parlor. Joe was the handsome young man who greeted me as I came into the house. He looked to be about thirty years of age. He seemed to be well educated, as well. Silas told me he didn't know what he'd do without Joe. He was their chief household slave and their main carriage driver.

"Mr. Arlington, if you don't mind, I would like to start with you. Do you want to go to your room? I would like to examine you thoroughly."

"My room would be the best. I'll tell Nestle, my housemaid, that we are not to be interrupted."

"Why don't you start by giving me your medical history? After that, I'll do an examination. How does that sound?"

Mr. Arlington was a funny gentleman. He had me laughing most of the time. I thought to myself, this man has to be a good man, by the way he talks and presents himself. I would bet he is good to his slaves as well.

After sharing his medical history with me, I began to examine him from head to foot. I discovered from talking with him that he had never gone to rehab after breaking his left leg. He explained that Dr. Weaver had set his leg, but that he hadn't returned to Dr. Weaver for additional examinations.

"May I ask why you never returned to see Dr. Weaver?"

"I didn't see a need to go back to him. He didn't encourage me, so I decided I could rehabilitate myself."

"Silas, have you taken any falls after the leg was set?"

"Why do you ask that?"

"I'm not one hundred percent sure, but I think you may have broken your hip as well."

"I do recollect falling a few times after returning home," he answered.

"Did your hip hurt after you fell those times?"

"Oh, yes, indeed it did!"

"Did you ever wonder if you may have broken it?"

"No, I just thought it was sore from the falls."

"Silas, your hip may be your biggest problem. I believe your leg is healed nicely, but I think your main problem is with your hip. If it's broken, I might be able to fix it through surgery."

"Oh, no! No surgery!" he said, very loudly.

"Not even if it would take care of your problem?"

"What would you have to do?"

"I don't know exactly. I would have to see how much damage you've done and then try to repair it."

"Do you think I might be able to walk without a cane?"

"If I can repair it, yes, you would be able to walk normally again, I would think."

"I'll study about it, Dr. Bradford. I'll give you an answer before you leave today."

Just as Silas was getting dressed, there was a knock at the door.

"I'm Melody Arlington, and you must be Dr. Bradford," Mrs. Arlington said as she entered the room.

"I'm pleased to meet you, Mrs. Arlington."

"Just call me Melody. Silas and I like to be called by our first name. Dr. Bradford, what do people call you?"

"You can call me Obadiah."

"Obadiah; that's from the Bible, isn't it?" Melody asked.

"That's right, Melody!"

"I like the name Obadiah, and I do believe you are the first Obadiah I've met. Well, is my Silas going to make me a young or old widow?" She laughed.

"I believe it's going to be a long time before he meets his maker," I replied.

"Melody, Obadiah will be examining most of our slaves today. He's also prepared to examine you today as well," Silas said.

"I will be last! I must get a bath first. I've been working in my garden. I don't think you want to examine me right now," Melody said as she left the room.

"Silas, I like your wife. She reminds me of my mother, Catherine Bradford."

"I don't know what I would have done this past year if it hadn't been for Melody. We've been soul-mates for some twenty-five years. She's a keeper!"

I spent the rest of the day examining Silas's slaves: his daughter, Susan; son George; and Melody. Other than Silas, the other family members were in good health. I was hoping Silas would come to El Dorado and let me do the necessary surgery. I was not one hundred percent sure, but I thought I might be able to repair the hip problem. If so, I think Silas will be in good health and could later throw that walking cane in the fire.

The majority of the slaves I examined appeared to be in fairly good shape. There were three that needed to be watched closely. Two were young slave girls who would be delivering a child in the near future. The other was a male slave with a persistent cough. I needed to give some thought to how best to treat him. I thought I could rule out tuberculosis at that time.

As I was getting ready to leave, Silas came to me and said, "Obadiah, I've decided to take you up on your offer to fix my hip. When do you want to see me in El Dorado?" he asked.

"When I get back to my office, I'll get Penelope to set up a time. I will have her send you the date by mail. How does that sound to you?"

"I'm good with that!"

I went ahead and scheduled a return visit to examine the rest of Silas's slaves.

I left Silas's plantation, feeling good about how he treated his slaves. In fact, if I had to compare him to plantation owners in Autauga County, I would rate him high on his treatment of his slaves. The slave housing wasn't as good as it could be, but it wasn't the worst I'd seen. The cabins had heat and ample room, and it appeared that the occupants had ample blankets to keep them warm.

On my way back to El Dorado, I felt good about my day. If all my house calls go as well as this one, I will be one happy camper in a new land, I thought!

CHAPTER 10

By the middle of March, it is getting close to potato-planting time. In another week the ground will be getting soft enough for cultivation. I have to find time to get with Hank and start planning for the spring and fall planting.

Hank and Nanny are expecting their second child. Nanny is about seven months into her pregnancy. Hank has been letting her help with the cooking at the bunkhouse.

Hank's little boy, Obi, is growing like a weed. He is Hank's shadow. Everywhere Hank goes, Obi is by his side.

I had Penelope clear my calendar for March 14 so I can meet with Hank, George, and Big Jim. They are the ones who will play a major role in getting the fields cultivated and ready for planting. We will plant several acres of white and red potatoes as well as sweet potatoes. Potatoes are a good food for the slaves, and they will be able to have potatoes year-round. I certainly don't want any of my slaves to go hungry.

I decided on March 14 to bring all my slaves together in the bunkhouse and address them all at one time. I haven't done that since moving to Three Oaks.

Hank, Big Jim, and George have handled my slaves' needs since we came to Three Oaks. I have been too busy to get involved. Today will be a special day. I have some of the best slaves in the country. I have treated them well, and in return, they have given back to me 100 percent of their work capacity.

The winter months were good. The slaves are healthy and ready for spring planting. They look forward to planting a big garden and share in having fresh vegetables to eat.

I will continue to follow my father's tradition during planting and harvesting time. The slaves will eat their breakfast around ten o'clock in the fields. Food will be prepared by Old

John and his wife, Lolo, and Mr. Sam and his wife, Beulah. Hank will make arrangements to transport the breakfast food to the slaves in the field.

At night, the slaves will eat in the bunkhouse or get their food and take it to their individual living quarters.

After my meeting with the slaves, Hank, George, Big Jim, and I got into a wagon and toured the plantation. We inspected the fields and selected the areas best suited for planting potatoes, corn, and cotton. We picked wooded areas where trees could be cleared for heating and cooking purposes.

The large garden spot will be located close to the plantation home. This will make it easier for the female slaves to dig baby potatoes to be used in soups and other dishes. I loved baby potatoes with sweet peas.

The slaves were pretty much free to do as they wanted during the winter months. They still had chores to do, but nothing like they will be doing during spring and fall planting and harvesting. Some of them have gained some weight, and that is a good thing.

My day went by fast. I enjoyed spending the day with Hank. He is one of my best friends. He is smart and knows exactly what I'm saying. He and I have sat down and made a list of supplies he will need for the spring planting. He will purchase the supplies at Virgil and Mary's general store in El Dorado.

While visiting with Hank, I inquired about his Sunday church service, being held at the bunkhouse.

"The services are going good, Master Obadiah."

"I'm sorry I've not asked you about this sooner. Is there anything you need?"

"There is one thing, if you would agree to it," he said.

"What might that be?"

"Do you think you could get us a few Bibles?"

"Who would be using these Bibles, Hank?"

"If you recall, Penelope taught a number of our young slaves to read and write back in Autauga County. I'm thinking if they had some Bibles, they could teach their family members how to read. I think they would understand my sermons and teaching better," he said.

"Hank, I think that's a great idea. If you want Bibles, I'll get you Bibles."

"Oh, thank you, Master Obadiah!"

"You are most welcome, Hank. I just may try to make one of your services sometime."

"We would love to have your whole family, Master Obadiah. I think that would be really special."

"Do you think missing a sermon in El Dorado will be worth hearing you preach?"

"Master Obadiah! Your teasing me, aren't you?"

"No, I'm really not. We may just visit your church service some Sunday and skip church at First Baptist. I'm ready to hear you preach and some good roof-raising gospel music from your congregation."

"You're welcome to come anytime. I'd love it!"

I explained to Hank that he will work closely with both Big Jim and George.

Big Jim will assume the duties and responsibilities of overseeing the cotton gin during cotton-picking time. He will also be in charge of equipment repairs and looking after the animals.

George will be in the fields with the slaves during the day. He will also be responsible for the slaves and housing needs.

I told Hank he'd be working with Penelope on financial matters. He is to report to me from time to time on the progress of crop planting and harvesting.

I informed Hank that Penelope will be responsible for the plantation's financial revenues and expenses. She will be working with him in approving supply needs and the collection of charged tickets associated with purchases for the plantation.

Everything was set in place on March 14. I was now free to get back to my daily job of being a doctor to a growing patient population. If the people keep coming, I may have to have that second doctor sooner than I thought. If that need occurs, I know exactly who I want.

My good friend Dr. Jim Burroughs is currently one of the staff doctors at Daniel Pratt's new hospital back in Prattville, Alabama. Jim and I went to school together at the Old Military Medical School in Augusta, Georgia. We lived in the Milton House in the historical district of Augusta. Jim, John Peters, Ben Murphy, Henry Dotson, and I were known as the five musketeers. We were always doing something together and became the best of friends.

Jim is the only one of the five who hasn't married. He was a groomsman at my and Audrey's wedding. I know he would come to El Dorado if I asked him. I've decided to write him a letter and ask whether he'd be interested in coming.

I can see, as the town grows, we will eventually need a hospital like the one in Prattville.

CHAPTER 11

Although the Emancipation Proclamation didn't immediately end slavery in the Confederacy, it did transform the character of the war. Those slaves who had been liberated were accepted as part of the Union Army and Navy, which brought on the saying, "The liberated are now the liberators."

The Civil War has not hurt the economy in Union County, nor have any battles come close. The Union Army hasn't seen the southern counties as a threat. To me, that's perfectly all right. I've seen enough of the war from my experience in the battles of Shiloh and Corinth.

Union County hasn't experienced any action in battle as yet, but there has been some action in regard to the war in the past few weeks. Young and middle-aged men have been coming to town on a daily basis to visit with Colonel Albert Rust, who is commander of the Third Arkansas.

Colonel Rust has spent the last two weeks recruiting soldiers for two companies out of Union County and the surrounding areas for the Third Arkansas.

Colonel Rust has gained a lot of respect from the citizens of Union County. The men he's recruited think of him as being an ideal commander, a giant in stature, with great endurance, a remarkable intellect, and reckless bravery.

He came here for the sole purpose of recruiting two companies for the Third Arkansas, and it appears he will soon accomplish his task.

The two companies he has organized consist of Company "E," which is composed of men from Hillsboro, Champagnolle, and the area around Champagnolle. To head up this company, he chose Thomas Nolan, a friend of mine, as captain.

Company "G" is headed up by Captain J. W. Reedy. Captain Reedy's enlistments came from Three Creeks, Lisbon, and the outlying area.

According to the El Dorado News-Times, Colonel Rust's Third Arkansas will be sent to Virginia to join General Henry R. Jackson's brigade. The Third Arkansas will consist of a regiment of some eleven hundred men and will be among the first to be sent to the front in Virginia.

As both companies were getting ready to leave Union County, I found myself sadden, knowing that several of these young and middle-aged men wouldn't return to Union County alive. The excitement of the war and being anxious to fight for the Southern cause are gratifying to them now, but when they actually become engaged in battle, that will probably change.

I had already experienced the real thing at Shiloh and Corinth, Mississippi, two of the bloodiest battles of the war so far. It wasn't nearly as glamorous as some soldiers had thought!

These young men, who have been signing up daily, have no idea of what they will eventually experience in battle. Some will be killed without firing a shot. Some will survive wounds that will leave them disfigured or handicapped for the remainder of their lives. Some will get lucky and return to live a normal life, but as a whole, the war will take a toll on them in different ways.

Once they engage in battle, they will quickly see that this is reality. It is kill or be killed! Their excitement will turn to fear. The war they once thought to be glamorous and exciting will turn into blood and guts. Oh, how I pitied each of them!

On Saturday, before the two companies left to join the Third Arkansas, a large send-off party was held on the El Dorado Court square. The churches in town provided the food.

I have never seen so much food. The east side of the court square was filled with tables of food and drink. The streets surrounding the courthouse were roped off, allowing an area for dancing and music.

My entire family was present for the celebration. Penelope is a lot like Audrey. She loves to dance. We spent a lot of time dancing, eating, and drinking punch. Although my mother will be turning sixty-five shortly, she still has the energy and endurance to dance. I believe she ended up dancing with every available middle-aged man in the city of El Dorado. It did my heart good to see her enjoy herself.

The celebration went on into the early part of the night, when the recruits left to go home to prepare for their early morning departure.

After Companies "E" and "G" left, things returned to normal around town. The city of El Dorado returned to its calm daily activities. I continued my daily schedule at the clinic and made several calls to the plantations in Union, Ouachita, Calhoun, and Columbia Counties.

While traveling from county to county calling on plantations, my thoughts turned to my good friend Dr. Henry Dotson. The last letter I received from Henry was well over a week ago. He was still in Vicksburg, Mississippi, where the siege of Vicksburg was under way.

In his last letter to me, he said, "Obadiah, if Vicksburg falls to the Union Army, it will greatly damage the South's chances of ever winning the Civil War."

I knew exactly what Henry was saying. Prior to General Ulysses Grant's campaign to capture Vicksburg, the city played a major role in exporting supplies down the Mississippi River to different parts of the Confederacy. If General Grant takes Vicksburg, the North will control the Mississippi and stop the exporting of goods to the South.

The El Dorado News-Times has been carrying short stories of the Union's attempt to take Vicksburg. General Grant's army tried unsuccessfully several times to capture Vicksburg. Every attempt made by the Union Army failed. Vicksburg has several advantages over the Union Army. It is well-fortified, and the terrain makes it impossible to break through the Confederate lines, which are positioned all around the city of Vicksburg.

In Henry's letter he wrote, "Obadiah, my greatest fear is if the Union Army captures all the small towns around Vicksburg, they will be able to isolate us from other parts of the South. General Grant could sit back and starve us to death without firing a shot. We are presently rationing food as I write to you."

I answered Henry's letter and mailed it to Vicksburg, hoping that it would get through to him.

Again, I count my blessings daily that I am presently in El Dorado where my family and I are healthy and safe from this terrible War. I do worry about Henry's well-being and the well-being of my nephew, Marion, Dent's oldest son. He, too, is stationed at Vicksburg. I pray daily that our God will protect them from harm.

Another important letter came yesterday. It was from my good friend Dr. Jim Burroughs. Jim wrote to give me an answer to whether he would be interested in coming to El Dorado to join me in my medical practice.

In his letter of response he said, "I'm definitely interested in joining you in your practice at El Dorado. I've giving my six weeks' resignation notice to the hospital board and plan to join you in El Dorado at the conclusion of my obligation here in Prattville."

Since receiving Jim's welcome letter, I have been excited. I know Jim is going to be a valuable asset to our clinic.

All in all, things are going well. Hank, George, and Big Jim are doing an excellent job with the plantation. The fields are being prepared and gardens are being planted.

Hank has established himself as my overseer, and people around town know who he is. He continues to work very hard in proving himself worthy of the position he holds. He and Nanny are expecting their second child anytime now.

Penelope is doing a great job as my receptionist. She makes everyone feel right at home as soon as they arrive at my office. She's very thorough and organized. She makes sure I'm not overbooked, and leaves a good hour open for us to have lunch together at Jake's Restaurant on a daily basis.

Mother is enjoying getting to make new friends at First Baptist and in town as well. She has her weekly card games and socials. She hasn't forgotten a thing about entertaining guests. Since she feels obligated to her grandchildren, while Penelope is working, she schedules most of her social events at Three Oaks.

Today I will make a visit to Mr. Benjamin Olson's plantation, which is located west of El Dorado, near the small community of Mt. Holly. From what I've heard around town, Mr. Olson doesn't have the best reputation or respect from other plantation owners in Union County. I am not sure what I will find during my visit at his plantation.

As I approached his plantation, I was impressed with the plantation house. It was well kept. The slave quarters appeared to be in great need of repair, and the barn looked pretty shabby as well.

I pulled in front of the house and was met by one of Mr. Olson's slaves. He greeted me and told me he would take care of my carriage. He pointed to the front door and said, "Master Olson is expecting you."

I thanked him and proceeded to climb the steps to the front porch. After reaching the front door, I knocked on the door, and a maid opened the door and asked, "How can I help you?"

"I'm Dr. Bradford. I'm here to see Mr. Olson," I said.

"Master Olson is expecting you. He told me to show you to the parlor."

I followed her to the parlor, where she asked me if I would like something to drink.

"I will have a glass of water, if that's not a problem."

"You have a seat, Dr. Bradford, and I'll get you a glass of water. We got some of the best water in these parts," she said.

I asked her what her name was and she said, "They call me Martha."

Martha hadn't been gone but a minute when Benjamin Olson entered the room.

"You must be Dr. Bradford," he said.

"Yes, I am, and you must be Benjamin Olson."

"Just call me Ben," he said as he reached out his hand to greet me.

As we sat down, I wasn't getting any bad feelings from his tone of voice, and I found myself questioning if what I had heard in town was true.

Mr. Olson began to share with me how he purchased his plantation after coming here from Rome, Georgia. He said he enjoyed harvesting timber as well as farming cotton and corn. He said he liked the Mt. Holly area because of its tall virgin pine. "One won't find these tall virgin pines in Rome, Georgia," he said.

He went on to say that he owned fifty-two slaves, fifty head of cattle, ten horses, and lots of hogs and chickens.

He informed me that his overseer was Mac Burton, one of the toughest overseers in these parts. He said Burton had put the fear of God into his slaves.

"There's only been one male slave who attempted to run away, and after a good flogging by Mac, he hasn't attempted to run away again."

"How do you want me to proceed in the examination of your slaves?" I asked.

"I've instructed Mac to round up our slaves so you can take a look at them. What will you need from me?" he asked.

"First of all, I'll need a place where there is plenty of light, water, soap, and towels."

"I figured you'd need those things, so I've instructed Mac to let you use his house to conduct your examinations. I've asked him to let Lula, his live-in, assist you in your examinations."

It didn't take me long to see that Burton had him a mulatto slave girl as his live-in. Her light skin reminded me of Mattie.

I instructed Lula to heat some water. After heating the water, I instructed her to bring a dishpan of warm water, soap, and some towels to be used in my examinations.

When I was ready, I walked out on the porch and told Burton that I was ready. As I turned, I heard Burton, crack his whip. I quickly turned and looked. The slaves were scared to death of this man.

"Y'all line up right here," Burton said, pointing to the ground.

The slaves quickly fell in line, with most of them trembling from fear of Burton.

It didn't take me long to see that Olson's slaves were malnourished. They were weak and skin and bones. Some of the older slaves were coughing. In fact, some were very croupy.

Some were suffering from high blood pressure; some had bad sores on their bodies.

I had to wash the dirt off several of the slaves before I could see the infected areas. After washing the dirt away, I immediately saw that the sores were infected. The sores resembled impetigo, which was quite prevalent among the slaves in Autauga County. Impetigo is treatable, and I had the ointment to treat these infections.

As I was washing away the dirt from slaves, who were wearing very little clothing, I was reminded of the day Dr. Banister and I visited a plantation where we found over a dozen slaves lying on a dirt floor, huddled together to keep warm. We found them in a hut, with no fire and no blankets to cover their half-clothed bodies. Since there was no heat, we found two slaves on the outer edge of the circle frozen to death. Several of the slaves had pneumonia.

While examining Olson's slaves, I found some suffered from poor eyesight. I had never seen this type of abuse. The more I examined, the more I became angered. It took me the entire day to complete my examinations. Out of fifty slaves, only about one-third of them would pass a physical. The others needed medical attention.

I asked Burton if he would show me the slave quarters.

"Why do you need to see the slave quarters?" he asked.

"I need to give Mr. Olson a report on my findings, and I can't make my report unless I personally see the conditions of the slave quarters."

"Well, I guess it will be all right," he said reluctantly.

I was appalled by the conditions I witnessed. My favorable impression of Benjamin Olson was decreasing fast.

After touring the slave quarters, I went directly to the plantation house to see Benjamin Olson.

Martha, Mr. Olson's maid, escorted me to the parlor where Mr. Olson was enjoying some hot tea.

"Come on in, Dr. Bradford, and have a seat," Mr. Olson said.

"Thank you, Mr. Olson," I said.

"Remember, you can call me Benjamin or Ben."

"I need to talk to you about your slaves," I said.

"How did you find them?" he asked.

"Not so good," I answered.

"Well, tell me about it, Dr. Bradford."

"You will not like what I'm about to say," I said.

"Oh, hell, Dr. Bradford! Just spit it out!"

"I'm afraid if you don't make immediate improvements to their living quarters, you are going to lose several of them."

"Come on now, Dr. Bradford! Surely it's not that bad!"

"Benjamin, I can assure you, it's bad!"

"Let me hear what you've got to recommend," Benjamin said.

"First, you've got to make improvements to your slave quarters. You need to add wood floors to each of the houses and get some proper bedding and blankets in each house. You need to provide firewood or something for the fireplaces. You also need better ventilation in most of them. A lot of the slaves have been infested with insect bites. I can give you medicine for that, but medicine is not going to do the job unless you clean those quarters up."

"Is that all, Dr. Bradford?"

"No, sir! Your slaves are malnourished. They need to be fed nourishing food. Some are so weak they have trouble walking. Some can hardly see. You've got to do something about them now if you want them to live."

"My slaves always look this way coming out of winter. They normally bounce back when we start raising fresh vegetables and corn."

"Benjamin, may I ask you how many slaves you lost this winter?"

"I don't know if that's any of your business, but I lost five. They were old and just couldn't survive the harsh conditions."

"Did it dawn on you that maybe they might have survived if they were better nourished and had better quarters to live in?"

"Now, you are meddling, Dr. Bradford. I hired you to doctor my slaves. That doesn't give you the right to tell me what

I should and shouldn't do. I appreciate your concern, but I'll decide what's best for my slaves."

"Indeed, you will, I'm sure!" I said.

"Dr. Bradford, I would have to spend a small fortune to make the improvements you've mentioned. I can't do that!"

"You asked for my recommendations, Benjamin. Now you have them. I guess you can do whatever you're led to do," I said as I got up from my chair to get ready to leave.

"Dr. Bradford, will you be leaving prescriptions for medicine that is needed for treatment of the infections and the coughs you mentioned?"

"I've written prescriptions for you. You can get the medicine at Bartley's Drug Store in El Dorado. I would suggest, the sooner, the better!"

Benjamin followed me to the front porch and bade me goodbye. As I left his place, I was very angry. I now fully understood what Dr. Banister meant when he said his hands were tied. There was little I could do for Mr. Olson's slaves.

The law was clear. Slaves were at the mercy of their owner. The owner could flog them, starve them, rape them, or do anything he wanted to them. He could literally kill them, and that's exactly what Olson was doing through his neglect. Oh, what a shame! Oh, Lord, have mercy upon their souls!

I arrived back in El Dorado just in time to see Penelope, Elizabeth, and Beth Ann. They too had a busy day.

I helped Penelope into the carriage, and off we went to Three Oaks. I was hungry. I hadn't eaten since breakfast and yearned for some of Betsy's and Mattie's home cooking. I was hoping for fried chicken but would be satisfied with anything.

Penelope and I had a good visit on our way home. There was never a silent moment between the two of us. Today, Penelope brought up the subject of the Emancipation Proclamation.

"Obadiah, today at lunch, Elizabeth, Beth Ann, and I went to Jake's Restaurant. As we were eating our lunch, I overheard a discussion between two ladies who were sitting at a table near us. They were talking about President Lincoln's Emancipation

Proclamation which freed slaves. Do you know why that hasn't been carried through on?"

"Well, the main reason is that the South doesn't feel they are part of the United States of America, and until this war is over, they will operate under rules of their own, as a Confederacy. If the North wins the Civil War and peace comes, the South will have to obey the proclamation."

"Does that mean all of our slaves will be freed?"

"Yes, that's what it means."

"Where will our slaves go?"

"That will depend on them, Penelope."

"How will they live?"

"That's a very important question. It will be awfully hard on slaves to find enough work to provide for their families."

"The ladies were also talking about sharecropping and tenant farming. I didn't quite understand all of that."

"I believe it will come down to sharecropping and, maybe, tenant farming if the North wins the Civil War. I've given some thought to what I would do. I think I would give my slaves an opportunity to continue to work for me at Three Oaks. I believe I would choose sharecropping over tenant farming.

"If my slaves choose sharecropping, they will do the farming and receive a portion of the proceeds that are made from the sale of the products. If they choose tenant farming, they will rent out the land from the plantation owner and farm it. They would pay the plantation owner for rental of the property and then receive more of the proceeds from the sale of the products. Does that make sense to you?"

"Yes, it makes a lot of sense to me when you explain it."

I put my arm around her and pulled her near me. I love this woman. She is very intelligent and doesn't miss a thing. That's why I trust her with our finances.

As we pulled up in front of our house, Charles and Belle were waiting on the porch, as usual, to greet us. As soon as we started up the steps to the porch, Belle threw herself into my arms. Charles preferred to hug Penelope first and, later, gave me a hug. I am truly grateful to God for giving me two wonderful children.

CHAPTER 12

The El Dorado News-Times continues to publish articles on the Vicksburg Campaign.

On May 12, 1863, General Ulysses S. Grant's Army of Tennessee began their conquest in capturing areas around Vicksburg. It began with the Battle of Raymond in Hinds County, Mississippi.

The Confederate forces under Lt. General John C. Pemberton failed to prevent the Union army from reaching the Southern Railroad and isolating Vicksburg from reinforcements and supplies.

On the morning of May 12, the Confederates had a two-to-one advantage in numbers, as they faced off across Fourteen Mile Creek against a single Federal Brigade. As the Confederates waited in ambush, the Union division secretly deployed into the fields beside the brigade, giving the union troops a three-to-one advantage in numbers and seven-to-one advantage in artillery.

The ranking Confederate officer, Brig. General John Gregg, attempted to achieve tactical surprise and rout the Union Army as it crossed the creek, but he was in turn tactically surprised and routed from the field by the Union XVII Corps under the command of Maj. General James B. McPherson. At the end of the Battle of Raymond, the Union army was victorious. During the battle, there were sixty-eight Union soldiers killed, 341 wounded, and 37 missing. The Confederate casualties were nearly double: 100 killed, 305 wounded and 412 captured.

The defeat of the Confederate Army at the Battle of Raymond played a major role in the Vicksburg Campaign.

Union interdiction of the railroad interrupted Pemberton's attempt to further consolidate his forces and prevented him from linking up with his commanding officer, General Joseph E. Johnston. As a result, Pemberton was limited to three options: abandon Vicksburg, withdraw into the city and accept a siege, or fight a meeting engagement against a superior force. Facing conflicting orders from his superiors and open insurrection from his subordinates, Pemberton was forced into the latter choice on May 16, 1863, at the Battle of Champion Hill.

After reading this article, my heart went out to the Confederate Army. It now appears that Henry's fear of Vicksburg being surrounded by the Union and being cut off from the outside world was set in place. If the Union Army captures all the surrounding towns, railroads, and waterways, it will be only a short time before Vicksburg will fall.

I prayed for Henry, Marion, and the officers and soldiers in Vicksburg. I wondered what would happen to Henry, Marion, and the Confederate soldiers should Vicksburg surrender to General Grant. Would General Ulysses Grant spare the lives of the Confederate soldiers? Would he imprison them, or would he kill them?

On May 14, 1863, we had an extremely busy morning, seeing one patient after another. The morning passed fast, and when twelve o'clock came around, Penelope and I went to lunch.

After lunch at Jake's Restaurant, Penelope and I returned to my office. As usual, Penelope went to her station behind the receptionist counter to check in our first afternoon patient. I had gone on to my office to ready myself for the afternoon patients' schedule. I had just sat down when I heard Elizabeth call out for me.

"Dr. Bradford, please come quickly!"

I ran out of my office to find Elizabeth on her knees, putting a pillow under Penelope's head.

"What's happened here?" I asked.

"Penelope fainted," Elizabeth said.

Penelope opened her eyes and asked, "What happen to me?"

"You fainted, my love." I said.

"I've never fainted in my life."

"Do you think you can sit up?"

"I believe I can."

By this time, Beth Ann had joined us behind the counter. The three of us helped Penelope into a chair. I examined her, and her blood pressure was fine. She was a little pale, but all of her vital signs were good.

"Do you remember anything?" I asked.

"No. I was feeling fine, and all of a sudden, I felt dizzy, and that's all I remember until now," she said.

"We're going to put you back in a room for a while and watch you."

"Who's going to see after the front?" Penelope asked.

"Elizabeth can take care of the front. You don't worry about that."

Needless to say, Penelope's fainting scared me. She has always been healthy. I don't understand what caused this. I will give her a thorough examination before we leave the office today. I wondered if it was something she had eaten at the restaurant.

The afternoon went by fast. After seeing my last patient, I went to see Penelope.

"How are you feeling?" I asked.

"I feel fine, Obadiah."

"Have you had any additional dizziness since fainting earlier?"

"Not one bit. I've been awfully bored back here with nothing to do. I found some old newspapers, and I've been catching up on some of the news."

"Good. I'm sorry we've been busy all afternoon. I have seen several patients who have flu symptoms. It's a little late for flu, but that's what it is. I hope you're not coming down with the flu, my love."

"I don't feel bad at all."

"I'm going to give you a thorough examination before we head home. Do you think you can give me a urine specimen?"

"Yes, I believe I can. I've needed to use the bathroom, but didn't want to go to the bathroom in case I got dizzy again."

After Penelope returned from the bathroom with her urine specimen, I gave her a full examination. I have to admit, I had never had to give Penelope a physical examination. It was a little odd, to say the least.

As I was analyzing the urine test, a strange thought entered my mind. Could Penelope be pregnant? We certainly hadn't used any methods to avoid getting pregnant.

As I finished the test, I discovered that Penelope was, indeed, pregnant. I was going to be a father again!

This is going to be the best news I could share with my beloved wife. Penelope wanted to give me a child in the worst way. She talked about it all the time. She wondered what it would be like to be a mother. I couldn't wait to tell her. When would be the right time?

As I entered her room, she looked at me with those piercing, blue eyes and a smile on her face.

"Obadiah, can I get dressed now?"

"Yes, you may! Come to my office when you finish."

In a few minutes, Penelope came walking into my office, smiling.

"You appear to be in a good mood, Penelope!"

"Something tells me you've got something exciting to tell me."

"Well, my beautiful Penelope, I may just have!"

"Come on, Obadiah. Don't keep me waiting!"

"Come here and sit on my lap. I need a hug and kiss."

"I'd be more than happy to give my handsome husband a hug and a kiss," she said as she pounced on my lap.

We were soon caught up in one of our passionate moods. When we came up for air, I looked at her and said, "Penelope, my love, you are pregnant!"

"Oh, are you sure?" she said as she looked into my eyes with the most exciting look on her face.

"Yes, the test was conclusive. I'm guessing right now, but you are probably two to three months along. I can't pin the time down yet, but will be able to as your pregnancy advances. I'm guessing the pregnancy caused you to faint."

"Obadiah, I am so happy!"

This was one of those moments in time that we both will never forget. God had given us some beautiful moments of memories together, but today would be historic.

Penelope and I decided we would wait until the weekend to share our good news. We had received news earlier in the week that my sisters, Sarah and Tanyua, and my brothers, Dent and John, and their families were coming to El Dorado to help celebrate our mother's sixty-fifth birthday.

They will be arriving by steamboat on Friday at Champagnolle. Virgil and I have made arrangements for wagons to pick them up and bring them to Three Oaks. They will be spending a full week with us. We have been excited about their visit. It will be like old times back at Twin Oaks. But this time, Penelope and I will be announcing the best news of our lives. Praise the Lord!

After dinner, Penelope and I turned in early. I was so tired and fell asleep holding Penelope in my arms. The night went fast. When I awoke, I looked across the room and watched Penelope brush her beautiful, black hair. I crawled out of bed, tipped-toed across the room, and wrapped my arms around her as I kissed her on the cheek. She smiled and raised her hands and touched my face. She had a glow on her face that I hadn't seen before. I could tell my Penelope was a very happy girl.

We met Mother and the kids in the dining room for breakfast. As usual, Mattie and Betsy had cooked a great breakfast. It was so hard for Penelope and me to keep our secret.

As I opened the El Dorado News-Times, I could see the headline. It read, "Union Forces Defeat Confederacy in the Battle of Jackson, Mississippi."

As I read the article, I realized that Henry's fear was becoming a reality as each battle was fought.

The article summarized the outcome and importance of the Battle of Jackson, Mississippi:

On May 9, 1863, General Joseph E. Johnston received a dispatch from the Confederate Secretary of War directing him to proceed at once to Mississippi and take command of the forces in the field. When he arrived in Jackson on May 13 from middle Tennessee, he learned that two army corps from the Union Army of Tennessee, the XV under Major General William T. Sherman and XVII under Major General James B. McPherson, were advancing on Jackson. The Union armies' goal was to cut the city and the railroads off from Vicksburg.

These corps, under the overall command of General Ulysses Grant, had crossed the Mississippi River south of Vicksburg and driven northeast toward Jackson. The railroad connections were to be cut to isolate the Vicksburg garrison. If the Confederate troops in Jackson were defeated, they would be unable to threaten Grant's flank or rear during his eventual assault on Vicksburg.

After learning that there were only 6,000 Confederate troops available to defend Jackson, Johnston ordered the evacuation of Jackson but left Brig. General John Gregg behind to defend Jackson until the evacuation was completed.

After Johnston's evacuation of Jackson, it was learned that Johnston acted prematurely in ordering the evacuation. He later learned that if he had waited until May 14, he would have had 11,000 troops at his disposal and by the morning of May 15, another 4,000. The fall of the former Mississippi State Capital was a blow to Confederate morale.

Jackson had been destroyed as a transportation center, and the war industries were crushed. But more importantly the Confederate concentration of men and materials aimed at saving Vicksburg was scattered.

In the Battle of Jackson, the Union army had 286 casualties to the Confederates' 850.

It was certainly not looking good for Vicksburg.

On May 18, 1863, the *El Dorado News-Times* carried the headline, "Union Defeats Confederates at Champion Hill, Mississippi."

> *The Battle of Champion Hill* was perhaps the most important battle in the conquest to take Vicksburg. This was one of the largest battles of the conquest. When the battle was over, the Union army listed 410 killed, 1,844 wounded, and 187 missing for a total of 2,457.
>
> The Confederate army listed 381 killed, 1,018 wounded, and 2,441 missing or captured for a total of 3,840.
>
> On May 19, 1863, the Union Army defeated the Confederates at the Battle of Black River Bridge.
>
> General Ulysses Grant had accomplished his goal of isolating Vicksburg by his final conquest of defeating the Confederates at Champion Hill and Big Black River Bridge. It would be only a short time before Vicksburg would fall.

A sharp pain hit my stomach when I read that General Ulysses Grant had achieved his objective. I hadn't received any mail from Henry. I'm assuming he wasn't able to respond to my letter, if he even got it. I didn't have a good feeling about any of this.

On the night of May 21, at 1:30 a.m., Mattie knocked on our bedroom door.

"What is it, Mattie?" I asked.

"Obadiah, Hank's at the door, and he's beside himself. He says Nanny's in labor and is hurting badly."

"Mattie, put a big pot of water on the stove and get towels ready. I'll go talk to Hank!"

"Hank, I hear Nanny's in labor?"

"Obadiah, she's hurting something awful."

"Calm down, Hank. Everything is going to be all right. I'll get my bag. You go back to your house, and we will be there shortly."

"Please hurry, Obadiah!" he said as he turned and left the house.

I had never seen Hank in such panic. He is normally a calm person. I'm sure he's concerned about Nanny, but if I hadn't missed something, she was having a normal, healthy pregnancy. I'm sure she'll do just fine in her delivery.

My mother, who is one of the best midwives that I've ever worked with, was accompanying me, and she and Mattie will assist me in the delivery.

Hank met us at the door and said, "Obadiah, she's screaming her head off. Please do something!"

"You go get Mr. and Mrs. Sam and bring them over to keep you company. You might want to start a fire in the cookstove as well. We may need more hot water."

Mother, Mattie, and I went directly into Hank and Nanny's bedroom. Nanny looked at us and screamed out, "Master Bradford, please do something. I'm hurting bad!"

"Try to relax, Nanny. Everything is going to be all right," I said patting her on the hand.

After examining Nanny, it was apparent why she was in such distress. The baby was big, and it was time for her to deliver. We didn't have much time to spare. Because of the size of the baby, I will have to cut Nanny more than normal. She will lose a lot of blood.

After explaining to Mother and Mattie what was happening, we went to work as a team. Mother and Mattie were naturals. When the blood started squirting out from the incisions, my mother was right there with her towel. It wasn't long before Nanny was able to push her second son through the birth canal. He was a big baby but was perfect. This gave Hank and Nanny two boys. I know Nanny wanted a little girl, but there would be plenty time for that.

During the delivery process, I made incisions that helped Nanny push the baby through the birthing canal. Nanny lost a lot of blood in giving birth to her new son, but she is in good health, and I believe she will be all right.

I sent Mattie to get Hank so he could see his newborn son.

By the time he arrived, Mother had the baby cleaned up and placed in Nanny's arms. Hank went directly to Nanny and sat by her on the bed.

There was a special glow on Hank's and Nanny's faces as they held and admired their new son.

"What name have y'all chosen for him?" I asked.

"We are going to call him Samuel after Nanny's father, Mr. Sam. We will be calling him Sammy."

"I think that's a good name!" my mother said.

"Hank, let's you and me go outside for a few minutes and let Mother and Mattie finish up in here."

After going outside, I congratulated Hank on his new son. I assured him all was well with the baby and that Nanny had lost lots of blood, but should be all right. I told him she needed nourishing food and to be closely looked after for a few days. I suggested he get her mother, Beulah, to take care of her for about a week. She didn't need to be doing anything strenuous for at least seven days.

I also assured him that I would come by daily after work and check on her.

Hank was so thankful! He hugged me and told me he loved me.

"I love you too, Hank!"

As it was now four o'clock in the morning, I was exhausted and needed to get a little more sleep before going to work. I asked Penelope to let me sleep a little longer than usual this morning. I needed about an extra hour of sleep in order to be alert with my patients.

CHAPTER 13

After closing my office at noon, we ate lunch at Jake's Restaurant and headed out to Champagnolle to pick up my brothers' and sisters' families.

I had earlier instructed Bill, George, and Hank to bring wagons to Champagnolle. As we pulled up at the Ouachita River Port in Champagnolle, they were already there. They had pulled the wagons under a big oak tree and were standing, visiting with each other, when we arrived. I was so fortunate to have trustworthy slaves. They had never let me down, and I trusted them with my life.

The steamboat was scheduled to arrive at three o'clock p.m. from Monroe, Louisiana. Virgil and I pulled our carriages up next to our wagons and went inside the port to have refreshments. I bought drinks for Bill, George, and Hank, and had them delivered to the big oak tree where they were waiting.

Mother stayed behind at Three Oaks to supervise the big homecoming event she had planned. She, Mattie, Big Jim, Betsy, and others were busy roasting a pig in a fire pit and cooking food to go along with the roasted pig. It would be a meal fit for a king. When my mother organizes a social event, she goes all out to make people happy.

After having refreshments, Penelope, Mary, Virgil, and I walked up a spiral stairway to a deck overlooking the river port. From the deck we could see every boat coming up and down the Ouachita River. We will be able to see the steamboat well in advance of its arrival at the port. As we waited, Penelope and I enjoyed the scenery directly across the river. The beautiful bluff that touched down into the Ouachita River reached upward to a height of some forty feet, with virgin pines growing on top. What a beautiful sight to be seen, and what a nice place to build a river port, I thought.

Penelope spotted the steamboat first. "Look, here comes the steamboat," she said with excitement.

"How far away is it?" Mary asked.

"I figure it's still a mile away," I answered.

"I can't wait," Mary said.

I was excited as well. I hadn't seen my brothers and sisters since leaving Autauga County. It would be nice to catch up on what's going on there and how things are going at Twin Oaks.

When the steamboat got within a quarter of a mile from the port, the captain started blowing his whistle. It reminded me of the days when I was a kid, living on the Black Oaks plantation at Cahaba, in Dallas County, Alabama. I would go to Selma with my father and watch the steamboats arrive and depart from the river port. As the steamboats arrived and departed, they would sound their whistles. It was so loud at times that it hurt my ears.

As the steamboat approached the loading dock, we could see Dent, John, Tanyua, Sarah, and a big portion of their families waving their hats and shouting.

It was a joyful time! My heart pounded with excitement.

The Bradford family has always been a close-knit family. It had been several months since we'd seen each other.

As the steamboat pulled up to the dock, my nephews and nieces were the first to exit the boat. They came running, with their arms wide open. We greeted each other with laughter and tears.

My brothers, Dent and John, were the last to leave the boat. They were checking to see if any personal items had been left on the boat.

There were so many of them. All my nephews and nieces were present, except Marion, Dent's oldest son. He had been drafted into the Confederate Army and was headquartered at Vicksburg.

Dent's oldest daughter and my favorite niece, Mary Catherine, threw herself into my arms. She is no longer a teenage girl. She is now a beautiful lady, just like her mother, Sara.

Finally, Dent and John approached me with wide-open arms. We just stood there embracing each other as though we'd never break. Finally, we came up for air and greeted each other like most Southern gentlemen would. We Bradfords don't mind showing affection for each other. We got that from our mother. After spending several minutes together on the landing dock, the family baggage was loaded into wagons. My nephews and nieces who were old enough, jumped into the wagons and off we went to Three Oaks.

The road to Three Oaks is narrow and dusty, and not as good as those in Autauga County. We hit several potholes that made things interesting.

When we arrived at Three Oaks, my mother, Charles, Belle, Mattie, Betsy, and Mattie's two children were standing on the front porch, waving. Mother was wearing her favorite apron and wringing her hands. She does that when she gets excited.

As usual, my nephews and nieces were the first to greet their grandmother. As I stood watching everyone, I stopped and thanked God for this grand occasion. Family is everything, and God has again allowed us to get together. The old saying in Autauga County was, "Absence makes the heart grow fonder." I certainly agreed with that saying!

Our home was overrun by nephews and nieces exploring the house and the surroundings. I didn't mind! They were excited to be here. Three Oaks would be their home for the next seven days. We were grateful to have them in our home. They came to celebrate their grandmother's sixty-fifth birthday. It will be a memorable occasion for all of us. Charles and Belle will get to know their cousins, and the cousins will get to know them. Penelope, Mother, and I will do our best to entertain them and make them feel welcome.

I knew Dent's and John's boys enjoyed fishing, so I previously made arrangements for Hank to accompany them and provide transportation to the best fishing holes on Calion Creek. Hank is one of the best fishermen in these parts and he will be the ideal guide.

The weather is nice and warm, so we will celebrate Mother's birthday by eating under the big oak trees in our front yard.

After Mattie announced dinner was ready, mother called everyone to the front porch for instructions. She first thanked them for coming and expressed how much this meant to her.

Since Dent was the oldest, she called on him to offer a prayer of thanksgiving. Dent's prayers are always long, but touching. He carefully gave thanks to God for all blessings he could think of. By the time he finished, we were starving!

The dinner was a success. If anyone went to bed hungry, it was certainly their own fault. Since the weather was nice, camping tents were set up under the oak trees in the front yard.

The older boys and girls had indicated they wanted to sleep in the tents. There were sleeping cots set up on the front porch and inside the house. For the smaller children, beds were made on the floor.

My mother was a little concerned about not having enough bathrooms. I wasn't too concerned about the bathroom situation. I knew from being a boy and living in the country, that boys don't worry about bathrooms. They take advantage of the outside environment when needing to relieve themselves. It is the younger ones who have not experienced the outdoors and might need a little help.

After dinner everyone was summoned to our big front porch to recognize Mother with birthday gifts. Mother was seated in her favorite rocking chair, with several of her grandchildren gathered at her feet. If she had problems opening a present, there were plenty eager grandchildren ready to help.

There were so many presents! I believe every grandchild brought Mother a present. Like my father, James Bradford, Mother was complimentary of everything she opened and had some personal remark to each giver. My father was so good at this. He had a special gift for making others feel good.

After opening the gifts, the ladies joined Mother inside the house while the children played games in the front yard.

The night was beautiful. The whole sky was lit up by a beautiful, glowing, full moon. There were lots of stars that twinkled and danced across the sky. One couldn't ask for a better night.

The children had plenty of light to play their games.

Dent, John, and I sat on the porch, visiting and watching the children play. Mattie kept us supplied with lots of lemonade.

"John, how are things going at Twin Oaks?" I asked.

"The winter went well, and we didn't lose any of our slaves, so I guess you can say we've had a good year."

"What about Black Oaks, Dent?"

"We had a good year, brother! The worst thing that happened to us this year was to see Marion leave for the war. Sara and I miss Marion something awful and worry about him all the time. We've not heard from him in some time."

"Let me tell you what I know about Vicksburg. About two weeks ago, I got a letter from my good friend Dr. Henry Dotson. He wrote in his letter that food supplies for the soldiers were getting lower and lower each day. He said rationing of food had already started, and he didn't know how much longer they would have food or drink. He said he thinks that General Grant's objective is to take Vicksburg by not firing another shot. He said Grant would just wait until the supplies ran out and let starvation be the key for the surrender of Vicksburg.

"Our local newspaper here in El Dorado has run stories on Grant's victories around Vicksburg. The Northern Army has defeated the Confederacy in every battle that's been fought in the past few weeks. I believe Grant's army is now in position to starve Vicksburg into surrender."

"I'm sure your friend Dr. Dotson is right on the starvation strategy. In Marion's last letter he confirmed what your friend said about rationing food. He stated the soldiers were all getting restless and were going to bed hungry. He said he didn't know how much longer they could survive on what little food they received daily."

"What do you think will happen to our soldiers if Grant takes Vicksburg?" John asked.

"I would hope General Grant would have some mercy and not kill every officer and soldier he finds in Vicksburg," I said.

"This war has turned into a nightmare," Dent said.

"I agree with that," John replied.

"Sara worries about Marion so much that she can't sleep nor eat. She's losing weight every day that passes. She did well as long as she heard from him, but now that we've not heard anything in several weeks, she's not the same. I think she believes he's dead," Dent said.

"Oh, Dent, I don't believe he's dead. Grant's tried unsuccessfully a number of times to take Vicksburg by force, and each time our soldiers have turned back his assaults. I can't see Marion dead. I pray daily that God will shield him from harm," I said.

"If you guys don't mind, I would like to change the subject. I don't like talking about this crazy war," Dent said.

"What about you and Penelope? How are things going with you two?" Dent asked.

"It couldn't be better. As you know, Penelope works for me at my office in town, as a receptionist. She's so good at it and enjoys every minute of it."

"She's still as beautiful as always. I'm so happy you guys are married," Dent said.

"John, what's going on with your children?" I asked.

"My children are doing well in school. Jake has an interest in politics. Jennie is becoming interested in boys, and Daniel wants to be a doctor," John said.

"A doctor! I knew there was something special about Daniel!" I said with excitement.

"Let me know if you think I could be of assistance to him. He might want to come here and do an internship under me, like I did with Dr. Banister."

"Who knows? We may need your help someday," John said.

"Dent, what about Mary Catherine, Everett, and Law? What are they interested in?" I asked.

"Well, Mary Catherine would like to do what Penelope did. She is interested in heading to Boston to Mrs. Adams' Boarding School."

"Really? I'm proud to hear that," I said.

"Sara and I have decided we're going to do what's necessary for her to go. There are several young men who want to court her, and we don't like any of them," he said, laughing.

"You asked about the boys. Everett and Law are doing well in school. Everett wants to be a minister of the Gospel, and Law wants to be a lawyer, of all things," Dent said as he laughed again.

"I don't see a thing wrong with either profession," I said.

"Neither do I, Dent!" John said.

"Now, little brother, tell us what's going on here, in the town of El Dorado, and at Three Oaks," Dent said.

"Well, it took a while to get settled in and get my practice started, but everything is running smoothly. Hank is doing a great job as overseer of the plantation. He's very smart and works hard. Everything is in good shape here at Three Oaks."

"How do the plantation owners compare to those in Autauga County?" John asked.

"There are some bad and some good plantation owners. The bad ones are the ones who abuse their slaves. I call on a few of them. We don't see eye to eye, but I guess we never will. I tell them what I think, and it goes in one ear and out the other."

"How's the economy here?" Dent asked.

"Right now, all is going well. We've not been affected by the Civil War like some parts of Arkansas. The plantations are doing pretty well, and cotton production has been really good."

"We're experiencing good fortune in Autauga County as well. So far, the Civil War hasn't come to Autauga County, and Daniel Pratt continues to bring new ideas to the city of Prattville. If it wasn't for old Daniel, I'm sure we wouldn't be doing that well," Dent said with a smile.

"I believe Daniel Pratt is one of the best businessmen I've had the privilege to be associated with. Who knows what would have happened to me if Mr. Pratt hadn't used his influence in making the right connections for me?"

"Is there anything special you want to do or see during the next seven days?" I asked.

"I want to see El Dorado, and I want to tour your plantation. I wouldn't mind working in some fishing," John said.

"I'm for seeing El Dorado and going fishing as well," Dent said.

"You can consider it done. We will do those things and more."

"Well, I'm getting sleepy. Where's that bed you were telling me about?" Dent asked.

Penelope and I decided to wait until the following day to announce our big news about her pregnancy. We had planned to make the announcement at Mother's homecoming celebration but decided to wait. We didn't want to take from Mother's special birthday celebration.

CHAPTER 14

The second day started off with a huge breakfast. It was like feeding an army. Mattie, Betsy, and Big Jim came through in flying colors. No one left the table hungry. After breakfast, we loaded two wagons and our family carriage, and off we went to El Dorado.

We spent the better part of the day with Mary and Virgil's family and touring the city of El Dorado.

Everyone was quite impressed with my doctor's clinic. While there, they had an opportunity to meet both Elizabeth and Beth Ann, who were holding down the fort, so to speak. Both ladies are very capable of handling minor emergencies and some diagnoses.

They were impressed with Virgil and Mary's large general merchandise store as well.

After returning to Three Oaks, we had an outstanding meal consisting of Betsy's fried chicken and all the trimmings. After dinner, we adjourned to the parlor. Our parlor is the largest room in the house and can easily seat all of the family. We announced at dinner that we had a special announcement to make in the parlor after dinner.

I saw my mother smile and wink at Dent. Could she know something already? I thought.

When everyone found a seat in the parlor, I began my speech by saying how much Mother, Penelope, and I were enjoying their visit. I motioned for Penelope to come stand by me. We held hands and smiled at each other. I've never been one who beat around the bush, so to speak, so I continued my speech.

"Penelope and I have some very special news to share with you. We wanted to wait until everyone was here so our good news could be heard by all. I'm happy to announce tonight that we are going to have a baby."

Mother rose from her rocking chair and said, "I knew it, I just knew it! Praise the Lord!" Applause was heard throughout the room.

After a short time of congratulations, Dent asked for everyone's attention. "I want to offer up a toast, if I may," he said.

"First, I want to say, this is the best news we could hope to hear on this trip. Secondly, knowing both of you, this baby is going to be the luckiest baby born in Union County. He or she will want for nothing. Thirdly, God certainly knew what he was doing when He brought you two together in holy matrimony. I commend both of you for waiting and pledging your lives to each other. May God give you a long life together and many children! We love you both!"

No sooner had Dent finished when John raised his wine glass and said, "Here! Here!" Everyone again applauded!

The adults stayed in the parlor while most of the children went outside to play. There was another full moon, which aided the kids in playing games.

On the third day, we shared in an early breakfast, loaded three wagons, and headed out to Calion Creek, which isn't far from our plantation and is known for its blue channel catfish, mud catfish, and lots of sunfish and bluegill bream.

To most fishermen, Calion Creek is the most popular. The Ouachita River is often swift and deep. The high, sloped banks on the Ouachita make it difficult to sit and stand. The Calion has several sandy bars suited for swimming, building fires, cooking, and setting up camping tents. It was ideal for our outing.

Dent and John requested we camp on one of the sandy bars.

Since Dent, John, and I are not good at cooking, we brought along Bill and Big Jim to do the cooking.

This is our night out for us men and our sons. Dent, John, and I remember our father taking us camping when we lived on the Black Oaks plantation in Cahaba, Alabama. We loved it and know it will be fun for the boys.

To make things interesting, we had a fishing derby. Whoever caught the largest fish would win a price. We separated the boys in two age divisions, making it fair for everyone.

The boys had from the time we got there until we left to vie for the champion fisherman.

Several catfish and bream were caught, more than enough for our dinner meal. When it came time to turn in for the night, Everett, Dent's son, and Obie, Hank's son, were leading the pack in catching the biggest fish. Everett had caught a five-pound catfish. After considerable tugging, Everett was able to drag the big catfish safely to the bank.

Obie was first in his age division. He caught a two-pound catfish that gave him a real struggle to bring in. He, too, was successful in meeting the challenge.

As dawn came, I smelled bacon and sausage cooking over the open fire. Bill and Big Jim were busy preparing breakfast for us. Our breakfast consisted of fried fish, eggs, bacon, and sausage. Mother packed some bread and jelly to go along with our breakfast meal.

As I left my tent for breakfast, I saw several of the boys fishing. They were determined to beat Everett and Obie at catching the biggest fish. They were having the time of their lives.

The biggest fish idea was certainly a motivational factor in bringing about competition among our boys. This trip will certainly be one they will remember.

The fishing was good for me. It gave me an opportunity to teach Charles how to fish. He caught several bream that were as big as my hand. Every time he caught a fish, he would say, "Daddy, Daddy, look! He's a big one!"

The second fish Charles caught brought to mind that I'd never taken my son fishing. I had been so caught up in my work and getting the plantation ready that I had neglected spending time with him. I decided right then and there, I would spend more time with Charles, especially taking him fishing!

After breakfast, we continued fishing, swimming, and just having fun with our sons. At three o'clock we decided it was time to break down the tents, clean up the camping area, and go home to Three Oaks. The fishing trip had ended, and Everett and Obie were declared the winners. Each of them received a new fishing pole and a duffle bag to carry their fishing supplies.

Hank had found us a great fishing hole. He and I agreed this was a good place to bring Obie and Charles back to fish.

Upon arriving back at Three Oaks, we were ordered by Mother to get ourselves cleaned up for dinner.

She said, "We are not going to put up with that awful fish stink while we eat our dinner!"

Mother was right, as usual; we did smell like fish. Because there were so many of us, bathing took an hour before we were presentable for dinner.

My family's seven days went entirely too fast. The ladies spent time in El Dorado shopping while we men continued to do some fishing, hunting, and visiting.

The boys joined us for one last fishing trip to Calion Creek. This time my son, Charles, won the grand prize in his division by catching a two-pound catfish, while Law, Dent's son, received the prize for his four-pound catfish. They, too, were awarded new fishing poles and bags to carry their fishing supplies.

On Sunday, we attended Hank's preaching service at Three Oaks bunkhouse. We filled every foot of the bunkhouse, except a small aisle down the middle. The singing service was outstanding, just as I remembered it being at Twin Oaks. I felt the roof was going to lift right off the building. The singing wasn't anything like what we white folks experience in our churches. The slaves seem to feel every word in their hearts and express it outwardly in their body language. I could feel the Holy Spirit working in me as I watched their moves and how they sang their songs. They are truly gifted when it comes to singing. I enjoyed every moment of it!

Some of the songs we sing came from the Baptist hymnals that Penelope had given them while she taught them back at Twin Oaks.

Several of the slaves had learned to read from the hymnals. As we sang, I made it a point to look around to see how my family was responding to the singing. I was pleased to see they were getting into the rhythm, especially the younger ones. This was certainly an eye-opener for them, since they had never been in a Negro church.

We were treated to one of the best sermons that I've heard. Hank's delivery of God's Word was nothing but perfect. It was convincing, and one would swear that the Holy Spirit filled his soul. There were amens everywhere. I noticed several coming from my brother Dent.

After the service, Hank greeted us at the door as we left. He thanked us for coming, and we were all grateful that we did. It had been a wonderful experience, one that my nephews and nieces would remember for many years to come. All they wanted to talk about at Sunday dinner was how much they enjoyed the singing and Hank's sermon.

On Monday, all good things will come to an end. My family will start their long journey back to Autauga County today. We loaded everyone in three wagons, except for Mother and the smaller children. They rode in the family carriage.

We arrived in Champagnolle around 10:30 a.m. The steamboat was scheduled to leave around noon. The steamboat will carry them to Monroe, Louisiana, where they will board a train to take them to Autauga County.

We said our good-byes, and they boarded the steamboat one by one. It was a sad time, especially for Mother. I knew she had to be hurting inside to see the majority of her family leaving, not knowing when she would see them again. I also knew she is a strong woman and she will endure it. She is Catherine Bradford, a woman of great strength and fortitude.

CHAPTER 15

Three days after my family left for Autauga and Dallas Counties, Alabama, I received a telegram from Dent, letting us know they made it home safely and all was well.

Things returned to normal at Three Oaks and El Dorado. I made several trips to different plantations as well as seeing patients three days a week in my office.

The June 16, 1863, issue of the El Dorado News-Times ran an article about the continued siege of Vicksburg. The newspaper told of failed attempts of the Union Army to break through the Confederate lines at Vicksburg.

The newspaper reported that General Grant had put a stop to any additional attempts to take Vicksburg by force.

It was reported that General Grant stated to his Generals, "We are going to out-camp the enemy and not incur any more Union Army losses."

General Grant had completely encircled the Confederate Army by a 6.5-mile radius. Lt. General John C. Pemberton and his Confederate Army were at the mercy of General Grant. There had been no sign of General Joseph E. Johnston, commander of the Confederate Department of the West, to come to Pemberton's aid. The starvation of the Confederate Army at Vicksburg was now set in place.

The newspaper reported that General Grant had over 77,000 Union soldiers in the area. The Confederate Army had around 33,000 troops.

General Ulysses S. Grant's Union Army of Tennessee had three corps in and around Vicksburg. They were: the XIII Corps, under Major General John A. McClernand; the XV Corps, under Major General William T. Sherman; and the XVII Corps, under Major General James B. McPherson.

Lt. General John C. Pemberton's Confederate Army of Mississippi, inside of Vicksburg line, consisted of four divisions under Major Generals Carter L. Stevenson, John H. Forney, Martin L. Smith, and John S. Bowen. One could easily see that the Confederate Army was far outnumbered!

General Pemberton was boxed in, with little food. His men were dying of starvation and disease, but he still wouldn't surrender. He kept hoping for a miracle.

I received a welcome telegram from my good friend Dr. Jim Burroughs. Jim will be here within a week. He asked me to find him a place to rent. I will ask my sister Mary today at lunch if she will help me find Jim a place to stay. She has more connections in El Dorado than I do.

I'm so excited to know Jim will soon be here. It will be great to renew our acquaintances and to be able to work side by side as doctors.

If nothing happens tomorrow, I will do surgery on Silas Arlington's left hip. Since my examination of him at his plantation, I've seen him in my office. I feel certain I will be able to help him walk normally again after his rehab.

I look forward to seeing him. I've decided he will need to stay a few nights in the clinic before I send him home. I know he's not going to like that, but it will be necessary to keep an eye on him for a few days. We are in great need of a hospital in El Dorado.

Penelope is doing well with her pregnancy. Her morning sickness has gone away, and she's keeping busy at the receptionist desk as well as keeping the finances of the plantation in order. She's one amazing woman!

The months of May and June were ideal for planting. The good weather made it possible for Hank to complete the planting of all cultivated acreage at Three Oaks. The chief crops are cotton, corn, and beans. There are several acres planted in sweet potatoes, Irish potatoes, tomatoes, and sugar cane for sorghum molasses.

We've been having fresh vegetables from the big garden close to the house. One of my favorite dishes has been sweet peas and new potatoes. We've also had fresh lettuce, onions, radishes, sweet corn, cabbages, and beans.

My slaves are really enjoying the fresh vegetables from the garden. I do believe their complexion is better, and several have put on needed weight.

As we returned to Three Oaks today, George asked if he might visit with me.

"What's up, George?" I asked.

"Master Obadiah, I need your help!"

"What's going on?"

"It's my Nellie and her man friend, Willie. I'm afraid they have gotten pretty thick since we've arrived here at Three Oaks."

"All right, George. Just tell me what's on your mind."

"I'm not for sure, Master Obadiah, but Willie may have my Nellie with child."

"What makes you think this?"

"Opal, she tells me she thinks Nellie is with child. You know Opal. She's knows about those things."

"Well, if Opal thinks that, I'm betting she's right."

"What do you want me to do?"

"Opal and I was wondering if you would allow Hank to marry them. We don't want our grandchild to be born without knowing who the father is."

"George, are you and Willie on good terms?"

"I'd like to kill him, Master Obadiah, but I remember how's I was when I was his age. Opal and I never got married officially, and we had our four children, Nellie, Samson, Henry, and Ham, without ever been married. I don't want that for Nellie."

"So, are you saying you want my permission for them to get married?"

"Yes, Master, I guess I am!"

"George, you don't need my permission. You're the father, and it's up to you to give them permission to marry. I do have one suggestion!"

"What's that, Master?"

"Why don't you and Opal get married at the same time as Nellie and Willie? I will get y'all a marriage license along with Willie and Nellie at the courthouse in El Dorado."

"You would do that for us, Master Obadiah?"

"I would be more than happy to do that, George. You and your family mean a lot to me."

"Oh, Master Obadiah, thank you, thank you so much!"

"By the way, we might as well start doing things correct around here. What last name would you like for me to put for you and Opal?"

"Master Obadiah, George is the only name I've had. I don't rightly know. Do we have to have a last name?"

"No, it's not necessary, but if you like a last name, I would be happy to get it added to the marriage document. If you and Opal decide to do the last name thing, I'll need Willie's last name as well."

"Let me talk with Opal about this. When do you need to know?"

"When do you want to get married?"

"We haven't talked about that yet!"

"Well, you talk about it and let me know."

"Yes, Master Obadiah, I will let you know real soon."

As George turned and went toward his house, I felt pain in my stomach. It had never dawned on me that my slaves, along with thousands of other slaves, have only one name. That name was given to them by previous slave owners or their current owner. How sad, I thought!

Before Hank and Mattie and Big Jim and Nanny got married, the slaves would find someone they liked and move in with each other and started having a family. Hank has done a good job preaching the gospel and the importance of getting married.

I know Hank preaches what the Bible says about marriage. That's where George was coming from when he inquired about marriage. I'm so glad Hank is doing this and am happy that religion has come to my slaves. Praise the Lord!

I will visit with Hank and get his input on how we need to help with George's problem in regard to Nellie and Willie. I'm hoping George will accept my suggestion so we can have a double wedding ceremony. This might just be the best thing that's happened at Three Oaks since we moved here.

I knew how busy I was going to be in the next few days, so I sent for Hank to come to my house.

Upon his arrival, I filled him in on my conversation with George. He immediately said, "Praise the Lord! They are listening to me!"

"Indeed they are, my friend. So what do we do and when?"

"We marry them, just like Nanny and I got married. We can do it on a Sunday after we get through with Sunday service."

"That sounds good, but we need to make it midafternoon. You forgot; we go to El Dorado for church, and we need time to travel home, eat dinner, and get ready for the wedding. Let's set the time for about three o'clock."

"I'm sorry, Master Obadiah. I wasn't thinking about the time. Three o'clock will be just fine with me."

"Hank, I think it's time you dispense with the Master and just call me Obadiah. We've been friends for a long time."

"I don't think I can do that, Master."

"Why don't you give it a try? Just say, 'Obadiah, we can do this.'"

"Obadiah, I will try, but when someone's with us, I'm going to address you as Master Obadiah."

"All right, have your way!"

"I want you to talk to George, Opal, Nellie, and Willie to find out what they want to do about the last name. Out of curiosity, I'd like to know if Nellie is pregnant. If she is, I need to examine her to see if things are all right."

"I'll talk to them and get back with you as soon as I know something," Hank said.

"By the way, Hank, a last name is something you might want to do yourself. You and Nanny were married without having a last name. When you got married, we presented you with a piece of paper that had only your and Nanny's first names on it."

"To be truthful with you, Obadiah, I've given the last name a lot of thought."

"That's good, Hank, because God has laid this matter on my heart, and I would like to do this for all my slaves.

"Hank, I'm going to share something with you. This has to be kept between you and me, okay?"

"You have my promise, Obadiah."

"It is my strong belief the North will win the Civil War. If they do, slaves will be declared free under President Abraham Lincoln's Emancipation Proclamation. I want my slaves to have last names. I need your help in informing them of this idea and helping them understand the importance of a last name. If they are interested, I will get my lawyer friend, Jack Spearman, in El Dorado, to draw up the legal papers."

"Obadiah, you are such a good man. God's going to give you a big mansion in Heaven someday!"

"Well thanks, Hank! This has been on my mind for some time now. I really want to do this!"

"Obadiah, I will be happy to do as you requested, and I'll let you know their responses. Thank you, Obadiah, thank you so very much."

This may not be a popular thing for me to do, should the other plantation owners find out I'm doing this for my slaves. But since when did a Bradford worry about that?

Silas Arlington's surgery went well. I was able to reset his hip. It will take time to rehabilitate his hip, but in time, he should be able to throw that cane away and walk normally.

Jim Burroughs is arriving today by steamboat at Port Champagnolle. I sent Bill with my carriage to pick him up. Bill will bring him directly to my office. I regret I wasn't able to meet Jim personally at Champagnolle, but Penelope had booked me solid throughout the day. After we visit, I'll have Bill take him to his new living quarters at the Watson Boarding House, located in the Mahoney District in El Dorado. The Watson Boarding House is one of the nicest places in town and doesn't cost an arm and leg to stay there. The longer a person stays, the cheaper the rate.

Jim has no idea what I have in mind for him. I love to play matchmaker and feel that I've done a good job with my slaves by bringing them together in Holy Matrimony.

I've decided that Elizabeth Parker, my head nurse, would be an excellent wife for Jim. I can't wait to see how all this might play out. I will give him time to get adjusted to his new job, and then I'll concentrate on getting them hitched.

CHAPTER 16

On July 4, 1863, the little town of El Dorado observed its annual celebration. The streets were roped off, and tables were set up on the east side of the court square. Food was in abundance. I believe everyone in Union County turned out for this annual event. People came from great distances to visit friends and loved ones. They spread their quilts on the ground around the courthouse and visited with their good friends. It was like a grand reunion.

There was a platform erected on the east side of the court-house, which faced the east street, where people danced and had a good time. The platform was used by the band and by politicians who wanted to make speeches.

My friend Jim Burroughs was impressed with the celebration. It was at this celebrated event that I introduced him to Elizabeth Parker. Elizabeth is both beautiful and single. She possesses beauty within as well as on the outside. Her dedication to her responsibilities as a nurse is much appreciated.

One time I asked her why she remained single. She looked at me and said, "Dr. Bradford, I consider my work as my companion. I'm perfectly content with doing service to others. I've never met anyone who was able to sweep me off my feet. If that person comes along, I just might marry him, providing he asks me," she said with a smile.

She came to El Dorado from Memphis, Tennessee, to be close to her older sister, Mrs. Millie Venders. She and her sister have a close relationship, and due to Mrs. Venders failing health, Elizabeth has become a real blessing.

As I introduced Jim to Elizabeth, I was hoping for a clue in their facial expressions. Much to my regret, I saw nothing that boosted my matchmaking ego. It was only cordial in nature as they greeted each other with a handshake. Although I saw no sparks during my introduction, I did notice they spent a lot of time together dancing and visiting while they ate. I considered that a good thing.

Penelope, being the mind reader she is, walked over to me and said, "Don't give up! I believe they are meant to be together."

"With that encouragement, how about dancing with me?"

She looked at me, with the prettiest smile, and said, "I'd love to dance with you."

As we danced, she said, "I had begun to think you'd never ask me to dance."

"You know that I'm not too high on dancing!"

"I'm well aware of that, Obadiah. I don't know why, because you are a good dancer!"

"Not nearly as good as you," I said.

We danced and we danced. I was getting very tired. My feet were hurting when my good friend Jim Burroughs rescued me.

"May I dance with your lovely wife?" he said.

As I left the dance floor, I went immediately to the food table and helped myself to a big glass of punch. As I stood sipping my punch, I watched my lovely wife being whirled around by Jim. She was still going strong and loving every minute of it.

By July 5, Vicksburg had fallen. The *El Dorado News-Times* headline read, "General John C. Pemberton surrenders to General Ulysses S. Grant."

In summary this is what was revealed in the newspaper article on the final Siege of Vicksburg:

On July 3, white flags began to appear above the Confederate fortifications at Vicksburg.

General Pemberton rode out to meet Grant in a no-man's land. Pemberton wanted open negotiation for surrender of the city and his army.

General Grant had earned the nickname "Unconditional Surrender" early in the war. He again offered Pemberton unconditional surrender, and Pemberton refused. Pemberton returned to Vicksburg and waited. General Pemberton had no bargaining power.

His men were starving and sick. Over half of his 33,000 men were suffering from scurvy, malaria, diarrhea, and other diseases. Starvation had become the Confederate soldier's worst nightmare.

General Pemberton knew his men couldn't hold out much longer. He knew he would have to do something soon. In his heart he knew what he had to do. If General Grant didn't change his mind, he would give Grant what he wanted.

His men had been faithful and loyal to the cause, but their future lives had to be more meaningful than to lie down and die of starvation. If Pemberton didn't hear something from General Grant by midmorning, he was planning to surrender to Grant and put himself and his men at Grant's mercy.

During the night, General Grant relented. He sent Pemberton a new offer. He agreed to parole Pemberton and his army. Pemberton quickly accepted the new offer.

The main reason Grant changed his mind was he didn't want the responsibility of feeding some 33,000 Confederate soldiers who were sick and dying, and who were so weak they were in no shape to march several miles to a Northern prison. He would end up having to transport them by train, which would take several days to accomplish.

General Grant was in hopes that paroling General Pemberton and his Army of the Mississippi would create a stigma of defeat to the rest of the Confederacy. He hoped the majority of the soldiers would stay at home and not return to any other unit of the Confederate Army.

On July 4, General Grant and the Union Army had taken control of Vicksburg. The capture of Vicksburg split the Confederacy in half and was a major turning point in the Civil War.

The fall of Vicksburg and General Robert E. Lee's defeat at Gettysburg by Major General George F. Meade the previous day crippled the Confederate states in the worst way.

The fall of Vicksburg cut off the states of Arkansas, Louisiana, and Texas from the rest of the Confederacy, as well as from communication with Confederate forces in the Trans-Mississippi Department for the remaining of the war.

I laid my newspaper down and prayed. My prayer was more of a thanksgiving prayer for General Grant's actions of paroling Pemberton and his Confederate Army.

General Grant could have made Pemberton and his men miserable by imprisoning them, but he chose not to do so. Although we were on the opposite side in the Civil War, I gained a lot of respect for General Grant for his humanitarian decision.

What General Grant's decision did for me was give me hope. If my good friend Henry Dotson and Marion Bradford, Dent's oldest son, were alive, they both would be returning home.

Dr. Henry Dotson will be returning to his home in Atlanta, Georgia, and Marion will be returning to Black Oak Plantation in Dallas County, near Selma, Alabama.

Oh, Hallelujah! Oh, Hallelujah, I said over and over in my mind. What I feared most didn't happen. I was afraid General Grant would imprison all the men and they would have to spend time in some overpopulated prison, where they would continue to die of starvation and disease.

But now, it appears they are being set free and given the opportunity to return to their homes and loved ones.

I looked up at the sky and said, "Lord, how do I find out if Henry and Marion are alive?"

I immediately felt a calmness come over me. I knew what to do. I would send Helen Dotson, Henry's wife, a telegram in Atlanta to check on Henry's status. I would do the same for Marion through my brother Dent.

When I shared the newspaper story with Mother and Penelope, Mother immediately cried out, "Praise the Lord, praise the Lord," as she sat down in her rocking chair.

I went over and knelt down by her and said, "I have this peace about me, Mother. I really think Marion and Henry are alive and that they are, right now, on the way home to their loved ones."

"I can't wait to find out," Mother said.

"As soon as I get to town, I'm going straight to the telegraph office and send both Helen and Dent telegrams."

CHAPTER 17

On July 10, I received a much-anticipated telegram from my good friend Dr. Henry Dotson. As I opened the telegram, I was so nervous that my hands were shaking and I had trouble focusing on the words. Penelope, perceiving I needed help, walked over and said, "Let me read it to you, Obadiah."

"Dear friend and colleague Obadiah Bradford. Stop. I bring you greetings from my home in Atlanta. Stop. I'm alive and well. Stop. Made it home today. Stop. A big letter will follow. Stop. Regards to your family. Stop. Dr. Henry Dotson."

My good friend is alive and well! What a comfort to know that he is back in Atlanta. I hope he stays there. I pray he will continue his medical practice in Atlanta so he can be with Helen and the kids.

Tomorrow, I'm scheduled to pay a visit to a plantation I've not visited yet. The plantation is owned by Lawrence Wilson, who lives about five miles south of Camden. I met Mr. Wilson during the July Fourth celebration. He shared with me that he bought his plantation in 1852 and moved here from Lowndes County, Alabama. It should be interesting to visit with him, since Lowndes County borders Autauga County.

Several people who know Mr. Wilson speak highly of him. They have been complimentary of his nice plantation and the way he treats his slaves.

Since I live five miles north of El Dorado, I'll leave from Three Oaks. Mr. Wilson's plantation is about ten miles north of mine. I've been to Camden one time since moving to El Dorado. I remember Camden as being a quaint, little town located on the Ouachita River.

As Penelope and I traveled down the dusty road leading to Three Oaks, she sat next to me on the driver's seat with her left arm wrapped around my right arm and her head leaning against my shoulder.

She is doing well in her pregnancy. Her face gives off a special glow that some women possess during their pregnancies. She's so happy to be pregnant and looks forward with great expectations to the delivery of our firstborn. I pray for her daily and thank God that she is healthy and happy.

Everything is going well at the plantation. Hank and Nanny are enjoying their newborn baby boy, Sammy. He's a big boy! I believe he's going to be bigger than his big brother, Obi.

Mother is still in good health. She looks after the children, just like our Mamie used to do when she was living. She reads to the kids and corrects them when needed.

Tomorrow will be a busy day for all of us. We now have two family carriages at Three Oaks. One will be used tomorrow by me to visit Mr. Lawrence Wilson's plantation while Bill uses the other one to drive Penelope to work at the clinic in El Dorado.

After a short night, I arose early, quickly ate breakfast, and took time to read an article entitled "General Robert E. Lee Retreats from Gettysburg."

The article was a summary of the Battle of Gettysburg, Pennsylvania, which was fought on July 1 to 3, 1863, and is considered the largest of the American Civil War. Gettysburg is in Adams County, Pennsylvania.

The Battle of Gettysburg was the bloodiest battle to be fought since the Civil War started. There were some 158,300 troops who participated in the three-day battle. Of that number, the Union Army had 83,289 men to the Confederates' 75,054. The Battle of Gettysburg and the Battle of Vicksburg were considered the turning points in the Civil War. The Northern Army was victorious in both battles.

General Robert E. Lee chose Gettysburg as the site of the battle because of the ten different roads coming into Gettysburg.

On the first day, July 1, fighting occurred at McPherson's Ridge, Barlow's Knoll, Seminary Ridge, Oak Hill, and Oak Ridge. There were 50,000 soldiers involved in the fighting, of which 15,500 were killed, wounded, captured, or missing.

The second day fighting, July 2, was the largest and costliest of the three days. The fighting took place at Devil's Den, Little Round Top, the Wheatfield, the Peach Orchard, Cemetery Ridge, Trostle's Farm, Culp's Hill, and Cemetery Hill. There were over 100,000 soldiers, of which 20,000 were killed, wounded, captured, or missing.

At the end of the second day, the Federals retained little Round Top and had repulsed most of Ewell's men.

On the third day, July 3, with a temperature of ninety degrees, the Confederate infantry was driven from their last toe-hold on Culp's Hill. After a preliminary 260-gun bombardment, Lee attacked the Union center on Cemetery Ridge. During Pickett's Charge, the Confederates pierced the Union line, but were driven back with severe casualties. There were 12,000 Confederate soldiers involved in Pickett's Charge. Stuart's cavalry attempted to gain the Union rear, but was repulsed.

On July 4, General Lee began withdrawing his army toward Williamsport on the Potomac River. It has been reported that General Lee's train for his wounded soldiers stretched more than fourteen miles.

The two principal commanders of the Battle of Gettysburg were Maj. General George G. Meade, who three days earlier had assumed command of the Union Army, and General Robert E. Lee, commander of the Confederate Army.

There were 120 generals present at Gettysburg; nine were killed or mortally wounded during the battle. Those Confederate generals who died were Generals Semmes, Barksdale, Armistead, Garnett, and Pender, plus Pettigrew during the retreat.

On the Union side were Generals Reynolds, Zook, Weed, and Farnsworth.

The newspaper article went on to say that the Union Army had 3,155 dead, 14,529 wounded and 5,365 missing, for a total of 23,049 casualties. On the Confederate Army side were 3,903 dead, 18,735 injured, and 5,425 missing, for a total of 28,063.

I laid down my paper, bowed my head, and prayed, "Our Heavenly Father, O merciful and kind God. Please hear my plea. God, please intervene in this awful Civil War. You are the only one who can stop this horrible war. Every day men are dying because of foolish pride.

"God, bring some common sense to those who are in charge. Please bring this war to an end and let us get on with our lives. Every day more and more men are dying and leaving behind families that need them at home. What's going to happen to the widows and children without husbands and fathers? Please hear our pleas for peace, O, Lord! In Jesus name I pray!"

My heart hurts for those who lost loved ones in this war. I personally have prayed over wounded men who died holding my hand. I've seen the horrible pain in their faces and felt their pain as they slipped away into darkness.

Bill brought my carriage around, and I said good-bye to Belle, Charles, Mother, and Penelope, and off I went to see Lawrence Wilson.

While traveling on the main road to Camden, I was blessed by seeing wild game crossing in front of me. The temperature was warm, but not extremely hot. It would get hotter in the middle of the day, but now it was just right. As I approached Mr. Wilson's plantation house, I was greeted by three nice-looking hound dogs. They gave me a friendly welcome, and I rewarded them by a gentle patting on the head.

Like most plantation homes, Mr. Wilson had eight steps leading from ground level to the front porch. As I stepped up, one of the hound dogs climbed each step with me. He stood beside me until the house attendant opened the door and invited me into the house. I patted my new friend on the head and said good-bye.

I was escorted to the parlor by a nice Negro maid named Missy. Missy was a friendly lady with a beautiful smile. She informed me she had been instructed by Mr. Wilson to make me comfortable in the parlor and to send for him upon my arrival.

Missy explained that Mr. Wilson was in the barn and she had sent someone to fetch him. She offered me a glass of water, and I accepted.

While I waited, I looked at pictures that lined portions of the walls in the parlor. There were several pictures that I assumed were Mr. and Mrs. Wilson, and family pictures that included three children, a girl and two boys.

In about ten minutes, Mrs. Wilson came into the parlor with fresh roses she had cut from her garden.

"You must be Dr. Bradford," she said.

"Yes, I am Obadiah Bradford."

"Pleased to meet you, Dr. Bradford. You can call me Angela," she said as she offered me her hand.

"I'm pleased to meet you as well, Angela."

"Did Missy send for Lawrence?" she asked.

"Yes, she did."

"I want to thank you for taking on our family and our slaves. I'm afraid we've been neglecting our own health as well as our slaves'. You're the first doctor we've met that does house calls."

I explained to Angela that I enjoy house calls. They give me an opportunity to get out of my office and meet people.

I visited with Mrs. Wilson until her husband showed up. Mr. Wilson came through the door with his work clothes on. Although he was somewhat dirty, he had taken the time to wash his hands.

"Dr. Bradford, how are you?"

"I'm doing well, Mr. Wilson," I responded.

"You caught me laboring a little, but my hands are clean," he said as he reached out to shake my hand.

"Oh, by the way, you can call me Lawrence."

"You can call me Obadiah, if you wish."

"If you two will excuse me, I must go wash up. It was nice meeting you, Obadiah," Angela said as she left the room.

"I'm at your disposal, Lawrence. What would you have me to do?"

"Obadiah, before you leave today, I would like for you to give Angela and me a good examination. We've neglected seeing a doctor for some time. I also want you to look at a number of my slaves. I've instructed my overseer, Jake Bentley, to round up those slaves who appear to need the most attention. We are going to let you use the parlor as an examination room. It's the cleanest place we have to offer.

"If you don't have time to see everyone today, maybe you could allow us another appointment."

"Let's see how the time goes today. I can spend all day with you and your slaves. While I'm here, I would like to do as much as I can."

"That will be just fine with us. I'll see that Missy sets another plate at our table for lunch. We'd love to have you as our guest."

"I certainly will accept your invitation," I said with gratitude.

I was impressed with having the use of the parlor for an examination room. I normally get stuck in a dark slave house or bunkhouse. This is certainly a pleasant change.

"Dr. Bradford, Jake is bringing our slaves to the front porch. He will direct them whenever you are ready. If Angela and I can be of additional help, please let us know. I'm going to join Angela and make myself more presentable. I'll bring Jake in and let you meet him. He's a pretty good guy. He's been with us since we bought this place in 1852."

He left momentarily. Upon returning, he said, "Dr. Bradford, this is Jake Bentley. He will help you with our slaves."

"Nice to meet you Mr. Bentley," I said.

"The feeling is mutual," he said.

"By the way, Dr. Bradford, make sure you give Jake a good examination as well. I'm sure he will try to weasel out of it. He doesn't like doctors!"

"I'm sure Jake and I will get along well," I said as I winked at Jake.

I spent the rest of the day examining most of Mr. Wilson's slaves. He was correct in stating that his slaves had been neglected—not to the point of being abused physically, but failure to correct problems that have led to such things as high blood pressure, contagious diseases, skin cancer, and constant coughing. Some of the older slaves were hard of hearing, had poor eyesight, and teeth that needed to be extracted.

I finally got around to Jake Bentley. "Jake, do you have a family?" I asked.

"Yes, sir, I do. My wife will need an examination as well. We have four children. They range in age from six to seventeen.

I didn't ask my family to come by for examinations. Master Wilson instructed me to seek out the worst ones with the most pressing medical needs. I believe me and my family are in pretty good shape. By the way, Doctor Bradford, you could see me the next time around if you'd like," Jake said.

"Jake, since you are already here, why don't we go ahead and do your examination today? I don't think Mr. Wilson would want you to wait."

"Okay, Doctor, what do I need to do?"

"Come over here and sit down. I'll do your blood pressure first."

It didn't take me long to discover that Jake was in bad shape. He smokes heavily and his clothes smell of nicotine. I didn't like hearing the rattling in his chest and the cough he had. I couldn't be certain until I examined him more closely, but Jake may have consumption.

I asked Jake if he could take me on a short tour of the slave quarters. I wanted to see the buildings where the slaves were housed. Seeing what kind of conditions they lived in would give me an idea when making my recommendations to Mr. Wilson. Jake agreed to show me the slave quarters and was very courteous in doing so.

Like most plantations, the slave quarters needed some repairs. The quarters were not nearly as bad as some I had experienced in Union County. No slaves had to sleep on dirt floors. Thank God for that!

If Mr. Wilson could make the needed repairs, several of his slaves' medical problems could be resolved through more sanitary conditions.

I returned to the main house where I examined Mr. and Mrs. Wilson and one of their sons, John David Wilson. Angela was in good shape, their son was in excellent shape, but Lawrence needed some attention.

He suffered from high blood pressure, poor hearing, bad eyesight, and a rattling in his chest, and I heard a heart murmur, which is not a good sign. I will have to do some more tests before I can diagnose Lawrence's medical needs.

Before leaving, I had my exit conference with the Wilsons. I related my concerns about his slaves' health needs, and the needed repairs to the slave quarters. I wrote out some prescriptions for his slaves and handed them to Mrs. Wilson.

"Lawrence, I normally have this exit conference with all my clients after I complete my examinations. I must tell you, I have some real concerns about some of your slaves, Jake, and you as well."

"You have some concerns about me?" he asked.

"Yes, Lawrence, I do! On a scale of one to ten, what do you think your pain level is?"

"I would say about a five. Now there are some days, I would say eight or nine. That higher rate is due to my arthritis."

"Lawrence, I would like for you to come to my office next Wednesday. I'd like to do some more testing on you before I come to any conclusions on your health needs."

"Do you think I have something life threatening?"

"Lawrence, I can't answer that question right now. Once I do the other tests, I'll give you a straight answer."

"Dr. Bradford, I'll make sure he's at your office next Wednesday," Angela said.

"Thanks, Angela! As far as my examination of you goes, it was good. I found nothing suspicious. You and John David are as healthy as you can be."

"That's good news," Angela said.

"I need to mention, one other thing! I need to see Jake in my office next Wednesday as well. I need to run more tests on him as well."

"So, it looks like Jake and I are being picked on," Lawrence said with humor.

"I'll see y'all next Wednesday. Lawrence, please consider making those improvements to your slave quarters when you can."

As I left the Wilson plantation, I was concerned about both Lawrence and Jake. I just didn't like what I heard when I listened to their breathing. I'm hoping it is something we can clear up with medication.

Carl J. Barger

As I headed home to Three Oaks, I was impressed with Lawrence Wilson's plantation and his respect for his slaves.

I believe he and Angela are good Christian people and well thought of in their community.

CHAPTER 18

On July 15, 1863, a messenger boy from the El Dorado telegraph office handed me a telegram from my brother Dent. Again, not knowing what was inside, I was nervous as I opened the telegram.

"Obadiah, Good news about Marion. Stop. Home safely with us and excited. Stop. Give Mother a hug and kiss. Stop. Marion will write you soon. Stop. Dent Bradford."

God is good all the time. He answers our prayers every minute of the day. "God, I thank you for sparing Henry's and Marion's lives."

I went immediately and showed Penelope the telegram. She rejoiced with me. God had lifted a burden from us. Penelope loves Marion as much as I do. He was always her favorite out of Dent's children. Marion always showed Penelope respect.

Marion wants to be a doctor and perhaps try his hand as a politician. I believe he would be good at both. Now he will have that opportunity.

Today, Penelope and I were joined by Jim Burroughs, Elizabeth, and Beth Ann at Jake's Restaurant. Penelope suggested that we close our office and everyone go to lunch together to celebrate Dr. Burroughs's first month on the job.

While sitting around the table, I noticed Jim giving a great deal of attention to Elizabeth. Penelope observed the same thing. Could our matchmaking be working?

We had a good time eating and relaxing over lunch. Jim has been such a big help to me. He's been able to take on some of my patients while I make house calls, as well as building up a large clientele of patients for himself. Jim loves El Dorado and has shared with me that he thinks he has found him a permanent home.

My examinations of both Jake and Lawrence Wilson revealed I was right about them both. As I feared, Jake does have cancer. It's bad, and I don't expect he'll be around longer than four months.

Lawrence, on the other hand, has a mild case of consumption but has some heart problems as well. I believe we can improve his health by treating him with medication.

I decided I would make another trip to Lawrence Wilson's plantation to give him the diagnosis. This is one part of my job I take no pleasure in. I want to break the news to them in their homes, instead of asking them to come into town.

As I approached the plantation house, I was again greeted by Lawrence's three bluetick hounds. Those dogs are the friendliest dogs I've ever been around. Again, the same dog stayed with me until I was greeted at the door by Angela Wilson.

"Dr. Bradford, welcome! Come in," she said.

"Thank you, Angela. Is Lawrence around?"

"Yes, he is. I'll send for him. Oh, by the way, is this visit in regard to his recent examination?"

"Angela, I'm afraid it is."

"I want to sit in on the meeting," she said as she exited the room.

In a few minutes, Lawrence and Angela returned to the parlor. As they entered the parlor, I got up from my chair and greeted Lawrence with a handshake.

"Good to see you, Obadiah!"

"Good to see you too, Lawrence."

"What's on your mind, Obadiah?"

"I have some health issues we need to talk about."

"That's what I was afraid of," Lawrence said.

"Let me start by telling you I don't think you are in any danger of dying."

"Well, that's good news!" Lawrence said.

"Lawrence, there is two things we are going to have to work on. You have a mild case of consumption, and you have some heart problems. I believe we can treat both by medication."

I looked at Angela as she let out a sigh of relief. I could see Lawrence was also relieved.

"Will this medication rid me of these health problems?" Lawrence asked.

"I can't assure you the drugs will cure your medical issues, but I think I can assure you that they will add years to your life."

"Thanks, Obadiah!" Lawrence said with a grateful attitude.

"Lawrence, do you think you could send for Jake and his wife? I would like for both of them to hear what I've got to tell Jake.

"I believe you might want to stay in the room and hear this as well."

"Is this going to be bad news?" Angela asked.

"Angela, I don't mind for you to know, but I believe I need to tell Jake first."

"We understand, Obadiah," Lawrence said.

In a few minutes, Jake and his wife, Velma, entered the room. We greeted each other as each of us took a seat.

"Jake, how are you feeling?" I asked.

"I'm feeling okay, Dr. Bradford," Jake responded.

"Jake, I wanted to meet with you and Velma today about the tests I ran on you at my office. I'm afraid it's not good.

"Go ahead, Dr. Bradford. Am I dying?"

"Jake, only God knows the day and time we are going to die, but I must be honest with you. You have cancer in both lungs. I'm afraid it's bad."

"Dr. Bradford, what are you saying?"

"Jake, what it means is that the cancer is a fast-growing cancer, and there isn't much we can do to stop its growth. I'm afraid you have it in your lymph nodes, as well."

Velma began to cry. Sharing my findings with my patients is the hardest thing about my job as a doctor. When cancer attacks the body, there is little I can do, other than give pain medicine and make the patient as comfortable as possible.

"Dr. Bradford, I've known for some time I was becoming weaker by the day but thought it was just my age. How long do you think I have?"

"As I've said, only God knows the answer to that question, but from a medical guess, I would say, maybe four months."

"Four months? Oh, my Lord," Velma called out.

Velma had gotten up from her chair and was standing by Jake when I gave him the bad news. Jake reached up and grabbed her hand as he looked up at her.

"There is really no treatment at this time," I answered.

"What can I expect during these next few months?" Jake asked.

"Jake, you will get weaker and you will experience more pain at the end."

Jake looked at Lawrence Wilson and said, "Boss, it appears that you might have to start looking for another overseer."

"Jake, don't you worry about that. We are going to do everything we can to make you comfortable here at the plantation. If the good Lord takes you home, we will make sure that Velma and the kids are provided for."

My heart went out to Jake and Velma. For Lawrence Wilson, I couldn't have been more proud of him. What he said to Jake was the right thing at the right time. His reassurance to Jake in regard to his family was certainly a sign of a Christian man at work. I immediately gained a lot of admiration and respect for Lawrence.

"I want everyone to know I'm ready to meet my maker, but I will worry about leaving behind Velma and the kids. Who will take care of them?" Jake asked.

By this time, I think everyone in the room was crying. Oh, what a sad time and situation. Jake's thinking of his family was what most men would do. God is giving Jake an opportunity to live long enough to figure out what is going to be the best for his family. I do think God will work things out for Jake and his family.

The trip to Lawrence Wilson's plantation had not been pleasant, but in my heart and mind, I believe God will use these circumstances to bring honor and glory to his name. For Jake and his family, I pray God will give them peace.

CHAPTER 19

The month of August is very hot. We have had some summer showers, which helped the crops, but the heat is typical for the month of August.

Penelope and Mother both are having problems with the heat. They hate it. Mother complains that she has to get up earlier to attend to her garden because of the heat.

I believe the humidity in Arkansas is worse than what we experienced in Autauga County, Alabama. We will just have to get used to it.

Hank made sure our slaves are given plenty of water and frequent breaks. So far, we've not had any heat strokes.

Despite the heat, it has been a month of blessings for me. I have received letters from both Dr. Henry Dotson and my nephew Marion Bradford.

I found both letters intriguing. As I read Henry's letter, I felt comfort in knowing he and Marion shared the same faith in God and possessed the will to survive during their days in Vicksburg.

I can't express how excited I was when I opened Henry's letter, which came a few days before Marion's. As I carefully unfolded Henry's letter, I noticed he had written six pages, front and back. With excitement, I read the long awaited letter.

> My Dear Friend Obadiah,
> I bring you good news from Atlanta, Georgia. I'm home with my family and enjoying life. I've decided to return to work as soon as I gain some of my strength back.
> I've come to the realization that the process of aging determines what I can and can't do. I never thought this would happen to me. While taking some time to

rest, I am eating everything Helen puts in front of me. I went hungry so many days in Vicksburg that I'm taking advantage of Helen's cooking, and lots of it. I don't think I'm hurting myself because I lost several pounds which is likely to be contributing to my fatigue.

The siege of Vicksburg played havoc with my health. I'm telling you, Obadiah, I thought we were going to die of starvation. We were down to our last crumb of bread when Lt. General John C. Pemberton surrendered to General Ulysses S. Grant. We couldn't have lasted much longer. We had men in the hospital who were so weak and dehydrated that they couldn't eat or drink, so naturally they died. There wasn't anything we could do for them. It was so sad.

We lost several soldiers before the surrender because of infections and diseases not related to battle wounds. I believe we lost more soldiers to diseases and starvation than those who lost their lives in skirmishes.

Obadiah, I know you are strong, and I know you want to hear my story so get ready. It's not going to be pleasant.

I was deployed from Tupelo to Vicksburg one month after you were sent home. At this time, the Union Army, commanded by General Ulysses Grant, hadn't yet surrounded Vicksburg. We were able to get inside the city and utilize the accommodations at the Vicksburg hospital. There had been skirmishes going on between the Union forces and Confederate forces off and on for some time, but the Union couldn't penetrate the Confederate lines.

General Pemberton and his officers had done a good job of fortifying the area around Vicksburg. The terrain at Vicksburg made it impossible for the Union army to win a skirmish.

Although, they weren't able to break through the fortified Confederate lines, there were still soldiers who died on both sides. The Confederate soldiers were brought to our hospital for treatment. I heard later that General Grant used some of the nicer homes at Vicksburg as hospitals.

We had six doctors at the hospital. We had an ample number of nurses but not nearly enough doctors. You saw first-hand the same situation when you were at Shiloh and Corinth.

I was placed in charge of the Confederate Medical Corp after getting to Vicksburg. The person in charge before I got there came down with an infection of some kind and died. I was at the right location at the right time to be given extra responsibilities. I didn't mind it. I'd rather be busy doing something than having idle time, but I can assure you, there wasn't much idle time.

I was able to stay in touch with Helen and the kids up until General Grant surrounded the city of Vicksburg and closed all avenues of sending mail or any other item out of Vicksburg. Our nights became long nights. Men were dying right and left.

Obadiah, I'm telling you, those were sad days!

I thought of you often. I asked myself many times how my friend would react to certain situations when it came to faith. It was hard, Obadiah. My faith was lacking on several occasions. I started writing a journal thinking if I was killed, or died of some kind of infection, Helen and the kids might later be given the journal and would know how much I loved them. There were many times I felt I wouldn't leave that rat hole alive.

Talking about faith! I did hold on to my prayer life. I think the many times I heard you pray while we were in Augusta rubbed off on me as well. I'm telling you, Obadiah, I am a believer in Jesus Christ as my savior. I wanted you to know that. I know there were times at school that I may have not left the impression that I was a child of God. You always were my inspiration. You had a faith like no one I'd ever known.

I truly admired you for your stand in not taking advantage of your slave, Penelope, who is now your beautiful and loving wife. You stayed the course with our Lord and Savior, and he blessed you in so many ways.

I believe with all my heart and soul, that God spared your life, so He could reward you for your faith in Him. I swear, Obadiah, you died on my operating table in Corinth, but God breathed life back into you. I've never seen that happen since. He loved you and knew your love for him.

Obadiah, I know it's only a matter of time that Atlanta will come under attack by the Union forces. Right now we are going about our business of contributing our resources to the Confederate Army.

I feel certain that General Grant will soon advance his Union Army into Georgia. When this happens, I'm afraid he's going to unleash that monster, Major General William T. Sherman. Sherman has no mercy on the Confederate Army. He will hit key areas in Georgia, Atlanta, being one.

From what I learned in Vicksburg, General Sherman is one vicious man. He will not stop at anything. He's focused on his march to the sea and if anyone gets in his way, he will do everything he can to eliminate those obstacles.

Obadiah, I am happy to know that your nephew, Marion Bradford, made it home to Autauga County safely. While he was here, I took the opportunity to look him up. He is a nice looking young man. Strong, like his uncle! I introduced myself as your good friend and we hit it off. We spent a good part of an hour talking mostly about you and his family back in Alabama.

He reminded me of you. He appeared to be a well-educated young man and said he might want to be a doctor and maybe a politician later. I shared with him my interest in politics as well. I'm glad he survived the odds at Vicksburg. I felt in my heart that he was a survivor, just like his uncle, Obadiah Bradford.

Helen and the kids are all doing well. Her father took real good care of her and the kids while I was away. You should see my kids. Henry Jr. is now fourteen; Robert is twelve and Dexter is ten. What am I going to do if I can't give Helen a girl?

You do know, according to genetics, a man determines the sex of the child. It looks like the odds are really against me fathering a girl. Well, anyway, I'm praying about it, and we certainly aren't doing anything to prevent Helen from getting pregnant. She wants at least five children!

Obadiah, I'm going to say this to you, in hopes it won't be repeated. I believe the South has already lost this war. The war will continue because of the South's stubbornness. Being stubborn and full of self-made pride got us into this war in the first place. Realistically, I can't see how the South can fight much longer.

All avenues of transportation have been stopped by the North. After the victory of both Corinth and Vicksburg, the North now has control of both the railroads and the rivers and river ports. Supplies to the South have been cut off. You can't win a war without supplies. It's only a matter of time!

How about your family? What's going on there in El Dorado? Tell me when you answer my letter how our dear friend, Jim Burroughs, is doing? Wouldn't it be fun to have a five musketeer's reunion? Oh, how I would enjoy that. Maybe after this war, we can do that. You take good care of Jim Burroughs. He's a good man. Find him a good woman to marry. He needs a family life.

Obadiah, we are still getting mail so answer this letter as soon as possible. I want to hear from you.

If I've calculated right, your and Penelope's baby will be born the last part of November or first of December. Oh, Obadiah, I'm so excited for you and Penelope.

I've not seen her, but I know she must be a beautiful lady from how you've described her. Please give her my greetings and tell her that someday our families will become good friends. I'm looking forward to good times ahead!

I believe God kept Penelope for you. After Audrey's death, Penelope became your hope, your foundation, and your reason to live. I know she's already brought an abundance of joy and love into your heart. I know, too, she will be a wonderful mother. She's already proved that in so many ways with Charles and Belle.

Please give your mother a hug and tell her that I said she did a good job raising you!"

God bless you my friend,

Dr. Henry Dotson

As I folded Henry's letter and placed it back in the envelope, I bowed my head and thanked God for a wonderful friend. He was the first one I met in Augusta, and he went out of his way to become a good friend. I believe we were destined to become close friends. We could share anything together and not be afraid that it would be talked about with others. We were there for each other, and above all, he and God saved my life on the operating table in Corinth, Mississippi.

I am so lucky and privileged to have Henry as a friend. If I knew I wouldn't be jeopardizing the lives of Penelope and myself, we would make a quick trip to Atlanta. I agree with Henry, Atlanta is still playing a major role in railroad shipping of supplies to the Deep South.

It was one week later after receiving Henry's letter that I received a letter from Marion. As I opened his letter, it, too, was thick! He had written on the front and back of each page, just like Henry. His letter was five pages long.

Dear Uncle Obadiah,

I'm trying to be proper in addressing you as uncle, although you've always insisted that I call you Obadiah.

Anyway, Father informed me that he made you a promise I would write you at the first opportunity. Well, please know my time as been awfully busy since I returned to Black Oaks Plantation.

Since arriving, I've gone fishing a few times with Law and Everett. Obadiah, my brothers have grown up. I wouldn't want to get in a fight with either of them. They are bigger than I am.

Although I'm skinny right now I should gain most of my weight back soon. I'm telling you, Mother is feeding me well. She makes sure I eat three meals a day and sometimes insist I have some of her apple cake and homemade oatmeal raisin cookies in between meals. If all goes well, I should gain my weight back soon.

Law, Everett, and I have been catching several good sized fish out of the Cahaba River. We have enjoyed some good meals of fish, hushpuppies, and potatoes. Come on, eat your heart out!

My father hasn't yet insisted I help at the plantation. I think he's waiting until I get my health and strength back. He has been extra nice to me. He's talked to me about going to school. I'm still very interested in becoming a doctor. He tells me when I'm ready he's got the funds to pay for my schooling.

I would love to go to Harvard University in Boston. I've read nice things about their degree offerings. I've not allowed myself to get too excited because the war is still raging on. I doubt seriously that a boy from the South who served in the Confederate Army would be admitted to such a prestigious university.

I feel certain that I'm finished with this awful war. Before being released at Vicksburg, every man had to sign a form saying he would not enter the Confederate Army again. I plan to obey that agreement. I guess if I wanted to fight again for the Confederacy that the Union Army couldn't stop me. That's not going to happen in my case. I signed that Union agreement without batting an eye. I wasn't then, nor would I ever be interested in reentering this awful, brutal, bloody war.

I never knew from day to day if I'd be killed. I've seen my buddies die right beside me. I wondered several times if the next bullet fired would hit me between the eyes. Obadiah, it was just awful.

I know you understand where I'm coming from since you had first-hand experience at Shiloh and Corinth.

I was never so happy to hear that General Pemberton finally surrendered to General Grant. Although we didn't know what Grant was going to do with us, we were just tired and hungry.

There were times we killed rats and ate them. I swear, I will never eat another dirty stinking rat. Although it was either that or starve to death. I didn't want to die!

I wish you could see my beautiful sister, Mary Catherine. She has certainly grown into a beautiful young lady.

Father is so strict on her. He doesn't allow her to go out on dates yet. Since arriving back at Black Oaks, I've escorted her to a community dance in Selma. She was the hit of the party. She reminds me of Aunt Audrey. She danced with every available unmarried gentleman at the community dance. She had the time of her life, and not like me, she does a great job at dancing. She never seems to wear down.

I'm not a good dancer, as you know, but I did get one or two dances in with her between those who were about to fight to see who was getting the next dance.

You know so well that Mary Catherine adores you. I'm hoping Father might agree to let me and Mary Catherine come spend some time with you and Grandmother in El Dorado.

After returning home from Vicksburg, Father shared with me about their trip to El Dorado. He made it sound so exciting, the steamboat travel, your town celebration, good Southern fried chicken, the big homecoming event at Three Oaks, and your beautiful plantation. He related also he had never seen a couple happier than you and Penelope. He also indicated that he'd never observed Grandmother Bradford being so happy and in such a good mood. He went so far as to say, he wouldn't mind living in El Dorado himself!

He also mentioned the camping and fishing trips you men made to Little Calion Creek. As he told his story, I could just feel and see the sand dunes, the cooking of the fish over a campfire, and the sleeping in the tents. Oh, how I would have enjoyed being there. Please let me know when a good time would be for you and Penelope to have some company.

This is the longest letter I've written in my life. I hope you don't get bored reading it.

I feel so blessed being back home in Dallas County and with my family at Black Oaks. God took care of me at all times. He's been good to me, and He's protected me in the heated skirmishes during the siege of Vicksburg. Why, I don't know, but I'm grateful, and I've thanked Him so many times in my prayers.

Obadiah, you too, have been a blessing to me as I've grown from boyhood to adulthood. You need to know you are my favorite uncle. You've always shown a genuine interest in me. Your kindness and attention always made me feel secure around you. Your ambition to become a doctor has inspired me to become a doctor. Your everyday faith in God has always amazed me. Your example of Christianity is unquestionable.

I've watched you set the example for all of us by respecting God's word in not taking advantage of Penelope when you could have easily done so. She was your slave, and you could have done anything you wanted with her, yet you didn't. You played it God's way. You may not realize it, but people were watching you all the time. They were waiting for you to mess up, but you never did. You held the course, and God, in the end, gave you the prize. I truly mean every word I've written. God bless you, Obadiah! I pray I'll be able to pattern my future years after you.

While at Vicksburg, I prayed a lot. I recognized I was nothing in myself, but with my savior, Jesus Christ, I was everything.

It is my Heavenly Father who gives me the air I breathe, the water I drink, the food I eat, and provides me with my every need. I just wanted you to know these things. It's because of Him that I live!

My Love to all,
Marion James Bradford

By the second week in September, the temperature was still hot. We had gotten a few rain showers, which cooled things down for short periods of time, but by midafternoon the temperature would be back in the high nineties. The crops at Three Oaks look good. We should have a bumper crop of cotton, corn, and beans.

Hank had two slaves who suffered dehydration and are currently recuperating back at their houses. I've examined both and feel they will be able to go back to work as soon as their body fluids are replenished. The biggest problem we have during hot days is getting our slaves to drink ample water.

Today I examined my beautiful, pregnant wife. Yes, I like to refer to her as my pregnant wife. She is showing every sign of carrying a boy. If she continues to gain weight, he could be a big one. As I was examining her today, the baby gave her a big kick. "Oh, give me your hand, Obadiah," she said grabbing my hand and quickly placing it in the area where the baby had kicked.

"Oh, there it goes again! Did you feel it?" she said with excitement.

"Yes, I did! What a kick!" I said.

"Oh, Obadiah, I'm so excited!"

"How do you feel?"

"I feel great! I don't know why some people don't want to be pregnant. I never felt so good!"

I believe she meant every word. As I've said before, she radiates that expression all over her face. Her complexion is beautiful. She smiled all the time.

As of late, we lie in bed with my hand on her stomach. She always wants me to feel the baby kick. We discuss possible names for the baby and why we feel those names are appropriate for a Southern doctor's son or daughter. Neither one of us expects this baby to be a girl.

Since Penelope is carrying the baby low and is constantly hungry and wanting to eat, plus the active kicking, we are convinced the baby will be a boy.

Penelope is so funny. She keeps me laughing with her mannerisms and the things she says. I love being with her. I know without a doubt our baby is getting the best mother in the world. Penelope has waited a long time to become a mother.

CHAPTER 20

Yesterday a telegram from Marion was delivered to my office. He and Mary Catherine will be here next week to spend a week or two with us. Mother is very excited. She is looking forward to having Dent's two oldest children under her roof. I think they look at Mother as both a friend and a grandmother. I know she's missed them since leaving Twin Oaks. Their visit will be good for her.

I've been a little concerned about Marion and Mary Catherine's trip from Selma to Monroe, Louisiana, especially since they will have to make a mandatory stop in Vicksburg.

Since Vicksburg is now under the control of the Union Army, I wanted to know what Marion and Mary Catherine might face upon arriving in Vicksburg.

The telegraph officials informed me their stop in Vicksburg would be safe. When the train stops to unload or take on new passengers, the Union soldiers will come on board, check each passenger's ticket and identification, and ask what business was bringing them to Vicksburg or Monroe.

After receiving the good news from the telegraph office, I laid my worries aside. I'm going to trust God to handle all the details.

Steamboat travel up and down the Ouachita River has not been interrupted by the Civil War. After they get on the steamboat in Monroe, it should be smooth traveling to Champagnolle.

I had no sooner returned to my office when Penelope informed me she needed to see me. She and I went to my office.

"Obadiah, I think we may have a problem."

"What kind of problem," I asked.

"While you've been out, Jim and Elizabeth have seen three people with smallpox. These people said they were aware of neighbors who had it as well."

"An epidemic of smallpox is definitely something we don't need. Did you come into contact with the patients treated by Jim?"

"I checked them in and that was it. Elizabeth and Jim are the only two who had direct contact with them."

"Did you touch anything belonging to them?"

"No, Obadiah, I was careful. I know if I got smallpox, I could get very sick, and it could affect my pregnancy. I'm well aware of what smallpox can do," she said.

Penelope is so smart. She is always reading about different diseases and how to treat them.

"Penelope, I want you to leave the office now and go to Mary's store. Tell her what you know and stay away from the customers. I'll come by and pick you up when I close the office. Don't come into contact with anyone. You hear me?"

"Yes, Obadiah, I'll do as you say."

I went back to see Jim, who was just finishing with a patient.

"Jim, what can you share with me about these cases of smallpox you treated?"

"Obadiah, those patients are pretty sick. I gave them vaccine shots and medicine and instructed them to go home, stay at home, and not to have contact with anyone other than family. Obadiah, if this becomes an epidemic, El Dorado could become a disaster."

"I've sent Penelope to Mary's store until we go home to Three Oaks. I don't want her to be exposed to smallpox."

"You made a good decision! Penelope doesn't need to get smallpox," Jim said.

"I'm wondering how many patients Dr. Weaver may have seen with smallpox?" I said.

"Why don't you send Beth Ann over there and check?" Jim asked.

After returning from Dr. Weaver's office, Beth Ann reported Dr. Weaver had treated five patients for smallpox. She said he treated two businessmen, who died unexpectedly. He's also running low on the smallpox vaccine.

"We need to get the pharmacy to order more vaccine, and fast," I said.

I took enough vaccine home to vaccinate my family. I went ahead and vaccinated Hank, since he comes into contact with people on a daily basis.

Since my slaves aren't leaving the plantation, I decided not to worry about them at this time. We need to reserve all the vaccine we have for those who are at a higher risk. We've ordered new vaccine, but it will be days before it arrives.

Penelope and I decided it was too risky for her to return to work. She will remain at home while we monitor this potentially dangerous development.

Today Jim and I saw six people with smallpox. We gave them shots and instructed them to go home and stay. We advised them to isolate themselves from healthy members of their family. We suggested they designate someone to bring food and drink. Whoever acts as the caregiver shouldn't stay any longer than necessary. Smallpox is very infectious, especially when the person has fever.

We also instructed them to wear a mask and wash their hands and clothing after each visit.

By the third day after treating our first small pox case, stories began to run rampant in town. There was a story being told that had everyone scared. It appears a Confederate doctor had sent some vaccine to a lady in town, whose husband was serving in the Confederate Army. The vaccine was for her and her kids. She decided there were people in town that needed it worse. She gave the vaccine to some people who had everyday contact with people in town.

It's been discovered that some of those people who received the vaccine had died within two days. The first victim was William Bennett, owner and proprietor of Bennett's Tavern. At the time he died, he was acting as deputy sheriff and was the caregiver to county prisoners.

A few hours after William Bennett died his neighbor, Jewels Redman, owner of Redman's hotel, died. He had just been elected as county judge and was also a much-needed citizen. The third victim was Miles Tigerton, a salesman in town. He came in contact with several people on a daily basis. The fourth victim was a Confederate soldier, Mason Donavan, who had been on leave of absence for only a few days. The fifth person, James Whitten, was a horse stable owner.

Jim and I decided we needed to get a bottle of this vaccine and analyze it. We were able to find a sample from the lady who first received it. She was very helpful. She had placed one sample in her kitchen cabinet. She told us that after receiving the vaccine, she passed it on to a nurse who was one of her best friends.

"I wanted the vaccine to be used by those who were public servants. I certainly hope this vaccine wasn't the cause of those deaths. You are welcome to this sample," she said as she reached in the cabinet.

After we analyzed the serum, we discovered it had been carelessly contaminated by germs of erysipelas.

What a shame! What started out as a good deed has ended in tragedy.

In a few days, things began to settle down. We saw fewer and fewer patients with smallpox on a daily basis.

The *El Dorado News-Times* reported that there had been fifty-two cases of smallpox reported, and nine people died.

Today Penelope and I picked Marion and Mary Catherine up at Champagnolle. They had no problems getting here. The checking of their identification and tickets at Vicksburg went without a hitch.

When I asked Marion how he felt being back at Vicksburg, he said, "It was a little frightening! I'm certainly glad we didn't have to be there long."

I had instructed Bill to stop at our plantation entrance. I wanted Marion and Mary Catherine to have an opportunity to see what Three Oaks looked like from a distance. The worst part of riding inside a carriage is not being able to see what is ahead.

I was aware that Mary Catherine enjoyed seeing beautiful things and felt she would enjoy the quarter-mile trip to Three Oaks. The scenery surrounding the plantation home is beautiful. The grass, trees, and flowers are still pretty and green. Mother's rose and flower garden can be seen on the east side of the house.

It, too, is still producing beautiful fresh flowers and fragrance for the house. The big three-acre garden can be seen to the east as well. There are still plenty of vegetables to be picked and preserved for the winter months.

Mother has been busy planning certain events for Marion and Mary Catherine's visit. She is aware of their interests and has planned activities accordingly.

She knows Mary Catherine enjoys dancing and made plans for all of us to attend the annual fall festival in El Dorado. During this two-day celebration, there will be dancing, political speeches, food, and drink, as well as lots of visiting around the town square. She planned shopping trips as well.

For Marion there would be fishing and camping trips. Mother made arrangements with Hank to help with the fishing and camping. She's also planning on Marion joining us for the fall festival in El Dorado.

I, too, want to show Marion around Union County and have cleared my calendar to work in a little fishing and horseback riding.

After dinner, we retired to the front porch for relaxation. There was a nice, cool breeze coming out of the west that made relaxing very comfortable. The temperature was so nice, not too cold or too hot—just right. It was now September, and I could feel fall coming on.

As we sat there visiting about old times and reminiscing of the days past, it was enjoyable watching Charles, Belle, Little Jim, Benjamin, Obi, and Samuel playing together in the front yard. They were having the time of their lives. I thought to myself, this is really nice that white and Negro children can play together without any fear of repercussions. Mixed-race friendships between blacks and whites have never been a problem on a Bradford plantation.

Mattie and Betsy kept the cool lemonade coming. I don't think anyone can make lemonade like Betsy. She's good at a lot of things, but her lemonade is always just right, not too sour or too sweet—just right. As I sat there on the porch watching Betsy serve her lemonade, I thought to myself, Obadiah, what will you do when the day comes that you will be setting Betsy and all the other slaves free? I knew it would be only a few years when I would be faced with that decision.

Betsy never married nor did she want to. I was in hopes she'd be with us until she died. I know Penelope felt the same about Betsy.

It was late when we turned in. Marion was a hit with Charles. It fact, you might say he was more than a hit, he was amazing.

Belle enjoyed playing with Mary Catherine as well. It was easy to see that Mary Catherine showed lots of patience when teaching Belle certain games, such as patty cake.

I decided to let Charles and Belle stay up late, since it was Marion and Mary Catherine's first night at Three Oaks. Tomorrow night they will return to their normal bedtime. Tonight, I would let them get to know their kinfolks.

Since the smallpox dilemma was still lingering around, I decided to work part time at the office. I will take off when the fishing and camping trips come up.

For several years now, I've been an early riser. While everyone else is still asleep, I get up, dress, and enjoy the cool breeze blowing across our front porch.

Reading the newspaper, sipping Mattie's fresh-brewed coffee, and watching the sun come up in the East is always an enjoyable time of the day.

This morning, after getting dressed, I went to the kitchen and helped myself to some of Mattie's coffee. While there, I visited awhile with Mattie, Betsy, and Big Jim.

On my way to the porch, I saw my newspaper lying on the dining table where my trusted friend Bill always puts it. I picked it up and carried it with me to the front porch, where I sat down.

As I unfolded the *El Dorado News-Times,* I could see the headline that read, "Confederacy Victorious in the Battle of Chickamauga."

The article was very informative. It wasn't long before I was completely consumed in reading about this important battle.

The Battle of Chickamauga was fought on September 19 and 20, 1863.

The location was in both Catoosa and Walker Counties in Georgia. The principal Commanders in the battle were General William S. Rosecrans and Maj. General George H. Thomas from the Union Army, and General Braxton Bragg and Lt. General James Longstreet from the Confederate Army.

General Rosecrans commanded the Army of the Cumberland, while General Bragg led the Army of Tennessee.

The *El Dorado News-Times* reported the following account of the Battle of Chickamauga, in sequential order of events:

> In early September, General William Rosecrans consolidated his forces which had been scattered in Tennessee and Georgia. He forced Bragg's army out of Chattanooga.
>
> As Bragg marched north on September 18, his cavalry and infantry fought with Union cavalry and mounted infantry which were armed with Spencer Repeating Rifles.
>
> On September 19, Bragg's men fought earnestly to break the Union line, but failed to do so. The next day Bragg resumed his assault.
>
> In late morning, Rosecrans received a misinformation report that a gap had been created in his line. This misinformation caused Rosecrans to start moving units to shore up the gap, and when he did, he accidentally created an actual gap, which fell directly in the path of the eighth-brigade which was led by Lt. General James Longstreet of the Confederate Army.
>
> Longstreet's attack drove one-third of the Union army, including Rosecrans himself, from the field.
>
> Union units spontaneously rallied to create a defensive line on Horseshoe Ridge forming a new right wing for the line of Maj. General George H. Thomas, who assumed overall command of the remaining forces.
>
> The Confederates launched costly and determined assaults on General Thomas's men, but Thomas prevailed until twilight. He later retreated back to Chattanooga.

The Battle was the most significant Union defeat in the Western Theater of the Civil War. This was the first major battle of the war that was fought in Georgia.

The Battle of Chickamauga was very costly for both sides.

On the Union side, there were 16,170 casualties and deaths. The casualties from the Union army totaled 1,657 killed, 9,756 wounded, and 4,757 captured/missing.

On the Confederate side, there were 18,454 casualties of whom 2,312 were killed, 14,674 wounded, and 1,468 captured/missing.

The article went on to list some interesting points about the Battle of Chickamauga:

It was the largest Confederate victory in the Western Theater.

The Confederate forces outnumbered the Federals.

The Union Army did not expect to encounter the Confederates at Chickamauga.

A fierce skirmish between Confederate General Nathan Bedford Forrest and Union troops at Reed's Bridge marked the opening of the battle.

The use of the Spencer repeating rifles played a decisive role in Col. John T. Wilder's famous "Lightning Brigade" ability to hold Alexander's Bridge on September 18. Because of the Spencer repeating rifles, General St. John Liddell's Confederates were delayed from crossing the creek.

The Spencer rifle enabled the shooter to get off fourteen rounds per minute, as opposed to the two to three shots per minute of an average Civil War rifle used by the Confederates.

The thick woods and swampy terrain made Chickamauga Creek a deadly place to fight.

Some say that, because of Rosecrans's confusion and actions brought about by his unconfirmed report of a gap in his line, the Confederates won the Battle at Chickamauga.

General George H. Thomas earned the name "The Rock of Chickamauga" for his steadfast defense of Horseshoe Ridge.

As I laid my paper down, Mattie came out carrying a fresh pot of coffee.

"Here is something special for you, Obadiah," she said as she handed me a plate containing a big apple muffin.

"What have I done to deserve this?" I asked with a smile.

"This is because you're my favorite son-in-law," she replied.

"My, my, Mattie, you've certainly increased your vocabulary haven't you?"

"I'm trying, Obadiah. Penelope has been giving both me and Big Jim some reading and writing lessons."

"So, that's where the son-in-law comes in?"

"I guess so. I just wanted to impress you!"

"Mattie, you impress me all the time. I'm so thankful to have you as my mother-in-law," I said as I smiled and took a big bite of the apple muffin.

"Penelope's been teaching me how to be a good mother-in-law," Mattie said as she refilled my coffee cup.

"Oh, she has now! Well, whatever Penelope is teaching you, I like it!"

"Thanks, Obadiah. I sure will be glad when my first grand-child is born. I believe it's going to be a boy."

"Why do you think that?"

"Penelope tells me you think it's going to be a boy. You're one smart man, and a doctor at that. I believe you're going to be right."

"Are you going to be disappointed in me if I'm wrong?"

"No, sir! I will be disappointed, because I'm counting on it being a boy, but a little girl would be good. Belle will finally have someone to play with."

"That's right! Belle will be thrilled, although she holds her own with the boys around here."

"She does at that!"

"How much longer will it be before breakfast?" I asked.

"I figure about thirty minutes. I know Mrs. Catherine is up, and Penelope was getting up when I came out here. You go ahead and enjoy that fresh apple muffin before it gets cold. It won't hurt your appetite!"

"Well, there you go again, appetite! Wow, I'm so impressed with you."

"Thanks, Obadiah! Oh, by the way, I'm singing tomorrow night at our church service. I was wondering if you and the family might come out to the barn for the evening service. Penelope told me to let you know and invite you. I thought maybe Marion and Mary Catherine might enjoy a different kind of singing than what they hear back in Selma."

"Mattie thanks for inviting us. We will all be there!"

"I'll be looking forward to seeing everyone."

"You have a great voice, Mattie. I know I'll enjoy hearing you sing."

"I'd best get back in the kitchen," she said as she poured me another cup of hot coffee.

As Mattie left to return to the kitchen, I felt blessed knowing Mattie is the mother to the love of my life. I've always believed God has a plan and purpose for each of us. In my case, purchasing Mattie and Penelope was in His plan for me.

When I accompanied my father to Selma, Alabama, to choose a replacement for our Mamie, I had no idea about Mattie and Penelope. When I saw them standing hand in hand with each other on the platform, I knew it was meant for me to bid on them, and hopefully be the winning bidder.

We are two of the happiest people in the world. What a blessing to have Mattie in the same household with Penelope and me. It is reassuring to me to have both Mother and Mattie living under the same roof. What else could be better than this? God, thank you, thank you, thank you!

CHAPTER 21

I held true to my promise to Mattie. We were all present at Hank's preaching and singing service in our barn at Three Oaks Sunday night. The barn was full of our slaves, eager to participate in the church service. Hank was glad we came. As we entered the barn, Hank escorted us to the front, where we took our seats on benches made by Hank and George.

The service started with a congregational song. The two following songs came from a Baptist hymnal, so I knew the words to the songs, but the rhythm was quite different from what I was accustomed to in my church. As I looked around over the congregation, I saw movement that would never be allowed in a white church service. I saw hands going up throughout the barn. Our slaves were certainly feeling the music as they felt the Holy Spirit come into their hearts and minds. What a song service!

We felt right at home as we joined in celebrating the word of God through great songs inspired by writers who surely used the Holy Spirit to talk to them when writing these beautiful songs.

Our driver, Bill, who reads better than most educated white folks, led the singing. He has a beautiful voice.

After the third congregational song, Mattie stepped forward for her special. It was a familiar song, "Swing Low, Sweet Chariot." I've heard the song several times in my life, but I can't remember it being sung so beautifully!

After she ended her singing, I immediately rose from my seat on the bench and applauded her performance. There were amens being shouted throughout the barn. Our slaves were on their feet, clapping and shouting glory to God. I, too, was filled with the Holy Spirit. As I looked at Mother, Penelope, Marion, and Mary Catherine, the expressions on their faces were of joy.

I thought to myself, This is what we need at First Baptist Church in El Dorado, Arkansas.

Hank came to the podium and delivered one of the best messages I'd heard. It was a message on love. His message was entitled "What the Heart Needs Most Is Love."

As I sat there absorbing every word into my head, I knew someday I would have to set Hank free, and when I did, I would help him get a church of his own in El Dorado. His ability to preach and win others to Jesus Christ would make him success-ful. Preaching would be his profession.

After hearing Hank preach, I felt a need to pray silently. I bowed my head and prayed, "Lord, thank you for this great day, your word, your songs, and for my slave friends, Hank, Bill, Mattie, and George. Thank you, Lord, for what they mean to this congregation of people. They are good leaders, and I pray your blessings upon each one of them.

"God, I also want to say thanks again for Penelope and the role she's played in bringing this church together. She's contin-ued to teach our slaves to read and write here at Three Oaks plantation, just as she did in Autauga County.

"When one of our slaves gets sick, she's always there to help me attend to them. She is respected and trusted by our slaves, and they accept her as one of them.

"Lord, I thank you from the bottom of my heart for Penel-ope. Thanks for allowing her to become a big part of my life."

As Penelope and I retired to bed, she rolled over and faced me and said, "Obadiah, I really enjoyed the church service today. What did you think?"

"Penelope, I felt the Holy Spirit in my heart today. I've not felt it being strong like that in some time. When Mattie was singing her song, I wanted to shout. She sang so beautifully, and her body language made it even more spiritual. Your mother has a God-given talent."

"You've explained it better than I could. I felt the Holy Spirit today as well. I want to be baptized, Obadiah."

I had forgotten Penelope hadn't been baptized. In fact, I can't remember visiting with her about her faith. We had been going to church at First Baptist in El Dorado for over a year now. Why hadn't I discussed all this with her before? I felt ashamed!

"I think that's a marvelous idea, Penelope. Are you saying that you've accepted Jesus Christ as your savior?"

"Oh, yes! I did that a long time ago, but I now think it's time I'm baptized. Isn't that what Jesus said we should do after we confess him as our savior?"

"Penelope, you are right! That's what Jesus teaches."

"Then I'm ready. I would like for Hank to baptize me, but I know I should be baptized at First Baptist in El Dorado. Isn't it the proper thing to do, to unite with our home church through baptism? I know I've been saved, but according to Jesus Christ's teaching I need to follow him in scriptural baptism out of obedience to Him. Isn't that right?"

Penelope is so smart. She has read all of this from the Bible my mother had given her.

"Penelope, I will speak to Brother Simpson at the church. He will make the arrangements for you to be baptized this coming Sunday. We will share your decision at breakfast with Mother and all the others in the morning."

I had just got those words out of my mouth when Penelope grabbed her stomach and said, "Oh, Obadiah, that was a big kick, and it hurt! Give me your hand. Do you feel that?"

Our baby acting restless reminded me of the Biblical story of Elizabeth, the wife of Zechariah. The Bible records that Mary and her cousin, Elizabeth, were both with child when they came together for a visit. They had not seen each other in months. When they greeted each other with a hug, John the Baptist leaped for joy inside Elizabeth's womb.

I've often thought of that scripture and what a joyous occasion that must have been.

"Penelope, this may sound crazy, but I believe our baby is letting you know that he or she is rejoicing with your decision of being baptized."

"I'm thinking you're right. He hasn't done this before tonight."

"So, you're convinced it's going to be a boy," I said.

"I really believe it's going to be a boy," she said, moving closer to me and lying on my arm.

"Oh, Obadiah, you've made me the happiest woman in the world. How did I get so lucky?"

"It was in God's plan, Penelope. He's always known that this would happen to both of us. He loves both of us and we love Him. When the time comes for you to give birth, please know He's going to be right there with you. He's going to see you through all of it."

"Obadiah, he's doing it again. Feel him!" she said with excitement.

"My, he's really active tonight!"

"I know it's not time for me to have this baby, but what if he comes early. Will it hurt him to be born early?"

"Eight-month babies normally have a good survival rate, but you're not dilating yet, and I don't think you will be having our baby anytime soon."

"We'd better get some sleep. It's going to be a long day tomorrow. Mother is taking you and Mary Catherine shopping in El Dorado. It is my understanding that Mary will be joining y'all upon your arrival at their store.

"We men are taking our boys and Marion on an overnight camping and fishing trip. We are going to do some serious fishing on Little Calion."

"Good night, my love," Penelope said as she rolled over and put her arm under her pillow.

Penelope sleeps exactly as I do. I sleep in my pillow, instead of sleeping on my pillow.

Hank, Marion, Charles, Obi, Little Jim, Big Jim, George, Bill, and I rose early and headed out to Little Calion in a wagon full of fishing gear, sleeping tents, campfire wood, and food. Yes, we took food, just in case the fish aren't biting.

Upon arrival at Little Calion, we put our tents together. The boys were very helpful, although they were anxious to get their hooks in the water. After getting the campfire ready, everyone grabbed a fishing pole and cast their hooks into the beautiful green stream of Little Calion. It wasn't long until the fish started biting. Obi was the first to catch a fish. Hank helped him remove the hook from the fish's mouth. Sometimes this is a difficult task, especially if the fish swallows the hook.

Hank put the fish on a string, attached the string to a nearby bush, and dropped the fish into the fresh, flowing water to keep it alive.

The first thing Charles said upon arriving at the camping site was, "Are you going to give the person who catches the biggest fish a prize?"

My response to him was, "Yes, there will be a prize for the person who catches the largest fish."

Charles remembered the fishing contest from a previous fishing trip. The competition made things exciting for the boys, and made a world of difference in accomplishing a task.

The boys watched closely as each fish was caught. At times I would hear someone say, "I've got the biggest one so far!"

Someone else would say, "No, you don't! I do!"

For lunch Mattie and Betsy fixed fried chicken and all the trimmings for us to eat. We would cook fish over the campfire for our evening meal.

By midafternoon, the boys decided to take a break from fishing and cool down while they swam in the Little Calion.

Hank had chosen a camping site with a nice clean sandbar. To the right of the sandbar was a beautiful swimming area, overshadowed by a tall bluff. There was a boulder protruding from the bluff, which the boys utilized for resting and diving into the water. Our boys could swim, so we weren't too concern for their safety. Bill and George kept a keen eye out in case someone got a cramp or got strangled.

Since there were no women around, we let the boys swim without any clothes.

We men decided to lie back and just talk while watching the boys swim. This was the first time I had a chance to really talk with Marion about his war experience.

"Marion, tell me from the beginning to the end what went on at Vicksburg. You were always at Vicksburg, weren't you?"

"That's right. Vicksburg was responsible for all my Civil War experience. I hated it! When I first arrived, there weren't a lot of things going on. We were able to spend lots of time in the town of Vicksburg. I made some friends, and we spent a lot of time in the pool hall. Don't tell Father, but we did take in a girly show now and then."

"What's a girly show, Marion?" Hank asked.

"Hank, don't you make fun of me. You know what a girly show means!" Everyone laughed!

"One day, our free time stopped. General Ulysses Grant's Union Army moved in and we had one skirmish after another. Several of our soldiers died defending Vicksburg. The Yankees tried to break through our lines on several occasions, but we were so well fortified that we drove them back each time. Each time we lost men, and so did they.

"I can remember when the yellow flags went up. That was an agreement that neither side would fire upon the other while each side collected their wounded. There were times I could have shot a few of them, but I didn't."

"Did the Union side ever get close enough to have hand-to-hand combat?" I asked.

"No, we would always drive them back before they got close enough to overrun our lines."

"Were you scared?" George asked.

"Yes, I was scared. There were times I got sick at my stomach. There were times when acquaintances of mine fell victim to the enemy's bullets. As soldiers fell to their death around me, I found myself in panic. I still have dreams of what I saw. There were young men, just like me, shot in the head, or in the chest, stomach, or shoulder, and sometimes arms were blown completely off by a cannon ball. I'm telling you, it was awful!"

"How many skirmishes occurred before General Grant called a halt to the fighting?" I asked.

"I believe there were at least ten that I was involved in. I'm not totally sure, because I've tried to wipe Vicksburg from my mind."

"What was it like after the Union stopped trying to take Vicksburg by force?" I asked.

"In a way, it was a relief, but in another way, it was still bad. General Pemberton ordered daily foraging expeditions on the riverfront that was still being controlled by the Confederate Army. I didn't mind the fishing part, but I hated foraging the nice gardens, stealing chickens and turkeys and other products from the residents in Vicksburg.

"General Pemberton had ordered the foraging because we were running short on supplies. Food had been rationed for weeks. We were losing weight, and some were starving to death.

"We didn't know it at the time, but the reason General Grant quit engaging us in battle was in hopes of starving us to the point that General Pemberton would surrender.

"I'm telling you, Obadiah, if there is a hell, which I believe there is, I believe we experienced a little of what hell is. I hope God doesn't punish me for all that foraging I did in Vicksburg."

"Marion, I want you to know that I have great respect for you. I admire you for doing what you had to do to stay alive. I don't think God is going to punish you for that! War forces us to do a lot of bad stuff; some things will affect us for the rest of our lives. God had a purpose for you. I know He did. He brought you home for a purpose. You just remember that," I said as I got up from where I was sitting and laid my hand on his shoulder.

"Marion, tell us more about how rationing of food affected the Confederate Army." Virgil requested.

"As time went by, we continued to bury soldiers who had been wounded or became sick with different types of diseases. Several died of starvation. They were already weak, and they got where they couldn't hold anything on their stomachs. They would just lie there and die.

"I believe we buried more who died from diseases and starvation than those who were killed or wounded in battle. It was just awful!"

"What is your assessment of the last few days at Vicksburg before General Pemberton surrendered to General Grant?"

"Our soldiers' morale hit bottom. They knew it was only a short time before we ran out of food. We had already started eating rats and anything we could get to supplement what little we were getting through our rations. Some resorted to eating leather from their shoes.

"General Pemberton's ranking officers pleaded with him to surrender before we all died. He first said, 'I'd rather starve to death than be captured and tortured and thrown into a Union prison and rot.'

"You know, hunger alters a man's thinking. I'm telling you, Obadiah, I was one of those who resorted to eating rats. It was something I thought I would never do, but you know, when you roast one of those hairy devils over a fire, the eating is not bad. I believe that it kept me alive."

"What were the reactions of the soldiers when General Pemberton surrendered to General Grant?"

"We all celebrated! When things settled down, there was a lot of speculation of what was going to happen to us. We didn't know if we'd be put on a train and shipped to some Union prison, where we would likely die of starvation."

"How did you feel when you found out that General Grant was going to let every Confederate soldier go home?"

"Obadiah, I can't describe to any of you how happy I was to hear that news. I got down on my knees and thanked my good Lord and Savior, Jesus Christ."

"We've never discussed how you got back home to Cahaba, Alabama."

"To gain our freedom, we had to sign an agreement that we would not become a soldier in the Confederate Army ever again. We were to go home and stay there. To tell the truth, I gladly signed the agreement. I was sick and tired of this war and was ready to get on with my life—what life I had left.

"The Union Army gave us three days of rations and told us to hit the road. We were given a paper to identify ourselves should we be stopped by other Union Army companies. I joined a band of Confederate soldiers who were heading to Alabama, Georgia, and other states, and never looked back."

"How long did it take you to get home to Cahaba?"

"It took me a week. I was scared, Obadiah!"

"Why were you scared?"

"I was afraid we'd run into other Confederate units along the way who would insist we join their unit. I was afraid if I said no, they would shoot me for desertion. We were lucky and didn't come in contact with any organized Confederate units."

"What did you do when you finally got home?"

"A farmer who lives in Selma offered me a ride to Cahaba in his wagon. The ride felt so good. My feet were killing me when he came along with his wagon. He was such a nice guy and carried me all the way to Black Oaks."

"Who was the first to notice your arrival?"

"Actually, I got home in late afternoon. The family was already seated, eating their evening meal. I quietly opened the door and slowly and quietly walked to the dining room. Before getting there, Buck, one of our servants saw me and came to meet me. He and I embraced, and I told him I wanted to surprise my family. He said, 'I understand, Master Marion.'

"The chatter coming out of the dining room was loud, just like always. We never were restricted by Father to remain quiet at the dinner table. As I reached the door, I just stood there until Father saw me. I can remember his exact words, 'Oh, my God!' He got up from the table, and by then, everyone knew I was there. From that point, everything turned into an emotional time for our entire family. As I received hugs from each member of the family, there was rejoicing and crying at the same time. I was crying as well.

"My mother was the last to get to me. She had tears of joy running down her beautiful face as she welcomed me home with open arms. 'I'm sorry, but I can't stop crying!' she said."

I had put Marion through all of this for a purpose. I felt if he was able to talk about what had happened to him at Vicksburg, he would be able to start a new life, one with a clear mind, and he'd have the ability to set goals and objectives for his life. I got up from where I was sitting near the campfire and went over and embraced him.

"Marion, this nightmare is over. You are now back where you belong. I know this has been the worst part of your life, but believe me, it's over. We all love you, and I promise you I'll do everything in my power to help you have a better life than what you've experienced. It's so good to be in your presence. May God bless you richly in the days yet to come."

The younger boys enjoyed the full day of fishing and swimming. Charles ended up catching the largest fish and was so happy. I do believe he was so excited about winning that very little humility existed when I presented him with his prize. Oh, well, I thought. We could overlook the lack of humility this time!

As we left Little Calion, I realized we had spent some real quality time with Marion and our sons. It was at Little Calion that many memories were made. There would be many more in the years to come. Thank you, God, for letting us share this time with Marion and build these blessed memories.

The time quickly passed, and it was time for the annual fall festival in El Dorado. We loaded a wagon full of food, drink, chairs, and quilts. All of these things would be needed as we joined hundreds of others who were camped around the courthouse, enjoying the music, dance, and other special activities, such as political speeches and the mayor's annual state of the union speech.

I didn't know it at the time, but Mary Ann and Elizabeth had been busy doing a little matchmaking for Marion and Mary Catherine. As soon as we reached our spot, Mary Ann and Elizabeth came walking up and introduced a young boy and girl to Marion and Mary Catherine. The two young people are members of our church and are sister and brother. Their names are Benjamin and Lindy Madison. Both are very polite and well thought of in our church.

After proper introductions, Benjamin asked Mary Catherine if she'd like to dance. She accepted, and away they went.

Marion, not to let Benjamin out do him, asked Lindy for a dance. She, too, gladly accepted.

From the expressions on Mary Ann's and Elizabeth's faces, I could tell they took pride in their matchmaking skills. "So, this is what you guys have been up to," I said.

"Obadiah, we felt Marion and Mary Catherine might feel a little out of place if they came to the festival not knowing any young people," Mary Ann explained.

"I think that was a very good idea," Penelope said as she voiced her opinion.

Mother was in agreement as well. After giving it a little thought, I wondered why I hadn't thought of it!

It wasn't long before Benjamin and Lindy had introduced Marion and Mary Catherine to several other young people of El Dorado. In fact, we didn't have much contact with them for the remainder of the evening. We'd see them dancing in the streets from time to time.

It wasn't long before my good friend Dr. Jim Burroughs and Elizabeth Parker joined us at our site. Penelope and I hoped that someday they might fall in love and get married.

Since Jim's arrival in El Dorado, he had concentrated mainly on getting his patient numbers up and worked long hours. In just the last month, we noticed he and Elizabeth had been seeing each other more. Penelope and I have decided that maybe, just maybe, this was the beginning of a courtship that just might lead to marriage.

By seven-thirty I was very tired. Penelope and I had managed to dance together a few times off and on during the day. As I looked at my beautiful wife, I knew she was getting tired as well. My mother was having the time of her life. She and Henry Batson, a good friend and deacon at First Baptist, were having a good time dancing and visiting.

I was ready to go home, but didn't want to say anything because everyone else who came with us was still going strong. I asked Penelope if she felt strong enough to take a stroll around the court square. She immediately said, "Yes!"

We excused ourselves and began our stroll around the square. We stopped and visited with friends as we made our way slowly around the courthouse. I noticed a few times that Penelope would touch her right hand over her stomach as we walked. I was wondering if the baby was kicking.

"Is the baby acting up?" I asked.

"Yes, he's telling me that it's not going to be long."

"You've got a few more weeks to go. You better tell him to calm down a little."

"You're so funny, Obadiah! Our son is alive and well in my womb. I just think he wants to see what this world looks like. You know, all he's ever known is darkness. I think he's tired of that!"

"You are some kind of lady! Where do you come up with all these analogies?"

"Oh, I think it must be because I have a very intelligent, good-looking husband!" she said as she gave me a kiss.

After rounding up our crew, we headed for Three Oaks for the night. We'd had a good time, but as I've already confessed, I was really tired. The next day would be Sunday, and we'd be driving back to town to attend church.

"Why don't we skip driving back to town tomorrow and attend Hank's service," Penelope asked.

I had thought about that myself. "That sounds like a marvelous idea," I said.

Mother was all for that as well, but I could tell that Marion and Mary Catherine are a little disappointed from the looks on their faces.

"Obadiah, we told Benjamin and Lindy that we would see them tomorrow in church."

"Let me suggest something to you. Why don't I have Bill get the carriage ready, and you and Mary Catherine can attend First Baptist Church? That away y'all can spend some time with Benjamin and Lindy. How's that sound to you?"

Marion looked at Mary Catherine, and she nodded in the affirmative.

"All right, let's do that! We are really tired and plan to stay home tomorrow."

"We perfectly understand," Marion replied.

Everything went off as planned. Marion and Mary Catherine were able to attend First Baptist and stay on for the afternoon.

Mother, Penelope, Charles, Belle, and I went to church service at Hank's church in our barn. Everything went great.

In three days, Mary Catherine and Marion will be leaving to go home to Cahaba, Alabama.

CHAPTER 22

On the day before Marion and Mary Catherine were to leave for Alabama, I took off work to spend my last day with them.

They will be sorely missed by everyone, especially Mother. I wish they could stay, but I know Dent and Sara are missing them. We have enjoyed their visit and hate to see it end, but as the old saying goes, "All good things must come to an end."

Penelope had gone to bed early. She had complained at dinner of being tired and sleepy.

Since tonight was Marion and Mary Catherine's last night, Mother and I decided to spend some quiet time with them on the front porch. At eight-thirty, Mattie came rushing through the front screen door shouting, "Obadiah, come quickly. I think Penelope is in labor!"

I was shocked. I hadn't examined her in the last two days but felt sure it was too early for her to be having the baby.

As we rushed to the bedroom, I turned to Mother and Mattie and said, "I may need your help. Come with me."

Marion and Mary Catherine stayed behind to take care of the kids. As I opened the door to our room, Penelope was rolling in our bed. She was in a lot of pain.

"Penelope, what's going on, my darling?"

"Obadiah, I think it's time! He wants out in the worst way, and it hurts so!"

"Let's take a look at you."

"Mattie, bring the lantern close so I can see her."

After examining Penelope, I knew she was right! Our baby wanted out. She had dilated a lot in two days. I could feel the baby's head when I examined her. We had to do something, and do it quick.

"Mother, she's ready to have this baby. You know what I need. Go quickly and tell Betsy we need lots of hot water and towels."

"Mattie, I'm going to need you to get some more lanterns and bring them over here. I've got to have more light. I will need your assistance in delivering your grandchild!"

Penelope was a true sport; she did everything I asked her to in pushing our baby through the birth canal. She screamed as any normal woman would when giving birth to a baby. I've never once delivered a baby that the mother didn't scream out with pain.

It was ten-thirty when Penelope gave birth to our son. Yes, I said our son! We were both correct in our prediction. He was a healthy, eight-pound and five-ounce boy. He had lots of black hair and was light in complexion.

One time Penelope asked me what I would do if he was black. I quickly said, "I'd love him even more!"

After tying and cutting the umbilical cord, I laid our baby boy on Penelope's breast. I sat down by her, and we examined his fingers and feet, which were absolutely perfect.

"You did well, Penelope. We have us a good-looking and healthy son."

"He is beautiful isn't he?" she said with those gorgeous, blue eyes shining brightly from the light of the lantern.

"All right, you two, what name have you chosen for my newest grandchild?" Mother asked.

We looked at each other and Penelope said, "We are calling him James Obadiah Bradford."

My mother cried out, "James would have been honored to have a grandson named after him. I truly appreciate what you have done."

I, too, found myself bursting with pride. This is my second son. He and Charles will carry on my bloodline. As I looked at him, I saw the things Penelope was talking about before he was born. He was experiencing light. He is taking everything in. Before he was born, he experienced only darkness; now he's seeing light for the first time. Before he was born, he heard muf-

146

fled noise; now he's experiencing real sounds. I've notice every time there is a sound, he tries to turn and look. He's already showing signs of real physical strength.

Penelope was right. He was tired of the darkness. He knew there was something else outside the darkness.

Penelope will absolutely enjoy our baby son. She will be a good mother. This baby will never want for anything. He will have our undivided attention as parents. We will do our utmost to protect him from the woes of this world.

He's blessed with two of the greatest grandmothers, who will love him and teach him God's great principles, and to top it off, they live under the same roof. What a blessing!

He will have his brother, Charles, and sister, Belle, to play with and to teach him valuable lessons of life. They will teach him how to share, I hope.

Penelope and I had decided should we be mistaken about the sex, we would call her Isabella. Since James made us right in our prediction, Isabella would have to wait for a while.

Mother had given us a few minutes to play with James before she came over to the bed and said, "Let me have Master James so Mattie and I can get him cleaned up. I'm sure everyone in this house will want to hold him tonight."

It was now almost midnight. Marion and Mary Catherine had put Charles and Belle to bed, with the help of Betsy. I was getting ready for bed when Marion knocked on the door and said, "Obadiah, I know it's late, but could you spare Mary Catherine and me a few minutes before you turn in?"

Although it was late and I was very tired, I couldn't deny Marion his request, especially since he and Mary Catherine were leaving for Cahaba tomorrow. I left Mattie and Mother in charge of James and Penelope as I left for the parlor.

As I entered the parlor, I took a seat across from Marion and Mary Catherine. I looked at both of them and asked, "What's going on?"

"Obadiah, we were wondering if we could impose on your generosity and stay here a few more weeks. Now that Penelope has had her baby, we thought we might be of some help to both you and the kids. Mary Catherine feels she could be helpful to you by filling in as the receptionist at your office. We both want to help out, if you think you could use us."

I knew Marion's request wasn't the main reason they wanted to stay. Something inside me told me there was something more important to them than volunteering their services to my family.

I looked at Mary Catherine and asked, "Mary Catherine, is this something you really want to do?"

"It is, Uncle Obadiah. It truly is!"

"I'm going to ask you one question. I want you both to be perfectly honest with me."

"All right, we will," Marion responded. Mary Catherine nodded her head in the affirmative.

"Does this extended visit have anything to do with Benjamin and Lindy Madison?"

Both Marion and Mary Catherine turned and looked at each other. At that time, I knew I had my answer.

"Obadiah, I may have found the love of my life in Lindy. I need some time getting to know her better, and I don't want to take off to Cahaba with the Civil War raging and not be able to come back and visit her at a later date. Does that make sense to you?"

"Yes, it makes a lot of sense. But, what will Dent and Sara say?"

"I believe they would want me to explore this relationship further!" Marion said.

"All right, Mary Catherine. Is this your reason as well? Is it Benjamin?"

"I like Benjamin. I think he's wonderful. I know my father would kill me if he knew I was even thinking about a boy. Uncle Obadiah, I've only known Benjamin a few days, but I have found him to be a perfect gentleman and a Christian. I wouldn't mind marrying a man like him. If I go back to Black Oaks, how will I ever know? I know, and you know Father. If he knew about Benjamin, he'd never let me come back here."

I sat there looking at two fine, young people who had met the loves of their lives. I felt both sorry and happy for them. It wasn't long ago I found myself going through the same thoughts and feelings about Penelope. I didn't want to make a mistake by sending them home, not knowing if these two people were to be in their lives forever. I may regret this for the rest of my life, but tonight I wouldn't deny my niece and nephew their request.

"You both are welcome to stay at Three Oaks. I expect you to let me know when and where you are going, and I expect you to telegram your father tomorrow and let him know you are staying on a few weeks longer. I also expect you to meet with your grandmother early tomorrow morning and share this information with her. You are to obey her as well. Is this agreeable to you?"

"Yes, sir," Marion and Mary Catherine said in a polite manner.

"All right, it's done. I'll have Bill drive you into town tomorrow for you to send your telegram. I don't want Dent and Sara worried about you. There is one other thing: I wouldn't share anything with your father and mother right now about Benjamin and Lindy. I know Dent pretty well, and this might just set off some kind of war. Do you know what I'm talking about?"

"I know exactly what you're saying," Mary Catherine said quickly.

"Good luck! I'm sure there will be a telegram coming from Dent as soon as he gets yours," I said with a smile.

As I left Marion and Mary Catherine in our parlor, I went back to my bedroom to spend my first night with my new son, James, and my love, Penelope.

On my way back to my room, I asked myself if I made the right decision. I believe I did, but time will tell, I guess!

CHAPTER 23

Aweek has passed since the birth of my son, James Bradford. He and Penelope are doing well. I insisted Penelope stay in bed for the first three days. On the fourth day she was up and around moving a little slow, but making her presence known. She is some tough lady! She nurses James every two hours, and he appears to be content with that feeding schedule. Penelope has an abundance of milk and has no problem given him the nourishment he desires. He has a very healthy appetite.

Marion and Mary Catherine sent their telegram to Dent on the day they were to start back to Cahaba. As we expected, Dent sent them and me a response right back. He wanted to know the real reasons Marion and Mary Catherine decided to extend their visit.

I decided not to respond with the real reasons but to share with him some good news that I thought would please him and meet with his approval. I decided to make Marion my assistant as I make house calls to the plantations, as well as in the city. Marion will shadow me as I did with Dr. Banister back in Autauga County. I have found myself needing an assistant several times since I started doing house calls.

This experience will give Marion insight into what is involved in being a doctor. Who knows, Marion might want to someday become a doctor. I would think Dent would be excited about that!

In regard to Mary Catherine, I decided to let her fill in for Penelope as the receptionist at my office. We could certainly use her, since we no longer have Penelope. She is now eighteen years old and well educated. She could easily do the job.

As I sent my telegram to Dent, I focused on those two reasons for their extended visit to El Dorado. I was in hopes the telegram would bring closure to Dent and Sara's fears. Dent is a smart man, and I'm sure he's beside himself trying to figure out why they were not ready to return.

I was hoping my telegram would buy us some time. I do hope Marion and Mary Catherine will arrive at a mature and intelligent decision in regard to their relationships with Benjamin and Lindy—the sooner the better for Dent, I thought!

We had bumper crops of cotton, corn, and beans. Hank and our slaves worked hard harvesting the crops. After the row crops were harvested, Hank planted winter wheat. As in Autauga County, I wanted to make use of my land year-round. Wheat is a good money crop that will aid us in our finances. Wheat is also a good food for our horses.

As each day passes, James does something to impress both Penelope and me. He's a very happy and healthy boy.

Every night when I come home, Penelope has a new story to tell me about James. According to Penelope, he's going to be a charmer. He's learned how to get her attention.

As of December 15, 1863, the Civil War has yet to come any further south than the Battle of Pine Bluff, Arkansas. The Battle at Pine Bluff was fought on October 25, 1863. The principal commanders were Col. Powell Clayton of the Northern Army and Brig. General John S. Marmaduke with the Confederate Army.

The *El Dorado News-Times* gave this account of the Battle of Pine Bluff:

> On September 17, 1863, Col. Powell Clayton of the Union Army was victorious in taking Pine Bluff. He and his brigade remained in town with the 5th Kansas Cavalry and the 1st Indiana Cavalry.
>
> The Confederates, led by Brig. General John S. Marmaduke, attempted to retake the town by attacking from three sides on December 12, 1863. The Union garrison, supported by 300 recently freed slaves, set up barricades in the courthouse square using cotton bales, along with nine cannons. Marmaduke made several attacks to retake the square but was unsuccessful.

After failing to take the square by force, the Rebels attempted to burn out the Union forces, but to no avail. The Confederate forces retired, leaving Pine Bluff to the Federals. The record showed that there were fifty-six federal casualties and forty Confederate casualties.

Again, the Union Army was victorious in this small battle.

For the past few weeks, I have been extremely busy with my work. Each morning I allow myself only enough time to glance at my newspaper, lay it aside, and do a few things I had been putting off. It has become apparent to me that my time-on-task skills are truly suffering with the type of schedule I'm keeping.

Today I decided to take a break from my hectic schedule and catch up on my reading. I asked Mattie to bring coffee to the parlor. As I sat down, I pulled my footstool close to me so I could put up my feet and relax.

There were several articles in the *El Dorado News-Times* that I hadn't gotten around to reading. From reading the first few paragraphs, I realized that most of the fighting was still taking place in Virginia, Tennessee, and West Virginia.

The first article I read was the coverage of the Battle of Lookout Mountain and the Battle of Missionary Ridge in Chattanooga, Tennessee.

The Battle of Lookout Mountain was fought on November 24, 1863. Union forces under Maj. Gen. Joseph Hooker assaulted Lookout Mountain at Chattanooga and defeated Confederate forces commanded by Maj. Gen. Carter L. Stevenson.

Lookout Mountain was one engagement in the Chattanooga battles between Maj. Gen. Ulysses S. Grant's Military Division of the Mississippi and the Confederate Army of Tennessee, commanded by Gen. Braxton Bragg.

The newspaper reported the Union Army's strength was 10,000 men compared to the Confederates' 8,726. When the battle was over, there were 408 casualties from the Union Army and 1,251 casualties from the Confederate Army. The Confederacy also had 1,064 soldiers either captured or missing.

On November 25, General Sherman of the Union Army attacked Gen. Braxton Bragg's right flank and made little progress. General Grant, in turn, hoping to distract Bragg's attention authorized Maj. General George H. Thomas's army to advance in the center of his line to the base of Missionary Ridge. A combination of misunderstood orders and the pressure of the tactical situation caused Thomas's men to surge to the top of Missionary Ridge, routing the Army of Tennessee, which retreated to Dalton, Georgia, fighting off the Union pursuit successfully at the Battle of Ringgold Gap.

Bragg's defeat eliminated the last Confederate control of Tennessee and opened the door to an invasion of the Deep South by General William T. Sherman.

The Battle of Missionary Ridge was costly to both the Union and Confederacy. The casualties and losses for the Union Army of Mississippi were 5,824. There were 753 killed, 4,722 wounded, and 349 missing. For the Army of Tennessee, there were listed 6,667 casualties, of which 361 were killed, 2,160 wounded, and 4,146 missing or captured.

I had just finished reading the summaries of the two Union victories at Chattanooga when Mattie came into the parlor with coffee.

"You look comfortable, Obadiah," Mattie said as she set the coffee pot on the end table next to my chair.

"I am. I decided to take a day off and catch up around here. I promised Penelope a carriage ride this afternoon. We wanted to wait until it warms up a little."

"That sounds mighty good to me! You and Penelope need that time together."

"Mattie, what do you think of your new grandson?"

"Oh, Obadiah, he's just precious. I can't keep my hands off him. He's going to be just like you. A wonderful gentleman and a charmer, at that!"

"It's funny you mentioned James being a charmer. Penelope has said that as well."

"You've not been around him as much as we have. If you were, you would notice how intelligent he is. He's doing things that I've never seen any baby his age do."

"Mattie, you might be a little prejudiced, since you are his grandmother."

"You just wait and see, Obadiah!"

"Mattie, I'm looking forward to Christmas this year. It's going to be nice celebrating together. I'm hoping with the good Lord's blessings, we'll always be able to celebrate Christmas together."

"Obadiah, I feel blessed too! Because of you and Mrs. Catherine, we feel safe and are honored to have an opportunity to celebrate with family. You and your mother are not like some slave owners. Some slave owners wouldn't give us the time of day. I'm proud to be treated nice. I'm proud to feel secure at night, and I'm proud to be living in this big house with my daughter's family.

"Big Jim and I consider ourselves to be blessed to be owned by a person of God. Just know we appreciate what your family has done for us."

"Mattie, let's talk a little about the future. I've been thinking about what's going to happen after the Civil War ends. In my opinion, it's just a matter of time until the North wins this war. When that happens, the South will again become a part of this United States of America. Slaves will be set free throughout the South. The slaves will be able to do whatever they choose to do. Have you given that any thought?"

"To be honest with you, Obadiah, I have. I must confess, it's scary to me. Where will we go, and what will we do? We don't have any money or land. We have two children to feed and clothe. I've worried lots about this, Obadiah."

"Mattie, you can stop your worrying. Penelope and I've been talking about this subject. We're in agreement that we'd like for y'all to stay on here at Three Oaks with us. We want to remain a family.

"Instead of you working as a slave, you will be free. You and Big Jim will earn money working for me. When that day comes, we will work out the details."

"Oh, Obadiah, I love you so! I want security for my boys, and I want them to be educated as well. You have just made my day. I can assure you, we won't do anything to disappoint you."

"That's never entered my mind. I look at you as family and I'll always look at you as being my mother-in-law, James's grandmother, and the mother to my Penelope. You will always be my special friend."

"Obadiah, it's going to be rough on slaves, isn't it? Who's going to take them in? Where are they going to work? Will they get enough work and earn enough money to provide for their families? This is all so scary!"

"Mattie, you are exactly right. It will be hard on them. I'm planning to offer my slaves jobs where they can stay here. I will pay them good wages. If they want to do sharecropping, we will work that out as well. I'm not too concerned for my slaves, but I'm afraid the future outlook for slaves as a whole will not be as good as they think it will be."

"Obadiah, thank you for what you do for me and my family. I want you to know I love you and pray for you daily."

"Mattie, that means a lot to me. Thank you!"

"I'd best get back to the kitchen. Betsy will think something has happened to me. I will be meeting with Mrs. Catherine this afternoon in regard to Christmas dinner. She's such a sweet lady. You are blessed to have such a sweet mother!"

"Indeed, I am. She is special!"

After Mattie left the parlor, I felt good sharing things with her. I wanted to reassure her that she and her family were members of my family and they would be taken care of when the slaves are declared free people. I wanted her to know when the war ends, she and her family will be provided for.

After the war ends, the government will move into a reconstruction period of rebuilding a new nation. It will not be a glamorous thing, nor will it be an easy task. It will be a time of heartaches and heartbreaks.

Several plantation owners will experience great hardship that will force them to sell their properties. They will no longer have free labor, and without free labor, profits will dwindle to the point that their indebtedness will exceed profits.

The remainder of my day was spent with Penelope. We made our trip over to Champagnolle to do some shopping at the port's merchandise store. The temperature was a warm sixty-two degrees, which wasn't bad for a late December day.

Our night together was just wonderful. This was the first night since James was born that we were really together as husband and wife.

"God, I thank you for my Penelope. She continues to make me the happiest man on earth!"

On December 19, the streets of El Dorado were crowded with Confederate soldiers who had set up camp on the outskirts of town.

This was the first time El Dorado had seen this many Confederate soldiers. General James Shelby had brought his company to Union County to establish winter quarters. His camp was located just north of Robert Goodwin's house, between the Smackover highway and the road to Norphlet. General Shelby made his headquarters in the home of Robert Goodwin.

Another battalion under the command of Major William Clarke Quantrill came with Shelby's brigade. This battalion set up camp a few miles northwest of Lisbon on the Lisbon and Mt. Holly Road.

Among its members were Frank and Jesse James, Cole Younger, and others from Missouri. Major William Clarke Quantrill had built a reputation of looting and killing innocent people. While camping near Lisbon, Major Quantrill made his headquarters in the home of William Young, about three miles west of Lisbon.

Another brigade who camped near Lisbon was General Thomas J. Churchill's. General Churchill made his headquarters at the home of Major Coulter. General Parsons of General Price's division also brought his brigade to camp near Three Creeks. His camp was known as the Kirby-Smith Camp.

When all these brigades started arriving in Union County, several residents wondered if some kind of battle was going to be fought in El Dorado. The main purpose for camping in Union County was the abundance of wild game, food, and ample water. There were also large, virgin pine trees that offered shelter from rain and snow.

Mother started her Christmas shopping early this year. She wanted to be sure that all Christmas presents were bought and wrapped to be shipped in plenty of time to our family members in Alabama.

Our family members there did the same thing for us. We were all ready for Christmas.

Penelope and Mother helped Hank decorate the barn for his annual Christmas program. Hank has gone all out to establish what Christmas really means. The slaves had become accustomed to the annual Christmas program. Since James was the youngest baby on the plantation, Hank asked Penelope and me to play the roles of Joseph and Mary, with James being baby Jesus. We gladly accepted his offer.

This year's Christmas was really special for Penelope and me. We were blessed by having both of James's grandmothers under the same roof celebrating Christmas together. Where else could you find this type of celebration in the South?

As I've said several times, slave issues have never been a problem with the Bradford family. I look at Mattie as a mother to my beautiful wife and the grandmother to my James. Someday, that legal document I keep in my parlor safe that identifies Mattie as a slave will be burned, and she will take on the legal aspect of a freed slave. If she wishes to stay on in my household as a mother-in-law, she will certainly be welcome.

We had a great, traditional Christmas. I read the Christmas Story to everyone. We opened our Christmas presents and enjoyed our annual Christmas dinner, which was prepared by Mattie, Betsy, Big Jim, and Bill.

At our table, we were graced by the presence of Penelope's family, Bill and Betsy, Marion, Mary Catherine, Virgil and Mary's family, and our special guest, Dr. Jim Burroughs, and his soon-to-be wife, Elizabeth Parker, as well as Benjamin and Lindy Madison.

Yes, Jim asked Elizabeth if she would marry him, and she said yes! They plan to be married on New Year's Day. They will be married at First Baptist Church in El Dorado and spend their honeymoon in New Orleans, Louisiana.

We are all excited about this marriage. In fact, Penelope and I have decided our matchmaking skills are working rather nicely. We are giving great thought to making it a second profession!

CHAPTER 24

The new year, 1864, started off with plenty excitement in El Dorado. The streets came alive with soldiers from the three different camps located nearby. From all indications, it appears the soldiers are not restricted to how they spent their off-duty time.

During the past two weekends, several soldiers have been jailed for being drunk or fighting.

My sister, Mary, shared with me a story that occurred at Dan's Tavern last weekend. It appears that Frank and Jessie James and two of the Younger brothers came to town to play some poker. While playing poker, one of the Younger brothers became intoxicated and fired his gun, with the bullet hitting the ceiling. She said Jessie and Frank immediately took his gun from him and escorted him out of the saloon and carried him back to the camp. There has been no arrest from the incident.

Marion and I have been making frequent trips to the three military camps, which are located just outside the city limits of El Dorado. Yesterday we visited the Kirby-Smith Camp, where we treated several soldiers for a stomach virus and some colds. So far, there haven't been any pneumonia cases.

The soldiers appear to have enough to eat and ample bedding.

On our way back to my office from the Kirby-Smith Camp, I asked Marion how his day had gone as he mingled among many of the Confederate soldiers.

He said, "It brings back memories both good and bad. The good was when my friends and I had plenty of food and drink and played horseshoes together. The bad were the times when the food was being rationed and seeing friends die of starvation and from disease."

"I can't imagine how that must have felt," I said.

"Obadiah, I know you've seen a lot of bad things as a doctor, but I'm just thankful you've not had to experience seeing your friends dying of starvation."

"I'm happy God blessed you with good health and strength during those hard times. I believe He had a purpose in seeing you through those hard times. One such purpose was to allow you to be here with me, helping me with my medical practice.

"Marion, I'm thankful for your dedication to the assignments I give you. You've not failed me yet. You are a mighty fine associate, one I'm happy to have as an employee—and maybe a doctor associate someday!"

"Thanks, Obadiah. I'm enjoying being here as well. I like being your assistant. I feel I'm learning a lot. I want you to be honest with me and tell me if I have any potential in becoming a doctor like you someday."

"At the rate you're learning, I think you have a very good opportunity of someday having your own medical practice. You are very conscious of what's going on. You're intelligent, and you learn fast."

"That's exactly what I need to hear. Please let me do things that you feel I'm capable of. I'll do my very best."

"Marion, I promise you I'll make it a point to give you things to do. Just be ready when I ask you.

"Oh, by the way, how are you and Lindy doing?"

"I'm glad you asked. I've been trying to build up the nerve to ask you something."

"Well, what is it? Don't be afraid. You can ask me anything and know it will remain between the two of us."

"Obadiah, I'm afraid I've sinned badly!"

"In what manner have you sinned?" I asked with some hesitation.

"Obadiah, Lindy and I have been intimate. After the first time, we both agreed it was a mistake. It was wrong in God's eyes, and we agreed we'd not do it again. But when we're together, our love for each other and the passion we feel for each other become stronger. We both realize right and wrong, but for some reason we can't control our feelings for each other. Obadiah, do you understand what I'm saying?"

"Marion, I know too well how your feelings for Lindy affect your heart and mind. Let me ask you a question, and I want you to be truthful in your answer."

"All right, ask!"

"You mentioned you and Lindy have been together more than once. Do you think this could be lust or true love?"

"Oh, Obadiah, I've asked myself that at least a thousand times. I know I love Lindy, and I know if this doesn't stop, she may get pregnant, and that would be disgraceful to not only her, but to our family as well. I just don't know what to do!"

"Have you prayed about this?"

"Yes, I have, and I've lied to God again and again. When I ask for forgiveness, I tell him it won't happen again, but when we're together, things just get out of control."

"Marion, only your father, Dent, knows what I went through with Penelope. I've experienced all those things, except we never gave over to our feelings. The hurting heart, the passionate moments, and the desire to go all the way—all of these I experienced. The only difference was my commitment to God, and my respect for Penelope was strong enough to wait for God to make things right for us."

"Obadiah, please tell me what I need to do," Marion asked with tears in his eyes.

As I looked at Marion, I felt compassion for him. It took courage for him to share his inward feelings and desires. He was reaching out to me for help, and I didn't need to let him down.

In my mind I was searching for the right words to say to Marion. I was silently asking God to give me wisdom in answering Marion's questions. I need to advise him in a manner which will be appropriate to his situation with Lindy.

I finally opened my mouth and said, "Marion, if you love Lindy, you need to marry her. You need to make this relationship right in the eyes of God. If you don't love her, break this relationship off and run from this temptation. Go home to your father and mother, and put Lindy behind you. This is my advice to you, dear nephew!"

"Thanks, Obadiah! Your advice is well taken! I need to ask you one other question, if I may."

"All right, what is it?"

"If we decide to get married, will you be my best man?"

"I would be honored to be your best man," I said as I laughed.

"Thanks again, Uncle!" Marion said.

"You're very welcome, my friend!"

Three days passed and I hadn't heard a word from Marion about our conversation. On the fourth day, as we headed toward Kirby-Smith Camp, Marion looked straight at me and said, "I guess you've been wondering what I've been doing."

"Well, to be honest, yes; I've been wondering every day if you were going to let me know what you are planning to do."

"The reason I haven't is that I had to wait to get Lindy's answer. Obadiah, we're getting married!"

"Congratulations, Marion!"

"Is that all you've got to say?" Marion asked.

"Well, what else did you expect?"

"I thought you would give me some kind of fatherly lecture or something!"

I couldn't help laughing. After seeing the expression on Marion's face, I just lost it.

"All right, tell me how you feel about getting married."

"I'm excited! We're going to visit with Lindy's folks tonight. Please wish us luck and say a prayer that all will go well."

"So, you and Lindy haven't talked with her folks yet?"

"Not yet! I proposed to Lindy three days ago, as soon as I got back from our trip to the Kirby-Smith Camp. She was so excited, but she wanted a few days to think about it. She gave me her answer last night."

"This visit with the Madisons may not be a piece of cake, you know!"

"What do you mean?" Marion asked with a disappointed expression on his face.

"What if they say, 'Lindy, you're too young to get married'?"

"Oh, Obadiah, do you really think they would do that?"

"What if they do? Are you and Lindy prepared to go ahead and marry without their consent?"

"Oh, Obadiah, you're making me a nervous wreck. You might as well turn this carriage around and take me back to your place. I'm not going to be any good to you today!"

"Hey, I'm only kidding around with you. I'm sure they will be pleased and give you their blessings. I know for certain the Madisons like you. They know you're intelligent and will be a good provider for their daughter."

I had no idea my kidding around with him would upset him so. All during the day, I made a point to encourage him in some way. I wanted to make up for the mess I'd created. I decided praying would be the best thing I could do. I prayed and prayed that the Madisons would be supportive of Marion and Lindy's request to get married.

As it turned out, the Madisons gave their blessing for Lindy to marry Marion, on the condition she and Marion would get married at First Baptist in El Dorado.

As soon as Marion and Lindy received her parents' blessings, Marion went immediately to the telegraph office and sent Dent and Sara a wedding invitation to his and Lindy's wedding. The wedding day was one month from today.

Marion's news to his parents will be a complete surprise and shock, to say the least. If I know Dent, he will rave and shout until he gets red in the face. I'm sure it will take Sara a few minutes to calm him down. After a while, he will accept it and work out a way to come to his first child's wedding. The only news that could top Marion's news would be for Mary Catherine to decide to marry Benjamin Madison on the same day, in a double wedding ceremony. That news would perhaps put my brother Dent in a cardiac arrest!

A few days later, Marion received a letter from Dent. It was long!

Dear Marion! We received your telegram. We were disappointed that you've kept us in the dark this long.

I've known all along it had to be something important to keep you and Mary Catherine in El Dorado. I never dreamed you'd be the marrying kind, especially this young. Lindy must be some kind of lady!

Needless to say, your mother and I were shocked when we read your telegram. I was angry at first, but after getting some sleep, I realized that this has to be important to you, or you wouldn't be getting married.

Your mother and I wish you well. You're an adult now, and it appears you've made an adult decision. I pray that your decision is a lifetime commitment, one that will make you happy. Please tell my brother that he will need to get his house ready for company. The entire family will be arriving around March 10.

You couldn't have picked a better time for your wedding. All the crops have been harvested at Black Oaks, so we are good until the middle of April when we start breaking ground for our summer and fall crops.

You indicated that Mary Catherine, Mother, and everyone else is doing well. That is good news. We have missed you and Mary Catherine badly. We're hoping that Mary Catherine will return to Alabama with us after the wedding. We need her to get ready to go to Boston for her advanced studies.

I want to remind you, Son, we are still willing to pay for additional schooling for you as well. We can talk about this while in El Dorado.

Please give our love to Mother, Mary Catherine, Mary's family, and Obadiah's family. We look forward in seeing y'all on March 10. If there are any changes in our plans, I'll send you a telegram.

Your loving father,
Dent Bradford.

As Mary Catherine, Marion, and I were riding home in my carriage, Marion handed me the letter. Mary Catherine asked,

"Uncle Obadiah, may I read it? I'll read it aloud for you, since you're driving."

I looked at Marion, and he nodded in the affirmative.

When she got to the part where Dent referred to her going back to Alabama with them, she stopped. She had a strange look on her face. I knew she wasn't in favor of her father's plans.

As soon as she finished reading the telegram, she began to cry.

I put my arm around her and asked, "What's wrong, Mary Catherine?"

"Uncle, Obadiah, I don't won't to go back to Alabama. I'm very happy here in El Dorado. If Marion stays, I want to stay as well."

"You know your father and mother will be very disappointed if you don't go back with them."

"I know that. It's been their dream to send me to Mrs. Adams' Boarding School in Boston. I, too, have looked forward to going there, but since I've been here in El Dorado, I no longer feel that away."

"Mary Catherine, does this have anything to do with Benjamin Madison?"

She cut her eyes toward Marion and then said, "Maybe."

"Oh, I see. I think we had better have us a good uncle-niece talk when we get to Three Oaks."

Mary Catherine bent over and screamed out, "Could we stop? I think I'm going to be sick!"

I immediately pulled the carriage over to the side of the road. Marion helped Mary Catherine from the carriage. She vomited and felt faint.

"I need to sit down," she said.

With Marion's help, she slowly braced herself against the wagon wheel and sat down.

"I'm so sorry. I've not vomited in years. Please forgive me!"

"You don't worry about that. You relax for a while. There is no certain time we have to be at Three Oaks."

After Mary Catherine regained her composure, we got back in the carriage and headed on to Three Oaks.

Penelope, Mother, and the children were waiting for us on the porch as we drove up. Samson, George's son, took the carriage on to the barn as we made our way up the steps to the porch.

Charles and Belle jumped into my arms. They are getting to be an armful. I always enjoy their warm hugs and kisses. Charles began to tell me about his day. He talked so fast that I had to tell him to slow down. I told him I wanted him to save some of his stories until dinnertime. I needed to spend some time with Mother.

"Can we boys play till dinner time?" Charles asked.

"I want to play, too," Belle said.

"I want you to stay within shouting distance. In fact don't go to the barn. Just play in the yard until dinnertime."

At this time Penelope came walking over with James in her arms and handed him to me as she laid a big kiss on my lips.

"I thought you might want to visit with your youngest son until dinner."

"Indeed, I would!" I said as I walked over and gave Mother a kiss on the cheek and sat down in my rocking chair next to hers.

Penelope noticed that Mary Catherine had gone into the house in a rush.

"I'm going to check on Mary Catherine. She looked white as a sheet." Penelope said as she turned and went into the house.

"What's wrong with Mary Catherine?" Mother asked.

"She got sick coming home today. I believe she's going to be all right."

"Maybe I need to go check on her as well."

"No, stay here, Mother. I've got some news to share with you. Penelope can take care of Mary Catherine."

"What news are you talking about?"

"I'm going to let you read a letter that Marion received today from Dent. I think you will find all of it quite interesting.

Marion, give the letter to your grandmother!"

Before he gave Mother the letter, he bent over and whispered in my ear. "She doesn't know I'm getting married, does she?"

I shook my head as a no.

The time Mother took to read the letter felt like an hour, rather than the few minutes she took. Finally, she laid the letter down on her lap, turned to me, and said, "I believe someone has some explaining to do, and obviously, it's not me!"

"First of all, Mother, I apologize to you, but in Marion's and my defense, we decided to keep it just between the two of us until all the preliminaries were worked out."

"How long have you two known about this?"

"We've known about the marriage date for about three days but wanted to wait for Dent's reaction before sharing things with you and other members of the family. We just got Dent's letter today."

"Marion, you come over here. I'm not going to bite you."

Marion slowly went over and stood in front of her.

"Do you really love Lindy?" she asked.

"Yes, I do, Grandmother. I love her with all my heart and soul."

"I like Lindy, too. I think she will make you a lovely wife. I can understand why Dent and Sara were upset with you. These secrets should not be practiced in this family. Your grandfather would clean your plow, young man!"

"I'm sorry, Grandmother, but all this has happened so fast. Obadiah is the only one who knew anything about this. I asked him not to share it until Lindy agreed to my marriage proposal. We also had to get Mr. and Mrs. Madison's blessing. It's been somewhat complicated. If you want to blame someone, blame me. I'm the responsible one!"

"Come here, young man!"

Mother rose from her chair and gave Marion a kiss on the forehead and a big hug. I breathed a sigh of relief. I knew Mother, and this was her way of saying to Marion, "I forgive you!"

My mother is a wonderful mother and grandmother. She wouldn't abandon any of her children or grandchildren. She'd fight to the death for any of us. She wasn't beyond scolding any of us for our wrongdoings, but in the end, everyone felt her love and affection.

"I need to ask a few questions. When do you plan to make your announcement of your upcoming marriage to Lindy?" Mother asked.

"I thought you might help me with that, Grandmother. I told Lindy that you were great at arranging weddings and getting out invitations and all of that. She was excited to know you would be willing to help with that."

"So, you were assuming I would do those things for you?"

"Yes, I thought you would love to do it."

"Well, it's been a while, but I think I can handle another wedding. I'll talk to Lindy and her mother, and we will see what needs to be done. By the way, where will the wedding be held?"

"It will be at our church, First Baptist of El Dorado."

"That's a good choice. Now, we'd best get ready for dinner. Before I go, I want to thank both of you for sharing with me. It makes me feel I'm still needed around here." She smiled all the way to the front door.

After Mother went inside, Marion sat down in his grandmother's chair and said, "That wasn't as bad as I thought it was going to be."

"Marion, I learned long ago that one has to handle Mother in the right way. Tonight, you came through in flying colors. That charming personality of yours came through for you. You knew Mother would jump at the opportunity to help plan a wedding. I'm telling you, Marion, you used the right charm tonight."

"To tell you the truth, Obadiah, I actually learned from you. I've watched how you handle Grandmother, and it always seems to work to your advantage. So, I thought I would try it!"

"You are truly a character!"

"It worked, right?"

"I think you need to go take a bath and get ready for dinner. Your head gets bigger by the minute!"

After Marion left for his bath, I enjoyed spending some time with James. As I held him, I began to talk to him. He just stared into my eyes as if he understood everything I was saying to him.

It didn't take me long to realize that James is special. Penelope has told me time and time again about the things he was doing at four months. She said, "Obadiah, our baby is doing things that most one-year-old babies do." As I talked to him, he responds with smiles. It is like he is saying, "Tell me more, Daddy!"

Mattie stuck her head out the door and said, "Obadiah, tell the kids it's time for them to come in and wash their hands for dinner. Dinner will be ready in about fifteen minutes."

"Thanks, Mattie!"

I rose from my chair and went over to the front door steps and hollered for Charles, Belle, Little Jim, and Benjamin to come in for dinner.

I noticed at dinner that Mary Catherine was very quiet and didn't eat much. I was concerned about her. It's not like her to be this quiet and not eat.

Every night when Penelope and I go to bed, we have a time of sharing together before going to sleep.

"Penelope, I'm curious about Mary Catherine. What can you tell me?"

"Obadiah, we've got a big problem."

"Well, don't keep me in suspense. What is this big problem?"

"Mary Catherine doesn't want to go back to Alabama after Dent and Sara come for the wedding."

"I knew Dent's letter upset her, but she will get over it."

"Oh, Obadiah, I'm afraid it's much more than the letter!"

"Penelope what are you trying to say to me?"

"Obadiah, I believe Mary Catherine is with child!"

"Oh, Penelope, what makes you think that?"

"Mary Catherine shared with me that she's not had her monthly period in two months. She, too, is afraid she's pregnant."

"What's going on here? Dent will never trust me with any of his children, ever again!" I said as I got out of bed, running my hands through my hair.

"Obadiah, this isn't your fault!"

"Penelope, you might as well know the entire story. I'm going to share something with you that only I know. You can't share this with anyone else."

"I always keep the things you tell me to myself."

"Marion and Lindy have been intimate for some time now. I don't think Lindy's pregnant, but what they've been doing is wrong. They love each other and are ready to make their relationship right with God.

"Penelope, both Marion and Mary Catherine were raised in a Christian home. They both are well versed in the Bible and have been taught right and wrong. They know very well that having relations before marriage is wrong. Why didn't they rely on God's teaching? I'm really frustrated about this!"

"Obadiah, please don't get upset with me for what I'm about to say. Some young people are not as strong as you were. Please keep in mind the times we almost disobeyed God's teaching as well. I was willing, but you wouldn't budge from your convictions. Please don't get me wrong. I know now it was right for you to stop when you did. I respected you then and I still respect you today. Try to remember, not every young couple has the strength to resist their emotions and desires for each other."

"Penelope, I know you are right. It still bothers me. Dent put his trust in me to see that his two oldest children carry on their Christian lives here in El Dorado. How will he ever forgive me when all of this comes out?"

"Maybe he won't have to know all the truth!"

"What do you mean by that statement?"

"Mary Catherine told me that Benjamin has asked her to marry him on several occasions. She said she kept rejecting his proposals."

"Did she say why?"

"Yes, she said she promised Dent and Sara that she would go to Mrs. Adams' Boarding School in Boston and felt compelled to fulfill her promise."

"Do you think she loves Benjamin?"

"Yes, I do. I asked her the same question, and she said she loved him with all her heart and soul!"

"I need to talk with her, Penelope. I would like for you to be there when we talk."

"I'll be there, Obadiah. But first, I think you need to determine if she's with child. This may make a difference in her decision to accept Benjamin's marriage proposal. If they get married, no one will have to know about their lovemaking before marriage."

"Penelope, you are so wise. Please know I appreciate your wisdom. If Mary Catherine is pregnant and if she loves Benjamin, she should accept his marriage proposal and give this child a proper name and a good home. A double wedding on March 15 is sounding better and better."

It wasn't long before Penelope and I were caught up in our passion for each other. I continue to praise God for Penelope daily. She knows how to please me. She knows when I need her. She rewards me daily with things she does for me. Our marriage is alive and well. Thank you, God!

CHAPTER 25

Today I've spent the biggest portion of my time with Mary Catherine, examining and counseling her in my office.

She is, indeed, pregnant. I figure she is about two and a half months along.

The first thing I said to her was, "Mary Catherine, you are pregnant. You have some very important decisions to make, and the sooner, the better."

Mary Catherine broke down and cried. She looked at me with those beautiful, blue eyes and said, "Uncle Obadiah, I'm so sorry for putting you through all of this. I know I've disappointed you and everyone else in this family. They will never forgive me for letting this happen!"

"Let's don't worry about that right now. I love you, darling, regardless of what you've done. Please understand this whole thing can be worked out. God will help us come up with a workable plan. I need to know how you feel about Benjamin."

"Uncle Obadiah, I love Benjamin. He's the only boy I've been with, and he treats me like a lady. He's good to me and I know he loves me."

"All right. If you know he loves you, why not marry him and make this right in the eyes of God?"

"Uncle Obadiah, I'm sure Penelope has told you that he wants to marry me. He doesn't know about the baby because I've not known for sure until now. I know now he will want to marry me even more!"

"So when do you plan on telling Benjamin you're pregnant?"

"We're having lunch today at Jake's. I plan to tell him then."

"Mary Catherine, what will you say to Benjamin if he asks you to marry him?"

"I've decided to say yes. I want my baby to be legitimate."

"I realize we are working against time, but how would you feel about having a double ceremony with Marion and Lindy on the fifteenth?"

"Uncle Obadiah, if we can make that work, I believe Benjamin wouldn't mind getting married on the same day with Lindy.

"But how do I explain this to my folks? They know Marion's getting married, but this will be a traumatic thing for them when they hear I'm getting married as well.

"I've mentioned Benjamin in my letters, but they know him only as the brother to my best friend, Lindy. Uncle Obadiah, what am I going to do?"

"First of all, you are going to discuss all of this with Benjamin over lunch. Then you're going to tell me what you have decided. After that, you are going to start being honest with everyone in our family, starting with your grandmother. She's going to be very upset with you, but she loves you, and she will do anything for you. She's going to be in charge of Marion and Lindy's wedding. I'm sure she'll be willing to take on some additional work for her first granddaughter."

"Do I tell grandmother about being pregnant?" Mary Catherine asked.

"I wouldn't say anything, but knowing Mother as I do, I don't think you will be able to pull the wool over her eyes. She's a wise lady, and if she questions you on why you're getting married, you can't lie to her. You must not lie to her. If you do, it will break her heart. You be truthful with her, and she will accept it, but with reluctance!"

"Obadiah, I'm so sorry for putting you in the middle of all of this. I assure you that your generosity and help will not go unappreciated."

"I'm not concerned about any of that right now. What we've got to do is let your folks know soon if Benjamin still wants you to marry him."

"Uncle Obadiah, tell me how to do that. How do I make that announcement, through a telegram?"

"You let me handle that. I know Dent, and he will be very upset and want to kill someone, but by the time he gets here on the tenth, he should have calmed down. As long as he's three hundred miles away, he can't do any of us harm. Time will give us an opportunity to work out a plan of action."

Mary Catherine threw herself into my arms and said, "How can I ever thank you and Penelope for what you're doing for me?"

"Mary Catherine, you will be a better person through all of this. Getting married right now is the answer. It is the beginning of years of happiness. As soon as you and Benjamin are through with lunch, let me know what you've decided."

As I continued my daily schedule, I couldn't dismiss Mary Catherine and Benjamin's problem from my mind. If I had just been more observant, maybe I could have stopped some of this.

My regret right now is that my brother, who trusted me with his children, is going to be so disappointed in me. He will blame me mostly for this, but by the grace of God, I will be able to handle it.

At four o'clock, I had some free time to visit with Mary Catherine. I asked Elizabeth to cover for me while I visited with her.

"How did it go with you and Benjamin?" I asked.

"It went well. He was shocked, at first, when I told him about the baby. He looked at me in disbelief, and then he took my hand and said, 'I love you Mary Catherine, and I want us to get married. Will you marry me?'

"I said, 'Yes, I will marry you, and I'll have this baby, and lots more if you desire. I want to live my live as Mrs. Benjamin Madison.'

"I asked him how we were going to handle this with his parents. He said he would take care of that. I explained to him that you suggested we have a double ceremony with Marion and Lindy. He agreed to that as well. You and Benjamin are smart people. He used the same phase that you used earlier, 'the sooner, the better!'"

"All right. We've set things in motion. I've got to talk to Marion and get his permission to share the stage with you and

Benjamin, so to speak. I'm sure he'll understand and be agreeable to our plans."

"Uncle Obadiah, Marion doesn't know I'm with child, does he?"

"No, he doesn't. None of us knew until today. Penelope suspected it, but we weren't sure. Now that we know, we have to act quickly. You now have the responsibility to talk to your grandmother about the wedding, and remember, no lying to her. She will be heartbroken if you lie to her."

"Uncle Obadiah, this is going to be the hardest thing I've ever done."

"Sometimes we benefit from doing hard things. It teaches us from a different perspective, and we grow by knowing there is a better way. Please share with me, or Penelope, how things come out with Mother."

On our way home to Three Oaks, I told Marion I needed to visit with him in private after we got home. He looked at me with a puzzled look and asked, "What's going on?"

"I'll tell you in private."

"You've got me worried, Uncle Obadiah!"

The first thirty minutes were spent with the kids. We had our normal play time, and then we let the kids play in the yard. It was still a little cool for this time of March, but the kids didn't seem to let the cooler weather bother them. They were always jumping and running.

I saw Mary Catherine looking at me. She was looking for a clue from me when she should visit with Mother. I nodded my head that I thought it was time. I saw her go to Mother and whisper in her ear. After a few seconds, Mother and Mary Catherine left for Mother's room to talk.

That presented a good time for Marion and me to take a walk in Mother's garden. There was a bench in the middle of her garden, which reminded me of the bench Penelope and I sat on many times at Twin Oaks.

"Obadiah, what's this all about? My curiosity is killing me!"

"Please sit down, Marion." I said.

At first, I remained standing. I wanted to see his facial expression when I was talking with him.

"Marion, I need you to promise me that what we're going to talk about will remain between you and me."

"Obadiah, I've always kept our conversations between the two of us in strict confidence. You can always count on that. Now, what's going on?"

"Something serious has come up in regard to your sister, Mary Catherine."

"Oh, I know that. She doesn't want to return home with Father and Mother when they come for my wedding."

"I wish that was all of it, but I'm afraid there's much more."

"Then what's going on with Mary Catherine?"

"Marion, your sister is with child. She is pregnant with Benjamin's child."

"You've got to be kidding me!"

I could see from his actions that he couldn't believe this.

"I'm sorry, but it's true. I'd say she's about two and a half months along."

"How could she let that happen?"

"Hold on, young man! You're not exactly a saint yourself, you know!"

"I'm sorry, Obadiah, I never would have dreamed Mary Catherine would let any boy touch her that away. She's been such a perfect lady."

"Let me tell you something, son, perfect ladies have feelings as well."

"Father will kill her, Obadiah!"

"No, your father won't kill her, because we may not have to tell him right now. This is where you come in."

"How can I help?"

"It's simple! All we need is your and Lindy's permission to share your wedding day with Benjamin and Mary Catherine."

"Oh, Obadiah, I'm afraid Father will never let her marry Benjamin, at least, not right now. He's going to think she's too young. It's going to kill him when he finds out his beautiful daughter is pregnant."

"Marion, as I've already said, he doesn't need to know that right now. There will be only a few of us who will know."

"Who will that be?"

"Right now it's Penelope, Mother, you, Benjamin, Mary Catherine, and me."

"Grandmother knows! Did I hear you right?"

"Mary Catherine is breaking the news to her as we speak."

"I think we need to stop right now and pray for Mary Catherine. Grandmother will kill her!" Marion said as he shook his head in disbelief.

"Your grandmother will be disappointed, but she will not lay a hand on Mary Catherine. In fact, she will side with me on this one. You don't concern yourself with that."

"I can certainly see the predicament we're in. I'll do anything for Mary Catherine. She's my sister!"

"I really think we have a crisis on our hands right now. It wouldn't be so bad if Dent and Sara weren't coming, but since they are, we can't let them know Mary Catherine is pregnant."

"Obadiah, you may have to help me out with Lindy."

"Marion, you can handle this with Lindy. I have all the confidence in the world that you can do this."

"I hear Mattie calling us for dinner. Let's go!" I said, as I reached down, took his hand, and helped him to his feet.

During dinner, Mary Catherine looked at me and winked. I assume from her wink and smile that all went well with her and Mother. If I know my mother, she will find some way to seek out a meeting with me after dinner.

I was right! No sooner had we finished our dessert than Mother came by my chair and whispered in my ear. "I need to see you in my bedroom."

I whispered back that I would be there.

After helping Penelope and Mattie get the kids ready for bed I went to Mother's room. As soon as I knocked on her door, she said, "Come in, Obadiah!"

As I entered her room she said, "Come over here and sit down."

"What's up, Mother?"

"We've got a big problem, don't we?" she said.

I knew not to beat around the bush with my mother. She is full of wisdom and not easy to fool.

"Yes, Mother, I'm afraid we have a challenge ahead of us."

"How many know about Mary Catherine's pregnancy?"

"Right now, Penelope, you, Marion, Mary Catherine, Benjamin, and me are the only ones I'm aware of."

"Then let's hope we can keep it that way—the fewer, the better!" she said.

"Mary Catherine shared with you our plan, did she not?"

"Yes, she did! I think it's a good plan. I regret this has happened, but we have to use common sense, handling this in the best way possible."

"I, too, regret this, Mother. Dent is going to be really upset that Mary Catherine is marrying Benjamin. If he knew she was pregnant with Benjamin's child, he would rant and rave to high Heaven."

"Your brother is a good man, Obadiah. He's also a good father. He will be disappointed in Marion and Mary Catherine getting married, but he will get over that. What he might not get over is that Mary Catherine got pregnant before she married."

"That's a great concern of mine. We must do whatever we can to keep her pregnancy a secret from Dent and Sara. It would break their hearts if they found out. I feel bad about keeping a secret. As you know, I just preached to Marion that we Bradford family shouldn't keep secrets. I don't feel good about it, but this might be the time to break that tradition."

"I'm in full agreement with that. I believe we can handle this if everyone is in agreement about carrying through with our plan. The only person that we may have to involve is Lindy. Marion is very concerned that she will want to know why, all of a sudden, Mary Catherine and Benjamin are getting married."

"Why can't Marion just tell her that Benjamin has previously proposed to her over and over, and that now that her folks are coming that it makes sense to go ahead and get married while they are here? To me, that would be convincing."

"That's a good idea, Mother. I'm going to pass that on to Marion."

"Obadiah, you can see why I've admired you so much for not giving in to temptation. You could have had several little Jameses running around here by now if you had given in to Satan and had your way with Penelope. I know Penelope was willing at all times. She loved you so and still does. I'm telling you, Obadiah, Penelope is a jewel, and you'd better thank God daily for her."

"Mother, Penelope and I have something special that lots of married people don't have. It's something I can't explain. God just worked it out for us to be together, and we're going to be together for the rest of our lives."

"When do you think I can start planning to include Benjamin and Mary Catherine in the wedding plans?"

"Marion will let me know tomorrow. He plans to have lunch with Lindy at Jake's Restaurant. I'll tell you tomorrow night."

"Then, it's a plan, if Marion is successful in getting Lindy to agree," Mother said.

"Everything except notifying Dent that Mary Catherine is also getting married on the same day as Marion."

"This is one time I'm thankful I live three hundred miles away from my firstborn. Oh, God, please have mercy on my son Dent when he reads the telegram. Please give him understanding and a forgiving heart," Mother said as she got up from her chair and gave me a goodnight kiss.

CHAPTER 26

Marion was successful in getting Lindy to agree to the double wedding ceremony, after explaining that Benjamin had asked Mary Catherine on several occasions to marry him.

He also used his grandmother's advice and shared the importance of having the wedding at the time of Dent and his family's presence. Our plan was now set. We could move forward in planning the wedding.

Dent had answered my telegram, and as expected, he was upset. He couldn't understand why there was such a rush for Mary Catherine to get married. He said, "We need to talk about this marriage upon our arrival at Three Oaks."

Tomorrow we will be going to Champagnolle to pick up Dent, Sara, Law, Everett, and my sister Sarah, who decided to make the trip with Dent and his family.

Sarah's husband, Jim Crawford, couldn't make the trip due to business obligations, but her two daughters, Amanda and Lilly, will be accompanying her. Sarah is coming, not only for the wedding, but to see Mother as well. She misses Mother and regrets her two daughters are growing up not knowing their grandmother.

The late arrival of the steamboat at five o'clock p.m. allowed me the opportunity to spend most of the day seeing patients.

Those meeting Dent and Sarah's family at Champagnolle were Bill, Mother, Penelope, and our kids, as well as Mary Ann and Virgil's family and Mary Catherine and Marion.

George and Hank brought a carriage and two wagons for the purpose of transporting the younger ones and the luggage back to Three Oaks. There will be a lot of family celebrating at Three Oaks tonight! All good, I hope!

After arriving at Champagnolle, several of us walked the spiral stairway leading up to the lookout station overlooking the dock and the Ouachita River. One could see everything approaching up and down the river. The surrounding scenery from the lookout is one of the prettiest places on the Ouachita River. The beautiful rocks and cliffs bulging out over the river, the beautiful, virgin pine on top of the mountain ridge, and the green water of the Ouachita River are just beautiful.

Mother, Mary Ann, Mary Catherine, Penelope, and the smaller children chose to remain below and enjoy refreshments at the little restaurant.

George, Hank, Bill, Marion, Virgil, and I accompanied the older children to the lookout.

We weren't there long before we heard the steamboat whistle. I looked to my right as Charles said, "Daddy, they're here!"

After we greeted each other, we loaded everyone into three carriages and two wagons and headed out for Three Oaks.

Dent asked if he could ride with me in the driver's seat to Three Oaks. I said, "You are more than welcome."

I knew he wanted to visit with me. I could tell he needed some answers before approaching Marion and Mary Catherine about the wedding.

We hadn't gone far when Dent turned to me and said, "Obadiah, we've got some serious talking to do."

"Dent, I'm truly sorry you are upset with Marion, Mary Catherine, and me. A letter wasn't a good way to address this situation, but it was the only way we had in reaching out to you."

"I realize that, Little Brother! When I got the letter from Marion, I was really disappointed and grieved for two days over the matter, until I got your letter explaining how you were going employ both Marion and Mary Catherine in your business. That helped a lot.

"But, when I got the telegram announcing Mary Catherine getting married as well, I literally flipped my lid! I went crazy, Little Brother! I mean, slap-dab crazy! Sara tried to reason with me, but I was drowning in my miseries and didn't listen to what she was saying at first."

"So, what do you want to know from me, Dent?"

"Tell me, in detail, why my two oldest children feel they need to get married," he said.

"If I told you it's for love, would that be enough?"

"I think you know the answer to that question Little Brother. Why don't you start telling me what you know?"

"Dent the kids' relationships started when Mary Catherine and Marion were introduced to Benjamin and Lindy Madison at the annual fall celebration. As you know, Benjamin and Lindy are brother and sister and come from a much-respected family here in El Dorado. Mr. Frank Madison is presently serving as our mayor, and he and his family attend First Baptist Church. Lindy plays the organ at the church, and Benjamin plays the piano. Both are gifted in music.

"Anyway, Marion, Lindy, Mary Catherine, and Benjamin started seeing each other. To make a long story short, they each fell in love and decided they want to spend the rest of their lives together."

"I expected more information than that, Obadiah!"

"Dent, what do you want me to say? I didn't follow them around. They both are considered adults now, and I figured you had taught them how to make adult decisions. I've watched them together, and I can swear to you that I believe they love each other with all their hearts. You need to swallow some of your pride and give them your blessings. That would be the best thing you could do for your oldest two children!"

"Obadiah, it's easier for you to say than for me to do. You know how much I love those two kids. I wanted them to choose a career and work toward accomplishing what it requires to achieve their goals. If they're married, how can they do that?"

"Dent, I believe they can still do that. You've got the money to send them anywhere they choose to go, whether they're married or not. I don't think Marion or Mary Catherine wants to abandon any of their professional interest.

"Marion has shown a great interest in the medical field. He can be married and still study to be a doctor. Mary Catherine is interested in some kind of medical profession. She, too, could still go to school.

"I wished you could see some of their work. You would be proud of both of them. They are highly conscious of what they do and are very intelligent."

"I'm not worried so much about Marion. It's Mary Catherine I'm mostly concerned about. Sara and I wanted her to go to Boston and get educated, just like Penelope. If she marries Benjamin, I'm afraid she will stay home, have several children, and get fat!"

"Are you saying, you don't want a bunch of grandchildren to play with?"

"Obadiah, don't try to make a joke out of this. It's not funny to me!"

"I can see that, Dent. I really can't tell you what you need to do as a father, but what I'm going to say is, whatever you say and do will affect your relationship with Marion and Mary Catherine for the rest of your life."

"I've thought about that as well. I realized if I don't give my blessing, I may be doing both of them an injustice. Sara and I have always had a good relationship with our children. I want that to continue. I don't want them to end up hating me for my actions."

"Dent, try to remember how much you loved Sara before y'all got married. Try to remember how I felt about Penelope and couldn't have her because of circumstances beyond my power. We both got the girl we wanted in the end. Have you ever wondered what would have happened if we hadn't?

"Sara and Penelope have made us happy. If you deny your blessings to Mary Catherine and Marion, you may damage them forever. Do you want to do that?"

"No, I really don't. I just need to know why all this is happening, especially with Mary Catherine."

"Why don't you talk to Mother tonight? You might feel better if you were to talk with her. She feels that Mary Catherine and Benjamin are making the right decision. I do too!"

"I plan to talk to all three sometime tonight. I know I need to bring closure to this matter, the sooner, the better. The wedding is only five days off. We need to get this right!"

"Big Brother, I was afraid you would blame me for all this."

"Obadiah, I learned a long time ago that the blame belongs to those who raised their own children and not someone else. I hold no resentment toward you."

"Thanks, Dent! That means a lot to me. I've missed our frequent talks. I wished we lived close to each other again."

"If my two oldest children decide to stay here in El Dorado, we just might sell out in Alabama and move here, too!" Dent said, smiling.

We arrived home to find out that Mother and Penelope had planned a big homecoming meal for our family from Alabama.

Mattie, Betsy, and Big Jim had been busy most of the day fixing a big dinner.

After washing up everyone met in the dining room. We increased the size of the dining table by adding leaves. Smaller tables were brought in for the younger kids.

The meal consisted of smoked pork, chicken, and all the trimmings. Mother knows Dent's favorite meat is chicken. After dinner, the children scattered. Some of us went to the parlor to enjoy coffee and dessert.

Dent and Marion went for a walk in Mother's garden.

Marion told me later that his visit with Dent was mostly cordial, and that his father actually gave him his blessings.

I learned from Marion that he invited Dent and Sara to lunch the next day at Jake's Restaurant. He proceeded to tell me that he was inviting Lindy, Benjamin, and Mary Catherine to the luncheon as well.

"I think the luncheon will give Father and Mother an opportunity to meet Benjamin and Lindy in an informal way," he said.

"That's a great idea, Marion!"

Dent still wanted to talk to Mary Catherine. Sara made it known to Dent that she wanted to sit in on the meeting with Mary Catherine.

While Dent, Sara, and Mary Catherine were visiting in my study, Mother and I went to the front porch. There was a chill in the air, so both of us wore our coats.

I related to Mother my conversation with Marion. She was pleased that Dent wasn't too rough on him. It was good to know that Dent gave Marion his blessing to marry Lindy.

"I suspected he'd come down on Mary Catherine harder than he did Marion. She's his only daughter, and he's not ready to turn her loose," Mother said.

"I'm thinking you are right on target about Mary Catherine. Dent's not going to give in until he finds the answer he's looking for."

"Obadiah, I know he's going to want to visit with me tonight as well. I've decided if he asks me if Mary Catherine is pregnant, I can't lie to him. I'll have to tell him the truth."

"You know this is going to create a big problem for us when he finds out. What if he loads her up and takes her home to Cahaba?"

"That would be a big mistake on Dent's part. I'm hoping that won't happen. I've got a few aces up my sleeve that might convince him not to react irrationally."

"Do I need to know what you're up to, Mother?"

"Not just yet! If it doesn't work, then I'll try something else. I won't let him do something that he'll regret."

"Mother, I wish you well. If anyone can persuade him to give his blessing to Mary Catherine, you can!"

"We'll see, Obadiah."

During Mother's meeting with Dent, he asked her the question we feared he'd ask.

He looked straight at Mother and said, "Mother, you've got to be honest with me. Is my Mary Catherine with child?"

Mother answered Dent's question with a question. "Dent, would it make a difference if she was with child?"

"It might!" Dent said.

"Dent, Mary Catherine is with child!"

"That's exactly what I thought. I told Sara it had to be that, for her to just up and marry someone. Tonight, I could just feel shame in her voice as we visited. I started to ask her if she was pregnant, but I knew if I did, she'd lie to me!"

"Dent, Mary Catherine is truly in love. Benjamin's a nice, young man. There isn't any doubt in my mind that his love for her is genuine."

"Mother, how could this happen? She's been taught differently. What has happened to my beautiful daughter? She's disgraced the Bradford name!"

"Dent, stop that nonsense! You're reacting emotionally. Let me remind you of something, son!"

"All right. What is it!"

"Your father and I knew you got Sara pregnant before you married her. We kept it to ourselves, hoping you were mature enough to do what was right, and you did. You married one of the best girls in Dallas County. She's made you a wonderful wife and has given you four wonderful children.

"Now you want to condemn your daughter for the same mistake that you and Sara made years ago."

"I never knew you and Father knew about Sara and me."

"That's right! We trusted God that He would lay it on your heart to do the right thing, and He did. Mary Catherine and Benjamin are trying to do the right thing."

"Mother, where do you get all your wisdom?"

"Son, I don't always have all the answers, but I lean on my God for wisdom."

"Mother, I'm so ashamed. You are exactly correct. Why should I condemn my daughter when her mother and I did the same thing?"

"Now you are making sense, Dent! We all make mistakes. When we make mistakes, the Bible tells us to pray for forgiveness and to repent of our sins. If we can do that, God forgives us. He forgave you and Sara many years ago. He will forgive Mary Catherine and Benjamin as well."

"Mother, what do I need to do?"

"Dent, you need to give both Mary Catherine and Benjamin your blessing. They need your support. This unborn child that Mary Catherine is carrying needs your support as well."

"I want to thank you, Mother, for being truthful with me. I realize now if I tried to stop the wedding it would be a mistake.

I can assure you, I will give Mary Catherine and Benjamin my blessing.

"Tomorrow, Sara and I will have lunch with Marion, Lindy, Benjamin, and Mary Catherine at Jake's in El Dorado. If I like what I see and hear, I plan to give Mary Catherine my blessing."

"Oh, son, that is music to my ear! You're doing the right thing. You will not regret your decision. I just know you won't!"

The luncheon with Sara, Dent, Marion, Lindy, Mary Catherine, and Benjamin went well. As we returned to Three Oaks, Dent asked me if he could see me in the parlor. He gave me his positive assessment of his and Sara's luncheon meeting. He and Sara were excited about Lindy and Benjamin. They both gave the four their blessing and wished them well in their upcoming marriages.

For the next three days, Sara and Dent got to spend time with both Benjamin and Lindy. Two nights before the wedding, Penelope threw a nice party at Three Oaks.

She invited local dignitaries and friends from El Dorado. It was certainly a grand event. Since moving to Three Oaks, we have had family celebrations, but nothing as big as this event. We had people dancing and visiting until midnight.

It reminded me of the big events Daniel Pratt of Prattville, Alabama, hosted in Autauga County.

This event was the first big event organized and hosted by Penelope. She did an excellent job!

Mother was extremely busy working on the double wedding ceremony and had little time to help Penelope with the planning and hosting duties.

I was impressed with Penelope as she mingled with our visitors. Every now and then, she'd come get me and pull me to the center of the room for a dance. She hadn't forgotten how to dance. Her long, black hair bounced off her shoulders as I led her around the dance floor. Her beautiful, blue eyes sparkled from the lights of the chandeliers above our heads. Dancing with Penelope was delightful!

I noticed from time to time that Dent and Sara danced with each other. Dent, too, liked to dance, and he danced with about every available unattached lady in the parlor, including Mary Catherine.

I felt good knowing Dent had overcome his hurt and was looking forward to being referred to as father-in-law. It's not every day two siblings from two different families marry each other. This is going to be a historical event for the Bradford family.

Before the dance started, we Bradford boys got together and decided that we'd all dance with Mother. I knew we wouldn't wear her down. She would love every dance. We decided that Law and Everett should be the first ones, and Marion would follow them. Dent and I would stand ready when our turn came around.

On the day of the wedding, the weather was nice. There was no rain, just a chill in the air. The carriage ride to El Dorado was pleasant. As tradition goes, Mother insisted that she ride with Mary Catherine. She had always been very protective of the brides. She had given me strict orders not to let Benjamin and Marion see the brides before they walked down the aisle of the church. She always said, "There can be bad luck in a marriage if the groom sees his bride in her wedding dress before the wedding."

I never understood where Mother got some of her beliefs, but if that's the way she felt, so be it!

The wedding went off without a hitch. Both brides were lovely. Mother did a good job in planning the wedding. Both married couples repeated their vows without stumbling over the words. Everything was perfect!

The wedding reception held in the fellowship hall at First Baptist was well attended. There was standing room only, and Mother arranged for a photographer to be present.

After pictures were made, rice bags were passed out as both couples politely walked out of the church onto a narrow walkway lined on both sides with people who enjoyed peppering the brides and grooms with rice.

Bill, our driver, had patiently been waiting with a carriage to take both couples to Champagnolle to board the steamboat.

They would be going to Natchez, Mississippi, for their honeymoon. Natchez had not yet been affected by the Civil War.

After the honeymoon, all four planned to return to El Dorado and continue their jobs.

This was the part Dent had the most trouble with. He was hoping Mary Catherine and Benjamin would return to Alabama with them to work in nearby Selma. He and Sara were hoping Mary Catherine would be close to them when the baby was born.

Another carriage was waiting to take Dent's family and Sarah and her daughters to Champagnolle. They will be riding as far as Monroe with the newlyweds. There they will split up and the honeymooners will journey on to Natchez while Dent and the others returned to Selma, Alabama.

It was an emotional time at Champagnolle as we said our good-byes. Laying aside the tension we first went through when Dent arrived, we had a great visit.

God's presence was with us each moment of the day. Praise to the Almighty God!

As usual, it was hard for Mother to see her children and grandchildren leaving for an area where she lived for several years. She would miss them, but she always considered their visit one she would treasure until the next one. She was one of those people who seem to radiate happiness and make it bloom all around, especially for us at Three Oaks.

CHAPTER 27

After spending three days and nights in beautiful Natchez, Mississippi, the newlywed couples returned and settled into their new homes on Jennings Street, three doors from each other.

All four have returned to their jobs. Mary Catherine looks good behind the receptionist desk. We missed her while she was away.

Marion has become a valuable resource for me. He is confident and dependable. He has developed an initiative of taking things in his own hands. I'm confident that he's leaning heavily toward committing himself to becoming a doctor of medicine.

Dent and his family are back at Black Oaks in Cahaba, Alabama. Dent is busy getting his plantation ready for planting.

Sarah and her girls, Amanda and Lilly, are back in Prattville and doing well.

I received a nice letter from Sarah, telling me how much she enjoyed the trip here and how much the girls enjoyed their grandmother. She wrote, "I believe our mother spoiled them, Obadiah! It may be good for me to live here instead of near Mother. My girls would be spoiled rotten!"

She went on to say that Jim Crawford, her husband, has had to travel a great deal for Daniel Pratt. She isn't too happy about that.

We are finally getting back to normal at Three Oaks. It will soon be fishing time, and I'm planning to take Charles, Little Jim, and Obie fishing. Of course, I'll have to make arrangements for Hank to accompany us on the fishing trip. With three growing boys, I don't know if I can handle all of them by myself.

Little James is growing like a weed. He has strong legs and arms. He's crawling and getting into everything. Penelope tells me she wants to get a guard dog to keep an eye on him when he's not sleeping. Of course, she was kidding!

Mother has started her bridge games back at Three Oaks. She and several lady friends meet once a week for bridge games.

From what Penelope shares with me, Mother and her friends seem to know about everything that's happening in the little town of El Dorado. Her friends are all long-time residents of El Dorado. Penelope tells me, "You're mother and her friends are problem solvers. They seem to have all the answers."

Besides playing bridge, Mother spends one day each week in El Dorado keeping Mary's three children, Frank, Nellie, and Julie.

In the past few weeks, Hank, George, Big Jim, and the other slaves have been busy getting the land ready for planting. They have been spending long hours in the fields.

We were blessed again this winter by not losing a single slave. There were the normal colds, but no one suffered from pneumonia.

Penelope makes sure our sick slaves are given tender, loving care, the right foods, and lots of liquids, and seeing that they take their medicine.

Penelope loves to minister to the slaves. She's thinks God has called her to care for the sick. I believe the good health of our slaves is mostly due to Penelope. She tells me who's sick and assists me in my examinations.

Sometimes I ask Penelope what she would do. She comes right back with an intelligent answer.

Penelope gets along well with our slaves. She is known as Miss Penelope to them. She enjoys teaching and watching the slaves improve in their reading, writing, and math skills.

She tells me that Charles and Obi are her best students. She said her brother, Little Jim, is pushing both Charles and Obi for a spot at the top. If Little Jim wasn't so lazy, he could be at the top. He's got a good memory and knows his skills, but he is really lazy when it comes to getting his homework.

Things have settled down a little at my office. I'm still making house calls and calling on the Kirby-Smith Camp located near Three Creeks.

The military units that spent the winter near Lisbon have moved farther south to join the Confederacy in Virginia and Tennessee.

When all the soldiers were camped here for the winter, they brought additional business to El Dorado, especially at the saloons in town. The presence of Major William Clarke Quantrill, Jesse and Frank James, and Cole Younger and his brothers brought some excitement to El Dorado also.

Several residents of El Dorado have voiced their appreciation to the soldiers for not shooting and killing someone. Their presence wasn't always quiet. There were some rowdy times as well.

For the past two months, I've been so busy with family and my business that I've not had time to relax to read my newspapers. Other than what I pick up from my patients, I know very little of what's going on with the Civil War.

Lately I've glanced at the headlines in the *El Dorado News-Times* to see if there have been any battles in our area of the state. So far, there hasn't been any action close to Union County.

Since tomorrow is Saturday, I plan to spend a few hours after breakfast catching up on my reading.

The first battle summary that caught my eye was the Battle of Elkin's Ferry, which was fought in Clark and Nevada Counties in Arkansas. The Union was victorious over the Confederate Army.

The *El Dorado News-Times* does a good job in summarizing battles. The Elkin's Ferry Battle was fought on April 3 and 4, 1864. The battle started when Confederate troops attacked a Union column deep in southwest Arkansas. This battle was the beginning of what became known as the Camden Expedition.

After capturing Little Rock in Pulaski County and Fort Smith in Sebastian County, in September of 1863, Union forces were in control of much of the state. From these two occupied cities, Federal troops could launch an attack into southern Arkansas, northern Louisiana, and eastern Texas.

In March 1864, an attack on northwest Louisiana and eastern Texas was launched from both Arkansas and New Orleans, Louisiana.

The Battle of Elkin's Ferry was fought near the Missouri River in Clark County. Those involved in the battle were Major General Fredrick Steele of the Union Army and Brigadier General John Marmaduke of the Confederate Army. General Steele's Union Army consisted of 8,500 men, while General Marmaduke of the Confederate Army had 7,500.

Losses on both sides in the Battle of Elkin's Ferry were light, with 18 Confederate soldiers killed and 50 wounded. On the Union side, there were 30 Union soldiers wounded.

When General Marmaduke realized he couldn't win, he retreated on April 4 and withdrew sixteen miles south to Prairie D'Ane the following morning.

The Battle of Poison Spring was fought on April 18, 1864, in Ouachita County, Arkansas. Because of dwindling supplies for his army in Camden, Arkansas, Union Army Major General Frederick Steele sent out a foraging party to gather corn that the Confederates had stored about twenty miles up the Prairie D'Ane-Camden Road on White Oak Creek.

The party loaded the corn into wagons, and on April 18, Colonel James M. Williams started his return to Camden. Brig. General John S. Marmaduke's and Brig. General Samuel B. Maxey's Confederate forces arrived at Lee Plantation, about fifteen miles from Camden, where they engaged Williams.

The Confederates eventually attacked Williams in the front and rear, forcing him to retreat north into a marsh, where his men regrouped, and then fell back to Camden. During the fight, Williams positioned the first Kansas Colored infantry, a regiment made up of mostly ex-slaves, between the wagon train and Confederate lines; these Negro troops repelled the first two offenses but ran low on ammunition and were beaten back by the third.

The Confederates refused to take the wounded Negro soldiers as prisoners, and instead brutally killed, scalped, and stripped them. The regiment lost nearly half of its numbers.

The Union lost 198 wagons and all the corn. Estimated casualties were 301 for Williams and 114 for the Confederates.

The victory at Poison Spring was a Confederate victory.

After reading the summary on the Poison Springs Battle, I laid my newspaper on the table next to my chair and dropped my head. My first thought was, What a shame. What an injustice to armed slaves with guns and probably very little training. This massacre of the Negro Union soldiers reminded me of what lies ahead for our slaves. I still believe it's just a matter of time before they will be freed. The war will be over. They won't have to fight and be massacred like those of Poison Springs, but the experiences they will face will bring on hardships they've never experienced.

I'm so afraid for my slaves, as well as slaves throughout the South. What will happen to them? Those slaves who were massacred thought they were going to have a good life, but look what happened to them. Their freedom was short lived. I looked up at the sky and said, "Lord, what a shame!"

I decided not to read any more for the rest of the day. It was depressing to read these stories. It appears that General Ulysses Grant's plan is to capture all the waterways in the South, such as the Ouachita River and the Missouri River. He wants to continue to cut off all supplies to the Deep South. His strategy is working. I expect that he has his eyes on all steamboats traveling up and down the Ouachita and Missouri Rivers. I'm wondering how long before it will be unsafe for anyone to travel south on steamboats or rail lines.

It's been two weeks since I sat on my front porch and read accounts of Civil War battles. In town, I've heard bits and pieces about two battles that have occurred in the past few weeks that were fought closer to home.

My next free Saturday came on May 12. I decided to relax and spend some time with Penelope and the kids.

Since I'm an early riser, I decided to get up, grab me a cup of Mattie's hot coffee, and do some early morning reading as I sit in my favorite rocking chair on the front porch at Three Oaks.

I figure it will be another hour before Penelope and the kids start stirring. This will allow me time to catch up on my reading.

I love to watch the sun come up in the East. I also like the quiet and calm of the early morning hours. During these early morning hours, the birds start chirping. At times, their chirping sounds like melodies. I know that sounds crazy, but it's like they are saying, "Good morning, Dr. Bradford. This one's for you!" Oh, how I love the country!

The first newspaper account was that of the Battle of Marks' Mill, which was fought on April 25, 1864. This battle took place in Cleveland County and was known as part of the Camden Expedition. The principal commanders were Lt. Colonel Francis Drake of the Union Army and Brig. General James B. Fagan of the Confederacy.

Major General Fred Steele of the Union Army sent a Union force to escort some 240 wagons from Camden to Pine Bluff to pick up supplies and transport them back to support his army in and around Camden, Arkansas.

When the Battle of Marks' Mill started, the Union escort rebuffed Rebel attempts. But it didn't take long for the Confederate troops who outnumbered the Union troops two to one to move in on the Union rear and front, causing a rout. The Confederate Army circled the Union soldiers. It became a slaughter. It wasn't long until the Union Army had to surrender. Most of the Union Army was captured, as well as all of the supply wagons.

At the end of the five-hour battle, the Confederate Army suffered 293 casualties: 41 killed, 108 wounded, and 144 missing. The Union suffered 1,600 casualties. The Confederates captured about 150 Negro freedmen and are believed to have killed more than 100 others.

The defeat of Drake's command had a significant impact upon Steele's position at Camden. The loss of Marks' Mills prevented Steele from obtaining much-needed supplies for his army. His men were already on reduced rations. Steele saw the writing on the wall. He had lost two key battles, and his men were weak. He did what most intelligent Union generals would do; he decided to silently slip over the Ouachita River on the night of April 26, abandoning Camden and began his desperate race back to Little Rock in Pulaski County.

The killings of the Negro soldiers at Poison Spring, paired with the large number of black freedmen killed in the Battle of Marks' Mills, enraged many in the Union Army.

The Battle of Marks' Mill was a big win for the Confederate Army. In all practicality, it was a good win for El Dorado as well. The talk was, when General Steele got things under control in Camden, he would concentrate on taking El Dorado, which would be an easy task since we had only the Kirby-Smith Camp here to protect us.

The Battle of Jenkins Ferry was fought on April 30, 1864, near Sheridan, in Grant County.

The Battle of Jenkins Ferry was the last important action of the Arkansas phase of the Red River Campaign.

This battle occurred three days after General Steele abandoned Camden and headed toward Little Rock, where the Union was in control.

The battle occurred when General Kirby E. Smith of the Confederate Army caught up with General Fredrick Steele's army at a swampy crossing at Jenkins Ferry on the Saline River, about fourteen miles from Sheridan.

On the morning of April 30, 1864, General Kirby E. Smith attacked the Union forces in the swamps at Jenkins Ferry. General Smith tried time and time again to break the Union forces' line, but to no avail. The big, fallen trees and swampy areas were an advantage to General Steele's army. After seeing that it was an impossible task to break through the Union Army lines, General Smith called an end to the battle.

It was reported that the Confederate casualties were 86 killed and 356 wounded, while the Union Army had 83 killed, 413 wounded, and 45 missing.

Although the Union Army was given credit for the victory, it did nothing to advance the cause of the Red River Campaign.

CHAPTER 28

After reading the Civil War articles, I laid my newspaper down by my rocking chair. I had just closed my eyes to pray when I heard a loud noise coming from the front entrance. As I turned and looked, I saw Charles coming through the front screen door in a big rush. He ran right to me.

"Daddy, Daddy!" he said as he jumped into my lap. "Daddy, can we go fishing today?"

I hadn't exactly given fishing a thought, but if my son wanted to go fishing, then fishing it would be. It was a nice day, and I was sure Penelope, Belle, and Little James would love to go along as well. We could make it a family picnic.

"Charles, that sounds like a great idea. Let's ask your mother if she and the others would like to go with us and make it a family event."

"Yea!" Charles screamed. "We're going fishing! We're going fishing!"

Mattie announced that breakfast was ready, and everyone entered the dining room about the same time.

"Penelope, Charles wants to go fishing today," I said.

"I'm well aware of that. He hit me up earlier, asking if I thought you'd take him fishing today."

"How would you and the kids like to go? We can have Mattie and Betsy prepare a picnic lunch."

"Obadiah, I think that's a great idea. I'm for it!" Penelope said as she smiled at Charles.

"I wonder if you'd let an old lady tag along with you. I've not been fishing since we left Alabama," Mother said.

"We would love for you to come along," Penelope said.

"In that case, I'll go put on my boots and fishing clothes."

"I'll go find Bill and tell him to get the carriage ready. I'll get George to hitch up a wagon for us to carry our fishing supplies. Penelope, go tell your Mother and Betsy to fix us a picnic lunch."

"This is great," Charles said as he ran out of the dining room to find his two best friends, Little Jim and Obi.

I looked at Penelope, and she looked at me and said, "What if Charles asks Obi and Little Jim to go fishing?"

"I really hadn't counted on that!" I said.

"Let them go, Obadiah. If Charles has his fishing buddies with him, he's going to be better satisfied," Penelope said.

"Maybe he won't ask, but if he does, I'll permit them to go."

"I'm going to go and see if I can find myself some fishing clothes. For the love of me, I don't know if I've got anything appropriate to wear!" Penelope said.

I'm happy Mother is going with us. She will come in handy in helping me put worms and crickets on the fishhooks.

Penelope was right; Charles invited his two best buddies, Little Jim and Obi, to go along with us. Naturally, I couldn't say no. I don't think I've seen young boys of their age get along as well as they do. In fact, I've never had to intervene in settling a dispute between them. They seem to find a common interest in everything they do and have fun doing it.

I will ask Bill to help Mother and me to keep them corralled and focused on fishing. I'm sure they will want to swim some when they get tired fishing. Although, the water may still be a little cool.

The picnic and fishing turned out to be a big success. After getting home, we were all exhausted. Mother ordered Charles and Belle to the bathroom for baths. They both smelled like fish.

Mother enjoyed her day of fishing. She got really excited each time one of the boys caught a fish. She helped Belle hold her pole and, with a little help, Belle caught some good bream.

Although Penelope didn't fish, she and James enjoyed playing in the sand. At times I joined them. I can't remember a time as a kid that I played in the sand. I had fun making castles from the wet sand. I found it both interesting and enjoyable. I was so excited about playing in the sand that I didn't mind getting my hands dirty!

Today, we built fond memories together as a family. It was memories we'll remember in years to come.

God has blessed me by sending Dr. Jim Burroughs to be a partner in my clinic. Without his help, I wouldn't have time to do what I did today. I'm hoping that Marion will want to become a doctor and become a partner in my clinic.

As El Dorado grows, I can see a need for a hospital, just like the one Daniel Pratt built in Prattville, Alabama.

As summer progresses, crops are being planted, and hay is being harvested and stacked in the barn for winter feed for our horses and cattle.

Hank's doing an outstanding job as my overseer. He's earned the slaves' respect, and on Sundays the entire space in the barn is filled with our slaves worshipping Jesus Christ as their Lord and Savior.

Penelope has taught Hank's wife, Nellie, how to play the piano. They now have music to go along with their singing.

In the past few days, Penelope has asked to be excused from the breakfast table. I didn't think too much about it at first, but today when she asked for the third time, I became alarmed. I followed her to the bathroom, where I observed her vomiting.

"Penelope, my love, what's going on?" I asked as I wet a clean washcloth and handed it to her.

"Obadiah, I'm so sorry. I didn't mean to alarm you," she said as she took the washcloth and wiped her face.

I took her by the hand and led her into our bedroom, where we sat on the bed.

"Is this what you've been doing each morning you've asked to be excused at the breakfast table?"

"Yes," she said as she wiped her face.

"How do you feel right now?"

"I feel a little dizzy, but it will go away in a few minutes."

"Why haven't you told me about this?"

"Obadiah, I wanted to be sure before I told you, but I think I'm with child," she said as she smiled and opened wide those beautiful, blue eyes.

"How long have you been feeling this way?"

"I've not had a period in two months. The morning sickness is exactly the same as I experienced with James. I really believe we're going to have another baby."

"Penelope, you truly amaze me! I love you so much. Another baby! Let's make sure! Take this container in the bathroom and get me a urine specimen. I'll take it to my office and run a test. I'll let you know for sure later."

"I want to make you happy, Obadiah. I told you once, and I'll tell you again, I want to give you as many babies as you want!"

Penelope has always wanted to please me. I believe being with child gives her a sense of personal pride, as well as pleasing me. She loves children, and I believe she wants to be a good mother, whether it is two or a dozen.

I took Penelope in my arms and held her. Her body next to mind felt so good. She's always told me my hugs are a sense of security to her. She said, "When you hold me, it's the best part of my day."

Each night, Penelope falls asleep in my arms. She can't go to sleep without me holding her. I used to worry I'd wake her up when I turned over, but over the years she's adapted and goes right back to sleep.

My God has given me wealth, love, and happiness, but above all, He's given me Penelope, who makes all things beautiful. Oh, how I love this lady! I love her more today than yesterday. In my mind I keep asking, God, what have I done to deserve Penelope and all of these other blessings?

CHAPTER 29

I arrived home a little before five o'clock. I went immediately to Penelope's classroom, where she was working with several of the smaller children who were not yet old enough to labor in the fields.

I quietly opened the door and stood as Penelope turned to see who had come in. She looked at me with an expression of curiosity.

I looked at her and smiled as I gave her a nod in the affirmative. Penelope immediately put both hands to her face, looked up to the ceiling, and said, "Thank you, God!"

She immediately dismissed her class and met me coming across the room. She jumped into my arms, and I swung her around the room.

"Obadiah, this is another great day in my life as Mrs. Obadiah Bradford. I am so very happy!"

"I rejoice with you as well. I'm hoping for a girl this time!"

"Are you going to be disappointed if it's another boy?"

"No, I won't be disappointed!" I said as I looked into her beautiful, blue eyes.

"I think I would like a girl this time as well," she said.

I embraced and kissed my lovely wife with passion.

Penelope wisely pulled back and asked, "How about helping me tidy up this room?"

I smiled and said, "I'd be happy to help you."

"When can we tell everyone, Obadiah?" she asked.

"We will announce it tonight in the parlor. We will do it right after dinner."

"Oh, I'm so excited," she said.

As we ate dinner, she'd look at me and give me that special smile of hers. I could tell she wanted dinner to be over. She was eating faster than normal.

At the end of dinner, I stood and said, "I've got a special announcement to make. I need everyone to join me and Penelope in the parlor as soon as the supper dishes are cleared away."

"Mattie, bring us a bottle of our best wine, and some sweet tea and lemonade for the children. Let's take our dessert in the parlor as well."

Wine is the only alcoholic drink in my household. My father and mother enjoyed drinking wine. Father used it on several occasions to make special announcements. Tonight we would have wine to celebrate our fantastic news.

"All right, everyone, please give me your undivided attention. I've asked you to come to the parlor tonight to hear some great news that we just discovered today. It is with great pleasure that I tell you Penelope is expecting our second child. If all goes well, she will be having another baby in about seven months."

The noise factor increased greatly as everyone was expressing congratulations.

Belle and Charles grabbed my hands, and Charles asked, "Is it going to be a boy or girl?"

"We don't know that right now. We will have to wait for about seven months to find out."

Belle said, "I want a little sister. I'm tired playing with all these boys!"

Mother said, "I knew it, I just knew it! I suspected it the first time she left the breakfast table."

Everyone in the room was excited about our news. It was certainly a grand time for all of us.

Mother said, "If you and Penelope have more children, we may have to do some remodeling or make additions to this house!"

"That would be just fine with me," Penelope responded as she grabbed my arm.

The weather during the months of June through August was extremely hot. It reminded me of the hot days in Autauga County, Alabama.

Hank was really good at not overworking our slaves. He made sure they got water breaks and rest from the blazing hot sun.

We had a bumper cotton crop this year. The Civil War had cut down on the demand for cotton, but we still made good money. Our corn crop and vegetable gardens had done well also. Our sorghum made several gallons of pure molasses. The sorghum molasses will go well with butter and biscuits this coming winter.

The slaves will not go hungry, either. Their contribution in working in the big garden reaped them several vegetable items such as sweet potatoes, white potatoes, corn, and beans. We've been blessed with lots of chickens for eggs, several hogs for slaughtering during the month of December, and several milk cows, who furnish us with milk and milk products.

As of late, I have experienced several incidents caused by a group of Jayhawkers from Kansas. The Jayhawkers are a group of bandits and renegades who make their living robbing and killing as they pass through communities.

On Friday of last week, the son of Major Edward Wright pulled his wagon up in front of my clinic. His son, Edward Jr., came running into my clinic, asking for help for his father.

Edward Jr. related the following story to me as we treated his father, who was in serious condition.

Edward Jr. said, according to his slaves George and Simon, the Jayhawkers arrived at their home near Mt. Holly in mid-morning. They demanded that Major Wright reveal to them where he hid his money and his silver.

Major Wright, being a strong man of convictions, as well as being a brave soul, refused the demands of the marauders. As a result, he was beaten and fastened with a leather strap to his neck, tied to a horse, and buried in a hole, with only his head showing. It was the Jayhawkers' objective that when the horse, moved the leather strap would tighten and choke Major Wright to death.

When the Jayhawkers left Major Wright's property, two of his slaves, George and Simon, who had been hiding in the bushes, went to find Major Wright's son, Edward. When they returned, it took all three of them to free Major Wright from the pit, which was cold and slimy.

We admitted Major Wright to my clinic for further observation and treatment. He's made some improvement, but the time he spent in the pit has done damage to his body. I'm afraid he will never regain the use of his legs.

In the past few weeks, I've treated people who have been beaten by the Jayhawkers. Some of them will have scars for the rest of their lives.

Our local sheriff's department hasn't had any success in capturing any of the Jayhawkers. As of late, it has been reported that they have moved on south into Louisiana.

The *El Dorado News-Times* keeps printing articles related to the Civil War. It appears that most of the fighting is taking place in the states of Georgia, Virginia, and Tennessee.

There are rumors also that General Robert E. Lee has lost a big portion of his Confederate Army and that the end of the war is close at hand.

I find myself wishing daily that the war would end. I realize it's going to bring chaos throughout the South. It's not going to be pleasant, but soldiers who are still alive will get to come home and live out their lives with their families. It will never be the same. Some will be wounded both mentally and physically, which will take time to heal.

Our slaves will be freed, but their freedom will not be what they thought it would be. Some will starve because of lack of work and food. Some will have nowhere to live. They will live in camps that will offer little shelter from the cold and heat. Some will beg for food and drink. Some will be killed because they will resort to robbing and stealing for the purpose of feeding their family.

There will be some who will struggle but will make it. There will be some who will choose to stay with their original owners and participate in working for a wage or sharecropping.

The government will go through a hard reconstruction period, and someday all the rebel states will be readmitted to the United States of America. It will take time for healing, but a hundred years from now, the only thing left of the Civil War will be in the history books.

There are so many unanswered questions. I know what I'm planning to do. I'm going to offer my slaves hourly wages or the opportunity to become sharecroppers. They should be able to have a better quality of life by staying at Three Oaks. For those who don't want to stay, I will try to help them any way I can. It's going to be a completely new world for them. In time, maybe, just maybe, someone will be able to make some sense of why this war has gone on so long.

CHAPTER 30

By July, 1864, the Civil War is threatening Atlanta, Georgia. I received the following letter from my good friend Henry Dotson:

> Dear Obadiah,
>
> It is now July 10. I'm praying this letter finds you and your family well. Right now all is well with me and my family. We are all worried about what's going to happen to Atlanta.
>
> I'm going to try to get this letter off today. Things are not looking good here in Atlanta for any of us. We are told General William T. Sherman and General James B. McPherson are on their way here with the purpose of capturing Atlanta and getting control of the Southerland Railroad. As you are aware, Atlanta is the hub of the Southerland Railroad and industrial and financial center for the Confederacy. If the North gets control of the railroad, the South is doomed to defeat.
>
> People are scared here and are leaving in large groups daily. Many are boarding up their homes and leaving everything they own behind. They've heard some awful things about General Sherman. He's made a reputation for himself already. He's been burning everything in his path. If he gets control of Atlanta who knows what he will do?
>
> Helen and I are not planning on leaving Atlanta. As you know her father is mayor here and he's not leaving. I figure Atlanta will make a stand and try to avoid being taken by Sherman and McPherson.

I'm told General Bell Hood of the Confederate Army has some forty thousand plus soldiers camped outside of Atlanta ready to do what he can to keep Atlanta from falling to General Sherman. When the battle begins we will need every available doctor and nurse we can muster up to treat the wounded. I figure there will be thousands of casualties in this battle.

Helen and I are sending our children to my sister's home in Augusta. We've heard Augusta is not in Sherman's plans to invade. I wanted Helen to go too, but she's stubborn and refuses to leave me.

Anyway, I must stop and get this letter in the mail. Please know I think of you often and after this war is over, we must make every attempt to get together. Give my regards to your mother, Penelope, and our good friend, Dr. Jim Burroughs. I'm assuming he and his new bride, Elizabeth, are doing well? By the way any chance of a baby in their plans?

I don't know how much longer we will receive mail here in Atlanta. You take care and keep up with us in your local newspaper.

Always your friend,
Dr. Henry Dotson

After reading Henry's letter, I folded it, placed it back in the envelope, and laid it on my desk. The next thing I did was say a prayer. My chest was filled with pressure. I found myself struggling to inhale sufficient air to fill my lungs. My mind felt emptiness, just as I felt during the battle of Shiloh. I was worried for Henry and Helen. If Atlanta tries to protect itself, I know what is going to happen. It will be a bloody battle. As long as any soldier needs attention for his wounds, he will be there. He will exhaust himself for the good of others. That's just the way he is!

If my good friend gets killed in Atlanta, I don't think I could ever find peace in my heart to forgive those who started this Civil War.

Before the Civil War, we fought together as a united country, and now we've divided ourselves to the point that we may never be able to patch things up. If we do, I'm sure it will take years. Oh, Lord, please protect my good friends in Atlanta. Please bring this war to a close soon.

The first thing I did on a daily basis was to check the *El Dorado News-Times*.

On July 22, 1864, the Battle of Atlanta started. It took over a month before Atlanta surrendered to the Union Army. It was a bloody campaign. The Union Army suffered 3,641 casualties, while the Confederacy suffered 5,500.

General James B. McPherson of the Union Army lost his life during the battle.

The *El Dorado News-Times* printed the following summary, "The Siege, and Closure, of the Battle of Atlanta, Ga.":

General Sherman tried unsuccessfully to take the city of Atlanta for weeks. He finally settled into a siege of Atlanta, shelling the city, and sending raids west and south of the city to cut off the supply lines from Macon, Georgia. Both of Sherman's cavalry raids were defeated by superior Southern horsemen. When Sherman failed to break the Confederates' hold on the city, he began to employ a new strategy. He swung his entire army in a broad flanking maneuver to the west. Finally, on August 31, at Jonesborough, Georgia, Sherman's army captured the railroad track from Macon, Georgia, pushing the Confederates to Lovejoy's Station. With his supply lines fully severed, General Hood of the Confederacy pulled his troops out of Atlanta the next day, September 1, destroying supply depots as he left to prevent them from falling into Union hands. He also set fire to eighty-one loaded ammunition cars, which led to a conflagration watched by hundreds.

On September 2, 1864, Mayor James Calhoun, along with a committee of Union-leaning citizens, met a captain on the staff of Maj. General Henry W. Slocum and surrendered the city, asking for protection to non-combatants and private property.

Sherman, who was in Jonesborough at the time of the surrender, sent a telegram to Washington on September 3, which read, 'Atlanta is ours, and fairly won.'

On September 7, Sherman established his headquarters in Atlanta.

After reading the battle summary, I had no information whether Henry was alive or dead. I took a chance that he would be alive, and sat down and penned him a telegram:

September 12, 1864. Stop. Dear Henry. Stop. I just finished reading the account of the Battle of Atlanta. Stop. I'm hoping that you can get a telegram there in Atlanta. Stop. I can't stand not knowing your status. Stop. I've been praying every day since the battle started that God would surround you with his protection. Stop. I hope all is well with you and Helen. Stop. If you get this telegram, please get right back with me and let me know how y'all are. Stop. Your friend, Obadiah Bradford.

Two days passed, and I still hadn't heard from Henry. The telegraph office said my telegram went through, but because of the turmoil there, it could be awhile before Henry could respond. I guess the Union officials are checking all outgoing telegrams before approving them.

On the third day, I received the most welcomed telegram from Henry. He is much alive! It read:

Obadiah, Helen and I are both well. Stop. The battle is over and of course you are already aware, the Union won. Stop. General Sherman has set up his headquarters here in Atlanta. Stop. He came into the hospital today to visit some of the Union soldiers who had been transferred to our hospital. Stop. I met him, and to my surprise, he was nice enough. Stop. Maybe it was because I'm a doctor attending to Union soldiers. Stop. My friend, we are well and I'm glad this ordeal is over. Stop. I will write you a long letter soon and give you the details. Stop. It's an experience I never want to have to repeat. Stop. The newspaper here said that the Confederates lost over 5,000 soldiers. Stop. What a shame! Stop. I believe the Union army lost over 3,000 soldiers. Stop. After you get this, write me a letter. Stop. They are letting mail come through now. Stop. Your good friend, Dr. Henry Dotson.

The El Dorado News-Times has done a great job covering the recent events of the presidential race between President Abe Lincoln, and his challenger, George B. McClellan.

The election was held on November 8, 1864, and President Lincoln was reelected by a landslide. Lincoln was reelected by a comfortable margin, with 212 out of 223 electoral votes. He won by more than 400,000 popular votes, on the strength of the soldier vote and military successes such as the Battle of Atlanta.

The Republican Party was also victorious by winning three-fourths of Congress.

Since the election of 1860, the Electoral College had expanded, with the admission of Kansas, West Virginia, and Nevada as free-soil states. No electoral votes were counted from any of the eleven Southern states.

President Lincoln is the first President to be reelected since Democrat Andrew Jackson in 1832.

At times during the election, things didn't look good for President Lincoln because of so many Union soldiers dying during the first three years of the Civil War. The North was tired of the war, and the many deaths angered a large segment of the voters. George B. McClellan took advantage of Lincoln's negative support and used it to increase his popularity among the voters. Things looked very good for George B. McClellan before the Battle of Atlanta was fought.

The fall of Atlanta and the success of the overall Atlanta Campaign were extensively covered by Northern newspapers and were a boon to Northern morale and to President Lincoln's political standing. The capture of Atlanta and General Hood's burning of military facilities as he evacuated showed that a successful conclusion of the war was in sight, weakening support for a truce.

Henry and I have been communicating back and forth by telegrams. Things are going well with him and his family. In his last letter he said, "General Sherman, after spending two months here in Atlanta, has left for Savannah, his next conquest in his March to the Sea."

By late November, Hank and the slaves have harvested most of our crops and are getting the fields ready for winter wheat. Thanksgiving is only two days away.

We were fortunate not to lose any slaves during the hot summer. Hank made sure our slaves were treated to water breaks every thirty minutes. He also made sure they had nourishing foods to keep their strength up.

Penelope is becoming more and more tired each day. She has gained more weight with this pregnancy. She has worried that she is getting too big and it will be hard for her to lose the excess weight after she gives birth. She tells me all she wants to do is eat. She said, "Obadiah, it's like I'm eating for three instead of two. I stay hungry all the time!"

I keep encouraging her not to worry about her weight. The food she eats has good nutritional value. Penelope believes this baby will be a girl. I'm in hopes she's right. It would be nice to have a little girl for Belle to play with.

My work at the clinic and my plantation trips in Union, Ouachita, and Columbia Counties pretty much keep me busy. There is just something about the traveling part that inspires me. The time I'm traveling gives me an opportunity to think.

Marion is taking advantage of an internship program that gives young men with medical interest an opportunity to become a doctor. He is doing his internship under me. After he completes the two-year internship, he will take a series of tests. If he scores high enough, he can get his license to practice medicine. Marion is a sharp young man. I have no doubt that he will be able to pass his tests at the end of the two years.

Yesterday was his first time to help deliver a baby. He was a little nervous, but he performed well.

"Uncle Obadiah, I don't think I've ever sweated so much!"

"That's because you knew you were dealing with bringing a new life into this world. You did amazingly well. I'm proud of you!"

"I'm sure it won't always be that simple!"

"That's correct! But if the person is healthy and there isn't a complication, such as breech delivery, women seem to be able to endure the pain and give birth without too much of a problem. Giving birth to babies is one of the functions that God gave women. If women refused to have babies, mankind would eventually die out!" I said as I laughed.

Our family members back in Autauga and Dallas Counties are all doing well. We are hoping that a majority of them can visit here for Christmas this year. Mother's age is not conducive to her making a long trip back to Autauga County. She's already writing letters to everyone to ask them to consider spending Christmas with us in Union County.

This will be the first Christmas for all my family to be present at Three Oaks. I'm betting my mother will be successful in achieving her goal of bringing them to El Dorado for Christmas. We have plenty of room. We will sleep some on the floor, and that will work out well, since the children enjoy sleeping on the floor.

As I left home this morning, Penelope wasn't feeling well. She ate very little breakfast. When I asked her how she was doing, she said, "I'm just miserable! I want this baby to hurry up and decide she or he wants out!"

I took her in my arms and said, "God knows the appointed time, my dear."

My schedule at the office is less demanding today. In fact, I plan to leave early to have more time with Penelope and the kids. I've instructed Mary Catherine to give Dr. Burroughs some of my patients for the next week or so. Something tells me that Penelope will have this baby any day now.

I was seeing a patient when Mary Catherine knocked on my door and said, "Dr. Obadiah, could I see you for a minute?"

I knew it had to be important, or she would never interrupt me. I excused myself and went outside the door.

"You need to go home soon," she said.

She handed me a note that Bill had brought from Mother. The note said, "Obadiah, come home quickly. Penelope has gone into labor and we need you."

I saw Bill in the waiting room. I went to him and gave him orders to return to Three Oaks and tell Mother I'm on my way.

I instructed Mary Catherine to shift the rest of my daily schedule to Dr. Burroughs and Elizabeth. I asked Marion to ride with me and to assist me in Penelope's delivery.

I don't remember driving my carriage faster than I did today. Nellie, my reliable horse, was laboring hard upon reaching Three Oaks. There were times I noticed Marion bracing himself as I made some speedy turns heading home to Three Oaks. From the expression on his face, I believe I scared him. I would look at him, smile, and say, "Did I almost lose you back there?"

As we arrived, Bill was waiting on the porch. He informed me that he would take care of the horse and carriage for me.

Marion and I quickly entered the house. Mattie met us in the hall as she was going after hot water and towels.

"Oh, Obadiah, I'm so glad you're here. Penelope is in a lot of pain! Mrs. Catherine is with her!"

As I entered the door, Mother left Penelope's side and immediately came to me.

"Obadiah, I think Penelope is in trouble. Do something!"

I quickly went to Penelope. She was screaming. "Obadiah, something is badly wrong!" she said.

"Try to relax, my darling! Let me take a look at you."

After examining Penelope, I discovered the baby's head was coming first. I was relieved we weren't having a breeched baby.

"Penelope, I'm going to help you as much as I can, but you're going to have to help me by pushing with all your might. Do you understand, my love?"

"Yes, I'll try!" she said as she began to push.

Penelope was a true sport. She gave it all she had and within three minutes she gave birth to our first little girl. She was perfect.

I was about ready to stitch up the incision when Penelope let out a loud scream.

"Obadiah, there is something wrong!"

"What do you mean?"

"I feel there's another baby trying to come out."

I again examined her and realized she was right. There was another baby in the birth canal. We started the process of pushing again. This time, I could see the baby's head. It wasn't long before the baby was completely out. All the time I was doing this, I was questioning myself, How did I miss this? Why didn't I know there were two babies inside of Penelope? I'm a doctor; I should have known this!

The baby I held in my hands was a healthy-looking little boy. Two more children! Twins!

Our little boy was perfect as well. Thank you, God!

This was certainly a big surprise for all of us. Especially, me! I still can't figure it out. How did I miss this?

As soon as I completed stitching up the incision, I sat down by Penelope as Mother and Mattie brought both babies and laid them on Penelope's breast. They were all cleaned up and looked beautiful! Penelope looked at me and said, "Obadiah, we thought our family was going to be six, but God has changed that, hasn't He?"

"He surely has," I said as I took the hand of our little girl. We decided earlier on that if it was a girl we'd name her Isabella. If it was a boy we'd name him Paul, after the apostle Paul.

As it appears now, we will use both names. What a blessing, I thought.

After making sure that Penelope, Isabella, and Paul were doing well, I excused myself for a walk in the garden. I needed a few minutes to myself with God. As I sat down on the bench in the middle of the garden, I gave thanks to God for his blessings. I thanked him for Penelope and our two healthy, twin babies.

The quiet time I spend with God is always good and fulfilling. To me, it's like He's standing right in front of me and I'm looking directly at Him as He listens to me. I know that sounds odd, but that's the experience I have with my Lord. I just pray this will never change.

Before leaving for the garden, I asked Marion to go to El Dorado and send a telegram announcing the arrival of our twins to our family members in Alabama.

I took the next few days off to be close to Penelope and the babies. Penelope is making good progress in her healing. For the last three days the only time she's been on her feet is to sit on the potty chair. We will start tomorrow walking a little. As before, Penelope has plenty milk for both Isabella and Paul. That's a blessing in itself. I've observed already that Paul has Isabella beat when it comes to appetite.

James, Belle, and Charles are big helpers to Penelope. She lets them hold the twins, under strict supervision, of course.

Belle thanks God every night in her prayers for Isabella. She says, "It's okay that I have another little brother, but Isabella is special. We are going to have fun playing dolls together."

Mother was successful in getting commitments from our families back in Autauga and Dallas Counties to spend Christmas holidays at Three Oaks.

John, who lives at Twin Oaks, volunteered to coordinate the trip with those in Prattville and with Dent, who lives in Dallas County. They will arrive at Champagnolle on December 23, 1864, where I'll pick them up and transport them to Three Oaks.

My mother is so excited and happy. She will once again have her family together for Christmas.

"It will be like old times," Mother said.

I'm pleased as well. Since mother has always been the nucleus to draw the family together, I hate the thought that, someday, God will take her to Heaven and these family get-togethers will be few and far between.

My brothers and sisters are scheduled to return to their homes in Prattville and Cahaba on January 2, 1895. We will have a little over a week together.

CHAPTER 31

Mother, who loves Christmas shopping, has spent several days in El Dorado buying Christmas gifts for the entire family. She's been very excited since finding out that the Bradford family from Alabama is coming to Three Oaks for the Christmas holidays. She has kept Bill busy taking her back and forward to El Dorado. In the past few days, I've seen that extra bounce in her steps. It's like she's out to win some kind of race. At sixty- seven, she is still in top-notch condition.

The parlor is decorated with a large Christmas tree, with lots of presents. Mother is fully organized, and unless she's forgotten something, we are ready for our big Bradford Christmas affair.

She's got my father's Bible laid out and ready for Dent to read the Christmas Story on Christmas morning. She knows where every child will sleep and what rooms she will use for the married couples.

She's made arrangements for the entire family to attend two special Christmas services. One will be at Hank's church in our barn and the other at our home church, First Baptist Church of El Dorado.

At Hank's special church service, everyone will have an opportunity to hear Penelope play the piano and accompany Mattie as she sings.

This will be the first time my family will have had the opportunity to see how much talent my beautiful Penelope and Mattie have when it comes to music. I'm sure they will be impressed with Hank's preaching as well.

On a special note, my family will have an opportunity to get to know James, Isabella, and Paul. They will be seeing them for the first time.

I, too, will enjoy their visit. It will be nice to sit down with my brothers and sisters and discuss the past and present. I'm anxious to see how things are going in Prattville with the hospital and if Daniel Pratt's leadership is still contributing to the growth of Prattville.

I'll be interested to hear how the Civil War has affected Autauga County and its effect upon the surrounding counties.

Their visit is going to give them the opportunity to see what it's like to have Negro and white families living under the same roof. This, too, will certainly be a little different from what they are accustomed to.

Mother made it plain that moving Mattie's family to a temporary location to accommodate our family members was out of the question. She considers them a part of our family, and that's the way it's going to be.

I'm trusting in God that all will go well and everyone will respect each other. Although we are different in some ways, God still makes it possible for us to have love for each other.

Mother and Penelope have worked hard planning menus for the Christmas holidays. Hank, George, Big Jim, Bill, and others have been busy killing and roasting hogs for the occasion. I gave them permission to roast two additional hogs for a Christmas dinner for the slaves as well.

Several chickens have been caught and caged for dinner meals. Mother is well aware that chicken is Dent's and my favorite meat dish.

I've made arrangements for three wagons and two carriages to be at Champagnolle at four o'clock p.m.

Mary, Virgil, and their children will meet us in Champagnolle. They will accompany us to Three Oaks for dinner and a visit, before returning to their home in El Dorado.

We arrived at Champagnolle around 3:30. As usual, we climbed the spiral stairway that led to the lookout deck that overlooks the Ouachita River. This is one of our favorite places at Champagnolle.

Today is a beautiful day. The temperature drops down to the low forties at night, but gets up into the sixties and seventies during the day. The mild winters are one reason I love south Arkansas.

Mother wanted to come, but decided she'd stay with Penelope to help with the kids and assist with the dinner meal. When it comes to food, Mother wants everything to be just right. The last thing she said to me was, "Tell them I'll be waiting with open arms to greet them at Three Oaks."

I could hardly believe my eyes as all my nephews and nieces started exiting the steamboat onto the landing deck. To tell you the truth, they have changed so much in three years. Dent and Sara's boys, Everett and Law, have grown into fine-looking young men. They are taller than Dent and me.

Tanyua's two daughters, Jane and Sally Ballard, are now teenagers, and beautiful girls, at that.

Jim Crawford and my sister Sarah's children, Amanda and Lydia, are as pretty as their mother. They have Sarah's blonde hair and blue eyes. Amanda is a year and a half older than Charles, and Lydia is a year younger than Charles.

John's three children, Daniel, Jake, and Jennie, have changed as well. They are no longer children. They are now teenagers. In fact, Daniel and Jake look like young men ready to take on the world. I can hardly believe three to four years can make such a vast difference in one's life.

Jennie is a beautiful young lady with long, black hair and blue eyes. She reminds me of Mary Catherine.

Daniel and Jake are very polite and came across as very distinguished young men as they shook my hand.

Dent was the last person to step off the steamboat. A young man had just exited the steamboat ahead of him. I stood there trying to figure out who this young, distinguished man could be. I was certain I'd seen him somewhere, but where? As they approached, it finally hit me. This was my deceased brother, Charles Alexander Bradford's, only child. His father was killed in a fall from his horse. He and his wife, Victoria, had one child and named him Alexander Jr. He inherited his father's share of James Bradford's estate.

Alexander has been away to college for the past several years. He has now graduated with a degree in law and has returned to his mother's home in Prattville.

When he heard of the Christmas gathering at Three Oaks, he contacted John and asked if he could tag along. Of course, John was happy for him to come.

When Dent asked me if I knew him, I said, "I believe this is Alexander Bradford, Jr."

"That's me, Uncle Obadiah!" he said as he shook my hand.

"Welcome to Union County, Alexander. It's good to have you here. Your presence is going to make Mother a very happy lady. She has no idea you were coming."

"I wanted it to be a surprise. I've not seen Grandmother in four years," he said.

Everyone carried their bags to the three wagons, and off we went to Three Oaks.

To get to know Alexander better, I asked him if he would like to ride with me in my carriage. He quickly said, "I'd like that, Uncle Obadiah."

On the way to Three Oaks, Alexander shared with me what he had been doing during the years he had been gone from Prattville. He had received his law degree and was looking forward to going to work with a law firm or setting up his own practice.

Besides becoming a lawyer, he intends to write as well. He loves historical books and is in the process of writing his first novel. His book will relate to the Civil War, its causes, and how the Southern plantation owners will cope without slave labor.

"It's my strong belief the Civil War will end soon," Alexander said.

"What makes you feel that way?" I asked.

"Well, for one thing, the North is now in control of the waterways and railroads throughout the South. The South is running out of supplies, and the Yankees are winning most of the battles. Without supplies, the Confederacy will not be able to fight."

I could tell that Alexander and I were going to get along nicely. I, too, feel the Civil War will end soon.

"My friend Dr. Henry Dotson of Atlanta, Georgia, feels the same way. He writes me all the time telling me what's going on in and around Atlanta. He says it's just a matter of time."

Alexander is now twenty-three years old and has not yet found the right girl to marry. He says, "Right now, I have bigger fish in the barrel to keep me busy!"

I knew exactly where Alexander's quote came from. I heard his father, Charles, say that many times when he was living.

Alexander is not only handsome, but he's intelligent as well. During the short time I've been with him, I've been favorably impressed with him. He's got a wide range of knowledge and knows how to express himself. Mother is going to be thrilled when she sees him.

As we turned onto the road that leads to the plantation home at Three Oaks, Bill stopped the carriage. It was at this time that I invited Alexander to ride with me and Bill in the driver's seat. From the driver's seat, he would be able to see the beautiful landscape leading up to the plantation house. There are two rows of red crepe myrtles that line the road to the house. During the summer months when the crepe myrtles are in full bloom, they are beautiful. I also wanted to explain a little about the layout of the property where he would be spending a little over a week.

As we got close to the house, Mother was sitting on the front porch waiting for us to arrive. As we pulled up in front of the steps leading to the porch, I heard Mother say, "Oh, Lord have mercy, it's Alexander!"

As soon as she could make it down the steps she moved quickly to my carriage and said, "Oh, my goodness, Alexander. It's so good to see you. Oh, I didn't know you were coming," she said as she embraced him and gave him a kiss on the cheek.

"I wanted to surprise you, Grandmother!" he said.

"Oh, my darling this is a wonderful surprise! I must now greet my other grandchildren and guests. You don't run off, you hear," she said as she made it to the first wagon, which had just pulled up behind us.

It was so wonderful to see Mother so happy and full of energy. This was good medicine for her soul. This was better than any medicine she could ever take. I am so grateful my brothers and sisters came all the way from Alabama to see Mother and my family. We are going to have the best Christmas. The only thing which would make this occasion even better is the presence of my father, James Bradford.

After dinner, Hank and his family joined us at the big house. Hank's father-in-law, Mr. Sam, George, and another slave by the name of Robert played the fiddle and banjo. They were good musicians and could play about any type of dance music.

It was a little cold, but that didn't seem to bother the young ones. They kicked up their heels and enjoyed dancing. To keep warm, we older ones gathered around a big bonfire that George and the slaves had built for this special occasion.

After watching the younger ones dance, I turned to Penelope and asked her to dance. She said, "I thought you'd never ask."

It wasn't long before my brothers and nephews were dancing with Mother. She loves to dance, and they love whirling her around.

Marion was the only grandson who previously knew about Mother's talent to dance. He started off with a slow dance. It wasn't long before Jake, Daniel, and Alexander broke in to dance with Mother.

After several dances with Mother, the boys began to back off. I think Mother wore them down. She could dance all night. It was fun watching my sixty-seven-year-old Mother hold her own with her young energetic grandsons.

My brothers, Dent and John, took the liberty of breaking in and dancing with Penelope. Dent, who had previously danced with Penelope, knew her to be a talented dancer.

About ten o'clock, things were slowing down. The older group was tired from the long trip from Autauga County and needed to retire.

Before retiring for the night, Dent walked up to me and said, "Obadiah, before we turn in, could we take a stroll in Mother's garden?"

I knew Dent well enough to know that, if he had something on his mind, he needed to get it off as soon as possible. I've always tried to oblige him.

We excused ourselves and took our stroll in the garden. As usual, we sat down on the big, iron bench that sat in the middle of Mother's beautiful garden.

"What's on your mind, Big Brother?" I asked.

"You know me like a book, don't you, Little Brother?" Dent replied.

"I believe I do," I said.

"Obadiah, things aren't going very well financially at either Black Oaks or Twin Oaks. The Civil War has drained big plantations down financially because of the decreased demand for cotton and corn crops. The shipping of cotton has gotten to be quite an ordeal this year as well. The price of cotton has fallen. We made very little money this year on our cotton crop."

"There was something about your last letter that gave me a feeling things weren't going well," I said.

"How are things going here for you?" Dent asked.

"We've not been suffering, but when this war ends and we have to start paying for labor, we, too, will be hurting."

"John and I have been discussing this very thing. We realize this will hurt us badly. We've got lots of money tied up in both Black Oaks and Twin Oaks."

"Let me tell you what I've decided to do when the slaves are set free. I'm going to offer them an opportunity to work for me for a wage or sharecrop. I've decided they will be better off staying with me than trying to make it on their own. At least they will have a decent place to live and something to eat."

"John and I have discussed doing exactly the same. I just don't know if we can hang on financially. This damn Civil War has affected us in a disastrous way," Dent said.

"I certainly agree with you on that subject, Big Brother. We may have to lower our standards of living, but with the help of God, who's always been with us, we can do it. We will make it work!"

"I'm praying you're right, Obadiah. It would kill me if I had to sell Black Oaks and my share of Twin Oaks to someone like Daniel Pratt. Mr. Pratt has more money than he knows what to do with. He's already bought out several plantations owners in Autauga County who have fallen victim to hard times.

"I'm telling you, Obadiah, I know he's a friend of yours, but this man very well could own most of Autauga County someday."

"Do you know if he's still interested in buying Twin Oaks?"

"I don't think he's approached John about Twin Oaks yet. If he has, John hasn't said anything to me."

"Since you are part owner of Twin Oaks, I'm sure John would have said something to you.

"Dent, may I ask you a pointed question?"

"What do you mean by pointed?"

"Since you and John are making payments to me for Twin Oaks, would it help y'all for us to renegotiate a new note that would lower the yearly payment?"

"Obadiah, we're going to be able to make our payment to you, but to be honest with you, it's going to increase our financial burden substantially!"

"I'm sorry to hear that, Dent. I'd like to help you and John. Let's pray about this. If you and John get in trouble financially, just know we can work something out that will help both of you on payments."

"Little Brother, that's very kind of you."

"I want you and John to know I never would encourage you to sell Daniel Pratt Twin Oaks or Black Oaks, but to be quite honest, he probably would be the only person around who would have the money to purchase your plantations."

"Obadiah, I'm not asking for charity. Please don't think that. John doesn't know I'm talking to you about this. I'm just trying to determine what steps we might take should the bottom fall out."

"Dent, I don't want you to grieve over this during your stay here at Three Oaks. Please enjoy your stay. Make some time with both Mary Catherine and Marion.

"That grandson of yours needs to get to know his grandparents. Have some fun! Christmas is only two days from now!"

CHAPTER 32

Our big house was completely full. People were bedded down all over the house. Everyone had their own little corner, and one could hear snoring going on throughout the house.

Penelope and I decided we were blessed to be a part of the big Bradford family. It was just like old times back at Twin Oaks.

We felt good not to have to travel. With five children and Mother, it would have been hard.

On Christmas Eve morning, people were waiting in line to use our three bathrooms. I encouraged the older nephews to step next door and use the bunkhouse bathroom if there was an emergency. The barn was another alternative, if needed. We men are a little more flexible than women, if you know what I mean.

Dent and Sarah plan to visit with Marion and Mary Catherine in El Dorado. This will help with the bedding and bathroom situation.

Mary and Virgil have offered their home for sleeping. Because of the busy shopping season, Mary and Virgil have to get up early and stay late at the store. Their sales have been very good, and they are reaping the benefits financially. Due to their working schedule, they wouldn't get to spend much time with their guests.

It is my feeling, since Mother is the nucleus of this family, most everyone will stay put at Three Oaks.

George, Big Jim, Hank, and Bill brought extra tables for the dining room and parlor. Mother wanted a place for everyone to be seated as they enjoy their meals.

This will be the first Christmas Eve breakfast that Big Jim, Mattie, and Betsy will be present. I, for one, am anxious to see how my family will react to sharing a meal with them at the table.

After everyone was seated, I returned thanks, recognizing God for his blessings of yesterday, today, and tomorrow. We were ready for a delicious meal consisting of eggs, sausage, bacon, white gravy, and hot biscuits, as well as good old sorghum molasses. There shouldn't be anyone leaving the breakfast table hungry!

Mother had everything arranged in an orderly manner. To help Mattie, Betsy, and Big Jim, she brought George's wife, Opal, and Sam's wife, Myrtle, to the big house as extra help.

As we began to eat, I looked around to see what kind of expressions were on my family's faces. As I mentioned before, this was the first time my family sat at a table with servants, who were now members of my immediate family. I was surprised everyone was handling this with the utmost respect. To tell you the truth, I was amazed!

Penelope looked at me and smiled; I winked and smiled back. Mother kept a family conversation going throughout the meal. As usual, Mattie, Betsy, and Big Jim had done a great job preparing our breakfast.

As soon as breakfast was over, Big Jim, George, and Bill, along with some of the nephews, carried the extra tables from the parlor to the front porch so we'd have plenty of room for everyone to meet in the parlor.

Mother, Penelope, and I had decided early on that we would have the family gift opening after breakfast on Christmas Eve. That will allow the families with small children the opportunity in years to come to establish their own family traditions for Christmas Day.

There was about an hour's break before we filed into the parlor for Dent's reading of the Christmas Story. We had to wait for the arrival of Virgil and Mary's family, Marion and Lindy, and Mary Catherine and Benjamin with their son, Benjamin William Madison.

When our family members from El Dorado arrived, everyone congregated in the parlor. There weren't enough chairs, so several stood while the smaller children sat on the floor.

Mattie, Betsy, Opal, and Myrtle stood at the door and passed out eggnog to everyone passing through the parlor door. Eggnog is a traditional drink that is served every Christmas Eve at the Bradfords'.

As usual, Dent's reading of the Christmas Story was a hit. The applause at the end was proof that it met with everyone's approval. Just like my father, he put his heart and soul in making it entertaining for all to hear.

After Dent's Christmas Story, Mother made her annual speech. As usual, she was very thankful for everyone's presence, especially for Alexander, who surprised her by coming to spend Christmas with us. She spoke of blessings God had given her for sixty-seven glorious years.

"Our God has been so good to me. Today He's brought my family together for the first time in four years. Hallelujah! Praise the Lord!

"When my dear husband, James, was alive, it was traditional for us to pause and share at least one thing during the year for which we were most thankful. Since we have everyone here, I would like for us to take time and share with each other that favorite blessing.

"I have many and I promise you, I won't bore you by naming too many, but since I'm the oldest, I think it's only fitting for me to be able to mention more than one thing. I hope that meets with everyone's approval."

Everyone applauded to show Mother our approval. "Who would even think about bucking our mother?" Dent said under his breath.

"The first thing I'm thankful for is God's blessing of allowing Marion to be with us today. This Civil War has brought sadness to many across the South, but Marion's return to us, safe and sound, has truly been a blessing."

No sooner had Mother spoken those words, than an applause was heard throughout the room. I could hear Alexander say, "Hey! Hey!"

"Secondly, I'm particularly happy to have my oldest grandson, Alexander, with us for the first time in four years." She looked at Alexander with her arms stretched out and said, "Welcome, Alexander. It means more than you know to have you here with us!"

Mother's third and last statement, perhaps, was the most gifted speech I'd ever heard her speak.

"We have a special closeness that few families have in this day and time. I pray for you daily and will continue to do that throughout the New Year. I have a strong feeling this Civil War will end this year. It's time we rebuild the United States of America. It will take people like us who find no fault in others who are trying to make a life for themselves. We Bradfords will do our share in bringing people together and working for a strong nation."

I didn't know my mother was such an inspiring speech maker. As I stood listening to the words of wisdom she was speaking, I thought, Maybe we need to elect my mother to some public office. As soon as she stopped, people were on their feet showing their love for a great mother, grandmother, and friend.

Mother had gotten everyone in the mood. She didn't have to call on anyone. Everyone was ready after such an inspiring speech. The sharing took over an hour, but it was worth every minute.

God has been good to all of us this year. Perhaps the best blessings were the new, healthy babies.

It was now time for the annual Bradford opening of Christmas presents. Another tradition in the Bradford family was watching each other open the first gift.

After the first present was opened, each person was free to open their presents at will. Sometimes it was hard to keep the little ones from jumping ahead.

Since Penelope and I were the hosts, we seated ourselves and our five children where we could see everyone in the room. It was fun holding the twins as they played around us. Charles, Belle, and James needed no help.

By the time all the gifts were passed out and opened, it was almost lunchtime. Mother announced in the parlor that lunch would be served around one o'clock instead of twelve. It hadn't been long since we had a big breakfast, and no one was hungry, especially, the kids, who were busy playing with their new toys.

A spell of extreme cold weather had hit Union County. We men decided to stay in the parlor and talk while the women went to the dining room to play cards, such as bridge and other games that mother had taught them over the years.

I noticed Alexander was getting along nicely with Marion, Everett, Law, and John's two sons, Daniel and Jake. Benjamin Madison, Mary Catherine's husband, had joined the clan as well.

Alexander was my oldest nephew, followed by Marion and his brothers, Law and Everett. I couldn't help noticing the strong personality of Alexander coming through as he visited with the others. He had everyone in his corner laughing. I felt sure his degree in law was going to be a big factor in his success. Since Jake was interested in politics, he appeared attentive and intrigued by Alexander's stories.

Dent, John, and I took seats near the fireplace. It wasn't long before we were right in the middle of telling each other what we knew about the Civil War.

"Obadiah, what are you hearing from your good friend Dr. Henry Dotson about the Civil War?"

"I received a letter from Henry last week. It's not looking good for General Robert Lee's Confederate Army. Henry said Atlanta was busy trying to rebuild from General Sherman's destruction. He says the damage has had a crippling effect on Atlanta and the entire Deep South.

"The railroads leading to the South are now under Union control. Henry thinks General Lee will soon have to surrender from lack of supplies and men."

"That's what I've been hearing around Selma as well. People there have little hope that the South can win. They are getting ready for the worst to happen. I must confess, I'm ready for it to end. We've had enough killing. It will take years for our country to get back to where we were before this war started," Dent said.

"I can agree to that," John said.

"I, too, want to see the Civil War come to an end, but to tell you the truth, we've got another war to fight that could be bad," I said.

After making that statement, I noticed Alexander nodding to the others that they should join us near the fireplace. They left their little corner and came over to join us.

"You're referring to the abolishment of slavery, aren't you, Uncle Obadiah?" Alexander asked.

"I am at that. I'm not too upset about the abolishment of slavery; however, I'm dreading what's going to happen to the thousands of slaves who will be out of work, no food to eat and no place to live. What's going to happen to them?"

"It certainly will be hard times ahead for not only them, but us as well," Dent said.

"Do you mind if I speak in regard to this subject?" Alexander asked.

"We'd be happy to hear what you've got to say," I said.

"I agree with Uncle Obadiah in his assessment of what's going to happen. This is going to be a dreadful time in our history. The key word in all of this mess is going to be reconstruction. What's going to happen is broad, broader than most people can comprehend.

"In law school we discussed this subject many times. We all agreed that both the plantation owners and slaves were equally going to suffer during this period of reconstruction."

"From your studies, how do you think all of this is going to play out?" Dent asked.

"I can't honestly tell you, but according to what we learned at Harvard, slaves are going to suffer a great deal. They will be struggling to stay alive.

"The big plantation owners are going to be fewer and fewer. The Confederate dollar isn't worth much, as I'm sure you can attest. Many of the plantation owners will either have to borrow money or sell what they have to the rich for a fraction of what their plantations are worth. The rich will get richer, and the poor will get poorer.

"The new government will have to create jobs or programs of assistance for the freed slaves. Without these programs many will perish. It's going to be a period that none of us want to experience, but unfortunately, it's going to happen."

"Did your professors have any solutions for us who presently own slaves and have depended on them totally for labor? What can we do to survive?" John asked.

"Uncle Obadiah has shared with me his idea of keeping his slaves at Three Oaks as wage earners and sharecroppers. I think that's a great idea. A plan like that would aid greatly the slaves' chances of survival. Something like that has to happen, because the government will not have the money and resources to rebuild the United States and to secure the survival of freed slaves.

"We, the people, will have to step forward and do our part in making things work. We will have to lay aside our prejudices toward the slaves and find ways to survive, ourselves."

"What do you plan to do with your lawyer skills, Alexander?" Dent asked.

"I'm going to try to find a place that I will be able to practice law to help others. Who knows? I may starve to death, but I think God wants me to help others. I'm thinking there'll be jobs created by the new government that will require my skills to help the slaves and others with their entitlements. Who knows? If I find myself starving to death, maybe I'll stay here in El Dorado and beg for a handout from Uncle Obadiah!"

I would love for Alexander to stay here and start his law practice in El Dorado. I just may approach him in regard to that matter.

In fact, I wouldn't mind for my entire family to move to Union County. I know without a doubt, Mother would love it.

CHAPTER 33

Everyone in the Bradford family was present for the Christmas Day dinner at Three Oaks—just like old times back at Twin Oaks.

The temperature on Christmas Day was extremely cold. It was too cold to be outside, so we decided our activities would remain inside the confines of the big house. Staying inside didn't seem to bother anyone. In fact, it gave us an opportunity to go from group to group, interacting with each other in either card games or conversational gab.

The closeness was a good thing. People were all over the house, going from one group to the other, getting to know each other. The little ones sometimes got a little noisy, but everyone understood they were just having fun in their own way.

A lot of our time was spent eating and drinking. Mattie and Betsy had prepared an abundance of finger foods, which could be found throughout the house, mostly in the parlor.

We call finger foods "grazing foods." The only problem with grazing is that we all tend to fill up and aren't hungry at mealtime.

Besides playing games, we had sharing times in the parlor. I loved this time of hearing others tell stories and what they remember about the years past. Dent, being the oldest, always seem to know more personal family stories. We all enjoyed his sharing.

Mother was able to take us back in time to when she was a little girl growing up in Georgia. She also worked in a little of her personal dating life with our father, James Bradford.

"Since everyone is sharing, I wonder if Penelope and Mattie could share with us about their lives before they joined the Bradford family," Alexander said.

You could have heard a pin drop in the parlor. Everyone was taken aback by Alexander's request. I know he didn't mean any harm in his request. I believe, since he was out of state going to school, he wasn't fully aware of the circumstances of Penelope and Mattie becoming part of our family.

I looked at Penelope as if to say, "I'm sorry!"

Penelope smiled, stood up, and said, "I don't mind sharing with you. In fact, I'd like for my mama to come sit by me as I share with you. After I finish, Mama might want to share with you some of her thoughts and memories. I do have one request. I would like for the children to be escorted to the playroom. Some of the things I share might not be appropriated for them to hear at this time."

"I think that's a marvelous idea," Mother said as she, Betsy, Minnie, Myrtle, and Sarah, escorted the children from the room.

I looked at Alexander, who was blushing because of his request for Penelope to share her story with everyone. I knew he wanted to take back his remarks, but it was too late. My beautiful, charming, brave, and loving Penelope was more than ready.

She had once said to me that there would come a time in her life when she would need to share her story with the Bradford family. She looked at me and said, "Tonight is a good night, Obadiah."

Mother and Sarah returned just in time to hear Penelope say, "If you don't mind, I'm going to take a seat here by Obadiah and Mama. My story may take a while.

"I was fifteen years old when I first laid eyes on my beloved husband, Obadiah Bradford. I can remember how scared I was standing on the auction platform in Selma, Alabama, hand-in-hand with my precious mama. I have never forgotten how I felt.

"Mama had assured me that Mrs. Charlotte Thompson, our owner, had promised her that we wouldn't be separated when we were sold. Whoever purchased us had to take both of us. We were grateful to Mrs. Thompson for her love and respect for us.

"As the auctioneer introduced us to the large crowd, I could barely stand on my feet. I was very frightened. Mama had shared with me when I was a young girl that she was separated from her mother and brothers when the Thompsons purchased her in Jones County, Georgia. She never knew what happened to them. I don't think I would want to live if I couldn't be close to my mama.

"Anyway there was a plantation owner by the name of Bishop, who came from Lowndes County, Alabama, looking for slaves who were mulatto. This Mr. Bishop was a mean-spirited man who liked to buy light-complexioned slaves and sell them for a big profit.

"He was very rude from the beginning. He came forward and pulled our mouths open to check our teeth. He checked for flogging marks, brand marks, and touched us in inappropriate ways. All during this time, I was thinking, Oh, God, please don't let this man buy us!

"I was so relieved when the bidding started and when Obadiah raised every bid that Mr. Bishop made. The bidding got higher and higher. I lost count of who had the highest bid when the auctioneer said, 'Sold, to the young man from Autauga County.'

"I looked at Mama and saw tears in her eyes. We looked at Mrs. Charlotte and she nodded as if to say, 'I'm happy with your new owner.'

"Mama and I were loaded into the Bradford wagon, which was being driven by Mr. George. We waited until Mr. James Bradford finished his bidding on four male slaves. Our Hank, who is now our overseer, was one of the slaves Mr. James bought.

"As we started back to Twin Oaks, I saw a young man run up to Obadiah and hand him a note. As I sat in the wagon, I wondered what the note was all about. I watched Obadiah as he read the note. After he finished reading the note, he turned to where Mrs. Charlotte was sitting and tipped his hat to her. I figured the note came from her.

"In later years, Obadiah shared with me the content of that note. I know the contents by heart and wish to tell you what it said. It read, 'Dearest Obadiah Bradford: You made me proud today when you stood your ground with that devil, Mr. Bishop.

I was praying hard he wouldn't out bid you for my special Mattie and Penelope. I saw compassion coming from your eyes and face today. I know now my slaves will have a good home with their new master in Autauga County. May God be with you and bless you. Thank you for this good deed you did today. Sincerely, Mrs. Charlotte Thompson.'

"It had been a long day, and I was very hungry. I was hoping that Obadiah was as hungry as we were and that he would find food for us soon.

"His father stopped at a general store in Selma and bought food. We stopped under a big oak tree, along the side of the road just outside the city limits of Selma.

"It was there that Obadiah made his first contact with me when he handed me food to eat. I acknowledged him by saying, 'Thank you, Massa.' It was like he was in a daze as he stood by the wagon gazing directly into my eyes. I didn't realize it until later that he was so shocked to see a slave girl with blue eyes.

"I want to go back now to the first fifteen years of my life at the Thompson's plantation. Our lives at the plantation were pleasant enough as far as being treated well by the Thompsons. There was some medical reason Mrs. Thompson couldn't have children. Because of that, in her own way, she kind of adopted me as her daughter. She dressed me well and treated Mama and me with the utmost respect.

"We were given the run of their big house. We each had our daily jobs to do and we did them well. We had only one bed, and Mama and I slept together during our years with the Thompsons. We didn't mind, because in the winter months it got really cold and we had no fireplace.

"Mrs. Charlotte taught me how to sew, and my mama taught me how to cook. I had two fine ladies who were my teachers.

"Mrs. Charlotte told me she'd like to teach me how to read and write, but that Mr. Thompson said a defiant no! So I had to wait until my good friend, and now sister-in-law, Sarah, taught me how to read and write at Twin Oaks. Sarah, I will always be grateful to you for teaching me to read and write and being my best friend!

"The years I spent at Twin Oaks were the best years of my life. Mr. James and Mrs. Catherine were some of the nicest Christian people who have walked this good earth. Mrs. Catherine made me beautiful dresses. She also taught me lifelong living skills, for which I am eternally grateful. Thank you, Mrs. Catherine!

"I fell in love with Obadiah Bradford on the first day I laid my eyes on him in Selma. My love for him has grown daily since that day. He is responsible for my being educated in Boston, Massachusetts, at Mrs. Adams' Boarding School.

"I would do anything for Obadiah. I want everyone to know that our lives together, before marriage, were pure. Obadiah was a patient man. We both knew God, but he seemed to be able to put his faith and trust in God into action better than I could. It was through Obadiah's faith that I become closer to God and his will for my life. His faith and patience are undisputable, to say the least. But I'm telling you today, this man is my love, my life, and my reason for living.

"I believe I'll stop now. To tell you the truth, I'm exhausted."

Everyone in the room rose to their feet and applauded Penelope's story. I knew my family loved her. She has truly been a supporter to me. She's always handled herself with poise and grace. She had never let me down. I could tell by looking at Alexander that Penelope had won his heart.

After the applauding stopped, Mattie stood and said, "I would like to share a little as well. I'll try not to repeat some of the things that Penelope has already said. I'll try to keep my remarks brief so as not to bore you.

"Penelope has already told you I was born in Georgia. My mother was a slave of light complexion. My father was a white man who my mother said died early on in life. When I was about seventeen, I was brought to my master's big house, where I was made one of the main maids of the household.

"My owners were big in entertaining. They had several dances and social events a year at their plantation. I was trained in the best Southern manners and was taught how to cook and serve in an elegant manner. Things went great for about four years. Although I was living at the big house, I still had opportunity to spend time with my mother and brothers. When I was twenty-one, the plantation owners employed a new overseer. He was a mean man who thirsted for young slave girls. He took a fancy to me since I was light complexioned. It wasn't long before I was with child. The only good thing that came out of that relationship was my beautiful Penelope.

"My owners decided to give up farming and move to Atlanta, Georgia. We slaves were all sold to the highest bidder. That's when my mother, brothers, and I got separated. I was sold to the Thompsons, and my family was sold to someone else. I don't know who. I had no idea who their owners were or where they were taken.

"It was the saddest time of my life. I cried for days. Finally, my sorrows were drowned out by Mrs. Charlotte's kindness. She made me her head servant. The Thompsons didn't know I was with child until later. When they found out, they didn't sell me or send me to the slave quarters. They showed compassion to me, and when Penelope was born, things were more like a family setting.

"Since Mrs. Charlotte couldn't have children, she treated Penelope like her own. Selling us was the hardest thing she ever did. She promised me she would not sell us separately and that she would see to it that we were purchased by good people. Between her and our Lord, she was successful.

"When Penelope was born, I was shocked when I saw her for the first time. I was expecting color, something like my own, but lo and behold, she was white. I started thinking, I'm half white, her father was white, I guess it's possible for Penelope to be white. What really got me was her beautiful blue eyes. These are the blue eyes that Obadiah said captured his heart. Obadiah, her blue eyes captured my heart as well.

"My life with the Bradford family has been the best part of my life. I could write a book about my days at Twin Oaks and now at Three Oaks. Because of Obadiah's Christian love and compassion, he has made my life one of the very best. Just as I thought Penelope was going to be the only child I'd have, God gave me a husband and two little boys."

A standing ovation went up all over the room for Mattie as well. We had just heard two courageous women share their life stories with us. As I listen to both Penelope and Mattie, my eyes filled with tears. I saw Bradford tears being shed throughout the room as well.

These two wonderful ladies are now part of my family. I believe with all my heart that God has been in every minute of carrying out this wonderful plan for us to be together. I'm just so lucky to have a family that loves and respects people regardless of what type of blood that runs through their veins. I praise God daily for my wonderful, happy life with my beautiful and loving wife, Penelope.

The day after Christmas, we all crowded into the barn for Hank's Christmas service. I have been anxiously waiting for this special occasion. I'm excited to see what my family thinks about attending a spiritual worship service with slaves.

As we entered the barn, we noticed the slaves had gathered together in one area of the barn and were sitting on bales of hay instead of the normal benches they were accustomed to. They had left all the benches open for us to sit on. We were their special guests, and it was an honor for us to be in their service.

Penelope had already taken her spot at the piano and was playing Christmas music. As we seated ourselves, I heard Mother tell Sarah that she was in for a real treat with Penelope's playing and Mattie's singing.

Hank came forward and welcomed everyone to the service. He introduced his small choir for special music that was led by Mattie and George. Both George and Mattie have beautiful voices. Mattie would sing at least one special song during the service. I'm hoping she will sing my favorite, "Swing Low, Sweet Chariot."

As she gracefully approached the podium, she looked out at the audience and said, "I want to welcome everyone to our service tonight. Obadiah has been good to us by letting us conduct our services here in the barn. There have been several improvements made since we've started having service here. It doesn't exactly resemble a barn now, does it?

"My daughter, Penelope, found us a piano and has been playing for us, along with Nellie and Nanny. We have truly enjoyed having a place to meet and the wonderful support Obadiah and Penelope have given us.

"Tonight, I want to sing for you my son-in-law's favorite song, 'Swing Low, Sweet Chariot.' He loves this song! I hope you like it too!"

Mattie's song brought everyone to their feet at the end. She did better than the last time she sang the song. As I looked around, I felt the Holy Spirit moving all around us. People were standing and clapping. What a great song service, I thought as we sat down.

Hank came to the podium and thanked everyone who participated in the song service. He said, "Tonight, I'm going to preach on Jesus Christ, our Lord and Savior. You are going to hear a message from the time he was born in the stable in a place called Bethlehem, where Mary laid him in a manger, to the time He was crucified on the old, rugged cross.

"You may be asking yourself how preacher Hank is going to preach on a time period which covers some thirty-two years. Well, all I can say, give me fifty minutes of your time and you're going to find out."

Hank had done it again! His sermon lasted for fifty-five minutes, just as he said it would. I was never so amazed by the words he spoke. How he condensed time periods and events into short remarks that were meaningful and spiritual, I cannot say. I can't describe what was happening, but the Lord's powers fell upon Hank, and his words of delivery were so strong and so powerful that we were all caught up in what he was saying. "Praise the Lord! Hallelujah!" was heard many times throughout his sermon.

The Bradford family couldn't have enjoyed any service any better than what they heard and witnessed from this barn tonight. What a blessing we had experienced!

During Hank's sermon, I realized that, when the slaves were set free, I had to help Hank get a church in El Dorado. His talent is a gift from God, and in my opinion, he will be an answer to many problems as the slaves are freed from the bondage of slavery. I want him to do well, and I want him to be able to grow a church where lost people can come to know Jesus Christ as their Lord and Savior. I will do everything within my power to see that someday he will become the pastor of the largest colored church in El Dorado, Arkansas.

CHAPTER 34

On Sunday the entire Bradford families were present for the Christmas service at First Baptist Church of El Dorado.

Benjamin and Mary Catherine had invited Benjamin's cousin, Jennie Madison, to church to meet Alexander. Jennie is a beautiful young lady who has just turned nineteen, and to quote Mary Catherine, "She will make some young man a great catch."

I could see matchmaking coming on ever so strong. After the service, Mary Catherine introduced Alexander to Jennie and invited him to join them at their house for dinner. Of course, Alexander accepted.

What started out as a planned introduction quickly turned into a busy relationship. Alexander didn't waste any time. Over the next three days, he borrowed our family carriage to court Jennie in El Dorado.

The Christmas holidays were quickly coming to an end. Our being together has made the Bradford bonding even stronger. The things we did and shared together will create memories that will last a lifetime. It was both fun and quality time—time that few families ever have the opportunity to enjoy. My father would be proud of his family.

It's been a long time since I've seen the vibrancy and excitement in Mother. She has been on cloud nine, you might say, from the first day the family arrived. This visit had certainly been good for her.

On the day before his departure, Alexander came into the parlor and asked me if I had time to visit with him in the garden. I took this as a private matter and said, "Yes."

"What's on your mind, Alexander?" I asked as we sat down on the cold metal bench.

"Uncle Obadiah, I need your advice."

"What's bearing on your mind, Alexander?" I asked.

"When I return to Prattville, I have no earthly idea what I'm going to do. I've been giving this a lot of thought the last few days. I've been thinking a lot about El Dorado. Do you think this little town could use another lawyer?"

"First, let me ask you a question. I'm being a little nosey, but does this sudden interest in El Dorado have anything to do with Jennie Madison?"

"Is it that obvious, Uncle Obadiah?"

"Well, I've noticed you've been spending a lot of time with her since meeting her at First Baptist Church."

"I'm trying to justify to myself that El Dorado might be a good place to start my law practice, and yes, to be perfectly truthful with you, Jennie Madison is stealing my heart away. I've never met anyone like Jennie. In fact, no girl has ever appealed to me as she has. I'm really confused! You might say I'm a lovesick puppy!"

"I do believe I see some of those characteristics," I said as I put my hand on his shoulder and laughed.

"I know it sounds crazy, but my heart and mind are constantly on Jennie."

"Alexander, I would be delighted to help you in locating a lawyer's position here in El Dorado. In fact, I have a good lawyer friend who is one of my patients. He mentioned to me a few weeks ago that he is thinking about adding a new staff member to his law firm. His name is Jack Spearman, and he is the only lawyer in El Dorado. I would be more than happy to introduce you to him."

"Do you really think you could get us together for a visit?"

"I believe I can arrange it. Whatever we do, we're going to have to act fast. Tomorrow is the day you and the others are scheduled to return to Prattville."

"That's why I want to know something now. If I have a chance of getting a job here, I want to stay in El Dorado."

"After lunch, we will break away for a few hours and drive into El Dorado to see Jack. If it looks promising, then you can make up your mind what you're going to do."

"That's sounds great to me, Uncle Obadiah. Oh, by the way, if I decided to stay, do you think I could stay with you until I get my feet on the ground?"

"Alexander, you are always welcome to stay with me and my family. Penelope, Mother, and the kids would love for you to spend time with us. We would be delighted!"

Our visit with Jack Spearman was successful. Jack hadn't found anyone, and he was very impressed with Alexander— so impressed that he offered Alexander a position in his law firm.

"Young man, your credentials are very impressive, and I feel you are just the person I've been looking for. Anyone related to my good friend Obadiah has to be a man of good character. Do you want to come to work for me?" Jack Spearman asked.

"When do you need me to start?" Alexander asked.

"How does next Monday sound to you?"

"That's fine with me!" Alexander said with excitement.

As Alexander and I left El Dorado, excitement was written all over his face. He looked at me and asked, "Uncle Obadiah, can we announce my decision tonight at dinner? I don't want to wait until tomorrow for everyone to find out I'm not returning to Prattville. I also need time to write Mother a letter explaining why I've chosen El Dorado to practice law. I'm sure Sarah won't mind hand-delivering my letter to Mother."

"I think that's a good idea. We will announce your decision at the dinner table tonight."

"Uncle Obadiah, thank you so very much for your help. I promise you, you won't be sorry you helped me. I won't let you down!"

"That's never crossed my mind. I told Penelope one time that I wish my entire family would move here to Union County. If you are right about the reconstruction, my brothers may want to sell out before all this mess hits. It's my belief that reconstruction may hit several of the plantations hard in Union County and the other counties. If that happens, there may be a number of good plantations and farms available, and perhaps, good bargains at that."

"Uncle Obadiah, I'm excited about my decision. This will give me an opportunity to practice law and at the same time find out where my relationship with Jennie is heading."

"Well, let me tell you. So far, those who have fallen in love here in El Dorado are very happy with each other and their marriages. If it's in God's plan, Jennie and your marriage should work as well."

"Uncle Obadiah, I wish I had some of your faith in God. You never seem to worry about anything."

"Alexander, I learned a long time ago that it doesn't do us any good to worry. In fact, the Bible teaches us that worrying is wrong. God's got everything under control. We just need to have faith that whatever happens was meant to happen. We then have to accept it and go on with our lives."

"I'm really going to try to develop that same faith, Uncle Obadiah!"

At dinner I asked for everyone's attention. "Since this is our last dinner together, I have a special announcement to make. I would like to announce that Alexander has decided to stay here in El Dorado and not return to Prattville. In fact, he accepted his first position with the Jack Spearman Law Firm today. He will start Monday of next week. I hope everyone here will join me in giving Alexander a hand of congratulations as he starts his career."

Dent stood and said, "Well, this is certainly a big surprise. I didn't know you were considering staying here."

"I feel it's the right thing for me," Alexander answered.

"I'm sure it is, Alexander. You are not tied to Prattville; you're single and free to do whatever you want. I must warn you, the young ladies around here seem to latch on to available young men like you."

"I have a feeling, one has already made her move on Alexander," Mother said as she got up from her chair and came over and gave Alexander a kiss on the cheek."

"I want to be the first one to say, I'm happy you are staying here with us. I wish everyone at this table would eventually move to El Dorado. It would be like old times. Just you remember my words. People move all the time. Several of you already have ties here; remember that!" she said as she looked directly at Dent and smiled.

Penelope stood and said, "Alexander, I'm happy about your decision. We can use another good lawyer in El Dorado. I have a feeling that Jack Spearman found the right person for the job. Congratulations!"

Alexander stood and thanked everyone for their congratulations and their support of him staying in El Dorado. He was also grateful for the opportunity to remain at Three Oaks until he got his feet on the ground.

After dinner, the ladies spent several hours packing for their early departure to Champagnolle. The steamboat is scheduled to depart at ten a. m.

The night hours passed too fast. When the roosters started crowing, I rolled over in bed, and Penelope was staring me straight in the face. "Good morning, Obadiah!"

"Good morning to you, my lovely Penelope!"

"This is going to be a big day," she said.

"Yes, it surely will be!"

"Do you think that it would be all right for me and the kids to accompany the family to Champagnolle? We've not been out of this house since before Christmas."

"That's a wonderful idea. It's going to be cold, you know!"

"I can get some blankets to wrap the kids in. They will enjoy the ride."

"I'll see Bill and make arrangements for another carriage."

Mother also wanted to make the trip to Champagnolle. She didn't mind the cold weather, so this wasn't going to be a problem for her.

We reached Champagnolle around 9:30, with plenty of time to get the baggage unloaded and checked for the journey back to Dallas and Autauga Counties. Everyone went into the small cafe at the port for hot chocolate and coffee. This was a change for Penelope and me, to have five little ones to look after.

As I looked around, I couldn't keep from thinking about Mother's encouragement for others of the family to move to El

Dorado. I decided right then I would ask God in my prayers to make this happen, providing it was in His will.

If hard times were to fall upon the Bradford family, especially during reconstruction, we would have a better chance to work through the difficulties if we were close to each other and were available to help each other. That is just plain common sense, I thought.

We all said our good-byes and watched the big steamboat leave the port with its whistles and smoke reaching high in the sky. It had been a wonderful Christmas season—one we'd all remember and cherish.

CHAPTER 35

The month of January, 1865, was the coldest month I had experienced since moving to El Dorado. Not only was it cold, we had two large snows, which complicated my getting to some of my patients who lived off the main country roads. I did my best, but on a few occasions, I had to wait until the snow melted to travel the small roads leading to their homes.

Penelope and Mother spend most of their time attending to the needs of Paul and Isabella. Charles and Belle are great helpers with the twins. But because of their other interests, they only help in short intervals.

James is a challenge. He's at the age where he expresses jealousy toward the twins. We are aware that his moods are normal for his age. In reality, he's still a baby, himself.

At times, Mattie and Betsy step in to help with the kids. They, too, are limited in time because of their meal preparations and housecleaning duties.

We've been receiving letters from my brothers and sisters in Autauga and Dallas Counties. They're doing well and experiencing basically the same type of weather we're experiencing here in Union County.

Alexander's mother was disappointed he didn't return to Prattville, but wants the best for him. Alexander is doing well in his new position with the Jack Spearman Law Firm. He's got plenty work to do, and Jack tells me that he believes he's found him a golden egg by hiring Alexander. Alexander and Jennie Madison's courtship is in full swing. I wouldn't doubt if wedding bells are not too far off. When I quiz Alexander about a possible marriage, he says, "I want to get my feet on the ground first, Uncle Obadiah."

The biggest news hitting our newspaper lately is the passing of the Thirteenth Amendment to the Constitution.

The *El Dorado News-Times* reported its passage in a recent article. According to the article, the Thirteenth Amendment, which formally abolished slavery in the United States, passed the Senate on April 8, 1864. However, the House at that time didn't follow suit.

On January 31, 1865, the House followed suit and passed the Thirteenth Amendment by a vote of 119 to 56.

President Abraham Lincoln immediately approved the Joint Resolution of Congress and submitted the proposed amendment to the state legislatures. The amendment now has to go to all of the existing states, minus the Southern Confederacy, for ratification. As soon as it is ratified by the required number of states, it will become the law of the land.

The Thirteenth Amendment to the United States Constitution provides that "neither slavery nor involuntary servitude, except as a punishment for crime, whereof, the party shall have been duly convicted, shall exist within the United States, nor any place subject to their jurisdiction."

In 1863, President Lincoln had issued the Emancipation Proclamation, declaring "all persons held as slaves within any State, or designated part of a State, the people whereof shall then be in rebellion against the United States, shall be then, thenceforward, and forever free." Nonetheless, the Emancipation Proclamation did not end slavery in the nation. Lincoln recognized that the Emancipation Proclamation would have to be followed by a constitutional amendment in order to guarantee the abolishment of slavery.

Everything is now set in place. Once the Civil War ends, slave states across the South will have to obey the Thirteenth Amendment.

I knew after the Emancipation Proclamation was passed in 1863 that President Lincoln would not give up until the U. S. Congress passed an amendment to the constitution to abolish slavery.

I pray daily God will speak to those in authority and convince them to come to their senses, swallow their foolish pride, and call this Civil War quits for the good of mankind.

The *El Dorado News-Times* continues to do a great job in keeping us informed on the happenings of the Civil War. Since January, there have been eleven battles fought in North Carolina, South Carolina, Virginia, and Florida. The Union has won ten out of eleven of these battles. The only battle the South won was the Battle of Natural Bridge near Tallahassee, Florida. This battle was fought on March 6, 1865. In this battle, the South was able to defeat the Union troops and prevent them from capturing the city of Tallahassee. Things continue to look bad for the Confederacy.

From talk I hear around El Dorado, "It's just a matter of time."

Recently, we've had a few soldiers return to El Dorado because of either desertion or wounds received from battles. Like most of the previous ones to return, these, too, will have some kind of handicap to live with for the rest of their lives.

From what I hear, those returning have been very vocal in speaking their opinions. They believe strongly that the South has lost the war and that General Robert E. Lee should surrender and stop this bloody war.

Many soldiers have deserted. They no longer believe the South can win. Every battle brings death to many. If they don't die, they are so crippled up they will never be able to plow behind a mule or horse again.

I was recently getting my hair cut at the local barber shop when I overheard a soldier say, "General Lee needs to recognize his limitations and stop this war. He needs to surrender. He needs to swallow his foolish pride. His pride continues to get more and more soldiers killed."

As I sat there listening to this soldier's words, I knew he was correct. We do need to surrender and concede that we've lost. I dread the consequences of our surrender, but I believe strongly it's time, and it's the thing to do.

Every plantation owner and farmer in Union County and the surrounding counties continue to prepare their fields for corn, cotton, and beans. We all are in hopes that our crops will be planted and harvested before our slaves are granted their freedom.

President Abe Lincoln recently won his second term as the president of the United States of America.

The El Dorado News-Times printed an account of President Lincoln's inauguration ceremony on March 4, 1865. I found it to be very interesting, since there were different parts of the inauguration address that gave reference to our Holy Bible.

President Lincoln used his second inaugural address to touch on the question of divine providence. He wondered what God's will might have been in allowing the war to come, and why it had assumed the terrible dimensions it had taken. He endeavored to address some of these dilemmas using allusions taken from the Bible.

President Lincoln reiterated the cause of the war was slavery. He went on to say, "Slaves constituted a peculiar and powerful interest. Everyone knew that this interest was somehow the cause of the war."

The phrase, "wringing their bread from the sweat of other men's faces" is an allusion to the fall of man in the Book of Genesis. As a result of Adam's sin, God told Adam that "by the sweat of thy face shall thou eat bread, till thou return unto the ground; for out of it was thou taken: for dust thou art, and unto dust shall thou return."

President Lincoln's phrase "but let us judge not, that we be not judged" is an allusion to the words of Jesus in Matthew 7:1, which in the King James Version reads, "Judge not, that ye be not judged."

President Lincoln quoted another of Jesus' sayings in Matthew: "Woe unto the world because of offenses; for it must be that offense cometh."

President Lincoln went on to suggest that the death and destruction wrought by the war was divine retribution to the U.S. for possessing slavery, saying that God may will that the war continue until every drop of blood drawn with the lash shall be paid by another drawn with the sword, and that the war was the country's "woe due." The quotation "The judgments of the Lord are true and righteous altogether" is from Psalm 19:9.

The closing paragraph on his inauguration speech contained two additional clauses from scripture: "Let us strive on to . . . bind up the nation's wounds" is a reworking of Psalm 147:3, and "to care for him who shall have borne the battle and for his widow and his orphan" relies on James 1:27.

After reading this part of President Lincoln's address, I felt compelled to put down my paper and pray.

My thoughts were on Lincoln's well-crafted words. What a brilliant man he must be! He had to put much time and thought into writing this great speech. When reading the excerpts from the newspaper, I found myself wishing I could have been there for his inaugural address. By his using the Bible to back up his speech, I'm convinced he is a Christian.

On April 8, I received a letter from my brother Dent:

> Dear Brother Obadiah,
>
> I'm afraid I bear bad news in this letter. You're probably aware by now that Selma has fallen to the Union Army. The good news is that my family is safe. We are still at Black Oaks going about our daily business. We are not leaving the plantation but find ourselves scared of what can happen should the Union soldiers come to Cahaba to forage for food and supplies.
>
> A friend came by Black Oaks and informed us of Selma being under attack by the Union forces led by General James H. Wilson. Everett and Law immediately wanted to go to Selma to help fight the Union Army. I put my foot down and refused to let them go. I am now so thankful I made that decision.
>
> We had heard for weeks that it was the Union's plan to capture Selma because of its arsenal and naval foundry. As you know, Selma has been a great asset to the Confederacy.
>
> The Battle of Selma was fought on April 2. Nathan Bedford Forrest was commander of the Confederate Army. He was greatly outnumbered. We've been told

that his 4,000 men were mostly young boys and old men. The Union Army consisted of 9,000 men. It's been told Forrest had been wounded the previous day at the Battle of Ebenezer Church and was in bad shape when he arrived in Selma. Although he was wounded and outnumbered, he and his men held Selma most of the day. It is reported that the Union lost 359 men and the South's loss was 2,700 men.

After realizing that the city could not be held, Bedford and others fled the city.

By taking Selma, General Wilson deprived the Confederacy of one of its last great manufacturing centers. His troops spent the next few days destroying the arsenal, machine shops, foundries, C. S. Navy facilities, and other factories in the city. After reaching their desired goal, they left Selma for Montgomery, Alabama. As you know that's just ten miles from Prattville. I'm worried that they will destroy the city of Prattville. As you know, Daniel Pratt has a big factory there.

Obadiah, I'm thinking really hard about selling Black Oaks and my share of Twin Oaks and moving to El Dorado. I'm serious about this. I want you to start looking for a farm. It doesn't have to be an established plantation like Three Oaks. I want something that I can make a decent living on. Without slaves, I don't want to own a large plantation when I might not have the manpower to farm it.

I bet you never thought I'd say this, did you? I'm sick of this Civil War and the effects it's having on people's lives. I know without any doubt, the South has lost this war. When General Robert E. Lee surrenders, we'll lose our slaves, as well as making major adjustments to our lifestyles.

Obadiah, Sarah and I miss Marion and Mary Catherine. We would like to live close to them so we could see them and our grandchildren. Mother isn't getting any younger and I would like to see her often as well.

251

I trust all is well with Marion and Mary Catherine. We've not heard anything lately from either of them.

Please give Mother and Penelope my regards and tell them we love them. I look forward to your reply.

Your brother,

Dent Bradford

The fall of Selma was a big surprise to me. Black Oaks is only about eight miles from Selma. I know Dent and his family had to be scared and disappointed when Selma fell to the Northern Army.

Dent and Sara attend First Baptist Church of Selma and spend a great deal of their time in Selma. This, perhaps, will change. I'm just praying that the Northern Army will not invade Cahaba and the plantations around Cahaba.

It appears that my prayers to God are working in respect to family members moving to El Dorado. I will start exploring the possibilities of finding some suitable property for Dent and, perhaps, John as well.

Alexander shared with me today that he and Jennie Madison have set a wedding date. They will be married on June 25, 1865.

Dr. Jim Burroughs shared with me today that he and Elizabeth are expecting their first child in November. This was great news as well! Naturally, I was pleased to hear the news and congratulated both of them accordingly.

I can't wait to tell Penelope and Mother the good news about Alexander and Jennie Madison's upcoming wedding, and about Jim and Elizabeth expecting their first child.

I know as soon as I share this news with Mother and Penelope, they will start planning a big celebration party for both couples at Three Oaks.

On April 10, I had just reached my office when I heard the big chapel bell ringing at First Baptist Church. Something of great importance had to be occurring. First Baptist Church only rings its bell on Sundays or for emergency reasons.

My staff joined me on the outside of my clinic as we observed people running up and down the street and around the courthouse. We then heard them screaming, "The war is over! The war is over! General Lee has surrendered at Appomattox. The war is finally over!"

We looked at each other, grabbed, and hugged each other as we joined in the celebration.

I had not received the morning edition of the *El Dorado News-Times.* I quickly walked across the street to the newspaper office, where I had to stand in line to purchase a copy. Sure enough, the *El Dorado News-Times* was carrying a news article about General Lee's surrender. I found out later, the newspaper was late getting out the morning edition because they wanted to include General Lee's surrender.

I quickly picked up my newspaper and hurried back to the office to read its account.

As I opened the paper, the headlines read, "The War is Over, General Robert E. Lee Surrenders to General Ulysses Grant at Appomattox Court House."

After a two-day engagement with the Union Army on April 8 at the Battle of Appomattox Station and the Battle of Appomattox Court House on April 9, 1865, General Robert E, Lee surrendered to General Ulysses Grant at Appomattox Court House.

When General Ulysses Grant of the Union Army and General Robert E. Lee of the Confederate Army met on April 9, 1865, at The McLean House in Appomattox the following agreement was approved by General Robert E. Lee:

In accordance with the substance of my letter to you on April 8, I propose to receive the surrender of the Army of North Virginia on the following terms, to wit: Rolls of all the officers and men to be made in duplicate. One copy to be given to an officer designated by me, the other to be retained by such officer, or officers, as you may designate.

The officers to give their individual paroles not to take up arms against the Government of the United States until properly exchanged, and each company or regimental commander sign a like parole for the men of their commands. The arms, artillery, and public property are to be parked and stacked, and turned over to the officer appointed by me to receive them.

This will not embrace the side-arms of the officers, nor their private horses or baggage. This done, each officer and man will be allowed to return to their homes, not to be disturbed by United States authority so long as they observe their paroles and the laws in force where they may reside.

The terms were agreed upon by General Lee. He felt the terms was generous and were the best he could hope for. He was thankful that the officers were allowed to keep their sidearms. In addition to his terms, Grant also allowed the defeated men to take home their horses and mules to carry out the spring planting and provided Lee with a supply of food rations for his starving army; Lee said it would have a very happy effect among the men and do much toward reconciling the country.

The terms of the surrender were recorded in a document handwritten by Grant's adjutant, Ely S. Parker, a Native American of the Seneca tribe, and completed around four o'clock p.m., April 9, 1865.

When General Lee discovered that Ely Parker was a Seneca Indian, he remarked, "It is good to have one real American here." Parker replied, "Sir, we are all Americans."

The treaty agreement accepted by General Lee came about when General Lee, himself, was surrounded by Union troops at Appomattox. When it was apparent to General Lee that he had no chance whatsoever in breaking through the Union's cavalry and two corps' advantage, he surrendered. He had no choice but to surrender. Any other decision would have brought slaughter to his North Virginia Army.

George Sawyer, the editor of the El Dorado News-Times, announced that the newspaper will focus on the battle and the surrender of General Robert E. Lee at Appomattox on a daily basis, as information is made available to him.

Robert E. Lee's surrender was the main topic of conversation in El Dorado. There is a lot of speculation about whether General Lee had the authority to surrender the entire Confederacy to the Union Army. The main question being asked, "Is the Civil War really over?"

If I know George Sawyer, the El Dorado News-Times will be finding out soon about what is taking place. Mr. Sawyer assured us that he and his staff are working hard in contacting other large newspapers, both in the North and South. Any information provided to them will be passed on to us as soon as it can be printed. He told us today, "My staff will be working around the clock to get you news about what's going on in Virginia and others parts of the South.

A few days later, a telegram came to the El Dorado News-Times announcing the assassination of President Lincoln on April 14.

George Sawyer put out a short leaflet on the court square announcing Lincoln's assassination. Mr. Sawyer felt it was important not to wait until the next edition of the newspaper came out.

The account of President Lincoln's assassination reads:

Shortly after 10:00 p. m. on April 14, 1865, actor John Wilkes Booth entered the presidential box at Ford's Theatre in Washington D.C. and fatally shot President Abraham Lincoln. As Lincoln slumped forward in his seat, Booth leapt onto the stage and escaped through the back door. A doctor in the audience rushed over to examine the unconscious President. Lincoln was then carried across the street to Petersen's Boarding House, where he died early the next morning.

I can't believe what I just read! How could this happen? Just as the war has ended, the man who played a major role in the beginning and the ending of the war is now dead. As I grieved his death, I asked myself over and over, What is coming next to our country? Will things ever get back to the way it was before the war? What's it going to take to pull our country together again?

I sat down behind my desk and began to pray. I asked God to show me what I needed to do to make freedom for my slaves a smooth transition. I don't want any of them to suffer. When our slaves are freed, we will see things happened that we have never experienced before. I know it's not going to be easy. I think it is going to be harder on them than on us plantation owners.

Over the next few weeks, the El Dorado News-Times revealed more about President Lincoln's assassination. The man, John Wilkes Booth, was shot and killed when he was trying to escape from Union soldiers. The whole country grieved the death of President Lincoln. As the nine-car funeral train carried President Lincoln home for burial in Springfield, Illinois, people showed up at train stations all along the way to pay their respects.

CHAPTER 36

By June, we'd seen little change in movement of slaves leaving their owners. The El Dorado News-Times has written a couple articles relating to the restructuring of state governments under the leadership of President Andrew Johnson.

President Johnson announced his plans for Reconstruction, which reflected both his staunch Unionism and his firm belief in States' rights.

In Johnson's view the Southern states had never given up their right to govern themselves, and the federal government had no right to determine voting requirements or other questions at the state level. Under Johnson's Presidential Reconstruction, all land that had been confiscated by the Union Army and distributed to the freed slaves by the army or the Freedmen's Bureau, which was established by Congress in early 1865, reverted to its prewar owners.

Apart from being required to uphold the abolition of slavery in compliance with the Thirteenth Amendment to the Constitution, swear loyalty to the Union, and pay off war debt, Southern state governments were given free rein to rebuild themselves.

As a result of Johnson's leniency, many Southern states in 1865 enacted a series of laws known as the "black codes," which were designed to restrict freed blacks' activity and ensure their availability as a labor force. These repressive codes enraged many in the North, including numerous members of Congress, which refused to seat congressmen and senators elected from the Southern states.

At this time, the Thirteenth Amendment was not being enforced in the Southern states. All the plantation owners in Union, Calhoun, and Columbia Counties decided to continue operating their plantations as though the Thirteenth Amendment hadn't been passed. Since Arkansas had not yet been readmitted to the Union, this gave the slave owners some time to adjust to what eventually would be forced upon them.

On June 18, I met with Penelope, Mother, Mattie, Big Jim, George, Bill, Betsy, and Hank.

The purpose of my meeting was to gain their advice on how I might best handle the transition of my slaves from being a slave to becoming a free person. I wanted to get their views on such items as sharecropping, working for a salary, and selecting a surname.

I discussed both the Emancipation Proclamation and the Thirteenth Amendment to the Constitution. I also gave my thoughts on when slaves in the South might be freed. I informed them that it was my understanding, that, before each Confederate State could be readmitted to the Union, it first had to ratify the Thirteenth Amendment.

I talked to them about their freedom and what some of the advantages and disadvantages were when they were set free. I wanted them to know, after they were freed, there would be some difficult times ahead. Jobs and food would be scarce, and a decent place to live would be hard to find.

I told them that every slave I owned would have a place to live and food to eat as long as they stayed at Three Oaks.

I shared with them that, at the present time, slaves were still under the ownership of their plantation owners. I wasn't able to give them a time when this might end or a time that they would gain full rights as a free person.

We also talked about selecting a surname, for legal purposes. If they chose to do this, I would engage Alexander to draw up the necessary paperwork to make their names legal. After they became free and purchased property, they would need a full name for the property deeds, credit, and other things. I emphasized that one's identity would be a part of their lives in years to come. It would mean everything to them.

I ended my talk by reemphasizing that my slaves have a place to live, with ample food, and certain freedoms.

At this time, I asked for their input.

"Please let me hear your thoughts," I said.

I looked around the room and noticed that everyone was looking at each other as if they didn't know who should start the conversation. Finally, my faithful and dedicated servant Bill raised his hand.

"Bill, what is it that you'd like to say?" I asked.

"Master Bradford, I believe I understood everything you talked about here tonight. I've been fortunate over the years to have a nice family to love me and appreciate the work I do. I'm an old man now, and I certainly don't want to start over again. I guess I'm trying to say, I want to stay here with you and your family, Master Bradford. I want to continue doing the same thing I've been trained to do. When this paper of freedom comes, I will feel good about it. But meanwhile, I'm one hundred percent sure the Bradfords are my family. I want to continue to live here at Three Oaks if you will have me."

"Thank you, Bill! I appreciate your remarks, and you will always be a part of the Bradford family. You will always have a home with us here at Three Oaks, as long as you desire one," I said as my eyes swelled with tears. As I looked around, Mother and Penelope were crying as well.

"Master Obadiah, I'd like to say something," George said.

"What would you like to say, George?"

"As you are aware, me and my family have been with the Bradford family most of our lives. The Bradfords are our family. You have always treated us fairly. As you know, I am now a grandfather and soon to be a grandfather again. My family is growing, and we want to stay put and live here at Three Oaks if you will grant that! El Dorado will be our home, and as Bill said, when those freedom papers come, we're going to be happy about that, but we want to stay here and work for you."

"George, thank you for those well-stated words."

The next person with a hand going up was Hank.

"Obadiah, I will always be grateful for the trust you showed in me when you made me your overseer. How many white plantation owners have a colored man as their overseer? I am, indeed, indebted to you, my loyal and good friend.

"My family wants to stay here in El Dorado and work here at Three Oaks. I want to preach the word of God as well, and I hope you will allow me the freedom and time to find me a church in El Dorado. You and I have talked about this before. I would like very much to proceed with these plans. I'm praying that you will be able to help me in this endeavor."

"Thank you, Hank! Indeed I will help you find a church in El Dorado."

Mattie was the next person to raise her hand.

"Obadiah, I'm speaking for Big Jim as well. I've longed for the day to receive my freedom and the freedom of my family. I know that time is near, and I appreciate you explaining why it's not here right now. When it comes, I don't think I'll know the difference. You see, where your family and home is, that's where your heart is also. We've been a part of the Bradford family for a good while now, and that's the way we want it to be. Where else can we go? Where else can we find good people like you, Mrs. Catherine, and my lovely daughter, Penelope?

"I hope we'll always be family. God has given me three children of my own, a great husband, and five of the sweetest grandchildren anyone could ask for. Why would I want to up and leave a wonderful family? We have our home and family right here at Three Oaks. We'd love to stay right here and be a part of this wonderful family!"

"Mattie, you are a jewel. I have loved you as long as I've loved your beautiful daughter. You will always be welcome in our home!"

The next hand that went up was that of Betsy.

"Master Bradford, you better not even thinks about getting rid of me. I will die and come back to haunt you if you do that!" she said as everyone laughed.

"The Bradfords are my family. You're the only family I've ever known. I've been with Mrs. Catherine since I was about twenty years old. That's a long time, I'm telling you! I'm too old to go looking for a man. If I wanted a man, I'd want Bill. He's probably one of the most educated colored men in El Dorado," she said, clapping her hands and laughing.

Everyone, except for my wife and Mother, had spoken. Everything had gone better than I expected. I looked at Mother and Penelope and said, "Do either of you have anything you'd like to say?"

Mother raised her hand and said, "I am so proud of all of you. I'm proud because all of you have a place in my heart. I've known for some time that the Civil War would end and we'd have to make some big decisions in regard to what Obadiah talked to us about tonight.

"I'm so happy that you feel the way you do, and I'm so proud that you would all stay here with us at Three Oaks. I know my son well enough to know that he's spoken with love, honesty, and hope. There isn't any doubt in my mind or heart that we can and will remain as one big happy family. We love and trust each other, and that's the way God would want it to be. Just know that as long as Obadiah has Three Oaks, we all will have a roof over our heads and plenty to eat. I have a strong feeling that after things settle down, Three Oaks will again make money and lots of it. I know Obadiah will be generous and share some of those profits with those who help him. Thank you for being a big part of my life!" Mother said as she began to cry.

Penelope rose from her chair and put her hand on Mother's shoulder to comfort her. She looked down at Mother and said, "We all love you, Catherine!"

She kept standing as she continued to speak eloquently. "I too have given this time period in our lives a great deal of pondering lately. I've read everything I can lay my hands on trying to keep up with the weekly happenings in Washington, D.C, the North, and what's going on in the South. I see the bureaus being established by the federal government, and hear that this time period will offer great opportunities to the colored man to become involved in politics and government.

"I'm not naive enough to think this is suddenly going to happen. Things don't work that way. I do think that many opportunities will be afforded to all colored men who work hard to achieve goals in life. I do think that the educated slave has an opportunity to someday project himself right to the top in politics.

"Obadiah and I have been thinking and talking a lot about my ambition of starting a colored school in El Dorado. If our people are to prosper, they must first be educated. They must know how to read, write, and do arithmetic. Those are the things I want to teach them. It will be up to them if they want this.

"Obadiah has a site in mind on the south side of El Dorado. There are more slaves living there than anywhere else, other than the plantations. He will help me get started. I've visited with Nellie and Nanny, and both of them have offered to be my assistants. I'm really excited about this possibility.

"Hank, I, too, look forward to you starting your own church in El Dorado. This is going to be very important in the reconstruction period, especially for the colored folks."

Penelope was given a standing ovation by those in the room. They see her as a slave who has made good in life. She is looked upon as being a pillar to all the slaves. She and Mother have been there for all the slaves who have suffered from colds and other sickness, as well as birthing babies. They have risked their own health for those in need.

I still think I'm a very lucky man, especially to have a wife like Penelope. She is full of knowledge and understanding. She has the ability to feel others' pain and to respond to their needs. She is as beautiful inside as she is on the outside. I feel strongly she will become known as the founder of the strongest colored school in our town.

As we finished the meeting, Mattie and Betsy brought in refreshments for everyone. While we were enjoying the refreshments, Hank walked over to me and said, "Obadiah, why don't you let me and George meet with our slaves. I know you have lots to do. I would like to do that for you. I've made a list of everything you shared with us, and I believe George and I can get them together and answer any questions they might have. If this will help you, we don't mind doing it."

"Hank, I appreciate you and George taking on that responsibility. You are both well respected, and I feel certain you can get my points across. What I need for you to do, first, is to contact each family, or single member, and have each of them select a surname. A name they will have for the rest of their lives. You and I have talked about this before. I believe you've been working on this.

"I also need a good count of those who may want to leave Three Oaks when Arkansas ratifies the Thirteenth Amendment and is readmitted to the United States of America. I need to know how many able-bodied men and women I can count on when I decide to plant certain field crops.

"My brother-in-law, Virgil Shamrock, who manages the only cotton gin in El Dorado, owned by Daniel Pratt of Prattville, Alabama, says that Mr. Pratt is planning on building two sawmills, near Mt. Holly and Norphlet. If, indeed, he follows through and builds those sawmills, the additional revenues for Three Oaks would be a small fortune. We have several acres of virgin pine just waiting to be cut. This could be an answer to the downturn of prices for cotton and corn products."

"That's good news, Obadiah. I've wondered why someone hadn't thought of timber production in Union County. Camden, which is not far from here, is doing well with their large sawmill. They have the advantage of shipping their logs and lumber to other parts of the country by way of the Ouachita River. It makes sense to build sawmills in areas where there is an abundance of virgin pine," Hank said.

CHAPTER 37

The day Alexander has been looking forward to for several months has finally arrived. He and Jennie Madison will be exchanging their wedding vows today at First Baptist Church in El Dorado.

After the wedding reception, they will leave for Champagnolle, where they will board the steamboat for New Orleans, where they will spend their honeymoon.

We are so blessed to have Jennie Madison coming into the Bradford family. She's a jewel of a lady. She's a very talented musician, and has been very active at First Baptist playing the organ and piano. She and Alexander are dedicated Christians.

I've been thinking a lot about Penelope's remarks at Three Oaks a few nights back. She made mention that there would be opportunities for colored as well as newcomers to be elected to a new legislature in Arkansas. The more I think on the subject, I could see Hank, Alexander, Marion, and Benjamin Madison as representatives, or maybe senators in the new legislature. We will need some strong representation from Union County to make sure El Dorado gets their share of what's coming down the road, so to speak.

As soon as Alexander comes back from his honeymoon, I plan to explore with him and the others the possibility of getting involved in politics, either on the county or state level. We need good, strong, reliable leadership. We need politicians who will be fair and open minded in crafting and passing realistic reconstruction laws.

Another pressing issue I must attend to is Dent's request to look for available land in Union County. I've been so busy lately, I've neglected his request.

Alexander and Jennie's wedding was absolutely beautiful. Their wedding brought people from all over the county and some as far away as Alabama. Alexander's mother, Susan Ragland, from Prattville, was able to be here. This was the first time we'd seen her in years. Susan came by herself because her husband, Michael Ragland, was having some heart issues. His doctor recommended he not make the trip.

Susan is very friendly and never seems to meet a stranger. I believe that's where Alexander gets his personality traits.

During her stay in Union County, she chose to spend her time at Mary and Virgil's home. She and Mary were close friends when they were growing up in Autauga County.

During the reception, I was fortunate to have a conversation with Melody, the widow of the late Silas Arlington. Before Silas died, he owned and operated a six-hundred acre plantation six miles from Camden and about five miles from Three Oaks.

Silas was one of the first patients I called on upon my arrival to El Dorado. When I first met him, I was able to relieve Silas of severe pain in his right hip. He had broken his hip in a horse accident. I was able to operate on his hip and reset it to relieve his pain. He became one of my most supportive patients and friends.

While visiting with Melody, she asked me if I knew anyone who might be interested in buying her plantation.

"Obadiah, I need some advice from you. Since Silas passed away, I have found the plantation to be a big responsibility. I'm afraid I won't be able to keep the plantation. I've tried hard, but things are just not working for me.

"I'm not getting any younger, and George, my son, who is mentally handicapped, isn't able to do much around the plantation. My daughter, Susan, is now married and lives in Camden with her husband, Ben. They have a son and another child on the way. You might say, it's just George and me now!"

Melody continued to share her deepest fears about the ending of the Civil War and not knowing how much longer she would have access to her slaves.

"I know, without a doubt, I couldn't keep the plantation when my slaves are freed. I ask myself every night why a widow woman needs a six hundred–acre plantation."

As Melody kept on sharing with me, it hit me that this six hundred–acre plantation might fit into Dent's plans.

"Anyway, Obadiah, I'm sorry if I'm boring you with my troubles, but since you know about everyone around here, I was wondering if you knew someone who might be interested in buying my plantation."

"Melody, you are not boring me, not at all! I might know someone who would be interested in visiting with you about the plantation. Can you give me a week or so to check this out?"

"You take as long as you need. My slaves have already planted most of the crops, and I'm not planning on leaving these parts any time soon. If I sell my plantation, George and I will be moving to Camden to be close to my daughter and her family."

After the reception, Bill, Penelope, and I took Alexander and Jennie in our carriage to Champagnolle to catch the steamboat to New Orleans.

On our way home, Penelope spent most of our time talking about the wedding.

She said, "At our wedding, I didn't know if everyone would be receptive to me being your wife. I prayed all the time that all would go well and we'd get to the part of saying our vows and the preacher would say, 'I now pronounce you husband and wife.' That's when I really felt comfortable being Mrs. Obadiah Bradford. Today was completely different. I was so relaxed. I was having fun watching Alexander and Jennie show genuine affection for each other. I guess when you're not personally involved, it's just different. Do you understand what I'm saying?"

"Oh, yes, I do! You are saying you weren't really certain you wanted to marry me!" I said with a smirk on my face!

Penelope's mouth flew open and the strangest look came over her face.

"What are you saying? I didn't mean to imply that I was dreading marrying you. In fact, I think I would have just dropped dead with disappointment if you had backed out of our marriage. Are you kidding around with me, Obadiah?"

I took her in my arms and whispered, "I love you, so very much, Penelope. I just had to have a little fun with you!"

She took my hand and put it across her heart and said, "I want you to feel my heart beating. You almost caused me to have a heart attack!"

"Like I said, I was only poking a little fun at you!"

"Obadiah, you will always be my man. You are my life, my encourager, my one and only soulmate. I shall never want any man in my life except for you. You remember that, my love!"

The next few weeks were extremely busy for us at the clinic.

Spring has brought on spring allergies, tick and mosquito bite infections, as well as the common cold. We are having some cases of pneumonia as well.

We have seen an increase in birthing babies. I'm guessing this is due to soldiers coming home from the war early and the influx of freed slaves moving into the south side of El Dorado. Several babies are being born on the plantations as well.

The Freedom Bureau has purchased up land on the south side of town to build slave homes for those slaves who have already been freed. Some slaves have moved here from other parts of the South. The Freedom Bureau chose El Dorado as a town they felt had the most to offer slaves after they were freed.

Penelope and Alexander have been negotiating for the first Negro school in El Dorado. If they are successful in obtaining support from the Freedom Bureau, Penelope will be the first education director and teacher. She is very excited about the possibility.

I, for one, think this will be good for Penelope. She is so intelligent and is a fantastic teacher. She has taught Nanny and Nellie everything they know. They will be assisting her in teaching colored children. She's got it all worked out in her head.

I believe it will be good for Penelope to be involved in this reconstruction process. She has so much to offer. Our kids are in good hands at Three Oaks. Mother, Mattie, and Betsy have already given Penelope their blessings and are more than ready to offer their service in taking care of our children.

Every time I go to deliver a baby, I take Marion with me. As of late, I've let him deliver all the babies being born. Every now and then we will have a breech baby, and I take on that responsibility. Someday I will let Marion handle that procedure as well.

Marion has grown so much in his knowledge of being a doctor. He studies all the time when he's not working. He is working so hard to become a good doctor. He and Lindy are expecting their first baby in October.

Since writing Dent about Melody Arlington's plantation, I've learned about another plantation that joins Melody's. It has five hundred acres. The plantation is owned by another widow, named Janet Saunders. Mrs. Saunders husband died last winter of pneumonia.

Mrs. Saunders is now left alone, except for her house servants and field slaves. She's fearful that if she doesn't sell soon, her property will be worthless should her slaves be freed.

Mrs. Saunders is not like Melody. She was totally dependent on her husband to manage and make all the financial decisions for the plantation. She is hurting financially and fears that if she waits any longer, she might have to sell her plantation for fifty cents an acre. Someone has really put a scare in her.

I'm thinking that Dent and John's property in Autauga and Dallas Counties will carry a value of three times the value of property here in Union County. It is my educated guess that they could purchase both properties and still have lots of money to live on.

I have visited with Mrs. Saunders, and she has expressed a dollar amount for her property. I felt that her asking price was fair, but explained to her that it depends a lot on when Arkansas ratifies the Thirteenth Amendment and is readmitted to the United States of America.

I explained to her that I couldn't speak for those who might be interested, but I would like a rock-bottom price should they think her asking price was unreasonable. She paused a minute, and said, "Dr. Bradford, I will take two thousand dollars less than my asking price, if it comes to that, but not a penny less."

Today, I received that much-welcome letter from Dent.

Dear Obadiah,

I apologize to you in not getting back with you sooner. I've been working with John on a solution that's best for us. Since I own half of Twin Oaks, I have to consider what's best for both of us.

We both have come to the same conclusion. We want to move to El Dorado, Arkansas. The hardest thing we've ever done was to approach your good friend, Daniel Pratt, to see if he was still interested in purchasing Twin Oaks. I have an excellent offer for Black Oaks and need to move on it fast.

Anyway let me return to Daniel Pratt. He's jumped at the opportunity to purchase Twin Oaks and is agreeable to give us market value. He's fully aware of the quality of land at Twin Oaks. As you are well aware, he's wanted Twin Oaks for years. He is ready to proceed.

Let me say that John and I are excited about the six-hundred-acre plantation near Camden. We have agreed to commit to that plantation and later look for property near Mrs. Arlington's plantation for John. He is fully in agreement with me on this proposal.

Daniel Pratt says he's very much interested in purchasing our slaves at Twin Oaks. He's fully aware that it's only a matter of time before the Thirteenth Amendment will set slaves free, but he knows when that comes about, he will have a laboring force already in place in continuing the everyday operation of the plantation.

Daniel Pratt says he understands that the Thirteenth Amendment to the Constitution has to be ratified by each of the Confederate States before that state can be readmitted to the U.S. of America. He says, "Who knows when that's going to be?"

Obadiah, is your understanding of the Thirteenth Amendment the same as Daniel Pratt's? If he's right, it could take years for all of the Confederate states to ratify the Thirteenth Amendment and be readmitted back into the United States.

We'd like for you to negotiate the deal with Mrs. Arlington for us. We trust your judgment. I've already told you that Daniel Pratt is prepared to pay us market value for Twin Oaks. We will have more than enough funds to purchase Mrs. Arlington's plantation. This doesn't include the money I'll get from selling Black Oaks. Who knows, I might be able to pay you back and still become a rich man!

If you don't mind, we'd like for you to telegram us as soon as possible and let us know what's going on. We want to know what you think of Daniel Pratt's offer. We need your blessings on this because, in all reality, you still own half of Twin Oaks.

I know this is a busy time for you, but we don't want Mrs. Arlington's six hundred acres to fall into the hands of someone else, especially the Freedom Bureau. We are afraid the way the Freedom Bureau is buying up land to give to the freed slaves they just might buy Mrs. Arlington's property.

John and I appreciate you, Little Brother, and look forward to hearing from you in a telegram soon.

Your big brother,
Dent Bradford

Because of the urgency of Dent's request, I decided to get together a proposal for both plantations. I enlisted the help of Alexander and Jack Spearman to help with legal proposals.

Jack's law firm has experience in drawing up contracts and knows what the fair market price of land is in Union County.

Upon the completion of their work I'll carry an offer to both Melody Arlington and Janet Saunders for their decision.

In the meanwhile, I sat down and wrote out a lengthy telegram of what I knew about Mrs. Arlington's and Mrs. Saunders' property. I advised John and Dent that I felt the land was very valuable, and like Three Oaks, both plantations had lots of tall, virgin pines.

At this point I informed them about what I was hearing about Daniel Pratt's intentions on building sawmills in these areas. I also informed them that Camden already had a larger sawmill in place and was shipping their lumber by barge up and down the Ouachita River.

My advice was for them to decide on making an offer on both plantations. Since the two plantations joined each other, they could partnership in different ways. Between Mrs. Arlington's six hundred acres and Mrs. Saunders five hundred aces, they would end up with eleven hundred acres. Since the plantations bordered each other, this would be an ideal situation.

Upon finishing, I went to the telegram office and sent the telegram. I informed Dent when I received the legal proposals from Jack Spearman's law firm, I would mail them a copy. This negotiation of property wasn't going to be completed in a matter of a week. If all parties are interested and can agree, John and Dent will have to make arrangements to come to El Dorado to sign the official deeds and sale agreements.

The only thing I worried about was that all parties already planted their fall crops. How will this play out in the long run, and what about the slaves?

I would hope that John and Dent will bring their own slaves with them. I know John's slaves from my time spent at Twin Oaks. They were once my slaves. I hated to leave them behind, but knowing they would be working for my brother, it made sense to leave them on the plantation to help with harvesting the crops. I would feel bad if either John or Dent negotiated their slaves into their selling price. When it comes time to make the final decision, I will encourage them not to do that.

I decided early on not to share any of my correspondence with Mother. I don't want to get her hopes up should this fall through. I have shared this with Penelope, and she's so excited.

Her remarks were, "Obadiah, this will make Catherine one of the happiest mothers in the world. She'll be getting her wish.

She won't have Sarah and Tanyua here, but she will have all three of her sons right here in Union County.

"I've been thinking! Since Jim Crawford, Sarah's husband, is Daniel Pratt's financial officer, he might let him come to El Dorado to oversee the building and management of those sawmills you've been talking about. Wouldn't that be wonderful?"

"You know, Penelope, I've been thinking the same thing. We have lived together long enough that we're beginning to think alike."

"Obadiah, you're just being polite to me!"

"No, I meant what I said as a compliment. You have a good financial mind. If I was Daniel Pratt, I would send someone like Jim here to manage those new sawmills."

Two weeks passed before I got Dent's answer to my telegram. His response came in a letter.

> Dear Brother Obadiah:
> I'm sorry for the delay of getting back to you. I know you must think we've been dragging our feet here, but I'm learning that we can't snap our fingers and expect everything to go our way in a short period of time. It has taken us awhile to work through this deal with Daniel Pratt in regard to Twin Oaks. I'm telling you the truth this man is a shrewd business man. I don't think I've ever run onto someone like him. He doesn't budge an inch!
>
> One big obstacle has been the slaves. John didn't want to sell his slaves to Pratt. He said, "I know what I have in my slaves and I want to take them with me. I don't think I could bear leaving them behind for Daniel Pratt."
>
> Daniel Pratt didn't like this part of the negotiation. He held out on making us an offer until yesterday. I think he thought John would change his mind, but John stood tall and strong.
>
> Obadiah, John wants you to make Mrs. Saunders a market value offer on her five hundred acres. He's

instructed me to tell you to offer her market value unless you can talk her down a little. He's leaving it totally in your hands.

I want you to handle the purchase of Mrs. Arlington's plantation for me. John and I are excited. I believe these plantations have a lot to offer each of us. From what you've described, we have ample cleared land for cotton, corn, and other products, plus those large virgin pines we can harvest. Who knows, we might make a small fortune in the lumber business if we play our cards right.

Obadiah, I'm in the process of selling Black Oaks to a Jonathan Marvel, a big time plantation owner from Georgia. He offered me market value for Black Oaks. I too have decided to take my slaves to El Dorado.

Sarah said, "It just wouldn't be right in the eyes of God to abandon our slaves and leave them with some stranger who was coming from Georgia."

As usual, my Sarah was right. Mr. Marvel didn't throw a fit like Daniel Pratt. He said he would bring his own slaves.

Oh, by the way, have you mentioned any of this to Mother? If you haven't, don't right now. If this all goes through we want it to be a surprise to her when we come to El Dorado to sign the deeds.

Your brother,
Dent Bradford

I'm relieved John and Dent decided to keep their slaves. This headed off a potential disagreement with my brothers. We can now move on with the negotiations.

I will speak to Alexander tomorrow about the progress of the two purchase proposals for Melody Arlington and Janet Saunders. In my opinion, things look good.

I am getting excited about John's and Dent's families moving to Union County. My prayers again have been answered. As it turns out, their plantations will be only about five to six miles from where I live.

Mother will be so excited to know her older two sons will soon be close to her. She's missed out on seeing their children grow into nice young men and women. She will now be able to see them often. If I know Mother, she will plan several social events to bring the Bradfords close together. She once said, "The more the Bradfords, the more power and voice we have in government."

God is good! He is good all the time!

CHAPTER 38

Alexander sent word this morning that he'd completed the proposals on Mrs. Arlington's and Mrs. Saunders' properties. He asked if we might meet at Jake's Restaurant for lunch and discuss the proposals.

After we finished a light lunch, Alexander handed me the two proposals. "I'm going next door to Virgil and Mary's to get an item for Jennie. While I'm gone, you can read through the proposals to see if there are any changes I need to make. The two proposals are basically the same, except for the selling prices. When I get back, you can tell me if you want anything changed."

While Alexander was away, I read through each agreement and found everything in good order. The proposals were professionally done.

I will now have Alexander make copies. I will go to Melody's plantation to see if she accepts the proposal. I will do the same when I go to Janet Saunders. If both ladies agree to the proposals, I will send both to John and Dent. I'll ask them to send me a telegram giving me the authority to pursue drawing up the legal deeds.

Upon their agreeing, they will make a trip here to meet with Melody and Janet to sign the official papers.

Alexander returned to Jake's Restaurant, looked at me with his elbows resting on the dining table, and asked, "Well, do the proposals meet with your approval?"

"Yes, they do, Alexander. You have done a great job. I feel certain both John and Dent will be pleased."

"I did my best, Uncle Obadiah. I want to see Uncle John and Uncle Dent move to El Dorado. It's going to be nice having them and their families close to us."

"You will need to send me a bill or bring one by my office for your services," I said as I reached across the table and shook his hand.

"Payment is made in full, Uncle Obadiah!" he said as he smiled.

"Alexander, you can't make a living doing charitable work for your uncle. I don't feel right not paying you!"

"This is my way of giving back a little for the generosity you and Penelope showed me while I was getting my feet on the ground. You and Penelope provided lodging for me for months before I had the money to purchase a house here in El Dorado. You didn't charge me a penny. This is the least I can do."

"I love you, Alexander. I'm so grateful God has planted you here. We are fortunate to have a man of your skills living right here in El Dorado. It's an honor to have you as my nephew."

"Thank you, Uncle Obadiah. That means a lot to me."

"How are things going with you and Jennie?"

"Great! Things couldn't be better. We are not doing anything to prevent getting pregnant. We both want to get our family started, rather quickly."

"Please let me know if I can do anything for you," I said.

"You have done enough already, Uncle Obadiah."

"One other thing before you leave. Have you given any thought to running for a county or state political office in the upcoming November election?"

"Yes, I have! Jennie and I have discussed it more than once. Marion, Benjamin, and I visited about this subject yesterday while having lunch here at Jake's. I believe we are interested but don't have enough information right now to plan any type of political strategies.

"I'm checking with the Arkansas State Government's legislative branch to find out how many representatives and senators will be certified for south Arkansas. Also, we've talked about the local races as well. We've heard rumors that the sheriff, prosecuting attorney, the county judge, and the mayor's office are going to be up for grabs.

"We are all in agreement that Virgil needs to be our next mayor. He would be excellent. He is well known, and everyone loves Virgil."

"You know, I agree with you on Virgil. Virgil would make an excellent mayor. I may encourage him to run. What a great idea!

"Tomorrow, I'll drive to Melody Arlington's and Janet Saunders's plantations. After they review the proposals, agree on the terms, and sign off, I'll return to El Dorado. I'll bring signed copies to you, and you can make copies to be mailed to John and Dent for their approval.

"If they agree, I'll set up a time for Melody, Janet, John, and Dent to meet at your office and put the finishing touches to the sale of these properties. By the way, I'm assuming that both plantations have legal abstracts and deeds?"

"Yes, I've checked that, and all is in order."

"Take care, Alexander! We'll get together soon. Give my regards to Jennie."

My visits to Mrs. Arlington and Mrs. Saunders were successful. They were very impressed with the offers and signed off on the agreements. I explained to them that I would mail the proposals to my brothers, John and Dent, for their approval.

"If they approve, I will make arrangements for all four of you to meet at Jack Spearman's law office to finalize the sale."

I returned to town and mailed the proposals to John and Dent. The major part of the job had been completed. We had an acceptance from Mrs. Arlington and Mrs. Saunders. We would now wait for the approval from Dent and John.

These past few weeks have been busy and demanding. I've had to shift several of my patient appointments to Dr. Burroughs. He's been really busy doing his work, as well as mine.

Penelope and I have been discussing how we can keep John's and Dent's visits a surprise from Mother. Last night, Penelope came up with a great idea.

We have been talking about a time to have a big celebration at Three Oaks to honor Marion and Lindy, Benjamin and Mary Catherine, and Dr. Jim and Elizabeth Burroughs. All three couples are expecting the births of their babies within the next three months. This will be the first baby for Marion and Lindy, and Jim and Elizabeth, but the second for Benjamin and Mary Catherine.

During the celebration, John and Dent will show up as a surprise. This should work if we play our cards right.

We know how much Mother likes to entertain and plan special occasions.

By the middle of August, the weather was hot and dry. August is certainly living up to its reputation of being the hottest month of the year. We've had only one rain, and the cotton and corn crops are suffering from lack of rain. If we don't get rain soon, I'm afraid the dry weather will severely take a toll on our key money crops. I suppose I need to pray harder for rain. We need it badly!

On August 17, I received Dent's long letter.

Dear Obadiah,

I apologize for taking so long to respond to your proposal on Mrs. Arlington's property. Just when I thought everything was in order to close on Black Oaks, Mr. Jonathan Marvel from Georgia, asked for more time. What could I do?

He was still interested but was having trouble getting his financial business in order to finalize our agreement. He asked me for five additional days, and I agreed. He was a man of his word and just yesterday, we closed on Black Oaks. I don't know what my decision would have been if the deal had fallen through.

Obadiah, John and I have agreed that we will arrive at Champagnolle on the afternoon of August 23rd. We will spend the night with Mary Catherine and Benjamin and close on the 24th. How does that sound to you? We will be available to surprise Mother on the evening of the 24th.

We look forward to signing the papers on our new plantations and making plans to join y'all in El Dorado sometime after the crops are harvested in October.

Let me know if these plans are in line with what you are planning. I'm making sure Mary Catherine doesn't tell Mother of our coming. We will need transportation from Champagnolle on August 23rd.

I look forward to hearing from you.

Your big brother,

Dent Bradford

Penelope and Mother immediately went to work planning the big celebration for the twenty-fourth. All plans have to be completed in six days. This was a short time frame, but I have confidence that Penelope and Mother will have everything ready.

I'm excited that everything has been set in place. It appears to me that God, again, has worked things out for the Bradfords. Once again, the Bradford boys will be living in close proximity to each other in Union County. This is going to be one of the best pieces of news Mother has received in years.

Thank you, God, for answering our prayers! Now, Lord, do you think you could send us some much-needed rain?

On August 23, God answered my prayer. We had a big rainfall on Union County. It was a soaker. It came down all day long. It was a slow rain, which really helped.

Mary Catherine is so excited about her family moving to Union County. She will accompany me to Champagnolle to welcome her father and John. They will be staying at her house tonight, and after completing all the legal work on the twenty-fourth, they will join us at Three Oaks for the big celebration and to surprise Mother.

August 23 is going to be a busy day. I awakened early, got dressed and joined Penelope, Mother, and the kids at the break-fast table. I hate it when I get in a rush. I'm always forgetting something. I quickly finished my breakfast, gave the kids hug and kisses, and returned to the bathroom to brush my teeth.

As I opened the front door I felt a gentle hand touch me on my shoulder. Penelope was right behind me. She joined me on the front porch as we waited for Bill to bring my carriage around. As we stood there, she brushed lint from my coat and gave me a kiss and hug.

Penelope can always tell when I am uptight. She practices doing extra nice things for me when she knows I am under stress. This morning was no exception. Her kiss almost changed my mind about going to work. She drives me crazy at times. If there were ever two people made for each other, it is certainly Penelope and me.

"Obadiah, it's going to be all right. You go on to work, and when you get home tonight, we will turn in early and get a good night's rest. Maybe I'll have a nice surprise for you, if you'll be good," she said with a devious look in her beautiful, blue eyes.

"Do you smell that pork roasting?" Penelope asked.

I had been so busy, I hadn't taken time to smell the wonderful fragrance coming from the pits near the oak trees. I took a deep breath and smelled it.

"It does smell good, doesn't it?"

"It certainly does. Big Jim and George have been working on the meat since yesterday. It should be good and tender."

Bill brought my carriage around. I had gotten so caught up with Penelope that I had forgotten my medicine bag.

"Obadiah!" Penelope screamed! "You forgot your bag," she said, as she quickly stepped down the steps and handed it to me.

"Thank you, my darling!"

"You have a wonderful day, my love."

As I drove away, I felt I was the luckiest man alive. God has provided my every need. Penelope provides everything I need in a woman. She is the reason I laugh, smile, and sometimes sing. She is truly my soulmate, and the reason I live. God, thank you for my woman!

My day at the office went fast. There was no time for boredom. My business has grown so fast. I am getting patients from as far away as Camden and Junction City, Arkansas. I will be so happy when Marion gets his doctor's certification. That will be a big blessing for all of us. Our patient load should decrease and make things easier.

I attribute a big portion of my growth in my patient load to my reputation of being the traveling doctor. The word of mouth from my patients, both inside and outside the county, has been good advertisement for me. My willingness to call on sick folks who have transportation problems has promoted my business tremendously.

At 3:30 p.m., Mary Catherine and I made our way to the carriage for our journey to Champagnolle to pick up Dent and John.

Mary Catherine asked me earlier on if she could ride with me in the driver's seat so we could talk and enjoy the beautiful scenery together on the way to the Champagnolle.

"Are you sure you can make it up here?" I asked.

"With a little help, I believe I can, Uncle Obadiah."

"All right, let's see if we can get you up here," I said as I reached out my hand and took hers. She placed her right foot on the first step of the carriage, and up she came. It didn't take her long to get herself situated in the front seat.

"You did that better than I thought you'd do, Mary Catherine."

"Benjamin made me a small stepstool to use when I get in our carriage. We use it wherever we go. With his help, I've been doing well. I may be getting big, but I'm healthy and very strong, at that," she said as she looked at me and smiled.

Mary Catherine was so excited that, come October, her whole family would be moving to Union County. She would soon have two babies for Sara and Dent to enjoy and spoil.

The steamboat was on time. We greeted each other with open arms. It was nice seeing both John and Dent looking so good. After loading their bags into my carriage, we headed back to El Dorado, where Dent and John would spend the night with Benjamin and Mary Catherine.

Tomorrow would be a day we'd all remember. Dent and John's presence at Three Oaks would be one of the greatest blessings our mother will ever experience. It will be like a homecoming, especially when they share with her their move to Union County.

Now that Dent and John are here, we can go ahead with tomorrow's closing.

The big day finally came. Penelope made sure I didn't forget my medicine bag. She carried it to the carriage and handed it to me as I got into the driver's seat of the carriage.

"We will see you this afternoon, Obadiah. You have a good day. I hope all goes well," she said as she stood there looking up at me with those gorgeous, blue eyes.

"I'll see you in about eight hours," I said as I headed out to El Dorado.

My day at the office was very busy. I had a full morning schedule, and when lunchtime came, I was ready to have lunch at Jake's. John, Dent, Mary, and Virgil joined my office staff and me for lunch.

At two o'clock, the three of us met Mrs. Arlington and Mrs. Saunders at Jack Spearman's law office to do the closings.

Alexander went over the final disclosures and deeds with the parties involved. He then passed the deeds around for original signatures. After signatures were secured, Alexander and I witnessed the deeds by signing our names. Alexander then placed his lawyer's firm stamp of seal upon each legal document.

Everything was now official. Alexander collected the two checks from Dent and John and handed the checks to Mrs. Arlington and Mrs. Saunders.

A date of October 15, 1865, was agreed upon by both the grantor and the grantee as the date the new owners would take possession of their properties. This date allowed Mrs. Arlington and Mrs. Saunders time to harvest their crops. The money made from the crops would remain with the original owners. This same deal was done for John and Dent back in Alabama.

We were now ready to concentrate on the big celebration at Three Oaks. Before I left the house this morning, Penelope gave me instructions on her planned arrival for Dent and John. They are to come with Benjamin and Mary Catherine, and they are to be the last to show up.

During the day, I made sure Mary Catherine was aware of this plan.

Mother still had no clue that John and Dent were in town and would be here tonight for the celebration. We were all eager to see how she would respond.

After getting cleaned up from a long day at work, I went to the front porch and played with the kids. While sitting on the front porch, I could smell the wonderful fragrance coming from the kitchen. The aroma of the fresh meats and vegetables was Heavenly. At one point, I thought about slipping off and going to the kitchen to sample the meat. When Penelope came to the porch, I immediately cancelled that thought.

As planned, tables, benches, and chairs were brought out and placed under the three big oak trees. Everything was now in place for the big celebration. All we needed now was for our guest and family members to show up.

Virgil and Mary were the first to arrive with their children. They were followed by Dr. Jim and Elizabeth Burroughs and Alexander and Jennie.

Penelope invited Hank and Nanny's family, George's family, and, of course, Bill. She also invited our pastor and his wife and several others from First Baptist Church of El Dorado. The last to arrive, as planned, were Benjamin, Mary Catherine, John, and Dent.

When Penelope saw Benjamin's carriage coming up the road to the plantation house, she quickly found Mother and asked her to come to the kitchen for one last look before supper was served. Penelope didn't want Mother to see Dent and John getting out of Benjamin and Mary Catherine's carriage.

After a short introduction of Dent and John to our guests, I asked John and Dent to join me on the front porch.

As Mother came through the door, she immediate spotted John and Dent standing by me.

"Oh, my, Lord! I can't believe my eyes. Am I seeing things?" she said as she reached out her arms to embrace John.

After giving John a hug and kiss she immediately reached for Dent. "Dent, did y'all come all the way for this? When did you get here?" she asked.

"We actually arrived last night but wanted to wait until today to be here for the big celebration," Dent answered.

"Oh, you don't know how much this means to me!" she said as she began to cry.

In order to get everyone's attention, I picked up a bell lying on a table next to my rocking chair and gave it a ring.

"Could I have everyone's attention please? As you can see, the arrival of my brothers, John and Dent Bradford, is a complete surprise to our mother. We planned it that way. Not only are we hosting this celebration tonight for our honorees, who will soon be expecting new arrivals to their families, but to make a very important announcement as well.

"It gives me great pleasure to announce that on October 15 of this year, Dent's and John's families will become permanent residents of Union County."

I had no sooner got that out of my mouth when Mother grabbed my arm and said, "Did I hear you right?"

Dent stepped forward and said, "Mother, we're moving to Union County. We closed the deal today on our plantations, which are only about six miles from here. We, too, are very excited," Dent said as tears begin to well up in his eyes. Mother was still crying and praising the Lord.

"Y'all don't realize how hard I've been praying. My prayers have been answered. I'm here to tell everyone, God answers prayers! Yes, He does! I am so happy! Praise the Lord, praise the Lord!" she said as she pulled us three together for a big hug.

"Now that God has answered half my prayer, I want to enlist everyone here tonight to pray in earnest with me that my daughters' families will someday join us here in Union County. Will y'all do that for me?"

Everyone said, "Amen!"

At this time, Penelope stepped forward and welcomed our special guest. She asked each expectant mother to step forward to receive a special present from her and Mother. Mother had knitted three blankets, one for each of the three new babies.

After the presentation of the gifts, Penelope announced that dinner was ready. Everyone gathered under the three oaks and was served by Big Jim, Mattie, Betsy, Bill, and George.

Penelope solicited George's and Mr. Sam's help in playing their fiddles while she played the piano.

Hank, Mattie, George, Millie, and Nanny provided the special music. Mother insisted they sing her favorite hymn, "When We All Get to Heaven." After the special music the dancing began. At ten o'clock the party ended. By eleven o'clock, our last guest, Virgil, Mary, and their family left for their home in El Dorado.

Dent and John stayed with us. They wanted to spend as much time as possible with Mother. In five days, they'd depart for Selma, Alabama. In the next five days, they would be extremely busy.

John and Dent wanted to visit their new plantations and do a close inspection of the plantation houses and the slave quarters, and explore the layout of the land. If repairs needed to be done, they had made arrangements with Mrs. Arlington and Mrs. Saunders to make the needed repairs before moving in during the month of October.

Dent asked Virgil to accompany them to the plantations to help with the inspections. If repairs were needed, Virgil would be responsible for getting materials and seeing that the work was completed. Mother wanted to tag along to offer her assistance in making remodeling decisions.

It had been a long day. By the time Penelope and I got the kids settled in, we were dog tired. When we finally got to bed, Penelope looked at me and said, "We did well, Obadiah!"

"I agree! You and Mother are the ones who did well," I said.

Penelope reached over and touched my left cheek with her soft hand. I looked at her and said, "Penelope, I love you so much!"

She smiled and said, "Not as much as I love you, my darling!"

We fell asleep in each other's arms. I don't know how long we slept like that, but at six a.m., when the roosters started crowing, we rolled over and faced each other. The night hours had gone too fast. I was still exhausted.

Since this was Saturday, I decided to accompany Virgil, John, Dent, and Mother to the plantations. I was curious about what condition we would find everything in. I had been to both plantations but hadn't had an opportunity to actually inspect the buildings.

CHAPTER 39

Mother was on cloud nine. In just one and half months, she would have all three of her sons living in Union County.

During our visits to both plantation homes, Mother was a valuable resource in helping John and Dent. She made several suggestions for needed repairs and remodeling ideas for both the plantation homes and the slave quarters.

Just like old times, she used her knowledge, planning skills, and experience in making good recommendations for needed repairs. These repairs would make Sara's and Deborah's jobs easier when they took possession of their new homes.

As I observed Mother at work, my thoughts went back to the time she and Penelope transformed our plantation home at Three Oaks into one of the finest and most attractive Southern plantation homes in Union County.

John and Dent were receptive and nice to Mother as she explained the need to make these changes. They would look at each other and nod their heads in the affirmative.

I found it amusing. When Mother made suggestions for the remodeling jobs, Dent would say to Virgil, "Make a note of that, Virgil!"

I had not inquired from either Dent or John about how much money they received from the sale of Twin Oaks and Black Oaks. From all indications, they must have done well. They were able to pay me what they owed on Twin Oaks and were still able to pay cash for their new plantations in Union County.

It has been three days since I took Dent and John to Champagnolle to catch the steamboat back to Monroe, Louisiana. I've been expecting a telegram from Dent.

After Dent and John returned to Alabama, things have returned to normal. Mary Catherine has given me a full daily schedule in order to catch me up. But that's okay. That's the way I want it. I feel I've neglected my patients long enough.

Today I received that expected telegram from Dent. He informed me that he and John were busy trying to get the crops ready for harvesting.

"Obadiah, my boys handled things very well here at Black Oaks during my absence. They are also looking forward to our move to Union County."

I also received a letter from John. He was in Prattville on business and ran into Daniel Pratt. He said that Mr. Pratt was serious about building the two sawmills in Union County. He said that he needed someone there to oversee the building and running of the mills. "I took the opportunity to say, 'Why don't you send Jim Crawford?' He looked at me and said, 'Jim Crawford is my financial officer. I don't think I could make it around here without Jim!'"

The letter continued, "'I just thought I'd mention him,' I said as I smiled. Mr. Pratt said, 'I know what you're up to, John Bradford. Your dear mother, Catherine, wants all her children in Union County doesn't she?' I answered, 'I'd say you're exactly right, Mr. Pratt.' Anyway, I tried. I planted a seed for Mother but I'm afraid it may not come up."

The month of September was really busy. Marion and Lindy's baby boy was born. They named him Joshua Dent Bradford. I was present for the birth, but Marion wanted to deliver his first child, so I just assisted him. He did a remarkable job. One could see the joy and pride on his face as he held his son in his hands and laid him on Lindy's chest.

A baby girl was born to Benjamin and Mary Catherine. They named her Catherine Jeanette Madison. Marion was present and played a major role in delivering his sister's baby girl. Benjamin and Mary Catherine now have two children. Their little boy, Benjamin William, now has a little sister to play with.

Dr. Jim and Elizabeth Burroughs were blessed with their first child, a little boy. He was born a few weeks early but was in good shape. They named him Thomas James Burroughs. I was there to assist Jim, but he too, wanted to deliver his firstborn. I am so proud of Jim. This little boy is about to change Jim and Elizabeth's lives.

We received good news yesterday that Alexander and Jennie are expecting a child. If everything goes right, the baby will be born sometime in March. The Bradford family is surely growing here in Union County.

Penelope has been working with the Freedom Bureau on her school. We discovered this week that before anyone could start a school, the school had to be approved by the Freedom Bureau. We are experiencing our first dealings with government regulations. If I know Penelope, she will get this school approved.

One bit of good news about the Freedom Bureau's approval is, there will be funds available for a headmaster's and teachers' salaries. The government will also pay for books and supplies. This is all good, providing the restrictions aren't too stringent.

The era of reconstruction in Arkansas isn't looking good. After reading accounts of what's going on in the other Southern States which were once members of the Confederacy, we find ourselves experiencing the same regulations and demands.

When President Lincoln was assassinated, the prospects for an easy reunification of the nation were severely dimmed.

On October 15, we picked up Dent's and John's families at Champagnolle. My sister Sarah and her two girls, Amanda and Lilly, surprised all of us by accompanying Dent's and John's families. Sarah and her daughters plan to stay through the Christmas holidays.

Jim Crawford, Sarah's husband, couldn't come at this time. Daniel Pratt had pressing business he needed Jim to handle. Jim does plan to ask Mr. Pratt for two weeks off during Christmas holidays, and if approved, he will join us here at Three Oaks.

If Tanyua's family can make it, they will accompany Jim Crawford here for Christmas.

Everyone has been extremely busy during the past two weeks. Dent's and John's families have worked hard on getting settled in their new homes.

Virgil was successful in getting all the repairs and remodeling jobs completed before they moved in. Everything looks great.

Penelope was notified yesterday by letter from the Freedom Bureau that her school had been approved and that she will be the headmaster. She was given the right to choose others to work with her. She had already decided that Hank's wife, Nanny, and George's daughter, Millie, will be her assistant teachers.

Everything was set in play, and after some needed repairs to the schoolhouse and ordering textbooks and student furniture, the school is scheduled to open on January 15, 1866. Penelope is very excited!

Sarah received a telegram from Jim today. He informed her he will be arriving here on December 21, and that John, Tanyua, Jane, and Sally Ballard will be accompanying him. This was another surprise. John has never been here before.

This news was another blessing to Mother, who was excited that all her family would be together again, just like the old times at Twin Oaks.

Mother is now sixty-eight years old. She is in good health, as far as I can determine. She doesn't complain about anything. She's a happy lady who enjoys life.

It is now Christmas Day at Three Oaks, and family members have been arriving since nine o'clock. Our parlor is full, and people are visiting all over the house. It will be like this for the entire day. There will be one thing different this year. Everyone but Tanyua's and Sarah's families will go back to their homes when things break up tonight.

This is a blessing in itself. Mother and Penelope won't have to worry about where everyone will sleep.

We continued our traditional activities, with Dent reading the Christmas Story, opening our Christmas gifts, and eating a delicious meal. After dinner, the men retired to the parlor where we visited, played cards, and sipped eggnog. It was cold outside, so most everyone remained inside.

Dent's and John's sons were about the same age and had some of the same interests. John's two boys, Daniel and Jake, were a little more reserved than Law and Everett, Dent's sons. Although they were a little different in personality traits, they still enjoyed being with each other and talking politics and playing cards. All four boys were outdoorsmen and enjoyed horseback riding and fishing. They all were in agreement that Calion Creek and the Ouachita River were their favorite places to fish.

The subject most talked about among my brothers and nephews was when we have to free our slaves.

This subject was getting a lot of attention in Union County.

Alexander, who keeps up with what's going on in the Arkansas State Legislature, answered with the following response.

"When the State of Arkansas ratifies the Fourteenth Amendment to the United States Constitution, Arkansas will be readmitted to the Union. If the owners of slaves do not cooperate, they will be held in contempt," he said.

"I'm wondering if we will have one year or two years before this happens," Dent said.

Alexander's reply was, "I don't know if anyone can answer that question right now. There is such discord in our state legislature. I'm looking for some strict regulations handed down to the Southern states from the national level.

"At the current time, we've been able to do about what we want to do, but I believe that will end in the next year or two. I don't think the United States will continue to give the Confederate states the leniency we now enjoy."

"So you think we will be all right to own slaves until the Fourteenth Amendment is ratified?" John asked.

"Yes, I do. I believe eventually every Southern Confederate state will ratify the Fourteenth Amendment and be readmitted into the Union."

"If we could get one more year with our slaves, I believe we would be pretty much established on our new plantation," Dent said.

"I have a question I want to ask. Has either of you met with your slaves to find out what they might do upon being freed?" I asked.

"No, I've not done that yet," Dent said.

"Neither have I," John added.

"You might be surprised if you ask. I've had such a meeting. My slaves want to stay on at Three Oaks and work for me. I plan to let them stay in their own housing and be paid a salary. I plan for them to manage their own money. I expect them to save enough money to purchase their food, clothing, and bedding. I want them to learn to be independent should they ever want to leave Three Oaks."

"That sounds like a good idea, Obadiah, but do you think you will have enough cash flow to pay them on a regular basis?"

"I've thought a lot about the finances. Penelope and I feel we can set money aside this coming year in a fund to be ready to pay our slaves when we're not getting money for our crops. We believe we can make it work. We are also going to let them have a garden to raise their own food. They will be welcome to cut wood from my land for heating and cooking purposes.

"I've decided, I don't want to get involved right now with sharecropping. I'm hearing some bad things about slaves being tricked into signing contracts that end up hurting them worse than when they were slaves."

"I want to hear more about this. This might work for John and me as well," Dent said.

The kids were in and out of the house. It was cold, but the cold weather didn't seem to faze them. They enjoyed running and chasing each other.

It was midafternoon when Mother came in the parlor and announced it was sharing time.

"Please round up the kids and have them come to the parlor," Mother said.

The parlor was full of Bradfords when Mother stepped forward and said, "If y'all don't mind, I'll go first."

No one was surprised when Mother offered to go first. The first thing she did was to thank everyone for being present for Christmas at Three Oaks.

With joy in her heart, she thanked God for allowing everyone to be healthy and able to be at Three Oaks. She encouraged everyone to pray hard this next year that God would make it possible for Sarah's and Tanyua's families to become residents of Union County.

She ended her talk by saying, "If you will join me in this prayer I want to hear a big Amen!"

Amens went up all over the room. Before Mother sat down, she asked who wanted to be next. Much to my surprise, Jim Crawford stepped forward.

"Since Catherine has brought up the subject of us moving to Union County, I decided to share some good news with everyone.

"A week before we left to come here, Daniel Pratt came to me and asked me if I'd move here to build his two sawmills and look after his financial interest here in Union County. I knew how much Sarah and the kids wanted to move here, so my decision was an easy one. I immediately said yes!"

Everyone in the room rose to their feet and was shouting and clapping. Mother was crying and saying, "Thank you, God! Thank you! Praise the Lord!"

After things settled down, Jim Crawford again stepped forward and said, "I would like for John Ballard to be the next person to share if y'all don't mind."

Everyone's eyes immediately turned to John, who was standing behind Tanyua, who was seated. This is the first time in years that John has been to our home for Christmas. In fact, I can't remember a time he's shared anything.

John stepped forward and said, "I'm not really good at speaking before a group, but what I've got to say will make Catherine happy.

"When Jim accepted Mr. Pratt's offer to come here, Jim approached me and asked me if I'd be willing to move to Union County and oversee the two sawmills and Daniel Pratt's cotton gin. I knew Tanyua wanted to be near her mother and family, so my decision was easy as well. I said yes!"

Again everyone stood and applauded. Mother's prayers and family prayers had been answered. The entire James and Catherine Bradford family was once again going to be together as residents of Union County. Oh, what a blessing from God. He is an awesome God! One I've known since I accepted him into my heart as a child. He's made it possible for all of us to once again be together.

As I focused on Mother, she was holding a handkerchief in one hand with both arms wrapped around Sarah and Tanyua. All three had handkerchiefs in their hands, and all three were crying. It was a joyful cry, I might add!

After things settled down, Alexander stepped forward with Jennie holding his hand.

"We rejoice with all of you in regard to Jim's and John's news. We also rejoice knowing God is good. He is good all the time. Praise His holy name!

"Jennie and I are expecting a baby. If nothing goes wrong, our baby boy or girl should be born sometime in March. Needless to say, we are excited. We look forward to being good parents and pray that our baby will come to know Jesus Christ as his or her savior.

"Jennie and I are blessed to be a part of the Bradford family. We ask for your prayers and want you to know we love you all!"

There were others who shared about nice things that had happened to them this past year, but nothing could top the announcements made by Jim Crawford and John Ballard. This was not only good news, but it was good medicine for Mother as well.

For the next few days, Jim and Sarah and John and Tanyua were busy checking out housing in El Dorado. Of course, Mother wanted to tag along with them. Their target date in moving to El Dorado is in May.

The months of January through March were cold and damp. We had three snows. The snows reminded me of what my father; use to say, "These snows will enrich our grounds with plenty of nutrients. We will have us some bumper cotton and corn crops."

Penelope's school is progressing well. She has several students, including children from our plantation and Dent's and John's plantations. She also has free slaves who are living on the south side of El Dorado attending as well.

Today she shared with me that the Negro children from Three Oaks were so much more advanced than the others. "Obadiah, I'm so thankful that you let me teach our kids on the plantation. I've got several of them helping with the slower children. They enjoy sharing their skills with the others. I love this job. I'm really fortunate to have Nanny and Nellie; they, too, are doing an excellent job. As you know, they were two of my earliest students. They both are bright and creative. God is surely blessing us!"

It is so satisfying to see Penelope doing something she really believes in. She had good training at Mrs. Adams' Boarding School in Boston. If anyone can educate the Negro child, she will be the one. She is talented in so many ways. Her only regret is that she doesn't get to spend much time with James, Isabella, and Paul. She knows they are in good hands with Mattie, Betsy, and Mother, and that's comforting.

As soon as she gets home, she makes it a point to spend as much time with them as possible before and after dinner.

She gives Isabella, Paul, and James their baths while I supervise Charles and Belle with their baths.

Charles and Belle are growing up so fast, especially Charles. He's turning into a little man. He is as sharp as a whip.

Every morning, Penelope takes Charles, Belle, Little Jim, and Benjamin to school with her. Charles is her top student in his academics. She brags on him daily. She's got him helping other children his age on their assignments. He told her one day that he wants to be just like her, a teacher.

Nanny and Nellie carry their children to school as well. Nanny's and Hank's children, Obi and Samuel, are fast learners. Penelope's little brothers, Little Jim and Benjamin, are good students as well. The Three Oaks children are well advanced in their reading, writing, and arithmetic.

CHAPTER 40

It is now March of 1866, and we've had lots of rain and windy weather. Our daffodils are in full bloom. I can feel and smell spring in the air.

I love spring. It's my favorite time of the year. When the sap starts rising in the trees, I can feel it rising in me as well. The trees are budding, and within two weeks, I expect them to start leafing out.

I can see the green grass penetrating through the dead grass of winter. It won't be long until our horses and cattle will start enjoying grazing on the lush, green, juicy grass.

Last week, I took my horse General for a ride. He's getting up in age, but we had a good time together. It had been some time since I'd ridden him.

It was a beautiful Saturday, and Law, Everett, Daniel, and Jake wanted to ride their horses with me. Since the community is new to them, I volunteered to show them around.

I asked George to meet us at Calion Creek with fishing poles. I also asked him to bring cooking utensils, in case we got lucky and caught enough fish to cook. The boys remembered Calion Creek from a previous fishing trip.

The fish were hungry, and much to our surprise, we caught a bunch of good-sized fish. Among our catch were several good-sized catfish. We also caught several good-sized bluegill bream and three large carp. Needless to say, we didn't clean the carp; they were too bony!

My nephews and I had a great time together. I had forgotten how much fun fishing and riding horses could be. We decided to do it more often.

My nephews had been busy in helping their fathers get ready for spring planting. They are all strong young men and don't mind working side by side with the slaves. They are not afraid of hard work. Both Dent and John have taught them good work ethics. I once heard Dent say, "My boys are going to do physical work. I don't want them to grow up being sissies!"

I spent most of March visiting my regular patients out in the county. I have several elderly patients who can't make trips to El Dorado.

Marion has been accompanying me on most of my home visits. In a few months, he will have finished his time requirement of being an intern and will start taking his state board exams. If he passes them, and I feel confident he will, he will become a full-fledged doctor of medicine. When that occurs, he will join our staff as a full-time practicing doctor.

If El Dorado continues to grow like it has in the last few months, we will someday need a hospital like Daniel Pratt built at Prattville, Alabama.

Daniel, John's son, wants to be a doctor as well. He will start shadowing me soon. I look forward to working with him as I have Marion.

Penelope's school is still growing. Since Sarah's and Tanyua's families have moved here, Penelope has seen a need to open the school for white kids as well. Sarah and Tanyua are well educated. Sarah has a degree as a teacher, and will become an assistant under Penelope.

Penelope has assigned Sarah the responsibility of enrolling white children and providing for their curriculum needs.

There are a few white families who want to send their children to Penelope's school. These are families who we are acquainted with and attend First Baptist Church of El Dorado.

They love Penelope and have confidence that she knows what she's doing and will provide a good education for their kids.

The white parents are willing to pay for their children's education, since the Freedom Bureau only pays for educating the colored children.

The children of the Bradford families make up the majority of the white students attending Penelope's colored school.

Penelope has quickly built a good reputation for her school. Since she's decided to increase her enrollment to take in white children, she is now faced with needing more classroom space.

Penelope and I have discussed how she might raise funds to add the additional classrooms to the present structure. I think her ideas are good, and I've encouraged her to pursue them. I'm betting, in the near future, Penelope will accomplish her goal in getting the money to build the needed classrooms.

Also in the month of March, Alexander and Jennie were blessed with the birth of a little boy. They named him Mason Alexander Bradford.

Alexander has decided to get involved with politics. He has decided to run for an Arkansas State Senate position in southern Arkansas.

Virgil has decided to run for the El Dorado mayor's position, and Marion has decided to run for a state representative position from South Arkansas.

Since the election will occur in November, we will be engaged in a great deal of politicking in Union, Ouachita, Calhoun, and Columbia Counties. I plan to promote all three of them as I call on each of my patients out in the counties. I want to believe all three can, and will be, elected.

In my honest opinion, Virgil, Alexander, and Marion have genuine reasons why they want to serve in these elected positions. They are all gifted speakers, knowledgeable, and will be good leaders. We need the very best in these positions representing our local interests in southwest Arkansas.

Dent and John, with the help of their sons, have turned their new plantations into some of the best looking plantations in Union County.

John has shared with me that his son, Jake, is interested in attending Old Military School in Augusta, Georgia, where I got my degree. He wants to study law.

John also shared with me that his daughter Jennie wants to go to Boston and attend Mrs. Adams' Boarding School. She said, "I want to be just like Penelope."

Dent told me this week that Everett is thinking about becoming a preacher. I've been watching Everett as he worships at First Baptist Church. I believe that the Holy Spirit is moving in him, and that's a good thing! Everett is a very good speaker, and if God is calling him to be a preacher, that's a good thing. It's about time we had a minister come out of the Bradford family.

Dent tells me that Law is thinking about going to Old Military School in Augusta, Georgia, to study law. If that materializes, Jake and Law will be there together. Who knows, they might end up staying at the Milton Boarding House on Telfair Street. That would be wonderful!

Today, I received a telegram from my good friend Dr. Henry Dotson of Atlanta, Georgia. He wanted to know if Penelope and I would be up for a visit from him and his family. This is the best news I've heard in some time. He stated that he was taking about two weeks off from his doctor's duties and was going to do some traveling with his family. He and his wife agreed that El Dorado, Arkansas, was where they wanted to go.

After discussing Henry's telegram with Penelope, we both agreed I should respond to him by saying, "Come on, we are excited, and hope to see you soon."

After Henry received my reply, he sent a second telegram, with the dates they would arrive in Champagnolle. They couldn't have chosen better dates. They would be arriving during the last week in May.

Penelope's school will be out for the summer break after May 15. I will be able to shift my patient load over to Jim and Marion. We will be well prepared for my best friend's visit.

The weather should be beautiful. While they are here, we will go horseback riding, fishing, and camping, and enjoy good Southern fellowship.

If I'm not mistaken, El Dorado is planning a big celebration the last weekend in May. The mayor will be recognizing our fallen soldiers as well as those who returned home from the Civil War. People will be dancing in the street, and tables of food will be in abundance. It will be a grand occasion.

I can't wait to tell Mother the good news. She met Henry at Audrey's and my wedding but hasn't had the opportunity to see him again. I know Mother will start planning delicious meals for every day that they are here.

By the middle of May, our field crops had been planted. My slaves had spent their extra time planting white and sweet potatoes, different kinds of beans, tomatoes, cabbage, okra, onions, and lettuce in the big garden. If we are blessed with good rains, there should be an abundance of fresh vegetables.

During parts of the spring, I allowed my slaves to work for other farmers and townspeople, to earn money to purchase items they wanted. Several of them used their money to purchase pigs to fatten and kill during the hog-killing months of late November and early December.

When my father was alive, pork was a popular source of food in a slave's diet. He always allowed our slaves to work for other plantations or farms to earn some money when they weren't needed on our plantation. I've always thought that was a good thing. I have continued the practice every year that we've been here at Three Oaks.

Today, Hank handed me a list of our slaves who selected surnames for their legal names. I will take the names to Alexander so he can process the names to make them legal. The surnames they selected will become their permanent names from here on out. By looking over the names, I have no clue where some of these names came from.

The important part of the process is that when they are set free, they will have a name to use to purchase land, mules, horses, homes, and all sorts of things in life.

Dent and John told me recently they were going to do the same thing with their slaves.

I've heard that slaves who were previously freed chose their owner's surname. I'm not sure that's a good idea, although Hank said several of our slaves wanted to use the Bradford name, but he discouraged them from doing that.

Tomorrow we will take two carriages to Champagnolle to pick up Henry and Helen Dotson and their children. Henry and

Helen have three boys. The oldest is Henry Jr., seventeen; then Robert, fifteen; and then Dexter, fourteen. I know the boys will enjoy fishing and horseback riding. I'm going to introduce them to John's and Dent's boys. They should get along well.

Henry was elected to the Georgia State Senate last year. I'm anxious to pick his brain while he's here. Henry is a very intelligent person. He knows a little about a lot of things. By him being in the Georgia legislature, he should know how the future looks for all of us plantation owners.

As usual, we got to Champagnolle a little earlier than the steamboat. We went inside the small restaurant and had some refreshments as we waited.

It wasn't long before we heard the steamboat whistle blowing. We knew the boat was getting close.

Bill, George, Penelope, and I made our way slowly to the loading dock.

Today, Penelope will meet my best friend and his family for the first time. She has been nervous for the past few days. She's aware that Henry and Helen know about her past. She knew they were aware that she was once a slave before marrying me. She has an inner fear that they might think she isn't good enough for me.

As the boat neared the dock, we spotted them leaning against the front of the big boat. We started waving, and they began to wave back. Penelope looked at me and said, "Obadiah, I'm so nervous!"

"Penelope, just relax! Be yourself and enjoy meeting these friends," I said, as I put my arms around her and comforted her.

The boys were the first ones to exit the boat, followed closely by Henry and Helen. As we approached each other, the boys stopped to allow their father and mother to move ahead of them to greet us.

"Welcome to Champagnolle," I said.

After a big hug, Henry turned to Penelope and said, "We Georgia people like to hug; is it all right with you?"

She looked at him with those beautiful, blue eyes, smiled, and said, "I'd be honored!"

As they hugged, I noticed Helen smiling.

After a hug, Henry turned to Helen and started his introductions.

"This is my lovely wife, Helen, and these are our three sons: our oldest, Henry Jr.; Robert, our second oldest; and last, but not least, our youngest, Dexter."

During each introduction, Henry's sons stepped forward and politely reached out and shook my hand. If Penelope was still nervous I couldn't tell it. She appeared to be very calm as she shook Helen's and the boys' hands.

I then turned to Bill and George and introduced them to the Dotsons.

"If it's all right with the boys, they can ride in George's carriage, while you and Helen ride with Penelope and me in Bill's carriage. This will give us time to visit on the way home to Three Oaks."

"That sounds like a good plan. Boys, help Mr. Bill and Mr. George with the luggage," Henry said.

The boys turned, grabbed their bags, and carried them to the carriages, where Bill and George placed them into the storage area in the carriages.

Before leaving, Henry Jr. asked if he could ride in the driver's seat with George.

"I've never ridden in a horse-drawn carriage before. I would like to see what it's like sitting up there."

"You are more than welcome to ride with me. I might just let you handle the reins at times, if you like."

"That would be awesome, Mr. George!" Henry Jr. said.

This would be the first time that Henry, Helen, and the boys visited a Southern plantation. They were city folks from Atlanta, Georgia. Henry and Helen's home is a large, six-bedroom home located on Madison Street, which is thought to be where the rich folks live.

CHAPTER 41

As Bill and George stopped our carriages in front of our plantation home, we were surrounded with a warm, Bradford family welcome.

Mother and Penelope planned a welcome dinner for Henry and his family. We felt a big get-together would be nice to introduce our big family to Henry and his family.

Henry's boys would need to be entertained by kids their age. John's and Dent's boys volunteered to spend time with them. Law shared with me some of things they were planning to do. One of the activities was an overnight trip on Little Calion Creek for fishing, swimming, and camping.

When we were discussing different ways to involve Henry's boys, Law said, "Uncle Obadiah, don't you give this a second thought. We will show Henry, Robert, and Dexter a good time during their visit here in Union County. You needn't worry; we'll handle everything."

I knew I could count on Law, so I dismissed my concern about Henry's boys and would leave everything in their hands.

George and Big Jim were responsible for roasting a pig. I don't think anyone around here can come close to competing with their skills in roasting a pig. The meat is always tender and juicy.

I informed Mattie and Betsy that Henry's favorite meal while we were together at the Milton House in Augusta, Georgia, was Southern fried chicken. The chicken at the Milton House was good, but as far as I was concerned, it was second to Betsy's and Mattie's fried chicken.

As planned, it didn't take Law, Everett, Jake, and Daniel long to involve Henry's boys. Henry and Helen appeared to enjoy visiting with my family. The food was simply marvelous.

As usual, I ate a lot. During the earlier part of the night, I found myself going back to the table and grazing. The Bible warns us against gluttony. I believe it says it's a sin. If that's true, I certainly sinned tonight.

About nine o'clock, I noticed Helen starting to yawn. The trip here from Atlanta was exhausting. To get everyone's attention, I made a little speech that included my thanks for everyone's presence in welcoming my good friend and his family to Three Oaks. I ended my speech by saying it was getting late, and we needed to let Henry and his family get a good night's rest.

It wasn't long after my speech that my family was saying their good-byes as they left Three Oaks to return to their respective homes.

Mother had made sleeping arrangements for every member of Henry's family. They would all have their privacy.

As Henry was headed toward the front porch, he came up to me and asked, "Obadiah, I've been wondering if you'd have time to show Helen and me around Union County and maybe some of the other small towns in the surrounding counties."

I informed Henry that Penelope and I had cleared our calendars for their visit and were at their disposal in doing traveling, fishing, horseback riding, or anything else that interested them.

"Thanks, Obadiah! When I travel, I love to see new things and experience the environment and beauty of the land. I wouldn't mind going fishing and camping one night with the boys. Do you do that type of thing?"

"That's one of my favorite things. In years past, when Dent and John came to visit from Alabama, fishing and camping was one of the things we enjoyed most. Yes, I love it!"

"We wanted you and Penelope to know that we'd love to attend church with y'all in El Dorado. We are Baptist, too, and attend First Baptist Church in Atlanta. Everyone in my family has accepted Jesus Christ as their Lord and Savior. It was during a revival last year that Dexter asked Jesus into his heart."

"That's wonderful news, Henry. I know you and Helen must be very happy knowing all three of your children know Jesus Christ as their savior."

"It is reassuring, Obadiah!"

"Oh, before I forget, on Saturday night Penelope and I want you to be our special guests at a big celebration in El Dorado. We have three to four celebrations a year. This one is to honor our fallen soldiers and to recognize those soldiers who made it home from the Civil War."

"Obadiah, we, too, enjoy celebrations. Helen's father, Frank Anderson, is mayor of Atlanta. He is noted for his big celebrations. Helen and I try to support him by attending every one he's involved with."

"Henry, wasn't Mr. Anderson instrumental in negotiating the surrender of Atlanta?"

"Yes, he was. He was truly a leader in that respect. General Sherman would have burned Atlanta to the ground if it hadn't been for men like my father-in-law. Frank and others struck a deal with General Sherman, and as a result of their agreement, General Sherman decided not to burn Atlanta.

"How long did General Sherman stay in Atlanta after he took possession?"

"After setting up his headquarters, he stayed on for twenty-one days before resuming his march to the sea."

"Did you ever have an opportunity to meet him?"

"Yes, I did. He came to our hospital one day and visited some of the Federal soldiers who we were treating."

"What was he like?"

"I was pleasantly surprised. He was a gentleman and appeared to have sympathy for both the Southern and Union soldiers."

"I know you must be exhausted from your long trip, but before we go in, I must tell you how much your visit means to me and Penelope. Penelope and I had hoped to visit you and Helen in Atlanta, but that got shot down when Penelope got pregnant with Paul and Isabella. Since their birth, we've been pretty much confined to Union County."

"Obadiah, I fully understand. Helen and I felt the same way when our boys were smaller. We, too, wanted to travel, but traveling with three small boys just didn't fit in our plans. Now that they are teenagers, we felt we could manage traveling.

"We, too, have been looking forward to making this trip to Union County to see you and your family.

"Obadiah, I shall never forget the day you took that bullet for me in the Battle of Corinth. I will always be indebted to you. You are my closest friend, and you will always be."

"Henry, I love you like a brother. If you hadn't saved me on that operating table, I wouldn't be here today. Your letter of discharge allowed me the opportunity to be what I am today."

"Obadiah, may I say one other thing before we go inside?"

"What is it, Henry?"

"Obadiah, it's been a blessing meeting your wonderful family. I don't want you to take this wrong, but I don't think I've ever seen a woman as beautiful as Penelope. My father would say, 'She's a knock-out!'"

"Henry, I thank you for saying that. I promise you, I'll never tell Helen about your kind words about my wife," I said, laughing.

"I now have a better understanding of your description of her when you talked about her in Augusta. Her feelings about you are very obvious. One can tell she worships you."

"Well, I don't know about the worship part, but I do know we love each other a lot."

"It is very apparent that God has richly blessed you with a wonderful wife and family, Obadiah!"

"That, I agree totally! God has been wonderful in meeting our every need. I praise him daily!"

"One more thing and we'll go in and get some shut eye," Henry said.

"Henry, I'm enjoying every moment of our conversation. In fact, I could stay right here on my front porch and visit with you all night long. It would be like old times!"

"We certainly had lots to talk about in Augusta, didn't we?"

"Indeed, we did! Those were some of the best days of my life."

"What I want to say to you concerns your trust and faith in God. I've never told you this before, but after getting to know you in Corinth and seeing you react under pressure during the battles, I found myself questioning whether I had ever truly been saved. I would look at you and ask myself, 'How does Obadiah do it? How does he stay calm? Is there something missing in me? Is my trust and faith in God lacking?' So many things entered my mind."

"Henry, when I was growing up as a child, our Mamie, who was our main household servant, treated me like a son. She was more like a grandmother than a slave.

"She taught me many things during my childhood. One thing, I remember well. She said, 'Obadiah, God created all of us in his image. I's don't know why I's colored and you's white, but what I do know, I'm no different than you in God's eyes.

"'Obadiah, you's be a very special boy. I believe that your feelings for people are genuine, and I think God has something special for you. You be the best you can be, and love our God the best you's can, and I knows my God will treat you special. You just hold to the truth, and trust God and He will do the rest. Do you understand, my child?'

"Mamie's words were written in my mind and heart. I've never forgotten her words of advice to me.

"Mamie was a slave who was uneducated in book learning, but she had a head full of common sense. She was the sweetest and most considerate person I've ever known. I shall always remember her talks with me. I've always strived to let God lead me by the way of His Word and to ask him for directions in what He'd have me to do. I give God full credit for where I am today, and what I stand for. Does that make sense to you?"

"I think I know exactly what you're talking about. I'm sure you don't know this, but you were an inspiration to me during our time together in Corinth. I could see the Godly spirit within you. I could feel your faith, and I could see your will to live.

"Obadiah, now that I've met Penelope, I know that God's plan for you has always included Penelope. He saved you for Penelope. You needed her and she needed you."

"Henry, thanks for saying those nice things. I could say the same for you. Helen is certainly the lady you described her to be. She's been your love for some time now, and she's given you three nice-looking sons. You and Helen have done a great job raising your sons. They are truly gentlemen. You must be proud of them!"

"Yes, I am! Life wouldn't be the same without my boys. I'm so thankful they weren't old enough to fight in the Civil War. I don't think I could have survived the worry of knowing they were somewhere being shot at and not knowing if they would ever return to us alive."

"Henry, we've been blessed so much. God has given us all we need. I believe in my heart and mind that he's not finished with us yet. He knows our future, and He's going to be there when we need Him.

"I predict that you will be one of Georgia's famous state senators, who will be known as one who played a major role in reshaping Georgia into being admitted again to the United States of America.

"I predict that we both will live long lives, long enough to see our children become adults, to see them choose their lifelong professions, and give us grandchildren. I believe all this, and I, for one, am looking forward to seeing all this come to be, right before my eyes. All right, friend, what do you think about that?"

"I tell you the truth, Obadiah, you sound like a prophet. I'm going to pray that your predictions come true!" he said, laughing.

"God knows, Henry! He's the one we must trust and place our faith in! Now, let's go to bed, my friend! Tomorrow's another day!"

Henry and I were the last two to enter through the front door. I said good night to Henry as I locked the front door.

I awoke early to the aroma of fried bacon. I was eager to enjoy a nice, hot breakfast with Henry and his family. I could be wrong, but I expect Henry and his family will thoroughly take a liking to our Southern-prepared breakfast.

At breakfast, I took my steaming-hot biscuit and split it in half. I then poured Mattie's white sausage gravy on top of it. I noticed that Henry and his boys were watching how I was fixing my biscuit and gravy.

Finally, Henry, who was sitting to my left asked, "Do you always put the white gravy on your biscuits?"

"Is there any other way to eat biscuits and gravy?" I asked as I laughed.

At that point, Henry and his sons did exactly as I had done. It wasn't long before they were asking if they could have seconds. Mattie's biscuits and gravy were a hit and remained a favorite dish each morning of their stay at Three Oaks.

"This is the best breakfast ever! I love it!" Henry Jr. said.

"It is great!" Robert said.

It wasn't long after breakfast that Law, Everett, Daniel, and Jake arrived on horseback. Today, they would take Henry Jr., Robert, and Dexter horseback riding to Little Calion Creek and, later, tour the town of El Dorado.

Henry had already informed me that his boys were not accustomed to riding horses. He said, "They are products of the city!"

I instructed George to pick three of our gentle horses for them to ride. Since they were not experienced at riding, I didn't want George to give them any of our spirited horses.

I suggested to George he saddle General for Dexter. General would be gentle with him.

Mother called Law to the porch and handed him seven sacks of food for their saddle bags. She reminded Law that, since they would be out most of the day, they would get hungry. Mother thinks of everything. I can tell right now she will end up spoiling all her grandchildren, now that they are close by.

I took the liberty of telling Law, in private, not to horse around with Henry Jr., Robert, and Dexter. I reminded him that I was holding him responsible for everyone's actions.

Law looked at me, smiled, held out his hand to shake mine, and said, "Uncle Obadiah, you need not worry. I've got everything under control!"

I love that boy. His cockiness sometimes gets a little under my collar, but I know I can trust him. He's so self-confident. He will make a good lawyer someday!

I was surprised to see that Law had organized the group in such a way that Henry Jr., Robert, and Dexter were visible at all times by the more experienced riders.

After the boys left Three Oaks, Bill brought our family carriage to the front of the plantation house, where Penelope, Helen, Henry, and I had been waiting on the porch for our trip to Camden. Camden is a quaint, little town located about ten miles from Three Oaks and is built near the Ouachita River. It is known for its river port and big sawmill.

The sawmill is the biggest employer in Ouachita County. The town of Camden is surrounded for miles by large virgin pines and big hardwood trees. There are several nice plantations in Ouachita County. The sawmill is considered a plus when it comes to the county's livelihood.

I shared with Henry about Daniel Pratt's future plans to build two sawmills in Union County. Union County is a lot like Ouachita County. It has an abundance of virgin pine and big hardwood trees. It is my belief the sawmills will play a major role in the future of the plantation owner, especially after the slaves are freed.

While we were out, we found a little restaurant near the river port that served Southern fried catfish. Oh, was it ever good.

"I have never tasted catfish this good," Henry said.

"Does El Dorado have a Southern catfish restaurant?"

"Matter of fact, they do. There is one on the road that takes us to Calion Creek."

"I just may want to eat another catfish meal while I'm here," Henry said.

After we had our lunch, we continued our tour of the little town of Camden. We visited the river port as well as the larger sawmill, which were the two key things to see in Camden. After seeing the highlights of Camden, Bill returned us to Three Oaks, where we sat on the front porch and visited.

During our porch visit, Law and the other cowboys arrived. Law let me know quickly that all went well and that they took a swim in their favorite swimming hole on Little Calion Creek.

Law said, "We found the camping area where we camped during our last visit from Alabama. It's the ideal spot on the

Little Calion to fish, swim, and camp. We'd like to go fishing and camping there this Wednesday if it can be arranged. What do you think?" he asked.

I looked at Henry, and he shook his head in the affirmative.

"That sounds good for us," I said, as Law shared the news with the other boys.

Later in the day, we left Three Oaks in time to tour Penelope's school before going to the courthouse area for the celebration activities.

Penelope wanted to give Henry and Helen a tour of her school. She takes great pride in offering a unique curriculum to both the Negro and white children.

Henry was amazed that this unique arrangement was taking place right here in the South. He was highly complimentary to Penelope.

It was at the El Dorado celebration that Henry fell in love with our town. It is such a clean, little town and is growing daily. I introduced him and Helen to several of my close friends, business associates, and other plantation owners.

Our mayor did a great job in recognizing those who gave their lives for the Southern cause in the Civil War. He gave a member of each family a certificate signifying the gratitude for serving in the Confederate Army. He then recognized several local soldiers who made it home alive.

There was dancing in the street and lots of delicious food on tables that stretched across the front of the courthouse.

We danced with our wives, changed partners, and rested while our sons and nephews danced with our wives. I believe Mother danced with all of her sons and grandsons. She never seemed to tire out!

Penelope introduced us to a few of the Freedom Bureau members who had approved her school. They appeared to be nice people.

On Sunday, Henry's family accompanied us to First Baptist Church. After hearing a nice sermon, we returned to Three Oaks for a big lunch.

Since there was lots of food left over from the big welcome dinner, Mother invited the entire Bradford family to Three Oaks to share in food and fellowship. Again, everyone had a good time.

Our next two days were spent touring the little towns of Magnolia in Columbia County, and Mt. Holly, Norphlet, Junction City, and Champagnolle in Union County. After two days of traveling, we looked forward to some relaxation on Little Calion Creek.

As usual George, Hank, Bill, and Big Jim were invited to come along to help with building campfires, putting up camping tents, and cooking. They also brought along their children to enjoy the overnight camping trip. Henry was amazed how well all the Negro and white children got along. I explained to him that we saw no skin colors at Three Oaks.

I related to him that my sons, Charles and James; Hank's, sons, Obi and Samuel; and Big Jim's sons, Little Jim and Benjamin have played together and gone camping with each other from the time they were little.

Little Jim and Benjamin are Penelope's little brothers, and they've lived with us in the same household while we were at Twin Oaks and here at Three Oaks.

"Henry, everyone at Three Oaks is treated as though they are part of the family."

"Obadiah, this is another example of God's grace coming out in you. I will be honest with you; I don't think this same arrangement could work in Atlanta, Georgia. People there are still very prejudiced."

"That's what I like about Union County. You do know that Hank's my plantation overseer? I put out the word that he was my trusted overseer, and the people of El Dorado have accepted him. They treat him with the utmost respect."

"Obadiah, that's the most gratifying thing I've heard about colored and white relations. You need to write a book about all this. I'm not kidding you! You need to write all these experiences down. The whole world needs to know that two races can learn to live with each other without worrying about repercussions.

"I'm so glad I've made this trip. You all have so much going for you. Praise the Lord for people like you, Obadiah!"

"Henry, I thank you for your nice comments, but I don't want you to think of me as a saint. I'm far from that! It's just that God makes all this easy for me. He's the creator of all things.

"To paraphrase the words of my dear beloved Mamie, I don't know why colored people became slaves to white folks, maybe greed. But what I do know, colored are human beings, and should be respected as human beings."

Mamie was a wise lady. She didn't learn to read or write, but she had lots of common sense. I loved that woman!

Our conversation went from discussing race relations to the fishing derby that goes on during each camping trip.

"Charles has been after me to explain the rules to our fishing derby. Whoever catches the biggest fish wins a price. I've extended it a little this year to whoever catches the largest fish and the most fish gets a prize.

"One year, Charles caught the largest fish, and I've never seen a boy any happier."

Charles was now big enough to bait his own hook and to take off his fish. He was ready to go. He looked at me and said, "Daddy, I'm going to do my best to catch the biggest fish in Calion Creek, but if I don't, I'll not cry. Whoever wins, I'll be happy for him!"

My little boy is growing up so fast. He is really mature for a seven-year-old.

The boys agreed that they would stop fishing and take a swimming break in midafternoon. As the boys swam, we older guys relaxed under a shade tree near the swimming hole. We enjoyed the diving maneuvers our boys attempted from the top of a big boulder in the middle of the swimming area. It was nice to watch them have so much fun.

At five o'clock, George and Bill built a large campfire. The boys who were big enough carried driftwood from previous flooding of the Little Calion for the campfire.

The Little Calion is the prettiest stream of water in these parts. Not like the muddy Ouachita River, the Little Calion's water is nice and green.

Where we camped, we could walk several feet out in the water before getting in water over our heads. It is nice for our children who are still trying to learn to swim.

At the end of the day we had a new champion. Henry Jr. had caught the largest fish. He caught a catfish that weighted around five pounds, just right for the big frying pan.

There were several other catfish and bream caught as well. The person catching the most fish was Everett.

Charles lived up to his early statement. Although he didn't win, he did come in second for catching the most fish. I decided he should get a consolation prize.

George got a kick out of teaching Henry Jr. how to clean a catfish. Henry Jr. had never caught a fish in his life. He was willing to follow George's instructions, but when the catfish wiggled in his hands, he immediately dropped it.

"That thing scratched me!" he said as he started slinging his hand.

George took Henry's hand and put some dipping snuff on the scratch and said, "Welcome to your first catfish finning!"

Henry Jr. looked at George funny and asked, "What does finning mean?"

George replied, "See those fins on that catfish's back? That's his weapon of defense. If you're not careful when you're skinning or filleting a catfish, he will try finning you to get loose. One has to hold a catfish just right, or he will fin you. Catfish can do some real damage. You're lucky that yours is just a scratch. Let me show you how it's done."

George took the catfish and held it with his hand tightly below the fins. He then cut the head off and filleted the meat from the bones. He looked at Henry Jr. with a big piece of fillet fish in his hand and said, "Sonny boy, when you eat this juicy meat you won't swallow a bone."

Everyone enjoyed a good campfire fish dinner, and when night set in, everyone gathered around the campfire to hear stories of the past. Most of the older boys wanted Marion to share his Civil War experiences.

I've heard Marion's story before, and I'm convinced that God had a purpose for saving Marion's life. Especially since so many soldiers died of starvation, disease, and battle wounds at the Battle of Vicksburg. As he told his story, there was quietness throughout the camp. The only time Marion's story was interrupted was when an owl or bull frog would make their unusual sounds in the background.

After Marion told his story, it was requested that Henry and I tell our stories.

Henry and I intentionally avoided the gross parts where we attended soldiers who were butchered up from fragments of cannons. Some soldiers had severe wounds to the stomach so that their intestines protruded from their stomachs. These wounds were called gut shots. There was little that we could do for these soldiers.

Several soldiers bled to death from horrible wounds to the legs and arms. To save their lives, we had to amputate many limbs. We had no pain medicine to give the wounded soldier when we removed their limbs. They would scream to the top of their lungs, and many would just close their eyes and die. I believe the pain was so unbearable that it made their hearts stop.

Some nights I wake up dreaming about those horrible experiences at Shiloh and Corinth.

The sharing of our stories seemed to be one of the highlights to our camping trip. The Civil War was a bad thing for America. Although it was bad, our stories needed to be told. The reasons for the war, the outcome of the war, and aftereffects to the world should all be made a part of our history. Never again should something like this happen to the United States of America. It will take a long time for resentment and hatred to run its course. Until then, we need to work together to make our country strong again.

The Civil War will go down in history as being the bloodiest war of all times in America. Never again should brother fight against brother or cousin against cousin.

Before I turned in for the night, I instructed George not to start breakfast until seven o'clock. By the time breakfast was ready at eight, everyone should be up and around. Was I ever wrong!

As usual, the little boys were the first to wake up. They wanted to start fishing early so they could catch more fish than the bigger boys. As we called the older boys to come to breakfast, there was only one sound that we heard, and that was snoring.

We decided to leave them alone and let them sleep. We were hoping they would finally smell the aroma of fried sausage, bacon, and eggs, and be encouraged to get up, dress, and enjoy a good breakfast.

As we sat around the campfire, my thoughts went back to when I was a small boy in Autauga County. My father and mother would take the entire family fishing and camping. We had such a good time together. I remember Father and Mother would let us sleep as long as we wanted to after a late night.

Henry, Dent, John, and I agreed this camping trip was mostly for the boys and not us. We would let them enjoy their extended time for sleeping while we would enjoy our hot coffee and morning fishing.

The younger boys soon discovered that the fish were hungry and were biting any bait they put on their hooks. Our boys were having the time of their lives catching good-sized catfish and bream.

At nine-thirty in the morning, Law came out of his tent. He was followed by the rest of our boys. "Where's the food, we're starved!" he said as he sat down by the campfire.

"Why didn't y'all wake us up?" Everett asked.

Henry, Dent, John, and I just looked at each other and laughed.

George passed out the tin plates and coffee cups and said, "Y'all dig in!"

They ate like starving teenagers. It was fun watching them enjoy their breakfast.

Dent asked, "Whose pole is this?"

"That's mine," Robert said.

"Robert, when I got up this morning, I saw this pole floating in the water out there. As I waded out to retrieve it, I pulled it back to the bank and found this little catfish."

Dent reached down in a big bucket and pulled out a large catfish.

"See what you missed out on, Robert?" Dent said.

"Since that catfish was on my pole, do I get credit for the fishing derby count?" Robert asked.

"I'm afraid not, Robert. The derby officially ended yesterday," Henry said.

"If you guys want to fish awhile longer after you finish your breakfast, we might catch enough fish for another meal. If we do, we'll eat lunch and then head back to Three Oaks," I said.

The fish were biting well. By eleven o'clock, we had caught enough fish for another big meal. George and Big Jim went to work cleaning and battering the fish. Within thirty minutes, they had enough fish cooked for our lunch.

There is something special about George's fried fish. I don't know the ingredients he uses in his batter, but whatever it is, it's good. There is something special about eating fried fish cooked in a black iron skillet over an open campfire.

CHAPTER 42

Today we accompanied Henry and his family to Champagnolle for their departure to Monroe, Louisiana. The steamboat will carry them down the Ouachita River to Monroe, where they will board a train for Atlanta.

As I waved good-bye to Henry and his family, I felt a strong emptiness in my heart. It was a feeling of sadness. I had never enjoyed anyone's visit more than Henry' and his family's. They are truly great friends. We will miss them.

As I closed my eyes, in silence, I prayed God would see Henry and his family made it safely home to Atlanta. When I finished my prayer, I caught myself wishing that Henry and his family could move here to Union County. It would be a great blessing to have Henry close by so we could share and confide with each other.

I quickly dismissed the possibility of Henry moving here because he has just recently been elected to the Georgia State Senate.

Dr. John David Banister from Prattville, Alabama, once told me that most people in their lifetime could count their true friends on one hand. I believe Dr. Banister was right. If he is right, Henry Dotson would rank number one as my trusted friend.

It is now September 16, 1866. The weather has cooled down considerably. The months of July and August were terribly hot. There were times I feared the heat and dryness would hamper the growth of our cotton and corn crops. But because of the scattered rain showers, I now believe we will have good cotton and corn crops.

In August, Jim Crawford was paid a visit from his boss, Daniel Pratt, from Prattville, Alabama. Mr. Pratt was in town to sign agreements on two sawmill locations.

Mr. Pratt's visit to El Dorado was a real treat, for not only me, but for Penelope and Mother. He is still a good-looking man at the age of sixty-nine. In June, he lost his wife, Jane, to cancer. She had been a driving force in his life.

When I first saw him at Jake's Restaurant, I took the opportunity to invite him to Three Oaks for dinner. He accepted, and we had a wonderful visit reminiscing about the good old days in Autauga County.

Somehow, Mr. Pratt had prior knowledge of my marriage to Penelope. What I didn't know was whether he knew Penelope was one of my household slaves at Twin Oaks. If he knew, he would never divulge that information to anyone back in Autauga County or Union County. He is a strong, Southern gentleman who respects the personal lives of others; he would do nothing to embarrass me or my family.

I wasn't in the least concerned about him knowing about Penelope. I wasn't worried about what people in Prattville, Alabama, thought about me marrying a slave girl. What was important to me was that I loved Penelope with all my heart and soul. Why should the past stand in my way of being happy?

Penelope and Mr. Pratt hit it off well. I could tell by the way they communicated that he was impressed with her. I believe that he found her to be charming.

Mr. Pratt is highly educated, intelligent, and very wealthy. One wouldn't know he was wealthy. He never put on airs. I've known Mr. Pratt for many years and have never seen him put anyone down.

I owe Daniel Pratt a great deal of gratitude. He was responsible for getting me assigned to Henry Dotson's medical corps in Corinth, Mississippi. During the first part of the Civil War, only one year of service was required to serve in the Confederate Army, and that's all I wanted to serve.

After the Civil War got in full swing, the big wheels in the Confederacy passed a new inscription law that would force everyone to serve three years. This was a bad thing for me. My whole purpose was to serve my one year, come home, and move to El Dorado, Arkansas, and marry Penelope.

Daniel Pratt knew people in high places. He made all the arrangements for my one-year commitment by pulling the right strings.

My mother liked Mr. Pratt, and he liked her. When we lived in Autauga County, Daniel Pratt invited Mother and Father to all his celebrated events. He and Mrs. Pratt loved to entertain. He loved to dance with Mother. Mother had been trained in all the social graces of being a Southern lady. When she and Daniel Pratt danced, everyone took notice.

During our visit, Daniel Pratt was very complimentary of Jim Crawford. He said, "Jim was my first choice to look after my financial interests here in El Dorado. He is intelligent, has remarkable financial understanding in management, and he is honest. I needed someone with those attributes."

As we enjoyed our dinner he made it a point to be extra nice and complimentary to Mother. He had always enjoyed her company. At one point during dinner, he looked at Mother and said, "Catherine, you may not know this, but you've got your son, John, to thank for Jim Crawford being in El Dorado.

"One day I was visiting with John in Prattville, and I shared with him that I was looking for someone to manage my sawmills and cotton gin in Union County. He looked straight at me and said 'Mr. Pratt, why don't you send Jim Crawford to El Dorado to handle your financial interest and get your sawmills started?'

"I'm telling you, I knew right then, Catherine Bradford had been praying for this to happen. So, I began to think about it a lot and decided this was a good thing. So, Catherine, God answered your prayers, didn't He?"

"Yes, He did, and Daniel, I'm so grateful!"

"It's also my understanding that Jim has hired you're son-in-law, John Ballard, to assist him in this new endeavor."

"Yes, that's correct! We're all excited to have Tanyua and her family here as well.

"Daniel, I'm well aware that your friendship has made a world of difference in allowing this to happen. I want you to know your kindness and generosity is appreciated. I am eternally grateful! Thank you, my dear friend!"

"I'm happy to do that for you, Catherine. That's what friends are for!" he said as he took another bite of Betsy's fried chicken.

Before leaving for Autauga County, Mr. Pratt assured me he would be returning to El Dorado from time to time.

"Upon my return, we must have dinner again."

"We'd love to have you as our special guest in our home at Three Oaks. There is no need for you to spend your time in a hotel. We've got plenty of room at Three Oaks."

"Obadiah, I will certainly take you up on that invitation. I feel comfortable around your family. I'll be looking forward to it. I've got to tell you before I go. I believe Betsy and Mattie's fried chicken is the best I've eaten. I can still taste that wonderful fried chicken!"

It is now December 1, 1866. Our crops have been harvested. We had bumper crops of cotton and corn. We had an abundance of beans as well.

My slaves have worked hard and are celebrating with some relaxation and getting ready for Christmas.

Christmas will soon be here. We are excited that the Bradford families live close enough to come and go for the traditional Christmas activities. This year, they can return home to sleep in their own beds. There won't be any more sleeping on the floor are waiting in line to use the toilets. It will certainly be different from what we've been accustomed to in the past.

For the past three weeks, Mother and Bill have made several trips to El Dorado, Christmas shopping. I don't know how much longer Bill can take Mother's rigorous schedule. I look for him to collapse at any time. He looks like he has worked all day in the fields. Mother doesn't let on, but she, too, is getting tired. On most days, Mary goes with her shopping, since Sarah and Tanyua are busy at Penelope's school.

Penelope decided that on Friday before Christmas she will close the school down until January 5, 1867.

"Everyone needs a long break, including me," she said.

Since most of the women in the Bradford family are working, Mother has done some of their Christmas shopping as well.

She didn't mind. I just hope she doesn't wear herself completely out.

Our Christmas at Three Oaks this year was awesome. I've never seen so many babies. They were everywhere. One would have sworn there had been a three-year epidemic. This was a good thing!

James, Paul, and Isabella have reached the age that they know exactly what to do with Christmas presents. I was amazed at the way they tore into their presents.

Dr. Jim Burroughs and his lovely wife, Elizabeth, and baby son, Thomas James Burroughs, shared Christmas activities with us at Three Oaks.

During sharing time, Marion announced he had passed his medical board exams and was looking forward to getting his Arkansas State doctor's license in the mail any day. He went on to personally thank me for allowing him to do his internship under me, where he learned the skills necessary to becoming a doctor of medicine.

Marion's announcement was met with cheers, clapping, and toasting with Betsy's eggnog. After Marion's announcement, I stood and announced that Daniel was going to start doing his internship under me starting January 1.

After two years, like Marion, he will start taking his state board exams. Upon completion and passage of his board exams, he will be joining us as a full-fledged, certified doctor in the Bradford Medical Clinic.

I went on to say that the rate of growth in El Dorado will someday support a hospital. We are doing our part in training up doctors to staff the hospital.

"I'll toast to that," John said.

At this point, Alexander stepped forward to ask for prayer for him and Marion as they leave for Little Rock, Arkansas. The legislative session starts on January 15, 1867.

"From everything I've been hearing, this year's legislature may be the one that votes to ratify the Fourteenth Amendment. If we do, Arkansas will once again become part of the United States of America. I'm predicting that both houses of Congress will accomplish this task. We need your prayers in helping us make the right decisions," he said.

Lindy Bradford stepped forward and announced that she was pregnant, and Marion and she would be having another baby in August.

"I'll toast to that," Dent said.

Mother was normally the first to start off the sharing time, but today she announced she wanted to be last.

Finally the time came, and Mother stepped forward.

"I know you've wondered why I wanted to be last. Well, to tell you the truth I've got a lot to say. Please excuse me if I get sentimental and emotional.

"I want to start by saying this year, 1866, has been the best year of my life. I can't think of another year that can top this one.

"One of the hardest things I've ever endured in my life was leaving part of my children and grandchildren behind in Autauga and Dallas Counties. I started praying after coming to Union County that someday God would bring those from Dallas and Autauga Counties here.

"Take a good look around this room. Today every member of my family is present. Praise the Lord for answered prayer!"

Everyone in the parlor started applauding.

"I know if James could be here, he would be praising the Lord and rejoicing with me.

"I want all you to know how much I love you. You are the reason I live. Every morning when I wake up, I thank my Lord for my large family. God has given me Godly children and marvelous grandchildren. Every day I look forward to getting up and helping Penelope with my grandchildren. There isn't a day goes by that I'm not thinking about every one of you and what amazing things you are doing in your lives.

"I'm very proud of all of you. You give me hope and something to look forward to daily.

"I'm amazed to see what my older grandchildren have already accomplished in their lives.

"Today, I want to do something I've never done at Christmas. Dent has already shared with everyone his traditional reading of the Christmas Story. He always does a great job. My story is a little different, in that it consists of certain events of the Bible that have sequentially come about because of God's plan for all of us.

"It means a lot to me and has given me reassurance over the years that we have a loving God, one who meets our every need. It's a story that we should remember all through our lives, a story that I've treasured throughout my adult life and from the time I first came to know Jesus Christ as my savior.

"Several years ago, I taught a girls' Sunday school class. It gave me great pleasure to work with those girls. At first, not all the girls knew Jesus Christ as their savior, but before I stopped teaching the class, every one of them had accepted Jesus.

"To pave the way to salvation, I taught them a brief history of who God really is. I did this through exposing them to Bible facts. Here is that story.

"In the beginning, God created the Heavens and the Earth.

"He then created man in His own image. He made the first man from clay and breathed life into him. God called him Adam.

"After God created Adam, He saw that Adam was lonely. He decided that Adam needed a helpmate, so he put him into a deep sleep and removed one of his ribs and made a woman. He called her Eve. Eve became Adam's wife and helpmate.

"God gave Adam and Eve a beautiful place to live, the Garden of Eden. God instructed Adam that he and Eve could eat any fruit in the garden, except that from the tree of knowledge of good and evil. God said, 'If you do, you will surely die.'

"In the Garden of Eden, Satan lived. Satan, with his craftiness, convinced Eve that she and Adam would not die if they ate of the fruit of the tree of knowledge of good and evil. They disobeyed God and ate fruit from the tree of knowledge of good and evil. Their disobedience brought sin into the world. As a punishment, God expelled them from the Garden of Eden.

"Although God was angry with Adam and Eve, He blessed them with three sons, Cain, Abel, and Seth. Cain killed his brother, Abel, out of greed and jealousy and fled the country.

"Many years passed, and the earth was populated with sinful people. God grieved that he had created man.

"God looked down from Heaven and spoke to a man named Noah. Noah was a Godly man who found favor with God, and God chose him to build an Ark. Noah filled the Ark with two of every kind of animals, reptiles, and anything that could walk, crawl, or fly.

"After the Ark was built, God caused a great flood to come upon the earth. The rain fell for forty days and forty nights and covered the entire earth. Every living human being and creature that God had created was destroyed except for Noah and his family and the life Noah took onto the Ark.

"After the rain stopped, the waters eventually receded into the seas and rivers. Noah and his family left the ark and started replenishing the earth. God blessed Noah and his family.

"Several years after the flood, mankind returned to their sinful and wicked ways. Instead of destroying mankind again, God sent His Son, Jesus Christ, to be born of Mary, a virgin, for the purpose of saving mankind. Jesus was born in Bethlehem of Judea. He grew up in the city of Nazareth. He worked with his earthly father, Joseph, as a carpenter.

"At the age of thirty, he started His ministry, by calling out twelve disciples to accompany Him in His ministry. He taught them many good things. Jesus enabled them to heal the sick and afflicted and perform miracles.

"During the three year period that Jesus ministered to the lost, he faced opposition every day from the Pharisees and Sadducees. They considered Jesus' teaching a threat to what they taught in regard to the Law of Moses or Jewish law.

"After seeing the many followers of Jesus, the Pharisees and Sadducees made plans to kill Jesus. They were successful in turning the heart of one of Jesus' disciples, Judas, to plot a way to have Jesus arrested. They were successful, and Jesus was brought before Herod and was later crucified on the cross.

"Jesus paid the price for our sins by dying on the cross. He was buried in a tomb with a large rock rolled over the entrance of the tomb. He lay in the tomb for three days and three nights.

On the third day, an angel of the Lord came and rolled back the rock from the empty tomb.

"After Jesus rose from the grave, He joined his disciples for a meal. Jesus continued his teaching to his Apostles and was seen by more than five hundred people during the forty-five days before ascending to his Father in Heaven.

"Our Jesus lives today in Heaven. He intercedes for us in our prayer lives. He's there for us to call upon any minute of the day. He's our one and only savior.

"The Bible tells us that whosoever believes that Jesus Christ is the Son of God can be saved. All we have to do is confess our sins, repent, and ask Jesus to come into our hearts and we will be saved.

"John 3:16, says, 'For God so loved the world that he gave His only begotten Son, that whosoever believeth in Him should not perish, but have everlasting life. '

"The Bible teaches us that God loves us in spite of our sins.

"He gives us a way to be forgiven of our sins by praying for forgiveness. It is not His will that any man should perish and go to hell. He has prepared a place called Heaven, where we will live with Him for an eternity.

"My whole point in telling you this story is to remind everyone here that we are all sinners. We are saved by grace and not by works. It is my hope that everyone in this room will come to know Jesus Christ as their one and only savior.

"I want to end my talk with these words of encouragement. It's worked for me all these years, and it will work for you as well.

"Always pray, keep your faith, trust Him in all you do, and sit back and count your blessings. There will be many; I can assure you of that!"

As soon as Mother finished her story, Dent walked slowly toward her. He reached out to her and gave her a big hug and kiss on the cheek.

My sisters were crying, I was crying. In fact, I believe that almost everyone in the parlor was crying.

The love in that room was powerful. Mother is the nucleus of our family, and today, she made it quite obvious that she meant to continue her family influence upon all of us.

Some people in the room may not know why Mother told her story, but I do. Sarah's and Tanyua's husbands, Jim Crawford and John Ballard, have never made a profession of faith. In fact, they only go to church on special occasions when the children are involved in some type of church program. This is not to say that they are bad husbands or bad fathers, because that's not the case. They are good men and love their wives and children. It's just that they were not brought up in Christian families and don't feel the need to get involved in church worshipping.

My sisters, Sarah and Tanyua, are born-again Christians who hardly ever miss a church service. They are the spiritual leaders in their families and strive to see that their children are receiving God's word by attending church.

After things settled down, Mattie stepped forward and announced that she wanted to invite everyone to Hank's Christmas program to be held in the barn the following night.

"If you've never been to one of our Christmas services, you have missed a real spiritual blessing. Please come if you can.

"You will love it, I promise you! You might want to bring some warm blankets. As you know, we don't have heat in the barn." Everyone laughed.

Everyone took Mattie's invitation at heart and was present for Hank's Christmas program. As usual, Mattie's musical performance in song was beautiful. She was so relaxed. It was as if God had His hand on her as she sang and swayed with the music.

As Penelope played the piano for Mattie, I watched her. At times, she would close her eyes and shake her head as she felt the music in her soul.

I sat there in awe, thinking about the time I purchased her and Penelope in Selma, Alabama. I never dreamed I would have this type of relationship with either of them.

I'm a firm believer God works in mysterious ways. He has a purpose behind everything that happens to us. In my particular situation, I believe He gave me Mattie and Penelope to bring joy into my life.

Mattie is good at so many things. She uses her God-given talent to entertain others. She's a good wife, mother, grandmother, and mother-in-law. I can trust her in all things.

As for Penelope, I find it impossible to describe my love and admiration for her. Her love for me and my love for her bring sunshine to my soul. She's my joy in the morning and my peace in the afternoon. She builds me up when I'm down. She's a great mother and a hard worker. She is my best friend.

As usual, the Holy Spirit encircled us as we listen to Hank's message. We took blankets as Mattie suggested, but during Hank's preaching, blankets were being thrown back and people were standing and shouting, "Amen! Amen!"

As I looked around at our family, I noticed that Jim Crawford and John Ballard both seem to be enjoying the service. They were very attentive as Hank spoke the word of God. Hank's delivery was not like what one would hear in our white churches. His preaching wouldn't let anyone sleep in church. He was loud and shouted out God's word in such a manner that one had to be caught up in what he was saying. There were lots of "Preach on Brother! Amen! That's right, brother! And, praise the Lord!"

CHAPTER 43

By the end of January, 1867, Marion and Alexander were right in the middle of chaos in the Arkansas State Legislature.

Governor Isaac Murphy had worked diligently since his election in early 1864 to promote reconciliation and to prepare the state for its return to the union.

In the elections of 1866, however, a combination of Democrats and former Whigs organized a Conservative party that swept away almost the entire Unionist ticket elected in 1864 and returned power to many of the same people who had run the state before the war. Governor Murphy survived only because his term was not up until 1868.

The old planter elites were also engaged in an attempt to restore their prewar economic status. Most of the members had retained control of their land, but with slavery gone, they had to bargain for the labor of their former slaves.

The seceded states were divided into five military districts. Arkansas and Mississippi constituted the Fourth Military District, each under the control of a military officer.

The states were required to draft new constitutions providing for universal male suffrage and to ratify the Fourteenth Amendment to the U.S. Constitution. Many former Confederates were disqualified from holding office or participating in the process.

Things in Union County had returned to normal. Everyone was going about their business without conflict of interest.

Virgil was our new mayor. He spent most of his time in the courthouse making decisions as mayor.

My sister, Mary, took on the responsibility of running their merchandise store. She didn't mind, because she's been working at the store since they first arrived in El Dorado. Mary has a good business head. She is good at organizing and had a good understanding of finances.

Penelope is back running her school. She and the Freedom Bureau are still getting along well. She believes in what she's doing and I believe the Freedom Bureau shares her goals as well.

In most cases, the Freedom Bureau is doing a good thing for the Negro children. Negro schools are springing up throughout the South. For the first time in their lives, Negro children are being educated.

On February 27, 1867, whooping cough hit Union County. We had several cases in Union, Columbia, and Ouachita counties. Some patients were very sick, and some have died.

It appears that no one is exempt from getting it. The germ is very infectious. Everyone who comes into contact with someone who has it should wash their hands thoroughly with hot, soapy water.

Thus far, we've lost six people in Union County from whooping cough.

As I was leaving Three Oaks, Mattie caught me in the hall.

"Obadiah, could I speak with you for a minute?" Mattie asked.

"What's up, Mattie?"

"I guess you noticed that Big Jim wasn't at breakfast. Obadiah, I left him in bed. He's got an awful cough, and he's running fever. I was wondering if you might look in on him before you leave."

"I did miss him this morning, but I assumed he was helping George do something in the barn. Let's go take a look at him."

After I entered the bedroom, there was an awful odor. It was like an odor of death.

I checked Big Jim's temperature, and he was burning up with fever. He opened his eyes, and they were yellow and bloodshot. He groaned, as he was hurting.

"Big Jim, how are you feeling?"

"I'm not feeling well, Master Bradford!" he said with a weak voice and then began coughing.

"Mattie, how long has he had this fever and cough?"

"He's been coughing for three days, but just last night his fever started."

"Mattie, I'm going to give you some medicine to start him on. When I get home today, I'll check him again. Meanwhile, don't let him get up and be stirring around. Keep him in bed and give him lots of fluids to drink."

"Thanks, Obadiah!"

"Walk out with me, Mattie."

"I don't feel good about this, Obadiah. Big Jim just doesn't get sick. I've never seen him sick!"

"Mattie, I'm afraid he's come down with whooping cough. We need to keep the kids away from him until he gets well. They don't need to be around him with this high fever, nor do you, but I understand you want to be near him.

"Here's what I want you to do. We need to get that fever down. The medicine I gave you should help, but I want you to use cold packs on his forehead and wipe his face and throat off and on during the day. Don't let him get up and be stirring around. If he needs to go to the toilet, bring him a bucket. We've got to isolate him from everyone else. Do you understand?"

"I do understand, Obadiah. I've heard whooping cough is killing lots of people here in Union County. Do you think Big Jim is in danger of dying?"

"Mattie, Big Jim is strong as an ox. I'm hoping his strength can help bring him through this. I would suggest that you make you a mask when you are working with him, and wash your hands after attending to him. I'm going to tell Betsy and Mother that you will not be helping with the food preparation until we get Big Jim through this ordeal.

"Mattie, you are putting yourself at risk by being around Big Jim. Are you sure you're fine with this?"

"Obadiah, Jim's my responsibility. I know the dangers involved, but he's my husband, and I want to take care of him."

"All right, I've got to go, but if he turns for the worse, you send Bill to town and get me."

"Thanks, Obadiah!"

After examining Big Jim I, too, had a bad feeling about him. He had a rattling in his chest as though he had lots of fluid building up. I hated this for Mattie. She didn't need to be around him, but I knew she wouldn't have it any other way.

I found Mother sewing in the parlor. "Good morning, Mother!"

"Good morning, Obadiah. I thought you'd already left for work," she said.

"I would have been gone a long time ago, but Big Jim has come down with whooping cough."

"Oh, my, whooping cough! Obadiah, that's bad!"

"I know, Mother. This is what I need for you to do. I don't want you to go near, Big Jim! Mattie is going to look after him. She's the only one that needs to be around him. I've covered all this with her already. I just need for you to help Betsy. If Penelope and the kids get home before I do, don't let them go near Mattie and Big Jim's room. Make sure Little Jim and Benjamin don't go into Mattie's room. We've got to isolate Big Jim from everyone.

"We are seeing several people at the medical clinic with whooping cough. I'm afraid this may become an epidemic. You know what that can do. I want you to tell Hank to survey all our slaves to find out how many may be coughing and running fever. I need that count when I come home tonight. We need to start taking extra precautions around here."

"Obadiah, I will get this done. You and the others at your office need to be extra careful in examining and caring for those who have the germ."

"You're exactly right, Mother, and we will do that. You have a good day, and I'll see you tonight. If you need anything today, send Bill to town and get me."

At the office we saw several who had contracted the disease. They were coughing badly and running fever. All we could do was to give them medicine and send them home to battle with this terrible disease.

This was the first experience Marion and Daniel had with whooping cough. I gave them the usual lecture of washing their hands very carefully after each patient they saw.

Tomorrow Daniel and I will be paying visits throughout the county for my follow-up visits to see my regular patients. I'm in hopes that the whooping cough has not hit them.

Big Jim has been on my mind all day long. I'm hoping when I get home that he will be better.

After we closed our office, I called a staff meeting. I related to them my concerns about those who have the whooping cough. It appears that we may have an epidemic confronting us. I went over some extra precautionary measures and said good night and headed home to Three Oaks.

Upon my arrival, Penelope met me on the porch.

After a brief hug and kiss Penelope said, "Obadiah, let's sit down."

We sat down in our comfortable rocking chairs and began to talk.

"When I got home today, Catherine told me what was happening with Big Jim. I went down to their room and knocked on the door. Mother came to the door and stepped out in the hall. Obadiah, Mother looked awful. She looked so pale!"

"Penelope, I didn't want you to be bothered by this at school. Mattie is just tired. She's lost a lot of sleep from Big Jim coughing so much. I hated to leave her alone with Big Jim, but she wouldn't hear about someone else taking care of him."

"I know; she told me the same thing as well. How bad is it, Obadiah?"

"I've got to go check on him. He wasn't doing well when I left this morning."

"Is there a chance he might die?"

"Penelope, my dear, there is always a chance he might die. We have been losing patients to the whooping cough breakout since it started. It could get worse."

"Before you go, what should we do with the kids? They are always running up and down the hallway."

"Let's make sure the kids stay away from Big Jim's room. Mother is going to find a place for the boys to sleep until Big Jims gets through this ordeal."

"Oh, Obadiah, what are we going to do if Big Jim dies?"

"Penelope, let's don't think about that right now. We must remain strong. You need to offer your mother as much comfort as you can at this time."

I went straight to Mattie's room. I knocked on the door and went in. As I entered the room, that same odor was still present, but stronger.

"Hello, Mattie, how are things?"

Mattie looked at me and shook her head in a negative way as tears streamed down her face.

"Mattie, it's not good is it?"

"Obadiah, I've got me one sick husband. I've tried everything you told me to do, but I've not been able to get his fever down. He's been talking out of his head all day long."

"Let me take a listen to his heart and lungs."

What I heard wasn't good. The fluid had built up even more from this morning. Mattie was right, Big Jim was a sick man.

"Obadiah, is there anything we can do?"

"Mattie, I'm afraid it's up to God from here on out. We don't have a cure for whooping cough. I wished we did, but we must now wait and see what happens.

"We can try putting socks soaked with a menthol and turpentine concoction around his neck to see if that would help his breathing, but other than that, I don't know of anything we can do differently."

"We can pray, Obadiah! We can surely pray!"

"We can do that, Mattie!"

"Will you pray with me, Obadiah?"

We held hands while Mattie held Big Jim's hand. I felt so bad for Mattie. She waited so long to have someone to love her and for her to love back. She now stands before the man she loves, who is the father of her two beautiful boys. She knows he's suffering, and there isn't anything she can do about it.

"Mattie, I'm going to get George's wife to come and sit with Big Jim tonight so you can get you some rest."

"No, Obadiah! I can't leave him. I'm going to be here for him. I don't want to put someone else in danger of contracting this horrible disease. I'm staying right here. If you don't mind, let George and Hank bring that small bed from upstairs in here. I'll sleep on the small bed. If you will do this, it will be much appreciated."

I knew that I couldn't argue with my mother-in-law. She is head strong when she wants to be. I will honor her wishes.

This is one time I wished we had a hospital. The next time that Daniel Pratt comes to El Dorado, I plan to hit him up with the idea of funding us a hospital. I hear he's doing quite well financially with the one in Prattville, Alabama.

About four o'clock in the morning, I heard a knock on our bedroom door.

I slipped out of bed and tiptoed over to the door. I opened the door and Mattie was standing at the door crying. Big tears were streaming down her face. I knew what had happened before she told me.

"What is it, Mattie?" I asked pulling the door closed behind me. I didn't want to wake Penelope.

"Obadiah, I believe Big Jim is gone. I don't think he's breathing."

"Let's go see, Mattie!"

By this time, Penelope opened the door and saw her mother crying. She went immediately to her and embraced her.

We all went to Mattie's room. I took my stethoscope and listened for a heartbeat. I checked the neck for a beat and then his wrist. Mattie was right. Big Jim had passed on to be with our Lord and Savior.

I turned to Mattie and said, "I'm so sorry, Mattie. He's gone."

Mattie let out a big scream. Penelope again embraced her, trying to console her. I quickly closed the door so others in the house couldn't hear Mattie's crying. Mattie was heartbroken. She had been through so much in the past, but this was going to be another hard challenge for her to overcome. She had lost the man of her life, a man who loved her and their children. They had made so many plans together. "Oh, Lord, please ease Mattie's pain," I prayed.

We buried Big Jim in the cemetery on a small hill north of our plantation house. It was close enough that Mattie and her sons could walk to visit his grave from time to time.

After the funeral, Mattie came to me and asked if she could talk to me.

"What's on your mine, Mattie?"

"Obadiah, I've been worried about what the future holds for me and my boys. Big Jim and I had decided that after we were freed as slaves we'd move into El Dorado and start a life of our own. What will I do, Obadiah, when you free me? Who will want a forty-nine year-old former slave? I will have two boys to educate and feed. Where will I go?"

"Mattie, Mattie, my dearest Mattie! You stop your worrying right now about what's going to happen. First of all, you, Little Jim, and Benjamin are family. You're not going anywhere. Your home is with Penelope and me. Did you think I would kick you out? Oh, my dear Mattie, we love you so much. You've got a home with Penelope and me for the rest of your life. I will take care of you as long as I live."

"Obadiah, do you really mean all of this?"

"I really mean it, Mother-in-law. You are the very best mother-in-law a man could ask for. You and the boys can stay here until you die."

"Obadiah, you have lifted much of my burden from my heart just now. Thank you, thank you," she said as she threw her arms around me.

"Mattie, there is one other thing before you go. Penelope and I were talking last night. It's time for us to burn that owner's paper my father gave me some fourteen years ago. After tonight, you will be a free woman. Your kids will be free as well. I've prepared a document to prove you're a free woman. You can come and go as you wish. You may want to accompany Mother to town from time to time. Instead of working for me, free, you will start earning a salary for your work. What you do with your money will be of no concern of mine.

"Your food and lodging will be free. The only thing I would ask is that you continue to help Betsy cook the family meals and help look after your grandchildren. I don't think I could do without your cooking!"

"Obadiah, I love you so much. You have been like a son to me all these years. You've treated me and Penelope with kindness. Your Christian love is something I've tried to pattern my life after. You've meant so much to us over the years. When I think about where we'd be or what would have happened if that Mr. Bishop had bought us in Selma, I shiver!

"I truly appreciate you letting me be part of this family. I assure you I won't let you down. I'll earn my keep, and I'll take care of my grandchildren and anyone else you want me to.

"Please know I'll always be thankful to you for what you've done for Penelope by making her your wife. You two were meant to be together in God's eyes. I truly believe that.

"I will miss Big Jim, but I know I must go on with my life. I've got two young sons to raise. I want them to grow up and be as successful as my Penelope. I also love my grandchildren and will do my very best to make them a good grandmother. I'm a very blessed person. Thank you Obadiah, and praise the Lord!"

CHAPTER 44

Big Jim was not the only slave we buried. Before the whooping cough epidemic was over, we lost Sam and John, who were our chief cooks at the bunkhouse. We also lost Myrtle, who was married to Samson. All three of these slaves had been with us since our years at Black Oak and Twin Oaks in Alabama.

John and Sam left behind their wives and children. Both have grown children who will be available to look after their mothers. We buried all three in the cemetery next to Big Jim.

Several others died throughout Union, Columbia, and Calhoun Counties. Those of us who administered to those having whooping cough were blessed by remaining healthy. We wore proper clothing, used masks, and washed our hands thoroughly after each time we touched a whooping cough patient.

Marion got his first taste of seeing patients die with this horrible disease.

He came to me one day and said, "Obadiah, I don't think I'm mentally ready for this epidemic. I never dreamed I'd see so many die of whooping cough. Every time I'd lose a patient, I felt sadness in my heart. I've questioned whether I've done enough for those I've treated."

"Marion, that's to be expected. I still question whether I've done as much as I can to save lives. This is something we will always question. We can pray and use our knowledge and skills, but God has to do the rest. It's always been my opinion that God has His own reasons for taking loved ones on to Heaven.

"Big Jim is a good example. He made Mattie a good husband, and the boys, a good father. He was a good man who knew Jesus Christ as his savior. He played a major role for us at Three Oaks. I can't remember one time that he was sick. Mattie and I tried everything to bring him through the crisis period, but the

Lord saw fit to take Jim home. It's hard to understand, but somehow we've got to shake things off and move on. There are still lots of sick folks out there who need our attention."

After the whooping cough epidemic, we found ourselves getting back to a normal routine.

One day, I was eating lunch at Jake's Restaurant when Mr. William George came in to eat lunch. Before he seated himself, he came over to my table and said, "Dr. Bradford, how are things going with you?"

"Things are going good now that the whooping cough epidemic has run its course," I answered.

"I know what you mean. My father was one of the many who died from whooping cough."

"I'm sorry to hear that, Mr. George."

"Thank you, Dr. Bradford."

"How are things with you?" I asked.

"Everything is going good for me. I saw you sitting here and thought I'd ask you a question, if that's all right."

"Do you want to sit down?"

"No, but thanks. My friend John Wisner is saving me a spot at his table. I was wondering if you might still be interested in my big storage building in south El Dorado."

"Mr. George, I just might be," I said.

"I'm interested in selling it. It was really my father's property, but he left it to me in his will. I don't really need the old building."

"Do you have time in the next few days to give me a tour of the building? It will have to be after my office hours."

"What about tomorrow?"

"Tomorrow would work for me."

"All right, I'll meet you at the building at five o'clock, if that's all right with you," Mr. George said.

"That will work for me, Mr. George."

"Just call me William, if you'd like. Everyone calls me William."

"William it will be," I said as I shook his hand. He then left to join his friend.

As I finished my lunch, I thought, Could this be one of those providential things that's meant to be?

After making the tour of the old building, I decided that was the building we needed to convert into a church for Hank. I made William an offer, and he immediately accepted.

The building would need some repairs before Hank could start his ministry. I figure by early spring of 1868, Hank would be able to utilize the building as his church.

I'm excited about this. Hank has really been praying for this to come about. He will certainly be surprised.

Hank doesn't know it yet, but I plan to give him and his family their freedom as a Christmas present. As a free man, he will have an opportunity to build his church congregation. He will still work for me and continue to live at Three Oaks until he gets his feet on the ground. I will continue to use him as my overseer.

It will be some time before the Negro congregation can financially support Hank's ministry. His main goal is to introduce Jesus Christ to the Negro population. The financial support can come later. He knows it will be a financial struggle for the freed slaves after they receive their freedom.

The weather in August of 1867 was typical, hot and dry. Although, the weather has been hot, our field crops are looking good. If nothing unforeseen happens, we will have goods crops of cotton and corn. The beans are looking good as well.

Hank has been busy both on the plantation as well as spending time in El Dorado working on his church building. He's pouring his heart and soul into painting the building and making repairs. Some of the slaves are helping him. Hank is a leader and is respected greatly among the other slaves. They would do anything for him. They, too, look forward to the day they can worship in the new church.

Jim Crawford has made much progress in building the sawmills at Norphlet and Mt. Holly. The target date for completion is sometime in January of 1868. He's instructed my brother-in-law, John Ballard, to start interviewing potential workers for the two sawmills.

For weeks now, we've seen several families moving to El Dorado. Some are free slave families and some are white.

Daniel Pratt, who is financing the sawmills, has also invested a great deal of money in building houses in North and South El Dorado. Being the brilliant businessman he is, he realizes he will need good labor to work at his sawmills.

As I've said many times, Mr. Pratt is both intelligent and a good business man. He thinks ahead and plans accordingly. By the time the sawmills are finished and ready to operate, he will have a labor force available.

Another thing Mr. Pratt is aware of is that sometime in the near future, the Arkansas Legislature will ratify the Fourteenth Amendment and Arkansas will be readmitted to the United States of America. He knows not to count on slave labor.

Penelope and Mother have organized a big Thanksgiving celebration at Three Oaks. George, Hank, and some of the other men have been busy roasting two big hogs for Thanksgiving. One of the hogs will be given to the slaves as they celebrate Thanksgiving in the bunkhouse.

It seems strange not to see Big Jim helping with the activities this year. We miss him a lot around here. Mattie has the boys to keep her busy. She's doing well but gets lonesome at times.

It has been my policy since taking over both Twin Oaks and Three Oaks to share my good fortunate with my slaves during July Fourth, Thanksgiving, and Christmas. When the Bradfords come together to celebrate, the slaves celebrate as well.

Our Thanksgiving celebration went well. We celebrated Mother's birthday as well. She turned sixty-nine years old last week. Everyone is amazed of Mother's youthful look and her good physical condition. She is very healthy and may live to be a hundred.

Hank and our slaves finished the harvesting of all our crops.

We also had our annual hog killings, and the meat is being preserved in the big smokehouse. Besides me, George, Hank, and Bill have keys to the smokehouse. It is George's responsibility to distributed pork to each family for their meat supplement.

The slaves are allotted a certain amount of corn, potatoes, and other dried vegetables two times a week for their needs. During the winter months, the slaves who have family members cook their own meals in their slave quarters.

The food for the single male slaves is provided in the bunkhouse. When Sam and John died from whooping cough, Hank selected Samson and Damon to replace them as cooks for the bunkhouse.

During the Christmas season, the slaves receive new clothes, shoes, and blankets. Our slaves look forward to Christmas each year. The new blankets are always much appreciated, as well as the clothes and shoes.

As usual, our Christmas was held at Three Oaks. All the Bradfords were present. We observed our traditional Christmas activities by toasting our achievements with Betsy's eggnog. Dent entertained us as usual with his rendition of the Christmas Story. We opened our Christmas presents and had our annual sharing time.

Alexander and Marion were the first to step forward and share that their good news was the upcoming births of new babies. Both Lindy and Jennie will be giving birth to babies in the month of June, 1868.

Alexander announced that he felt sure that the Arkansas Legislature was going to vote on ratifying the Fourteenth Amendment this coming year. He said, "It's going to happen! We'd best get ready for it. If the Legislature ratifies the Fourteenth Amendment, Arkansas will be readmitted to the United States of America."

At the conclusion of our sharing time, I walked to the center of the parlor and asked for everyone's attention.

"Today, I asked my good friend, Hank, and his family to be present so I could make a special presentation to them.

"As you know, Hank and I are the best of friends and have been since we brought him home to Twin Oaks. Hank and his family are special to us in many ways. As my overseer he has worked hard in developing Three Oaks into one of the best plantations in Union County.

"It is with my love and appreciation for Hank and his family that I've declared this day, in my home, the Hank Banister day!

"Hank has chosen Banister as his legal surname. He and his family will be known from this day forward as the Banisters. He chose Banister because of his love and respect for Dr. Banister of Autauga County.

"Today, I want to recognize Hank and his family and honor them by presenting to Hank this legal document that reads, 'From this day forward, I, Dr. Obadiah Bradford, declare that Hank Banister and his family are free from the bonds of slavery. From this day forward, he and his family are free people.'

"Hank, I love and respect you and your family, and it's a great honor for me to present you with this document that declares you as free. May God bless you and your family."

"Obadiah, I'm so humbled by this great gift. I'm at loss for words. Please forgive me!" he said, dropping his head.

He stood there for a few seconds and then raised his head with tears running down his face and spoke.

"There is something I've wanted to say to the Bradford family for several years. I trust this is the appropriate time to say what's on my heart. Since Obadiah became my master and friend, I haven't felt like a slave. The Bradford family has always made me feel comfortable.

"Mrs. Catherine, you've treated me like a son, I thank you for that and will always treasure your kindness and what you've done for me and my family!

"Penelope, you and Sarah taught me to read, write, and do arithmetic. The communication skills you taught me have allowed me to become an educated man.

"Obadiah, you led me to Jesus Christ by explaining the plan of salvation. From there, I studied my Bible, and God's called me to preach.

"You've supported me in my ministry in so many ways. I shall never forget what you've done for me in making it possible for me and my people to worship in a real church. I will always be beholden to you for making this happen.

"There have been many times I've thanked the good Lord for Master James Bradford, who outbid that horrible man, Mr. Bishop. If Bishop had bought me, I probably would be dead by now. I wouldn't have met my Nanny, and we wouldn't have our two boys.

"Obadiah, I can assure you, you will not regret making me a free man. My family and I will make you proud of us.

"Thank you for this wonderful piece of paper. I will cherish this document and hide it away to become part of my heritage for as long as I live. This paper will be handed down in my family from one generation to the next."

As soon as Hank ended his talk, Dent stepped forward.

"Let's toast to Hank and his family!"

"To Hank and his family," John said as everyone enjoyed more eggnog.

I don't think there was a dry eye in the room when Hank completed his talk.

The day after our Christmas celebration at Three Oaks, our family was blessed again by attending Hank's Christmas program in El Dorado. This time, instead of having to sit in a cold, damp barn, we had the privilege of sitting in a warm, comfortable church house.

Hank and many of his friends labored long and hard to have the building finished by Christmas. The program was heartwarming, as usual. I know God is going to bless Hank's ministry in El Dorado. As I've said all along, Hank is a great spiritual leader, one who has the ability to lead and influence the lives of those he touches.

Among those in our family who were present for Hank's Christmas program were Jim Crawford and his family and John Ballard and his family. Mother looked at me, smiled and winked, as if to say, maybe the Lord is working on my sons-in-law. All through the preaching service, Jim and John were very attentive as Hank preached the word of God.

Everything went well during the cold and damp winter months. We had three snows, two in February and one during the first week in March.

Hank and our slaves were successful in getting our fields ready for planting. In early March, the potatoes were planted. In a few weeks, we will see the potatoes peeping through the soil. It will soon be gardening time. The daffodils are in full bloom, and green grass is popping up all around Three Oaks.

Penelope's school gets larger by the month. She's enrolled several more colored children who have moved into El Dorado. The colored children's families have moved here in anticipation of working in one of Daniel Pratt's sawmills.

Penelope's white population has increased as well. Several white families have moved to El Dorado for the same reason as the free slaves, to work in the sawmills.

CHAPTER 45

On June 15, 1868, I received a telegram from Alexander. He wanted to share with me about a very important vote coming up in congress. The vote would be on the ratification of the Thirteenth and Fourteenth Amendments. He said, "Get ready, it's going to pass."

The Reconstruction Act of March 2, 1867, outlined the readmission of the onetime rebel states. The Act divided the former Confederate states into five military districts.

The Reconstruction Act required each Confederate state to write a new Constitution that had to be approved by a majority of state voters, including newly emancipated slaves, before being considered for representation in Congress. In addition, each state was required to ratify the Thirteenth and Fourteenth Amendments to the Constitution.

The Arkansas legislature was dominated by radical Republicans who had established universal male suffrage while disenfranchising former Confederates, mostly Democrats. One of the good things they did was to enact a free universal public education system in Arkansas.

The state of Arkansas has come under racial violence in some parts of the state by the Ku Klux Klan, comprising mainly former Confederates. It was so bad that the U.S. Army and the Arkansas Militia had to intervene to keep order in some communities. The Klan was very active in fourteen counties in Arkansas. Union County was not one of them.

It was on June 22, 1868, that Arkansas was readmitted to the Union. Arkansas became the first rebel state to be readmitted to the Union.

By June 25, 1868, Louisiana, Florida, North Carolina, and South Carolina were readmitted to the Union.

After Arkansas was readmitted, the slaves were freed throughout the state. In Union County, the majority of the slaves stayed with their previous plantation owners. Some took their chances and moved into town or elsewhere in the state.

Some, with the help of the Freedom Bureau, took up share-cropping with their plantation owners. This practice proved to be the least popular because of cheating tactics used by some plantation owners.

One hundred percent of my slaves stayed at Three Oaks.

They were allowed to have free housing and freedom to make gardens, and were provided an area so they could raise chickens and hogs. They were given complete freedom.

In return for free lodging, garden spots, and a place to raise their animals, they committed themselves to me during planting and harvesting time. They were paid a wage for that.

Hank split his time between working for me and doing his ministry in El Dorado. He became popular fast among the Negro population. His church was always full of worshippers. As I predicted, his leadership qualities had gained him the love and respect from his church family as well as other Negroes on the south side of town.

Because of the financial support of the Freedom Bureau, Hank started a feeding program to feed the hungry at his church.

What I feared most about the freedom of the slave had already raised its ugly head. There are so many slaves who are hungry. They can't find work and have inadequate shelter to live in.

Hank is doing everything he can to help them survive. If it wasn't for Hank's feeding program, many of the freed slaves would starve. He is surely living up to the commandment of the Bible where it instructs us to help the poor and needy.

In 1868, Congress passed the Free Education Act that guaranteed a free education to all white and Negro children across the United States

The white patrons who had been paying Penelope tuition for their children's education were no longer obligated to pay.

Penelope was approached by state education officials to become the headmaster of the first white school in El Dorado.

This offer meant she would have to resign her present position as the headmaster of the colored school due to the rule colored and whites were to be segregated.

After visiting with the Freedom Bureau, she convinced them to let Sarah run the colored school, and she would take the white school. The state education officials agreed to her terms, and she was made headmaster of the first free white school in El Dorado.

The white school was built on the west side of El Dorado, while the colored school remained on the south side.

The year of 1868 would certainly go down in the history books in Arkansas.

Powell Clayton, who was a Union General during the Civil War, was elected governor on July 2, 1868.

Governor Clayton immediately went to work to keep the Confederates out of power and protect the newly freed blacks. His political appointments were from Northern states, leading his opponents to paint him and his allies as carpetbaggers.

In order to build Arkansas's infrastructure, Clayton raised taxes, another unpopular decision. Financial incentives of $9 million dollars went to railroad companies who laid 662 miles of track by the end of reconstruction. The state also paid out $193 million dollars on several other infrastructure programs.

After Clayton was elected governor, many residents were frustrated by the radical Republicans who had taken control of most county offices.

The KKK began what was called white-capping throughout Arkansas, and Governor Clayton declared martial law in ten counties, and later added four more.

Clayton used the state militia throughout the state to suppress violence. His declarations of martial law in fourteen counties in 1868 successfully ended the Klan activities within the state.

I was happy we weren't one of those fourteen counties who participated in the KKK. The people of El Dorado, on the whole, are good, decent, Christian people.

Among Governor Clayton's accomplishments during his three-year administration was the construction of several railroads. He created Arkansas' first free public school system. He established the first Arkansas industrial university, the basis for the future University of Arkansas in Fayetteville. He also established the Arkansas School for the Blind and the Arkansas School for the Deaf in Little Rock.

In September of 1868, several interesting political developments occurred throughout the South. One such development happened in Georgia.

The El Dorado News-Times ran an article that made me sick to my stomach. The article reported that Negro elected officials in the Georgia State Legislature were ousted from the legislature. The story printed a quote, "The Negro is unfit to rule the state," the Atlanta Constitution declared.

On November 3, 1868, General Ulysses Grant was elected President of the United States. The Electoral College vote was 214 to 4 over his Democratic opponent, Horatio Seymour of New York. Grant received 3,013,650 popular votes, giving him 52.66 percent of the vote, while Seymour received 2,708,744 votes, or 27.21 percent of the popular vote.

By December, things began to settle down and most people started concentrating on Christmas.

On Christmas Day, the temperature reached about seventy-four degrees. Instead of having all our activities inside the house, we moved to the front porch.

The children enjoyed playing in the yard. We older people enjoyed sitting on the front porch sipping eggnog, eating Betsy and Mattie's Christmas desserts, and playing cards. As usual, we discussed politics and predicted what the future held for all of us. I, for one, wasn't worried, I figured God knew best for us and would continue to bless us according to our needs.

In late January, 1869, the Freedom Bureau was instrumental in starting up nearly three thousand schools, serving over one hundred fifty thousand students in the South. Who would have ever guessed that there would be that many children attending public schools across the South?

Penelope continued to run the first white school built in the city of El Dorado. Her goal is to make her school the best school in the South. Her background training and experience at Mrs. Adams' Boarding School in Boston has equipped her with the knowledge and understanding necessary in running an efficient school.

She's always looking for ways to improve. She has employed some really good teachers, who are dedicated and expect the best out of their students.

Sarah continues to do a great job as the headmaster at the colored school. She, too, has employed qualified teachers to help her. She and her teachers expect the very best from their students as well.

On February 26, 1869, Congress passed the Fifteenth Amendment to the United States Constitution. This amendment addressed violence in the South, and the amendment stated that the right to vote cannot be denied on the basis of "race, color, or previous condition of servitude." It was sent to all the states for ratification.

The month of March lived up to its windy nature. It was really cold in the mornings, but by noon the temperature was just right.

Due to the cold, damp weather in March, we had an unusual number of bad colds and pneumonia. In fact, we had several die of flu-like symptoms and pneumonia.

We lost several older whites and Negroes throughout Union County. Mother got sick for the first time in years, but she pulled through, with Mattie's help. Mattie's good health was a strong asset in taking care of both Mother and the kids. Mattie demanded that Mother drink lots of fluids and get lots of rest, and that's exactly what Mother needed.

During the first part of March, tragedy hit Three Oaks. We were saddened by the deaths of Myrtle and Annie, widows of our deceased slaves, Sam and John. They were both getting up in age and were too weak to fight off the effects of pneumonia. We buried them in the same cemetery up on the hill, east of our plantation house, next to their husbands, Sam and John.

Daniel Pratt's two sawmills are now in full operation. Dent, John, and I have started cutting the large virgin pine and hardwood trees from our plantations. We are getting a good price for our logs. The extra income has come in handy in providing income to pay our freed slaves.

It is my hope the price of cotton, corn, and beans will make a comeback in future years. I do believe when all the Confederate rebel states are readmitted to the Union that the price of our money crops will return to normal.

In April, the El Dorado News-Times reported that the U.S. Supreme Court, in a 5 to 3 vote in Texas v. White, declared Radical Reconstruction constitutional, stating that secession from the Union is illegal.

The summer brought on some good rains, which helped our cotton, corn, and bean crops. In fact, it appears we will have a bumper crop of all three money crops. My freed slaves have been true to their word. They were present for cultivation, planting, and now for the fall harvesting.

The money I pay them normally goes for clothes, shoes, and the purchase of hogs, milk cows, chickens, and household goods. They raise most of their food from the gardens.

On Sundays, I let George use the plantation wagons to transport the freed slaves to Hank's church in El Dorado. Sometimes it takes four wagons to haul everyone.

There continues to be violence against Negroes across the South. In Georgia, a Negro legislator, Abram Coby, was kidnapped and whipped. In some states, laws are being made that favor the old, established, Democrat party that was in office before the Civil War. They are now winning back their legislative positions, while Negroes are losing their legislative representation and influence throughout the South.

The laws that were part of Reconstruction after the Civil War gave favor to Negroes and gave them a better opportunity to get elected to state legislatures. But now, these laws are beginning to change, and Negroes are being voted out across the South.

I can see how this could get worse. Equality is not here yet. It may take years before the Negroes can feel secure in the South, especially in the Old South.

It's apparent from what I see and read that the freed slave is not, and will not, be treated as equal in the eyes of most Southern people. I'm afraid this violence that we are seeing across the South will continue.

I continue to pray that the Thirteenth, Fourteenth, and Fifteenth Amendments to our Constitution will someday be the answer to fair and equitable treatment for all races.

As for me and my family, we will do our part in seeing that equality is afforded to our freed slaves and all who we come into contact with. It may take years of suffering, but eventually, just maybe, the Negro population will come to be accepted for who they are in our society.

On December 20, 1869, the public schools shut down for a two-week Christmas break. Because of the Christmas break, the city of El Dorado has come alive with lots of Christmas shoppers.

One such shopper is Mother. For several days in a row, Bill has been driving Mother to El Dorado. Since Christmas break started, she's been joined by Penelope, Sarah, Tanyua, and Mary.

I am so thankful I have a legitimate excuse not to do Christmas shopping. I hate shopping in the worst way. To me, shopping is for women. I do manage to take off enough time to purchase Christmas gifts for my immediate family members. For some reason, Penelope always manages to drag me along with her when we shop for our immediate family.

Penelope is like Mother; she has the names of everyone we buy something for. She normally knows exactly what she wants to get for each particular person. How do they do it?

On Christmas Day, we noticed Mother didn't show the bounce in her step that she normally has at Christmastime.

We just assumed her age of seventy-two was catching up with her, and all the Christmas shopping had worn her down a bit.

The family again celebrated Christmas at Three Oaks. As long as Mother is alive, we will continue to host Christmas activities.

The Bradford family continues to grow in numbers. Since last Christmas, Mary Catherine gave birth to a boy. She and Benjamin named him Johnny Lee Madison.

Jennie gave birth to a girl. She and Alexander named her Susanna Bell Bradford.

Marion and Lindy were blessed with another boy, and they named him William James Bradford.

We had one wedding this past year. Jennie Bradford, John's daughter, got married to Sam Mason in an October wedding ceremony at First Baptist in El Dorado.

During the Christmas sharing time, Daniel announced he had passed his entire Arkansas state medical tests and was patiently waiting for his license to practice medicine.

We are all excited that Daniel will be joining our staff at my clinic. Like Marion, Daniel is going to be a fine doctor.

During the past few months, I've been praying earnestly that God would provide a means for us to have a hospital in El Dorado.

During Daniel Pratt's last visit to El Dorado in October, he and I had an interesting talk about a partnership in a hospital.

Mr. Pratt has done well financially from the hospital he built for Prattville. The hospital is making good money and, at the same time, fulfilling the medical needs of the residents of Autauga and the surrounding counties.

I was able to present my ideas to him in regard to a hospital and asked him if he'd consider being a business partner with me in making this happen.

Much to my surprise, he said, "I'll consider it! I'll give you my answer in a few months."

"I need to tell you that Dr. Burroughs is interested in sharing in the building cost as well."

"Obadiah, you're proposal is sounding better the longer we talk," he said with a smile.

"Then, you will consider it, right?"

"I promise you, I'll consider it, on one condition."

"What is that?"

"If you will promise me you will be the chief of staff."

"I'll make you that promise right now. I'd be honored to be chief of staff."

"All right, let me sleep on this for a couple of months, and I'll give you an answer."

I've never known Daniel Pratt to forget a conversation, especially when it comes to finances. I feel confident that he will give me an answer soon.

CHAPTER 46

On the morning of January 15, 1870, we awoke to one of the biggest snows I'd seen since moving to Union County. In some areas, we had as much as a foot of snow. The snow came at a good time. It fell during Friday night, giving us two days of sun to melt some of the snow off the roads before we had to go back to work on Monday.

The deep snow gave Penelope and me an opportunity to spend some quality time with the kids. I didn't realize how quickly kids could wear me down. They went from one activity to another and expected me and Penelope to participate in every game. It wasn't that I didn't enjoy playing with them, but they just wore me down. I realized that I had to start doing something to get myself in better physical condition.

We were blessed to have Charles, Belle, Little Jim, and Benjamin to help us with James, Isabella, and Paul. Charles and Little Jim were big enough to ride the sleds with the younger ones. This gave me and Penelope a much-needed break.

On Sunday morning, Mother didn't come to breakfast as she normally did. I was worried about her, so I excused myself from the breakfast table to go check on her. I knocked on her door and I heard her say, "Come in!"

She was still in bed, and the room was chilly because the fire in the fireplace had burned down to mostly ashes.

"Mother, it's cold in here."

"I haven't noticed! I've got these quilts to keep me warm."

"I'm going to put some more logs on the fire, if you don't mind."

"Go ahead. I need to be getting up soon anyway."

"Mother, is there something wrong?"

"To tell you the truth, Obadiah, I don't feel very well. I stay tired all the time."

"I'll be back in a few minutes. I'm going to get my stethoscope."

On the way to my room, I stuck my head in the dining room and told Mattie to put my food in the warmer.

Penelope, noticing something was wrong, followed me to our bedroom and asked, "Obadiah, what's going on?"

"Mother's not feeling well. I'm going to get my stethoscope and go back and examine her."

"Is there anything I can do?"

"Not right now. Have Mattie and Betsy help you with the kids."

When I returned to Mother's room, the room was heating up from the new fire in the fireplace. It felt good.

As I examined Mother, I could hear a rattling that sounded like she had fluid buildup. Her heart was beating erratically as well.

"Mother, can you tell me how long you've been feeling this way?"

"It started after I had pneumonia. I've not really felt good since then."

"Why haven't you mentioned this to me?"

"I thought it would go away. I just thought this was normal after someone had pneumonia."

"I wish you had said something!"

"Obadiah, you and Penelope have your hands full attending to your work. I didn't want you to worry about me."

"Do you feel like dressing yourself?"

"Of course I do. I don't need any help dressing myself."

"All right! Do you feel like coming to breakfast?"

"As soon as I get myself ready, I'll come down and join y'all."

By now, everyone was finished with their breakfast. After the kids gave their grandmother hugs and kisses, Penelope took them to the parlor to play.

"How do you feel now that you are up and stirring around?"

"I'm weak, but I feel better now that I'm up."

"After you finish your breakfast, I'm going to give you another examination."

As I observed Mother taking deep breaths, I became alarmed that this could be a serious matter. She would eat a little and wait for a minute before taking another bite. She ate very little.

"Mother, you need to eat!"

"Obadiah, I don't have an appetite."

After breakfast, I took Mother back to her room, where I gave her a thorough examination. After examining her, I was convinced Mother was suffering from congestive heart failure.

"Okay, I want to know the bad news!" she said.

"Well, for one thing, you've got to limit some of your daily activities. Maybe afternoon naps every day will help your situation."

"Obadiah, I've never had an afternoon nap, and I don't plan on start now."

"It's not going to hurt you to take an afternoon nap. There are lots of people your age who take a nap every afternoon."

"I can't promise you I will do that."

"But, you will try, won't you?"

"If it's the doctor's order, I'll give it a try, but don't expect me to sleep," she said as she smiled.

"Although you will have to limit some of your activities, I see no reason why you can't continue crocheting, knitting, and playing your weekly bridge games, providing that your friends come to Three Oaks."

"Does this mean I'll have to stop going to El Dorado shopping?"

"Well, that will depend on how much you shop. You can't make a full day of it."

"Obadiah, you and I need to talk."

"Talk about what, Mother."

"I think I'm dying, Obadiah!"

"Don't say that, Mother!"

"Obadiah, I've been having these dreams. I had one last night where James was standing over me in a white robe with his arms reaching out to me, like he was welcoming me into Heaven."

"Mother, I don't think you're in any immediate danger of dying."

"Obadiah, I'm ready to go to see James. God has blessed me by bringing all my family together here in Union County. That was, indeed, the highlight of my life. I've enjoyed these past few years that I've had the opportunity to visit with my big family. It's been wonderful, but now if God is ready for me, I'm ready to go be with my Lord and Savior and to see James."

"Mother, what if we're not ready for you to go? I'm not ready for you to leave my family. I want my kids to grow up knowing their grandmother. I want them to get to know you as I know you. I want them to have an opportunity to benefit from your Godly influence. You were the greatest teacher I had when I was growing up. It's because of you that I have my faith and trust in Jesus Christ."

"Obadiah, thank you, for those kind words! But you must know that James and I were the lucky ones. God gave us a special son. We knew you were special on the day you were born, when you looked at us and smiled. Most babies sleep during those first hours after birth, but you opened your eyes and we talked to you, and you smiled at us. As a child, you related well with everyone. You were the peace maker.

"Your father and I noticed how you treated our slaves as a young boy. You felt their needs, and every day, after a long hard day of laboring in the fields, you'd carry water and bread to them.

"That was a sign of compassion. Not every child is born with those qualities!

"Our slaves loved you and still do. That's the reason they decided to stay here with us at Three Oaks. They respect you and feel safe around you. Your kindness and goodness are their proof of trust.

"I've never known anyone who's shown any more faith and trust in God. Every decision you've made has been based upon what you think God would want you to do. As a kid, you spent more time studying your Bible than most people do in a lifetime."

"Mother, you are my shining light! I appreciate these flattering remarks, but as I've mentioned all ready, my character as a man wouldn't be anything without you, Father, and my Lord, Jesus Christ. If I hadn't had Godly parents, I would not be where I am today.

"Mother, you were there when I needed you. You answered my questions. You comforted me with your warm hugs when I was saddened. You encouraged me to do my very best, and you were responsible in teaching me to love and respect others who were less fortune. Now can you see why I need you to stay around to help me with my children? I want them to have the Godly qualities and principles that you've taught me."

"Obadiah, I want you to promise me something."

"What is it, Mother?"

"I would like for you not to share my health problems with my other children."

"Mother, why would you ask me to do that?"

"I don't want my children to know how bad this could be. I don't want them to worry about me. I don't want them to wonder or worry about how long I have to live. Will you please honor my request? If I should linger at the end, you can tell them."

"Mother, I will honor your request. It's going to be hard because, when they come around Three Oaks, they're going to see how weak you've become and start speculating about your health condition.

"I will have to share your health condition with Penelope, Mattie, Betsy, and Bill. I will ask them not to share anything with any of the other family members. I plan to bring in Missy, George's youngest daughter, to help Mattie with the children. This will give Mattie time to meet your needs as well."

"I'll promise you right now, Obadiah, I'll try my best to get better from this day forward. Who knows, God may have other things He wants me to accomplish in this life. Who knows, those afternoon naps might be nice once I get the hang of it," she said with a giggle.

Mother's condition appeared to be getting better. She was taking the afternoon naps and getting extra rest. I felt much better about her health condition. She is a tough lady, one who keeps her promises. She was doing everything that I asked her to do.

On Tuesday, Daniel received his doctor's license from the Arkansas Medical Board Division in Little Rock, Arkansas.

To celebrate this accomplishment, we decided we'd have a come-and-go reception at the doctor's clinic on Friday afternoon.

The reception was well attended, and Daniel was excited when meeting and greeting his many quests. He enjoyed the congratulatory remarks, as well as those who commented on his accomplishments.

The celebration came alive when Mother entered the reception room. She patiently waited her turn in the reception line. When she reached Daniel, she took his hands in hers and said, "Congratulations, Dr. Daniel Bradford! I'm very proud of you!"

"Thanks, Grandma!" he said as he put his arms around her and gave her a big hug. "I'm so glad you were able to be here."

"A herd of wild horses couldn't have kept me away," she said as she smiled.

If I hadn't known about her heart issues, I wouldn't have guessed anything was wrong. She was her usual self and enjoyed every minute of the reception while visiting with friends and family.

The *El Dorado News-Times* reported this morning that the state of Virginia was readmitted to the union on January 28th. The Civil War essentially ended in the state of Virginia. Because of its vote of approval of the Thirteenth and Fourteenth Amendments, it was readmitted to the United States of America.

The town of El Dorado is growing daily, and as it grows, our patient load increases. Since we are getting new patients daily, I decided to give Marion half of my house call business. Marion loves to do house calls. The patients love his bedside manners. In the short time he's made house calls, his reputation of being friendly and caring has spread throughout the county.

The only thing we need now is for Daniel Pratt to return to El Dorado and give me some good news about a much-needed hospital.

Mother continues to do well. She continues to take her afternoon naps, which seems to be helping with her lack of energy.

At times, I still hear some irregularity in her heartbeats. That is something she may have to endure as long as she lives.

On February 28, 1870, the *El Dorado News-Times* carried an article about the passage of the Fifteenth Amendment to the United States Constitution.

The Fifteenth Amendment to the United States Constitution prohibits the federal and state governments from denying a citizen the right to vote based on that citizen's "race, color, or previous condition of servitude." It was ratified on February 3, 1870, as the third and last of the Reconstruction Amendments.

The newspaper also published a short article on the rebel state of Mississippi being readmitted on February 23.

The month of March brought on lots of rain and cold, windy weather. Hank and the freed slaves were busy getting my fields ready for spring planting. We would again plant cotton, corn, and beans.

By March, 1870, Texas was readmitted to the United States of America. One by one, the rebel states ratified the Thirteenth, Fourteenth, and Fifteenth Amendments to comply with the United States Constitution.

On July 15, Georgia became the last rebel Southern state to be readmitted to the Union.

When Georgia was readmitted to the Union, this completed the long, drawn-out process of putting our country back together. Never again would we kill our cousins, brothers, and other relatives in a Civil War.

The Freedom Bureau continued to support Sarah's efforts in educating the colored students. In the middle of the year, the Freedom Bureau started paying for a child's lunch. The colored children were coming to school hungry and were having trouble concentrating on learning. The free lunch is a good thing.

I've been surprised at the governmental regulations of running a school. This is not just the white school, but the colored school as well.

On July 20, I was awakened by a noise coming from our bathroom. The noise sounded like someone vomiting. I opened the door and saw Penelope bent over the toilet seat. I wet a wash cloth and started washing her face.

"Penelope what's going on? How long have you been doing this?"

"I've been having morning sickness now for about two weeks."

"Did I hear you right? You're having morning sickness?"

She looked at me with those beautiful, blue eyes and said, "I was going to tell you, but you have been so busy that I haven't had the right opportunity to talk to you about this."

"Are you telling me you may be pregnant?"

"I do believe I am."

"Penelope, my goodness, are you serious?"

She gave me a look I'll never forget and asked, "Are you disappointed?"

"Penelope, I'm speechless! I'm not disappointed at all. In fact, this is the best news I've heard in some time."

"Why don't I give you a urine sample and let you take it to your office and see if I'm really expecting a child?"

"Yes, that's a good idea!"

"Obadiah, needless to say, I feel exactly the same as I've felt when I was pregnant before."

After arriving at my office, I went immediately to our lab and performed the test. It didn't take long to see that Penelope was, indeed, pregnant. I can't believe this. Another child! I had thought the twins would be our last.

I've decided to take the afternoon off and go home to share the good news with Penelope.

Penelope was sitting on the front porch with Mother and the kids as I drove up. Mother looked at Penelope and said, "Why is Obadiah coming home this time of day?"

Penelope got up from her chair and met me at the porch steps. James and the twins were there to greet me as well. They are growing up so fast. James is now eight, and Isabella and Paul are six. Time is certainly flying by. I can't believe that it's been six years since the twins were born.

As soon as I had the opportunity, I looked at Penelope and nodded my head in the affirmative that she, indeed, was with child. She threw herself into my arms and whispered, "I love you!"

"I love you too!"

Mother called out from her chair, "Why are you home so early?"

"Mother, Penelope and I have some good news for you."

"Well, what is it?"

"We are going to have another baby."

"I knew it, I just knew it. I've been watching Penelope's reaction every morning at the breakfast table. She normally eats a good breakfast, but lately she's been really picky. Oh, I'm so happy for you both. When are you expecting the baby to be born?"

"We don't know for sure, but it's going to be either the last of March or early April, 1871."

"Well, that does it! I've got to start praying that God will allow me to live awhile longer. I want to be here when he arrives."

"Mother, what gives you the idea it's going to be a boy?"

"I just know!"

"Do you know something we don't know?"

"I just have that feeling. Normally, I've been right one hundred percent of the time when I have that certain feeling."

Penelope decided she would resign her job as headmaster at the all-white school because of her pregnancy and her desire to stay home with the kids. I thought this was a great idea. She could also help look after Mother.

Sarah was hired as Penelope's replacement as headmaster at the all-white school. She loved working with the colored children but had become discontented with some of the policies that were passed down by the Freedom Bureau. Politics had got involved, and there had been bickering back and forward because of a white lady heading up the colored school.

When she got the headmaster's position at the white school, she brought Nellie and Nanny with her.

It was now October, and Hank and George were successful in getting our crops harvested. Hank and his strongest men continued to cut logs and transport them to Daniel Pratt's sawmill in Norphlet. Norphlet is now a thriving, little town that is growing in population because of the sawmill.

The extra income from the virgin pines and big hardwood logs comes in handy in paying for the plantation's labor.

Hank was still doing well at his church. Penelope and I visited his church occasionally. I loved his service. I always come away filled with the spirit. The music always set the tone for Hank's messages in God's word.

Mattie continues to worship at Hank's church and continues to sing specials. "Swing Low Sweet Chariot" will always be my favorite song.

In mid-October, Daniel Pratt was back in El Dorado, checking on his two sawmills. I had waited a long time for his return. During this visit, he was our honored guest at Three Oaks. He and Mother were always engaged in talk on the front porch.

It was hard for me to have patience and avoid bringing up the subject of the hospital with Mr. Pratt. In months past, he had told me he'd get back with me in a few months and give me his decision on the hospital, but several months have passed without hearing a word from him.

Finally, at the dinner table, Mr. Pratt leaned over close to me and whispered, "Obadiah, I'd like to visit with you tonight about the hospital."

Those words were music to my ears. I'd waited for months to visit with him about the hospital.

After dinner Mr. Pratt and I went to the parlor to visit. Mattie brought us some fresh tea and some dessert. She was doing her best to please Mr. Pratt, or, I might say, to "butter him up."

"Obadiah, I'm assuming you've thought I'd forgotten you on the hospital here in El Dorado."

"No! I felt at some point during your visit you would give me a yes or no answer."

"There's a reason I've not given you an answer sooner. After returning to Prattville, I was involved in a carriage wreck. My driver had a heart attack driving me to a client's house. The horses were spooked and ran out of control, and my carriage flipped, and I was thrown out of my carriage. I suffered a broken right leg and right arm from the accident. So, my friend, I've been pretty much occupied in getting rehab for the last four months."

"I'm sorry to hear that. If I had known, I would have contacted you."

"I didn't want people to know about the accident, so I went to Birmingham for rehab. There were reasons I didn't want people to find out about my accident. I could have gotten good care at our local hospital, but I didn't want people feeling sorry for me or bothering me. I just wanted some privacy.

"My stay in Birmingham was some of the best days of my life. It was quiet there. I wasn't bothered by people wanting me to make decisions every minute of the day. I was able to get some good rest and adapt to a solitary lifestyle, something I'd not had in years.

"The physical and occupational therapist and the nurses at the rehab center were excellent and worked with me daily.

"Although I'm getting up in age, the fractured bones healed well. Now let's talk about a hospital for El Dorado, Arkansas. Is it still needed?"

"Indeed, it is! The town of El Dorado and Union County continues to grow. Your sawmills have brought several families to our area. The Negro and white populations continue to increase daily. We have outgrown my medical clinic.

"I now have Dr. Jim Burroughs and my nephews, Dr. Marion Bradford and Dr. Daniel Bradford, on my staff."

"Obadiah, to save us time, I'm going to say right off, I'm ready to help you build a hospital."

"Oh, that's great good news, Mr. Pratt. All of us have been praying that you would help us with this project."

"How much financing do you need to make this happen?"

"Jim Burroughs is willing to put in 20 percent, and I can do 30 percent if you could do 50 percent. How does that sound to you?"

"Obadiah, I thought I would be putting in something like 75 percent. You and Jim Burroughs must be doing well here."

"God has blessed both of us."

"Obadiah, I'm prepared to do more than 50 percent if it comes down to needing more funds. During my experience in building hospitals and homes, I've learned that, in most cases, the building cost exceeds the estimated budget.

"Don't you have a nephew by the name of Alexander Bradford, who is both a lawyer and state Senator?"

"Yes, I do. He's well respected in Union County."

"That's what I've been hearing. Why don't you let him figure out the financial mechanics of our agreement?"

"I can do that. I'll talk to him as soon as possible."

"Just get everything in order and send me the contractual agreement. I'll sign it, and you can get started on building our hospital."

"You don't know how much this means to me and my staff. It will mean even more to our patients here in El Dorado and Union County. Thank you so much for helping us make this happen. You will be proud of this joint adventure."

"I have no doubts you will do an excellent job in getting this project completed in a timely manner. Now, if you don't mind, I'm going to have some more of Mattie's cake and tea. Why don't we celebrate again?" he said.

CHAPTER 47

Penelope and I hosted another traditional Christmas on December 25, 1870, at Three Oaks. Again, every member of the Bradford family was present. Mother's health had improved over the past few months, and she was the life of the party. She had a strong desire to live, and that's the biggest contributor for older people to cling to. I've seen some older people give up on life. They have no will to live and just die. Mother has been just the opposite.

She tells me her daily prayer includes her request to live long enough to see her new grandchild born. She takes good care of herself by taking a midafternoon nap almost every day.

She also takes time to baby Penelope. She wants this baby to be healthy. She goes out of her way to make sure Penelope drinks lots of fruit juice. Some of her daily hours are spent knitting and crocheting. She also sews for the other grandchildren. It gives her pride to see them wear what she makes. Lately, she's been crocheting a blue baby blanket. She still believes our baby will be a boy.

El Dorado continues to grow. The hospital is about half finished. We are all excited about getting it built so we can move in. As of right now, I'm somewhat apprehensive about becoming the chief of staff. Besides being the chief of staff, I will continue practicing medicine at the hospital. I don't plan to be just an administrator. I still want that daily association with my patients.

I've spent several weeks now interviewing for staff members for the new hospital. I hope to have everyone hired by the time we have our grand opening.

Dr. Jim Burroughs will become the head doctor at the hospital. I have been interviewing for two additional doctors, three nurses, and other support staff for the hospital.

Marion and Daniel will remain at the clinic, where they will continue seeing our established patients. Marion will continue to do house calls. Both Marion and Daniel will refer all patients who need hospital care to the new hospital. They will make visits to the hospital and help during emergencies.

Penelope is doing well in her pregnancy. She's gained more weight this time than she did with the twins. The weight gain doesn't alarm me because, if Mother is right, and if the baby is a boy, this is expected. If it's a boy, I'll have four sons to carry on the Bradford name.

Penelope and I have decided six children are all we need. We will consciously work hard to avoid another pregnancy. We love kids and would like to have a dozen, but we know how challenging it's going to be to feed, clothe, and educate them.

The month of March was beautiful, not too hot, and not too cold—just right. We couldn't have asked for better weather. We had several good rain showers and the daily temperatures ranged from mid-sixties to the mid-seventies.

The baby hasn't arrived yet. Each day, I find myself dreading to go to work because of my fear Penelope will go into labor and will need me.

I've instructed Mother, Mattie, and Betsy to keep a close eye on Penelope. If she goes into labor they are to send Bill immediately to get me. It's not that I don't have confidence in Mother's and Mattie's knowledge and experience of birthing babies; it is my desire to be present to deliver my own child. So far, I've delivered all my children and don't plan to miss this one, either.

I'm getting a little worried because Penelope hasn't gone into labor. My examinations indicate that she's ready. The baby's heartbeats are strong, which leads me to believe all is well. I tell myself to be patient because the time will get here soon.

There was something about this day that bothered me all day long. I decided to go home a little early. I had worked really hard seeing patients that I needed to see.

As I pulled up in front of our house at Three Oaks, I saw Penelope sitting on the front porch. As I stepped on the porch, she and the kids met me.

"How are you feeling?" I asked as I put my arms around her and kissed her.

"I'm doing okay. I've had some discomfort today that comes and goes."

After greeting Mother and the kids, Penelope and I went to our bedroom, where we could have some privacy.

After examining Penelope, I was convinced that she had dilated enough to have this baby anytime.

"What do you think, Obadiah?"

"I think you will have this baby soon."

"I'm more than ready. I want this baby to be born. Maybe it's my age, but I don't remember having these feelings with the other babies."

"I want to try something, Penelope. Let's take a walk through Mother's garden. Maybe the walking will bring on your labor."

"That sounds wonderful to me. I know I need to walk more, but the pressure hurts."

"We will stop and rest on the bench when you get tired. You just let me know when you need to sit down."

We spent an hour in Mother's garden walking, sitting, and visiting. It was like old times! As the sun settled behind the barn, we returned to the house to get ready for dinner.

After dinner, Mother, Penelope, and I were sitting on the porch while the kids played in the yard. Mother was telling us about a conversation with my sister, Mary, when Penelope screamed out.

"Obadiah, come quickly."

"Show me where you are hurting."

"Right here," she said as she pointed to her lower abdomen.

"All right, I'm taking you to our room."

She stood, took a few steps, stopped, and let out another loud cry. This time she bent over in pain.

"I've got you, Penelope," I said.

We hadn't gone far when her water broke.

"Mother, go tell Mattie to get plenty of hot water ready and lots of linens. I believe Penelope is going to have this baby soon. Get Betsy to watch the kids and keep them outside. I will need you and Mattie to help."

After getting Penelope to our bedroom, I undressed her and put her gown on. She looked at me and said, "Obadiah, I believe he's going to be big."

Her contractions continued to increase. "Obadiah, I don't know if I can stand this pain," she said as she squeezed my hand.

"Hang in there, Penelope. You need to push for me as hard as you can."

By this time, Mother and Mattie arrived with the water and linens.

I looked at them and said, "Ladies, get ready. We are going to have us another little Bradford in a short period of time."

It didn't take Penelope long to push our son through the birth canal.

She was correct. Our newborn son was big. He weighted nine pounds and seven ounces. He was twenty-one inches long and full of life.

Mother smiled big and said, "I told y'all it would be a boy, didn't I?"

"Yes, you did, Mother!"

"What are you going to name him?" Mother asked.

Penelope looked up at me and said, "We are going to name him Obadiah Patrick Bradford, Jr."

"That's a wonderful name, Penelope," Mother said.

"Our baby will carry Obadiah's name as long as he lives."

I felt honored! Penelope and I had tossed names around for days. I finally told her she had the responsibility to name our son, and she chose Obadiah Patrick Bradford, Jr.

When Mother and Mattie finished cleaning Obadiah Jr., Mattie laid him on Penelope chest. She and I began to play with his little hands and feet. He kicked when we touched his feet. He was perfect in every way.

By this time, Mother and Mattie came over to join the party.

Mother said, "I've dreamed that Obadiah Jr. will grow up and become a recognized national figure in our society. He will make you proud. He will be a Christian and will be responsible for winning many lost souls to our Lord and Savior Jesus Christ.

"He will be just like his father and mother. He will have a kind and considerate heart, one that will reach out to the poor. He will marry and have you several grandchildren. He will be a blessing to y'all as long as you both shall live.

"I'm going to get the kids and let them see their new brother," Mother said.

The first one through the door was Belle. She ran straight to the bed and said, "I want to be the first to hold him."

Belle got her wish. She crawled up beside Penelope as Penelope put Obadiah Jr. in her arms. She kissed his face time and time again.

Charles approached the bed with caution. He wasn't sure he wanted to hold his little brother. Penelope looked at him and said, "Charles, do you want to hold him?"

"I think I'd prefer to wait awhile. Let James hold him!" he said backing off a few steps. James crawled up on the opposite side of Belle and held Obadiah.

It was now the twins' turn to hold their new brother. Isabella and Paul needed a little help. It would take them a little time to adjust to having a little brother in the house.

After seeing everyone's excitement, I knew right away that this child will be spoiled rotten. He will be the center of attention for some time. Penelope will have lots of help as Obadiah Jr. grows into childhood. I guess that's one advantage of having six children in the household. The older ones can help raise the younger ones.

Obadiah Jr's siblings were not the only ones who would be spoiling our new son. There were two grandmothers living under the same roof who would be contributing to that as well.

Penelope and I decided having this many people available to help with Obadiah Jr. might be a blessing!

Seeing Penelope was exhausted, I asked the children to continue their playing outside. I asked Mattie to remain with Penelope and Obadiah Jr. while Mother and I excused ourselves to spend some time on the front porch.

"Obadiah, you and Penelope have done it again. He's a beautiful, little boy," Mother said.

"Yes, he is. I see a lot of Penelope in him."

"I love his dark hair. He has more hair than James and Paul did when they were born."

"Mother, I need to ask you some very important questions."

"What are your important questions?"

"You said from the beginning that we would be having a boy. You seemed to be very sure of that. Did you guess?"

"Obadiah, it wasn't a guess. I dreamed he would be a boy."

"So, this came to you in a dream?"

"Yes, that's correct!"

"So, these things you said about Obadiah Jr. a short time ago was from your dreaming as well?"

"Those things were in my dreams as well. I've been dreaming a lot since I started having my heart issues. This particular dream came as the result of your announcement that you and Penelope were going to have another child. The dream seemed to go on and on, like a continuing story. You are the only one who knows about my dreaming."

"Do you think God was speaking to you about the future?"

"Obadiah, I don't know, because most people believe dreams are of the subconscious mind, not from God. All I know is, after that dream I prayed even harder that God would let me live long enough to see this child."

"Mother, you are a wise person. You've been blessed in so many ways. I want you to know that I'm going to keep your dreams a secret, but I will tell you this. You've been right so many times that I will do everything I can to see that Obadiah Jr. gets an opportunity to explore his interests."

"Is there anything I need to be doing to get ready for all these future happenings?"

"Obadiah, stay true to God, obey Him, see that your children come to know Him, use the wisdom He gives you to make good decisions, treat others as you'd want to be treated, and spend time with your family.

"If you will do this, your days will be blessed, and your skies will be blue."

EPILOGUE

After Obadiah Patrick Bradford, Jr.'s, birth, the Lord blessed Catherine by giving her four more years of life. She died in her sleep at Three Oaks, at the age of seventy-six. The Bradford family decided not to transport her back to Autauga County, Alabama, to be buried by her beloved James. Instead, they buried her in the Bradford Cemetery up on the hill overlooking Three Oaks plantation.

For several years, Dr. Obadiah Bradford and his brothers, Dent, John, and several of his nephews bought timber and farmland in the Norphlet and Smackover communities.

On July 4, 1891, the Camden and Alexandria Railroad was built and ran through the Norphlet and Smackover communities, the city of El Dorado, and on into Louisiana. The timber business increased throughout Union County. Instead of hauling the timber to Champagnolle to be shipped, it was now transported by the railroad.

In 1904, Mattie fell victim to pneumonia and died at the age of seventy-two. She raised her two sons in the same household with Obadiah and Penelope. She continued her responsibilities as the family cook until she died. She, too, was buried in the Bradford Cemetery on top of the hill east of the Three Oaks plantation house.

Mattie's two sons, Little Jim and Benjamin, attended college in Boston. Penelope wanted her brothers to get a good education, so she insisted that they get their education in Boston. They both remained in Boston after they finished their degrees. Little Jim became a lawyer, and Benjamin became a teacher. Little Jim married Lucy Tackett, and they had three boys. Benjamin married Jessica Nelson, and they had two girls and two boys. Penelope and Obadiah made several trips to Boston to visit them.

Betsy continued to live with Obadiah and Penelope until her death in 1910. She, too, was buried in the Bradford Cemetery.

Bill lived to the ripe old age of ninety-two. He moved in with Obadiah and Penelope ten years before his death in 1915. He died of complications from liver cancer. He was buried in the Bradford Cemetery.

Hank and his family moved to El Dorado in 1872. He continued as pastor of the church he organized. He also served in the Arkansas State Legislature for two terms and, later, became involved with local politics in El Dorado. Hank and Nanny's children received college educations. Obi became a lawyer and practiced law in El Dorado. Samuel, Hank's youngest son, became one of the first colored airline pilots for a national airline company.

George, Obadiah's faithful and dedicated servant, also moved to El Dorado with his family. George involved himself in city politics and the board of education at the colored school. He died in 1912 and was buried in the Bradford Cemetery alongside his wife, Opal, who died in 1906.

On January 10, 1921, the first oil well was completed in Union County. It was a giant producer. The well produced from three thousand to ten thousand barrels a day. The oil was found 2,233 feet below the surface of the earth.

The discovery of oil in the county was the beginning of big money for the citizens of Union County. The Bradfords benefited from oil wells on their property.

Charles, Obadiah's oldest son by Audrey, made a career in the armed service. He became a Lt. Colonel and was stationed in Europe for several years. After retiring from the service, he returned to El Dorado with his family. He was the father of three sons and two daughters. He and his family were members of First Baptist Church in El Dorado.

Belle, the second child of Obadiah and Audrey, married Josh Mahoney, from one of the richest families in El Dorado. Josh and his family were later involved in the oil business. Belle gave birth to three girls and one boy, and she and her family were members of First Baptist of El Dorado.

James, the first son of Obadiah and Penelope, followed in his father's footsteps and became a doctor. He studied medicine in Augusta, Georgia, and became a surgeon. He married Susan Fisher of Augusta. They had two sons and one daughter. He worked at the El Dorado Hospital for several years before his retirement.

Isabella and Paul, twins of Obadiah and Penelope, went their separate ways after graduating from El Dorado. Isabella moved to Boston and attended the same boarding school her mother attended during her early years. Isabella became the wife of Franklin Bishop of Boston. She remained in Boston and had two daughters and two sons. Mr. Bishop was associated with shipping.

Paul also studied medicine in Augusta, Georgia. He returned to El Dorado after graduation and became a partner in the Bradford Medical Clinic, where Daniel and Marion were practicing. He married Bridgette Madison of Augusta, and they had three boys and one girl. They were members of First Baptist Church of El Dorado.

Obadiah Patrick Bradford, Jr., lived up to Catherine Bradford's dreams. He went to Harvard University where he majored in law. He practiced law in Little Rock, Arkansas, for several years. He later was elected to the United States Senate. He married Belinda Jefferson from Virginia. He and Belinda had five boys and two girls. While living in El Dorado, Obadiah Jr. became a preacher. He was known as the traveling preacher. He preached throughout the southern counties in south Arkansas. While preaching, he continued his law practice.

Obadiah lived to enjoy eighty-eight years of quality life. He and Penelope never lost their love for each other. As they grew old together, they enjoyed their comfortable life together at Three Oaks. They raised all six of their children at Three Oaks and helped raise Mattie's two boys, Little Jim and Benjamin.

Obadiah died in 1920 of complications from a lung disorder. He died one year shy of the first oil well drilled in the Smackover field. During Obadiah's last years of his life, he was involved with the Southern Baptist Convention.

At his funeral service, which was held at his home church of First Baptist of El Dorado, there was standing room only. Because of his reputation as a doctor and his work in the Southern Baptist Convention, people came from all over to pay tribute and respect to an extraordinary man. Obadiah was buried in the Bradford Cemetery next to his mother, Catherine Bradford.

Seven years later, on July 10, 1927, Penelope went to be with her beloved husband in Heaven. She was eighty-nine when she died in her home at Three Oaks. She was surrounded by all six of the children she raised. She, too, was well respected and admired for the contributions she made in Union County. She died from complications of pneumonia. She was buried at the side of Obadiah in the Bradford Cemetery.

CPSIA information can be obtained
at www.ICGtesting.com
Printed in the USA
FFOW02n1812100418
46196246-47449FF